FREEFALL

ROBIN BRANDE

RYER PUBLISHING

FREEFALL
by Robin Brande

Published by Ryer Publishing
www.ryerpublishing.com
Original Copyright 2012 by Robin Brande writing as Elizabeth Ruston
Revised Copyright 2014 by Robin Brande
All rights reserved.
Cover photos Dreamstime.com
Cover design by Robin Ludwig Design, Inc.
http://www.gobookcoverdesign.com
ISBN: 978-1-952383-34-2

✿ Created with Vellum

ALSO BY ROBIN BRANDE

Romance

Love Proof

Freefall

Heart of Ice

Fire and Ice

Winnie Parsons Mysteries

The Genius Track

A Man of Appetites

A Drop of Sweat

The Long Gray Hook

The Slip of a Rib

Dove Season Series

Dove Season

Finder

Seeker

Believer

Bradamante Saga

Book of Earth

Book of Water

Young-Adult

Evolution, Me & Other Freaks of Nature

Fat Cat

Doggirl

Replay

Parallelogram-Series

Into the Parallel

Caught in the Parallel

Seize the Parallel

Beyond the Parallel

Collections

The Love of a Good Dog

Mountain Tough

Self-Help

What If You're Doing It Right?

What If You're Doing It Right? For Teens

FREEFALL

1

It was her last column for *Outdoor Adventure.*

Their last column.

Eliza had waited three months until she could write it, could bear to look at the picture of him taken on that last day—the picture she knew she'd have to let them print at the top of the page. Because their columns always came with a picture.

She could have waited longer—people understood, no one was pushing her—but she wanted to write it while she was still angry at him, because those had always been their funniest columns, those he said-she said renditions of some disastrous adventure they'd both just barely survived.

This one wasn't funny at all.

Is it better to die doing what you love, or to be more careful so you can stay alive and keep doing it? Jamey and I had those fights all the time—when he'd go diving with sharks in baited water. Or backpacking alone, deep in grizzly country during a salmon run, no contact with the outside world until a plane was scheduled to pick him up a week or ten days later. Or climbing in a country where even the toddlers carried guns.

Or that time we were hiking up Conundrum Pass in Colorado, and a freak storm blew in early in the morning, trapping us high on an exposed ridge above 13,000 feet. The hail beat down on us as lightning flashed all around. A bolt slammed the ridge right above me, blinding me for a moment with light I didn't know could be that white.

And what did Jamey do? He pulled out his camera. He stood on that ridge with electricity raining down on top of us and he pulled out his damn camera.

"What are you doing?" I screamed as I topped the hill and prepared to keep running down the other side.

"It's so beautiful!" he shouted back, aiming at the sky.

"You're going to die, you a**hole!" I'm not proud to say I shouted, and as I tore down the hill desperate for the safety of treeline, it went through my head that those would be my last words to my husband, and some time a few hours later, when the storm passed, I'd have to trudge my way back up that mountain to retrieve his lifeless body. I actually started working out how I was going to carry him down. It kept my mind occupied and pushed out the terror of being struck by lightning myself. Cursing helped, too, and I had an awful lot to curse about with a husband who was such a reckless idiot.

But of course he didn't die. Because Jamey was incredibly lucky that way. Everyone knew it—it's what made being with him and reading about all his exploits in the wilderness so exciting.

But this time he is dead. From doing something so easy, something he'd done twenty, forty, fifty times before. Climbing up one of our local pitches, perfect blue-sky day, no wind, no weather, just Jamey and his friends out for a leisurely afternoon. He was supposed to be home by five. We were going to an early movie.

But it doesn't matter how lucky or handsome or funny or charming or well-loved—fiercely-loved—you are, you can still die when you're 29 and leave behind a bewildered, pissed off wife who doesn't know how to be a widow any more than she knew how not to fall in love with the likes of you, Jamey Shepherd, from the first time I saw you in our college English class 11 years ago. You hooked me in the first time you spoke, and even though I was a lifelong chicken you somehow turned me into an adventurer, into a partner who could do half the crazy things you did, and I know if we'd have had time to start that family we talked about, our children would have been more like you than like me, because everyone always wanted to be you.

But now that's over and that's it, and all the amazing, daring, hilarious things you would have done and written about for all of us to see will never happen. Because of a stupid anchor bolt.

Wasn't that a history lesson? "For want of a nail, the shoe was lost; for want of a shoe, the horse was lost; for want of a horse, the battle was lost..." Because little details matter. Sometimes little details are all that matter.

The point is, Jamey, you robbed us. You went out one day with just a kiss at the door, and you promised to come back and you didn't. You took that joyous, carefree life of yours and played with one too many risks. And now you're never coming back, and there's nothing any of us can do about it.

We should all be monumentally pissed.

Eliza passed the kitchen window on the way to her mother-in-law's back door. Daisy sat on guard duty just inside. She started barking before Eliza could knock.

"Good," Hildy called to her. "I've got coffee."

Eliza opened the door slowly, her foot extended to prevent Daisy from dashing. Still, the dog tried. Eliza reached down and scooped her up. "Why would you run away? Not spoiled enough here?" The dog panted. "Brat."

Eliza set the terrier down and gave her mother-in-law's thin shoulders a squeeze. "How are you feeling?"

"Rotten." Hildy's voice was deep and throaty, with the broad tones of her New York girlhood still intact. "The phone never stops."

"Take it off the hook—you're allowed. I did when Jamey died."

"That's because reporters were calling you. It's just my friends calling me—but they won't stop."

The phone rang to prove her point.

"Leave it," Eliza said.

Hildy shrugged. Eliza freshened her mother-in-law's cup of coffee and poured one for herself. At the fifth ring the answering machine took over.

"*Hi,*" Hildy's deep voice cut in, "*Ron and Hildy can't come to the phone...*"

"I'll have to change that," Hildy mused, a slight break in her voice. She quickly doused it with a sip of coffee. "So, how you doing?"

"Fine. I thought you might like some company. Did you sleep much?"

"I'll take a nap later..." Hildy paused to listen to the end of her friend's message.

"*—so give us a call—any time—I mean it. We're thinking of you. Bye now.*"

"That's nice," Hildy said. "They're all so nice."

"You should take them up on it, you know. That was the mistake I made—I hardly left the house for weeks."

Hildy patted her daughter-in-law's hand. "It's not the same, is it? Jamey was such a surprise. Ronny...well, we knew about that for a long time, didn't we?"

A stroke had destroyed Ron Shepherd's great engineering mind, but left his body still relatively untouched. He deteriorated more slowly than he wanted to, Eliza suspected, knowing all along that his mind would never return. When finally his body began breaking down, he made it clear he was ready to go. Then a cold brought on pneumonia, and Hildy abided by his wishes not take any extraordinary measures. He had died quietly in his bed a few nights ago while Hildy sat holding his hand.

"I've been thinking," Hildy said. She took another sip of coffee, then leaned back in her chair and peered at her daughter-in-law. "You're going to say I shouldn't, so let me tell you right now my mind's already made up."

"Okay," Eliza said with a smile. "That's typical."

Hildy fidgeted with the edge of her placemat. "I've still got the house, you know—in Careyville."

It had been Jamey's childhood home in a small suburb of Syracuse, New York. He had left it for college at the opposite end of the country, deliberately choosing the hottest, brightest place he could find after a lifetime of cold, dark winters. Eliza had grown up in Henderson, Nevada, close to Las Vegas, had never left, and was grateful for it when Jamey showed up that first day of college at UNLV. Jamey's parents had followed him to the desert a few years later, enticed by the warm winters.

Ron and Hildy had rented out their Careyville house to a series of tenants over the years, and the last family had been a disaster. After bouncing several rent checks, they moved out without notice and left the house in disrepair. The property manager had called with the bad news only a few days before Ron's death.

"I was thinking I should go back and take care of that."

"Why?" Eliza asked. "Let the management company do it —that's what you pay them for."

"No, I mean live there—move back there. Stay there."

Eliza took a moment to absorb the news. "But why? I thought you hated New York—it's too cold."

"I don't hate it," Hildy said. "I just stopped liking it for a while. But maybe I can like it again—who knows?"

"But you have all your friends here. And me."

"I have friends there, too. I don't know, honey, it's hard to explain. I just don't feel so...right here anymore. First Jamey, now Ronny—all my boys are gone. I don't think I want to live here without them anymore."

"But your work—"

"I can get it going up there, too. Some of those people still remember me. I can work for a caterer, maybe, while I build my clientele back up again."

"But Hildy..." Eliza cast about for a better argument. What exactly, she wondered, was her objection?

"I'm only sixty-nine," Hildy continued. "I'm not ready to curl up and die yet. My mother lived until she was ninety-one, the mean old bag—"

"Hildy..."

"I have at least ten or fifteen more years of good honest work in me." Hildy reached for her daughter-in-law's hand. The older woman's skin was warm and soft, and Eliza's fingers were still cold from her early springtime walk.

"Lizzy, you've always lived here, so you don't know what it's like to miss your home. I never thought I'd say this, but I actually miss those miserable winters in Syracuse—at least you know when it's Christmas. Here I can hardly get in the mood for it—some years I'm still wearing my bathing suit on Christmas Eve."

"That's not true."

"Close enough. What I'm saying is, maybe I forgot how

much I hated it, but I swear I miss it. I think it's time for a change. Again. I want to go home."

"You are home," Eliza urged. "You can move in with me if you don't want to live alone."

"I don't mind living alone. I like the quiet—you know that. Besides, I've been living alone the past few years, haven't I? The way Ron was."

The two women sat in silence for a few minutes, each absorbed in her own thoughts.

The decision came easily, almost unconsciously. Eliza was almost surprised to hear herself say it. "Then I'm going with you."

"No, you're not."

"Yes, I am."

"You wouldn't last a winter," Hildy said.

"I'm a hardy girl—you've always said so. Besides, it would be good for the book. I could fill in all the details about Jamey's childhood—I wouldn't have to rely on just you and what Jamey told me and a bunch of old pictures."

"Sweetheart, there's nothing for you there. Believe me."

"Hildy," Eliza answered softly, "there's nothing for me here anymore, either. I'm coming with you. You might as well get used to it."

It wasn't entirely true, that part about there being nothing for her there. Eliza still had her own family— mother, stepfather, two brothers and their wives and a niece and nephew.

Which was why her mother couldn't understand the

impulse to go.

"I just want to see her through this year," Eliza told her mother. "Make sure she's okay. Jamey would want me to."

"A whole year?" Joyce said.

"At least through Christmas. Come on, Mom, you know it's the right thing to do."

Joyce sighed. "But what about our movie dates? And all the birthdays and holidays you'll miss? It's only March—how are we going to do without you the rest of the year?"

Eliza had those same misgivings. It's why she hadn't gone away to college. She liked being close to everyone and everything she knew. But Jamey had already drawn her out of that shell, teaching her the pleasures of travel and outdoor excursions. She would just have to look at this as one longer expedition. Once it was over, she could come home again and burrow back into her routines.

"I think a change would do me good for a while," Eliza said, hoping to convince herself as much as her mother. "I haven't been able to work on the book at all—I've been too distracted. The publisher already paid me a good chunk of money for it. I'm supposed to deliver a manuscript by next year."

"It's just so long," Joyce argued. "And what about your house?"

"It'll be okay. The neighbors can check it every now and then. Really, Mom, it'll be fine."

ELIZA DECIDED TO PACK LIGHT. It was a skill she learned from living with Jamey for so long. He could get an assignment, get an invitation to go climbing or rafting or caving, and he'd be packed and out the door in a few hours. No puzzling over what to wear for formal versus casual events, what to wear if the weather went south—just his standard kit of zip-off pants, a few synthetic shirts, rain gear, and a layer of fleece.

Eliza had developed her own standard kit in the two years since Jamey died.

A widow's wardrobe, she once told her readers, *can play tricks on the eyes.*

It's like a nun's habit. It draws attention to the woman, but it also allows her to hide behind it.

Think of the last time you saw a nun in the grocery store. You couldn't help but stare at her—right?—no matter how briefly. But did you really see her? What color were her eyes? Were her lips full or thin? Did she have freckles or moles or a scar above her lip? Admit it: All you saw was the outfit. You forgot that behind it she was somebody's daughter once, and that she had a life before she became what her clothes said she was.

Eliza fished through her widow's wardrobe now: the black fleece pants and jacket, the gray sweaters and dress, the black dress pants and matching jacket. She added a few pair of jeans, some shorts and T-shirts, then considered her packing complete. She wasn't going to Careyville to try to impress anyone. She was going to be a companion to her mother-in-law.

And to finally force herself sit down and write the book she had agreed to write. Even if it was going to hurt.

3

S now covered the daffodils. They, like Eliza, had been tricked into believing spring had come to Careyville to stay.

Eliza layered long johns under her sweatpants and coat, and snugged a gray fleece cap over her ears. She left her long brown hair out of its customary ponytail so it could keep the back of her neck warm.

"Come on, Daisy."

The terrier leapt from her sentry post on top of the couch. She had been sitting there since dawn, erect in front of the second-story window, eyes trained on the street below to guard against cats invading the Shepherd yard. So far she had warned away three.

This time of day Daisy faced south. Later, at a shifting of the guard Eliza still didn't understand, Daisy would pad toward the window on the opposite side of the house, take up her station on one of the kitchen chairs, and guard the back yard instead. Eliza had to admit that the dog had adjusted to their new life in Careyville far faster—and better —than she had. For Eliza it was still a work in progress.

"That mutt has it too good," Hildy said as Eliza scratched the terrier's ears and then clipped on a leash.

"She won't think so when I'm out there dragging her through the snow."

"Eh, it's good for her—remind her what a Syracuse dog is supposed to be like. She's gotten soft—haven't you, Daze?"

The dog raced down the stairs and waited for Eliza at the bottom. "We won't be gone long," Eliza said. "It's probably too cold for both of us."

"I've got that meeting at Walsh's this morning," Hildy reminded her. "I might not be here when you get back."

"Good luck," Eliza called, then she and Daisy stepped out into the morning chill.

It had been two weeks since they arrived—two weeks of unpacking and organizing and cleaning and otherwise avoiding the reality of the situation. For Eliza, at least, it was all still make-believe. She wondered when it would finally sink in that she had left the city where she had lived all her life, left friends and family and the familiar routines of her day, to hide in a strange town for the next eight and a half months.

"Daisy, stop." Eliza tugged back on the leash and the dog strained forward. It was a daily contest for superiority, and Daisy, despite her size, normally won. Eliza didn't have the heart to discipline the dog, even though the terrier sorely needed it.

Among her other personality defects, Daisy seemed to

object to every four-footed creature she met. She couldn't pass a Husky or a Doberman without lunging at it. She was less aggressive toward dogs her own size, but still growled at every one of them. And cats—why were they even allowed? Daisy seemed to have made it her personal mission to chase every single one of them off the earth.

Eliza and the dog puffed their way up the steep slope at the west end of Careybrook Lane. Eliza's boots slipped in the snow, but Daisy continued on. She might be handy in the Iditarod, Eliza thought, if only someone would believe in her and give her a chance.

"Hold on," Eliza warned, tugging back on the leash while she steadied her feet on the steep hill. But the dog ignored her and lunged ahead, leaving Eliza no choice but to keep scrambling.

At the top of the hill, to the north, was a web of cross-country trails where lately Eliza did her best thinking before writing. In addition to working on the book about Jamey, she also had her syndicated newspaper column to write every two weeks, and regular monthly assignments from various women's magazines.

It had been a struggle, these past two years, to keep the magazines interested. During Eliza's adventure days she could always sell her essays easily, and for good money. She'd even been able to compile some of her best ones into a book which sold reasonably well. Not as well as Jamey's books—those were still popular, and maybe even more so with certain people now that he was gone.

As the dog pulled her along, Eliza practiced saying what

she meant to write as soon as she got around to it that afternoon.

Change is inevitable. The cells moving through your veins right now aren't the ones that were there last month...

Is that true? Eliza wondered. She'd have to check on the Internet when she got back.

Change is inevitable. You can stand where you are and let the waves crash over you, or you can dive in head first to meet them...

Well, Eliza thought, at least the first line was all right, but she'd have to keep working on the rest. It was her monthly essay for *Outdoor Woman,* and even though Eliza hadn't been outdoors for more than a walk or a run since Jamey died, so far the editor hadn't seemed to notice. As long as Eliza still had lessons to draw from the life she used to lead, she hoped she could continue writing the words that might inspire other women to do what she used to do.

Eliza and Daisy passed a wooden bench dedicated to one of Hildy's old neighbors who used to rest under that particular maple tree. Then they strode up a small incline, toward a fork in the trail. To their left was the path leading to the lake and some of the fancier homes in Careyville, to their right a trail across the meadow. It forked further on, offering a choice between the woods or a long walk out in the open beneath a power line.

"No, Daisy, I want the sun," Eliza said, fighting with the

dog to stay left. But Daisy must have caught some scent in the woods, Eliza realized, because the dog was set on going that way.

Eliza gave in, as usual.

They were trotting along the path to the woods when Eliza heard a loud grunt, and then the sound of something bounding down the trail behind her. It sounded like an animal—something big.

"Bear!" a man shouted.

Eliza whirled around. She barely had time to register that there were bears in that part of New York, when a huge mass of black fur came tearing toward her and Daisy.

Eliza stumbled back just as Daisy lunged forward, jerking the leash from Eliza's hand. The terrier attacked, leaping into the face of a large black Labrador, snarling and snapping and barking.

"Daisy! Stop!" Eliza tried to grab the leash, but it was lost in the tornado of teeth and bodies.

"Call your dog!" the man shouted, racing to catch up.

"I'm trying! Daisy!"

The Labrador's owner, a man in sweats and a T-shirt and running shoes, immediately tried to break them apart. He hoisted his dog by the collar and kicked Daisy to keep her off.

"Hey!" Eliza shouted.

"Well, get your dog!"

"I'm trying!"

Eliza reached for Daisy's collar just as the man kicked again.

"Ow! Damn it!" Eliza collapsed to her knees and cradled her wrist.

"I'm sorry—"

"Damn it!"

Meanwhile the terrier continued her insane assault. "Daisy, would you *shut up!*" Eliza managed to reach over with her good hand and grab the dog's leash. She jerked Daisy to her side.

The man pulled his own dog a few feet off the trail. "Bear, sit." The Lab plopped his tail into the snow and panted in a friendly way.

"Are you all right?" the man asked.

Eliza rotated her wrist to test it. "I'll live. You didn't need to kick her."

The man's voice was icy in return. "You should learn to control your dog."

You should learn to control yourself, Eliza thought, but she didn't say it. Because the truth was Hildy's dog was a menace.

Eliza pushed to her feet and faced the jogger. And wasn't prepared for his reaction.

The man took a step backward. "You're...I'm...I'm s-sorry." He suddenly seemed very interested in the trees off to the side.

Eliza yanked on the leash. "Come on, Daisy. Miserable dog."

"I'm sorry," the man said again.

Eliza sighed and looked at him. "No, I'm sorry. She's just... protective. Or possessed, whichever one you believe."

The man still wouldn't meet her gaze. "It's...f—" He

seemed to struggle with the word. "Fine. Come on, Bear." He headed left and continued jogging down the trail that followed the power line.

Eliza's shoulders slumped. She knelt down beside the terrier. "Daisy, you are beyond a doubt the worst dog in the world—you know that, don't you?"

Daisy's soft tongue swept Eliza's nose.

"Don't even try it." Eliza straightened and gazed out over the white-encrusted field to follow the progress of the jogger. He moved quickly, and she understood why she hadn't heard him before she did. With her mind occupied and Bear and his owner running at that pace, she never had a chance to react.

"Thanks a lot," Eliza muttered to the dog, who happily set out for the woods. It was a full ten minutes before Eliza felt her heart beat slow down.

They completed their loop and emerged back on Careybrook Lane at the opposite end from where they had started. Birds fluttered from branches as Eliza and the dog passed, sending showers of snow to the frosty lawns below.

They had just passed a house with a basketball hoop chained to the mailbox at the end of the driveway when Eliza heard a girl call out, "I like your dog."

Eliza turned and answered wearily, "I don't. You can have her."

"Really?" A chestnut-haired girl of about ten wearing a purple coat and matching wool hat bounded from her front steps down to the edge of her driveway.

"No, not really," Eliza answered with a smile. "I'm just not a big fan of hers at the moment. But she's not mine—afraid I'll have to take her back home."

The girl squatted beside the dog and stroked her back. "What's her name?"

"Daisy the Destroyer. Daisy the Demented."

The girl laughed.

"What's yours?" Eliza asked.

"Katie."

"Hi, Katie, I'm Eliza."

The girl stood up and offered her hand. Eliza was impressed to find the girl's grip so strong. And unlike some girls Eliza had met, Katie had no trouble looking her directly in the eye. It was a mark of confidence Eliza loved to see in girls of any age.

"Isn't today Monday?" Eliza asked, looking at the date on her watch. She often lost track of the days of the week—they were all the same to her unless she had some reason to remember, like a deadline. "Does school start this late here?"

"The teachers had a meeting or something this morning," Katie said.

A woman emerged from the house carrying an armful of blankets. "Katie—oh." She hesitated when she saw Eliza, but quickly recovered and smiled. "Hello."

"Hi, I'm Eliza Shepherd. I live just down the street."

"Oh. Hilda Shepherd's girl, right?"

"Well, sort of—her daughter-in-law."

"Oh, that's right. Come on, honey, we have to go." Katie's mother set the blankets on the back seat of the car and walked around to the front.

"Well, see you later," Eliza told Katie.

"Okay." The girl scuffed her boots up the driveway and made room for herself in the back seat.

"I'm sorry," her mother said, walking toward Eliza. "Where are my manners? I'm Carolyn Jackson. I've never met your mother-in-law, but my husband knows her. He's lived here for ages."

Eliza shook her hand. "Nice to meet you. I won't keep you." She waved to Katie and set off down the street.

The car slowed as it passed her. Carolyn rolled down the front passenger window. "I'm sorry—I meant to stop by when I saw you moving in. Is everything all right? Are the two of you settled?"

"Yes, thank you."

"We should have coffee sometime. I'm free Thursday morning—maybe then?"

"Sure. That sounds nice. I don't know if Hildy—"

"I'm sorry, I really have to hurry," Carolyn interrupted. "We're late. Why don't you walk down Thursday. Around nine-thirty?" She waved and drove off before Eliza could answer, but what would she have said except yes? Now that the initial flurry of moving was over, Eliza had begun to realize just how isolated she was. She had never been the new girl in school, never had to begin from scratch building a life with friends and activities and new routines. She felt unsteady, and that was what she was struggling to convey in her *Outdoor Woman* essay. *Like waves crashing against your shins...*

She'd have to keep working on that.

.   .   .

"Well, it took some canoodling, but Teddy Walsh finally agreed."

Eliza looked up from her laptop. "To classes?"

"No, better," Hildy said. "We're going to cater his new opening."

"*We?*"

"Just one night—do you mind? I'll do all the cooking, but I told him there'd be two of us to dish it out."

"Hildy—"

"There'll be lots of other tables—ours will be just inside the door when they first walk in. I thought I'd make my champagne potatoes..."

Eliza squinted skeptically at her mother-in-law. Hildy had talked her into gigs like this before: "Just a few hours...you won't have to do a thing...it'll be fun…"

Eliza saved the work on her laptop and sat back in her chair. "Tell me."

Hildy smiled, as if she already knew she would get her way. "I met with Teddy—I was expecting his brother, but for some reason it was Teddy, but that was all right because I know him even better from when Jamey was growing up—"

"Cut to the chase."

Hildy laughed her husky laugh. "It's just for one night—just a few hours. I thought you might like a behind-the-scenes look at some of the people around here."

"What do I have to wear?"

"Black. I know you've got plenty of that."

To Hildy's credit, she didn't seem uncomfortable making the crack about Eliza's clothes. Hildy, more than anyone else, had always been willing to acknowledge the death of her son and talk about it openly. It was a skill Eliza was still trying to learn.

Eliza sighed. "When is it?"

"A week from Friday."

"And this is for what?"

"The Walshes are opening a new store in Monarch—it's the town just over."

"I thought you were going to talk to them about holding classes."

"Teddy says he'll think about that, too. We talked about doing some wine-pairings like the ones I did at Fancy Foods."

In addition to running a catering business and teaching cooking classes, Hildy had worked out an arrangement with the largest specialty grocer in Las Vegas to combine cooking lessons with wine-tastings that would highlight the store's selection. Every other Friday night she would haul her hot plates and cooking supplies to the store, and teach groups of half-inebriated customers how to whip up something besides cheese and crackers to go with their pinot noir or chilled chardonnay.

"Your dog got me yelled at today," Eliza tattled. She recounted the morning walk. "Oh, and I met Carolyn...Jackson, I think she said."

"Hmm, must be Willy Jackson's wife."

Eliza smiled. Everyone was a "y" to Hildy—Ronny, Jamey, Teddy, Willy, Lizzy. Eliza wouldn't have been surprised to hear her mother-in-law call the President by a nickname if he had grown up in her neighborhood.

"She invited us for coffee Thursday morning."

"If I can," Hildy said. "You should go, though. You need to start making friends."

"Thanks, I think I noticed that."

"It's not good for you to hang around with an old woman all day."

"That's why I keep walking her obnoxious dog," Eliza said. She awakened her sleeping computer. "I've got to get back to work. I'll be happy to be your servant girl next Friday."

Hildy smiled. "Good." She bolted from her chair as if all her earlier relaxation were just an illusion. "I have to go shopping. I told Teddy Walsh I'd bring by a few samples tonight."

"I thought you already had the job."

"You don't know Teddy," Hildy said. "That boy has always loved to eat."

ELIZA WONDERED if she had made a mistake. Somehow she'd let Hildy talk her into going with her to Ted Walsh's.

"We'll just pop in and out," Hildy said. "But you should see how the other half lives—the Walshes have always had the best houses."

They sat in Hildy's car, lights off, taking in the view.

"How big do you think that is?" Eliza asked.

"Three story—I'm sure there's a basement. Mmm, maybe five or six thousand square feet? It's not as big as his parents' house used to be, but it's still plenty big."

"And he lives there by himself?"

"I know—what a waste," Hildy said.

"What do people do with houses that big?"

"Wander from room to room counting all their toys."

Eliza shook her head. "All I can think of is having to clean it."

"That's what cleaning women are for."

"Wouldn't you feel lonely in a house that big?"

"Let's go ask him." Hildy exited the car, leaving Eliza to wonder if her mother-in-law really would ask that question. Yes, she decided, Hildy probably would.

Eliza followed Hildy to the door, feeling more like a fraud with every step. Here she was—semi-famous writer, lecturer, former adventurer—dressed in her nicest pair of pants and her one dress sweater, walking up the heated concrete driveway to Theodore Walsh's home, hot dish cradled in her arms, prepared to pretend she was Hildy Shepherd's assistant chef just so she could steal a peek inside and satisfy her curiosity about the lifestyles of rich people.

Research, she told herself. For that novel she might write some day. Or for a magazine piece on the trap of possessions versus the freedom of the wilderness. Or something like that.

"I'm just going to carry this in and leave."

"No, you're not," Hildy scolded. "You'll stand there and let me introduce you and you'll talk like a normal human being."

Eliza rolled her eyes. "He doesn't want to meet me."

"Of course he does—he just doesn't know it yet. And you're going to try to talk fast and scoot right out of there, but I'm not going to let you. It's time you practice making small talk."

Eliza suppressed a smile. "You're a bossy old witch, aren't you?"

"You're not going to sit around every night watching my hair turn gray."

"It's already gr—"

The door swung open. A man in his early thirties stood before them dressed in jeans, wool socks, and a Syracuse University sweatshirt.

Eliza felt overdressed.

"Hi, Teddy, here we are," Hildy said, sweeping past him into the front room.

From Hildy's comment about how much Ted Walsh liked to eat, Eliza expected him to be overweight. To the contrary: He was handsome and fit, with sandy brown hair, wire-rim glasses, and a charming half-smile that he directed toward Eliza.

"Hello," he said.

"Hi."

She kept her head down and followed Hildy.

"Where's the kitchen?" Hildy demanded.

"Through there," Ted said, pointing straight ahead. He and Eliza followed. "Bossy, isn't she?" he murmured.

"I was just telling her that."

The kitchen looked new and unused. A half-eaten microwave dinner sat on the counter beside the sink. Eliza took in the cherry wood cabinets, the oak floor, the clean granite countertops in muted grays and greens. The room was cozy, despite how enormous it was. But it lacked something. The appliances all looked brand new—not even a smudge on their black and stainless steel exteriors. The track lighting cast a cheery glow, but what was wrong with this picture?

"I see you made yourself dinner," Hildy smirked, setting her casserole dish on the counter.

"Yes. Cooked it myself," Ted said. "Would you like one?"

Hildy made a face. "I don't know how people eat that garbage. Why don't you bring yourself home some soup from your store? I saw some nice ones in there today."

"I didn't have time to stop," Ted answered. "I was expecting some ladies."

"Oh, well we'll get out of your hair—"

Ted smiled at Hildy. "I meant you two."

Hildy laughed. "Well, you could have dressed up a little more."

"I didn't want to shock you."

Hildy squeezed his arm. "It takes a lot to shock an old woman like me."

Eliza watched in amazement. She couldn't remember ever seeing her mother-in-law so flirtatious. And Ted Walsh seemed to be enjoying it as much as she did.

"Well, let's see if we can feed you something better," Hildy said, unveiling her creations with a flourish. "Take your pick."

Ted withdrew a spoon from a drawer and sampled what was in the casserole dish. "Mmmm..."

"Horseradish mashed potatoes," Hildy said with pride. "I like to serve those in champagne glasses—people really get a kick out of that. Of course we can use plastic glasses if you like."

"I think we'd better. People get awfully sloppy at these

things." Ted leaned over the counter and continued sampling Hildy's work. He reached for a stuffed mushroom.

"That one has garlic and—"

Ted held up his hand. "Let me guess." He maneuvered it over his tongue while he gazed at the ceiling for inspiration. "Lemon, maybe some curry—"

"No," Hildy said.

"Butter—"

"Of course—"

Ted turned to Eliza. "Did you make these or did she?"

Eliza wasn't prepared for any attention. "Uh...no, she made them all."

"You're the assistant she talked about?"

"Yes."

"Will you be cooking for this event?"

Eliza glanced at Hildy.

"She always does," Hildy lied. "What difference does it make?"

"Just asking." Ted made another selection. With his mouth full of smoked salmon and capers on crostini, he asked Eliza, "How long have you worked for Miss Hildy?"

"Uh, off and on, a few years."

"Hm," he said, swallowing. "That isn't what I heard."

Eliza tensed. "Oh?"

"I heard you're Hildy's daughter-in-law Eliza Shepherd, you're about thirty-one, grew up in Nevada, two brothers, you majored in English, you're a writer—what else have I missed?"

Eliza stared. "How could you possibly know all that?"

Ted shrugged and picked up another mushroom. "Word gets around."

"Gossip," Hildy said.

"But it's true, isn't it?" Ted asked.

"So far," Eliza confirmed. "Did anyone guess my height and weight?"

Ted considered her. "Five foot four, maybe? Weight about...nah, I'm really bad at that. Let's just say under two hundred—"

"Close enough," Eliza said.

"Truth is, I met you once."

"You did? When?"

"Maybe ten years ago? Long time. You and Jamey were up here visiting the folks."

"Must have been the year after you got married," Hildy said. "'Cause we moved out to Nevada—"

"I don't remember," Eliza interrupted. She wanted to head them both off before they felt it necessary to talk about Jamey. "Remember meeting you, I mean. I'm sorry."

"I'm not surprised," Ted answered. "As I recall, you only had eyes for Jamey."

She nodded politely. It was still hard for her, hearing people talk about him so easily. With Hildy it was one thing—Eliza had learned to listen without flinching while Hildy reminisced about this or that from her son's life—but she still had trouble hearing about Jamey from strangers. She supposed people felt entitled to talk about him. His life in the public eye made him other people's property, not just hers.

"I saw something you wrote once," Ted said.

"You did?"

"Some trip you did with Jamey—Antarctica, maybe? Somewhere where there were a lot of glaciers."

"I didn't go with him on the Antarctica trip," Eliza said. "It must have been either Alaska or France."

"Right—Alaska. Jamey took some great pictures, didn't he? I liked the one of you climbing that frozen waterfall—"

"Listen," Eliza said, "I don't really—"

"I liked your article, too. Really vivid."

"Thanks." Eliza felt a mix of emotions: pride at the difficulty and success of that trip, joy at the memory of sharing it with Jamey, the pain of knowing that part of her life was over.

"Lizzy writes beautifully, doesn't she?" Hildy said.

"She does. You do."

"They made an excellent team."

"I'm sure," Ted said. "Anyway, I was sorry to hear about Jamey."

Eliza cleared her throat. "Yeah, well.... So, will any of this food do?"

"All of it," he said. "Can we do that?"

"Sure," Hildy answered. "I'll set it out in shifts. Start with the mushrooms—"

"However you want it," Ted said. "Set up by four o'clock. I expect it'll go till around eleven."

"All for a grocery store?" Eliza asked before thinking it might offend him.

"Not just a grocery store," Ted corrected her, "a shopping and dining *experience.*" He stood erect and placed his hand over his heart and recited solemnly, "'At Walsh's we don't just promise the finest selection of foods in central New York, we promise a shopping and dining experience your family will want to return to again and again.'" He rotated his hand in the air. "And again and again and again. Seriously, we put up some great stores. Have you been in one yet?"

"No, sorry, I haven't gotten out much." Eliza thought guiltily about a conversation she'd had just a few days after arriving, when Hildy had suggested they stock up on groceries at Walsh's.

"That place?" Eliza had said. "Too big, too loud, too trendy." She'd driven past it a few times and always kept on going. She preferred the small, homey market just up the street from Hildy's house. They might not have every food and gadget Walsh's did, but at least Eliza could shop there in peace without having to compete with the crowds.

"I'll leave all these for you," Hildy told Teddy. "You can give me back my dishes later."

"No, here, take them now." Ted swiftly transferred the food from Hildy's dishes into some of his own. When Hildy reached for her casserole dish, Ted pulled it back and rinsed it in the sink first.

Hildy nudged her daughter-in-law. "Wow, what manners —huh, Lizzy?"

Eliza shot Hildy a warning look. "Yes. Very nice."

"So, Teddy," Hildy said, "we'll see you next Friday, then? Or maybe before? We just got here, and Lizzy doesn't know many people yet—"

"That's okay—"

"No, Lizzy—Eliza," Ted said, "Hildy's right. I should show

you around the greater sights of Careyville before too long. Have you seen the post office yet?"

"I'm pretty busy."

"Doing what?" Hildy scoffed. "Walking the dog? Clicking at your computer? You should go."

Eliza glared at her. Hildy shrugged.

"You could come by the store tomorrow," Ted said. "Oh, no, wait, I have to be at the Delmar store tomorrow. How about Thursday—lunch? I'll give you a tour so you can see the full Walsh's shopping experience. Maybe even sneak you a free lunch."

"No, thanks, I'd pay—I mean, if I came—which I probably won't—"

Ted smiled and there was mischief in his eyes, making Eliza feel even more flustered. She wasn't used to men looking at her that way anymore. In fact, she had made a point over the last two years of not inviting any attention at all. She dressed plainly, usually in jeans and a black or blue shirt of some kind. She wore little or no makeup, kept her long brown hair pulled back in a ponytail, and had switched from contacts back to glasses.

"I have to go," Eliza said. "Come on, Hildy, I still have work to do."

"Writing something?" Ted asked.

"Her magazine column," Hildy said.

"Yeah, and it's due day after tomorrow." Eliza pulled at her mother-in-law's sleeve. "We have to go. Nice meeting you—um, seeing you again."

When they were safe in the car, Eliza turned to the older woman and said, "What was that?"

"What?" Hildy answered innocently.

"I'm not that lonely."

"He's a nice man—and very good looking, don't you think?"

"I'm sure he is, but I'm not interested."

"He's very nice."

"How do you even know? When's the last time you talked to him before today?"

"He was one of Jamey's friends in school."

"Oh, I see, so we're talking historically here. Well, they can't have been that good of friends—Jamey never mentioned him."

"It was when they were younger."

"Hildy, honestly—I'm not looking for male companionship."

"Honey, you're going to have to start thinking about it some time. I'm not going to have any more sons, you know. You're going to have to start looking around."

Eliza groaned in frustration. "Please, *please*, don't do that again. It's embarrassing."

"Why? He's good looking, you're gorgeous, if you'd fix yourself up a little—"

"Hildy, I'm serious."

Hildy laid her hand on Eliza's wrist. Eliza winced—the wrist was still tender from having been kicked that morning.

"It wouldn't hurt to be a little friendly. You need the practice."

"I'm plenty friendly." Eliza gave her best fake smile. "See?"

"You know," Hildy said, "I might get married again, for the right man."

"No, you wouldn't."

"I sure would. You think I'm too old for that? You think no one would want me?"

"No, of course I don't think that. But even if you did, that's you, all right? I'm perfectly happy with the way things are."

"You think you're going to live with me until death do us part? No way," Hildy said. "The first sign someone's interested in me, you're out on your can."

"Start the car. I'm freezing."

"He's cute, isn't he?" Hildy pressed.

"He's rich and he's charming, and you know I can't stand either of those things."

"So that's why my Jamey never made a success."

"He was plenty successful and you know it."

"He could have been a millionaire," Hildy said wistfully, "but he loved his wife too much..."

"Start the car."

"I can't," Hildy said. "He's coming."

Eliza slunk down in her seat. Hildy started the engine and rolled down Eliza's window.

"I forgot," Ted said, leaning in. "I can't do Thursday lunch —I have a meeting. How about dinner instead?"

"Um...no, thanks. I can't."

"Yes, she can," Hildy said.

Without turning her head Eliza flicked her hand against Hildy's thigh. "I really can't. Sorry."

"Okay, too bad," Ted said. "Maybe some other time."

"Yeah, maybe. Good night."

"'Night."

Eliza rolled up her window and mumbled from the side of her mouth, "Can we please go now?"

Hildy waved to Ted before backing into the street. "He's a very nice man."

Eliza's breath steamed the window. *I had a nice man*, she thought. *One was enough.*

4

E liza awoke just after five o'clock Wednesday morning and put the coffee on. She sat at the kitchen table and booted up her laptop. She checked her essay one more time, then e-mailed it to her editor.

Change is inevitable.

When Eliza first stopped writing what she thought of as her Widow Columns, she received mixed reviews from her readers.

"Glad you're moving on..."

"You understood exactly what I was feeling. I wish you the best, but I'm not ready..."

"Thank God. You were depressing the hell out of me..."

"I am a single white male, 35, non-smoker..."

It was Jamey's idea, six years ago, that she taper off writing outdoor adventure articles and concentrate instead of writing more personal pieces. "You're getting bored."

"No, I'm not," Eliza had argued.

"I can tell—your writing's gotten flat."

"Thanks a lot."

Jamey tilted his head in his irresistible puppy doggish way. "Liz, you know what I mean. I love having you on these trips, but you shouldn't feel like you always have to come. Maybe it's time you started writing other things."

"Go ahead and say it—you have a girlfriend."

"It's true."

"She's five foot-ten, blonde, an expert mountain climber, and you'd rather have her belaying you than me."

"It's all true, but that's not why I'm saying this."

"Then why?"

"Simple—I think you're a great writer."

The compliment had pleased her more than he could know. Jamey Shepherd had worked with some of the best outdoor writers in the world, and even though Eliza knew he was biased, she still soaked up his praise.

"And I think you have more to say than this," Jamey continued. "A lot more."

That one discussion had led to a whole separate career for Eliza. She began with a compilation of essays on over-coming her fears to become an outdoor adventurer, and that in turn led to a book about other women who embraced the risky life. Soon Eliza caught the attention of various women's magazines, and for the last few years she had made her living through a combination of freelance work and the modest royalties from hers and Jamey's books.

She also managed to make some money here and there

from teaching and speaking fees. She taught writing work-shops a few times a year, and she was often invited to speak at conferences around the country.

One of her more popular talks arose from an article she once wrote about creating a Life List. The first group to invite her to speak about that was a conference of women executives who wanted to be inspired in their personal lives. Eliza handed out several sheets of loose leaf paper to each woman, then over the next half hour she had them write quickly, without self-editing, listing every single thing they wanted to do before they died.

"Let's hear some of them," Eliza prompted when the half hour was over.

A dignified-looking woman in her mid-fifties stood and read, "I want to learn French."

"Go hiking in the Alps," said another.

"Learn to make a great chocolate mousse."

Some ideas were simple—learn to drive stick shift—some more complicated—"Finally let go of all my anger." Before she dismissed the group, Eliza made them all stand, raise their right hands, and pledge to begin pursuing just one thing on their list that very day.

"Can you go to Greece this afternoon? Probably not," she said. "But you can get on the phone or the Internet and check out prices and make a plan to start saving and get yourself there next year or the year after that. Right?"

"Right," the crowd agreed.

"How many of you said you wanted to learn a foreign language?" Hands went up. "You can call your community college as soon as you get back to the office and sign up for the next class. Or you can buy yourself a software program and practice for an hour every night. Right?"

"Right," they all agreed.

"Okay, then. Don't make me come back here," she threatened, and the women cheered.

She had been invited back there three times so far. Other engagements around the country followed.

But that stopped when Jamey died. Eliza started turning down offers. She lost the urge to leave home. She lost the urge to tell other people what to do—she had forgotten what to do herself.

Instead she turned inward and wrote about what she found there, and the offers to speak dwindled. She wondered if her readership did, too.

Over the past year she had been working to bring them all back. She played at being upbeat again, funny—ready, she pretended, to enjoy life along with everyone else.

Daisy's tags tinkled against her bowl as she drank. The terrier followed Eliza into the living room for the next stage of their routine.

Eliza flicked on the reading lamp beside the couch, and nestled beneath the lap quilt Hildy had made for her husband. Then Eliza opened her journal and prepared to tell the truth.

Her readers thought they saw her—knew her—but Eliza was well aware the woman she seemed to be in her columns was an illusion. Her essays were designed to inspire, challenge, uplift. More times than not Eliza used the columns to convince herself of changes she needed to make in her own life, even though she knew people reading the essay probably assumed she already had everything figured out.

But here in her daily journal she could be as petty and angry and awkward and stupid and pitiful as she really felt inside. Some days she might cover a sheet with lists of things to do, or whine about how someone had mistreated her, or go on and on for pages about how unfair it was that Jamey had died so young, just when they had talked about finally slowing down and raising a family.

Eliza had bent every ear around her for months after Jamey died, but she knew that even her dearest friends and her supportive family had their limits. No one wants to be around someone who cries all the time—a little goes a long way. Eliza learned to temper herself—to keep things breezy and light, to avoid certain topics that were sure to set her off —and then wait until she was alone with her journal pages to pour out the mean, ugly, pathetic truth.

She knew before she set pen to paper exactly who her topic would be that morning. She had already lost sleep over him last night. But first she needed to warm up, to dawdle.

Another cold morning, but sunny. Underslept. Got the column off just now. Maybe go to the bookstore later today? Get a copy of John Steinbeck's journal. Maybe get a haircut?

Eliza searched the window for the first rays of morning. She stood, stretched, refilled her coffee. Daisy dozed on the couch—her sentry shift had not yet begun.

Eliza curled up on the couch again and rambled for another paragraph or two before finally acknowledging what was on her mind.

All right, he was cute—I admit it. But so what? The world is full of cute men. So what are you afraid of? Everything. Sex. Falling in love. Feeling guilty. Upsetting Hildy. Even though she claims she wants me to date, I know it would kill her to see me fall in love with someone else. Back to sex—not ready <u>at all.</u> I don't even know where the parts go anymore. I embrace my new virginity. Let's leave it at that.

Okay, so what's the worst that can happen?

I take him up on his offer and go out to dinner some time. We laugh, I like him, he takes me home, I pause before opening the car door, he leans over, kisses me. Good? Bad? Probably good. But then what? Second date, isn't he expecting more? You like him, it's going well, then you're some place and you're naked and—

Eliza closed her eyes to imagine it. She had tried this once before, envisioning herself with a friend of one of her brothers who kept asking her out last year, but she couldn't get very far in the daydream without running into this same barrier.

—you see Jamey. You're thinking of him. You remember how he looked and smelled and laughed and kissed you and made love to you.

"Forget it," Eliza told the dog. She closed her notebook

and gave Daisy some attention. She stroked the terrier's ears and waited for enough light to walk. It would be a long walk this morning, she decided. She needed to numb herself with the cold.

The dog huffed up the hill. The previous afternoon's sunshine had melted much of the snow. The flowers would have their chance again to prove it really was spring.

Eliza pondered her options. She had told herself when she moved there that she would stay only through the end of the year. If Hildy seemed to be getting along—plenty of friends, a thriving business, sturdy health—Eliza might consider coming home even sooner. Even after only a few weeks she was already homesick. She missed her family. She missed her normal life.

But she still knew she had done the right thing by coming. The thought of Hildy rebuilding her life alone filled Eliza with the kind of emptiness she felt in the first weeks after Jamey died. Maybe Hildy was hardier, or maybe it was different when you watched your husband deteriorate over the years. Maybe Hildy wouldn't have those nights of anguish over being left alone after so many days and nights with the man she loved.

In any case, eight months—or maybe only six—seemed a reasonable commitment. Eliza felt fortunate that she could do her work from anywhere, and had: mountaintop cabins, tents, hotel rooms. A few months' retreat to Jamey's childhood home might be just what she needed to find her way again.

Snow crystals shimmered in the morning light. Eliza paused at the edge of the meadow to take in the cold serenity of the place. Her breath fogged her sunglasses.

"Shall we try the lake today?"

Daisy pulled toward the right.

"Not this time, evil beast." Eliza asserted her weight and dragged the dog after her toward the left.

The trail markers promised a three-mile walk to the lake, where Eliza could then link into another path and circle the water for several more miles. She'd warned Hildy it would be a long one, and Hildy reminded her the dog might not be up for it.

"I'll take my pack," Eliza said. "I can carry her if I have to."

"You really think Daisy will stand for a pack?"

Eliza envisioned trying to load the thrashing dog. "Well, maybe not."

"If you're home by ten you can come to Monarch with me," Hildy told her. "I've got some shopping to do."

So Eliza had agreed to shorten the walk, all for the sake of setting eyes on a town Hildy described as "the snootiest place you've ever seen."

Eliza liked snooty. She liked to dress a place down by showing up in jeans and a T-shirt. It was one of the things Jamey claimed to love about her, that she dressed however she wanted to, as comfortably as she wanted to, no matter what the occasion. Eliza wondered what he would have thought of her widow's wardrobe. Jamey always hated her in black.

Eliza and the dog had just turned back and were heading

home when Eliza saw two familiar figures in the distance, running down the trail toward them.

"Great. Try not to kill him this time, will you?"

As the jogger and his dog came closer, Eliza drew Daisy off the trail beside a wild rose bush and waited for them to pass.

Some habits are hard to resist, Eliza realized, and her southwestern friendliness was one of them. "Morning."

Daisy didn't even try to resist her own habit. She snarled and lunged at the Lab. Eliza jerked the leash. "Daisy—"

The man nodded once and kept on running without saying a word. Eliza's greeting hung uncomfortably in the air.

"Pompous ass," Eliza muttered once he was out of earshot.

Daisy barked once more for emphasis.

"Making friends," Eliza complimented herself and the dog. "Yes, sir."

"So Monarch is a town, right?" Eliza asked, looking out the car window at the Victorian houses and fancy shops they passed.

"Right," said Hildy.

"And you—we—live in Careyville, which is a village in the town of Monarch?"

"Right. And there's both a village and a town of Monarch."

Eliza shook her head. "This is all too complicated. And they're all suburbs of the city of Syracuse?"

"Yes."

"How do you people keep it all straight?"

Hildy shrugged. "It's what you know." She pointed to the right. "There's where the fanciest houses are, up that street. Should we go look?"

"Sure." Eliza felt relaxed, having turned in her work for the week. Now she was on her own time.

Hildy eased the sedan up the hill. The posted speed limit of twenty made it perfect for gawking. The houses were refined and enormous, with skillfully arranged lawns, sheltering trees, and perfect, orderly flower beds.

"That's Suzy Walsh's house, I think," Hildy said. "She's Teddy and Davey's sister. Different last name now—forgot what it is."

"Who's the oldest?"

"Davey, then Suzy, then Teddy."

"What's Suzy like?"

"She was a nice girl. Haven't seen her in a long time. Who knows, maybe she's as stuck up as Davey now. But Teddy's the sweet one—probably because he was the baby."

Eliza knew many youngest siblings who were anything but sweet, but she didn't feel like arguing the point. She was more curious about the Walshes at the moment, and whether any of them would be worth interviewing for her book.

"Was David a friend of Jamey's?" she asked.

"Not really. He came around sometimes with Teddy, but he wasn't really in Jamey's group."

"But Ted was?"

"On and off. Look there." Hildy pointed out a white

three-story with dark green trim. "That used to be Lucy Greaves's place—stuck up old witch. I catered a party for her once, and she complained the whole time, even though her guests loved every single thing I made. Then I had to send my bill three times before she finally paid it. Then she deducted ten percent because she said the sandwiches were soggy. Old hag."

Eliza laughed. "No, how do you really feel?"

"There are rich people who know how to make good use of their money, and then there are the ones like Lucy Greaves who hate to part with a penny of it, even if someone deserves it. She's pretty stingy with her compliments, too—like telling me something was good would kill her or something. I swear I'd never cater a party for that old hag again no matter how much she promised to pay me. It isn't worth it."

They had reached the end of the block. "Do you want to see more, or should we go back down?"

"I've seen enough. Is there a bookstore around? I wouldn't mind looking for a few things."

"Sure. It's close to the fabric store. I'll drop you off and come find you when I'm done. Will half an hour be long enough?"

"Or longer, if you need it. I can entertain myself."

Eliza entered the bookstore and immediately smelled the coffee. She would save that pleasure for the end. Back in Henderson that had been her treat: to browse for as long as she wanted, then take her selections into the adjoining café and savor good coffee and something new to read.

She headed for the magazine rack first. She had written a quiz for a girls' magazine, and wondered if the issue was on the shelf yet. She found it—noting with satisfaction that her quiz was highlighted on the cover—and turned toward the biography aisle to search for the John Steinbeck journal she had read about in the introduction to *East of Eden*, which she had just finished reading before the move.

When Eliza loved a book, she loved it all the way, and wanted to know as much about it as possible. She hoped Steinbeck's journal would help her understand how he wrote such a rich, textured story. Maybe that, in turn, would teach her how to do it herself.

Not finding the journal on the shelf, Eliza settled for special ordering it. She paid for her magazine, bought her coffee, and sat at a table ready to enjoy reading her own quiz. She always loved seeing what photos and illustrations the various magazines paired with her articles. It made her feel like she was part of a creative team, even if she never met the artists.

Another customer had come into the café. Eliza didn't recognize him at first, but something about the way he carried himself and spoke to the young woman behind the counter caught Eliza's attention. Ever since her days of waitressing, she was alert for rude customers.

The owner of the black Lab wasn't rude, exactly, just cold and direct. "No, I said non-fat." The barista emptied the cup and began again. "To the top this time, please," he directed her.

Eliza and Hildy both hated bad manners—especially if

the person was wealthy. "They can afford charm school," Hildy liked to say.

With his back to her, Eliza had the chance to study him: In his mid-thirties, with short blond hair that looked like it was growing out of a buzz—the kind you want to bristle your hand over to see if the stubble hurts. Nice sturdy form from all those miles running. Not a bad profile.

He wore dark olive slacks, brown loafers, and a button-down shirt under a navy crewneck sweater. He checked his watch and turned toward the rest of the store.

Eliza dove behind her magazine.

As he walked toward her table, Eliza wished she weren't hiding behind *Adventure Girl.* For once she wished she were reading *Smithsonian.*

Why? Eliza chided herself. *Why should you have to impress him?* She straightened in her chair, fully prepared to defend her selection: "Yes, I read *Adventure Girl*—so what? They happen to have great quizzes in here."

But he walked right by her. Eliza slouched again, knowing the rest of her relaxation had been ruined. She drank the last of her coffee, tossed the cup in the trash, and went outside to wait for Hildy.

Within a few minutes Hildy drove up in front of the store and Eliza opened the door.

"Oh, look," Hildy said, nodding her head toward the bookstore door.

Eliza turned. Her jogger was just emerging.

Eliza scooted into the car. "Let's go."

"Hold on, I should say hello."

"Say hello?"

Hildy had already rolled down Eliza's window. "Davey!" The man looked up, confused, and Hildy waved. "David!"

Eliza slumped down in her seat. "Please don't—"

He stepped up closer to the side of the car and peered in.

"Hi, Davey, it's Hilda Shepherd—remember? Jamey's mother."

David Walsh nodded vaguely. "Oh, yes..." He glanced at Eliza, then back at Hildy. Eliza slumped down even further and shielded half her face with her hand.

"I was supposed to meet with you yesterday," Hildy continued, "but they said you had a meeting or something."

"Yes, I—"

"So I met with Teddy instead, which was fine."

Hildy's accent had never sounded so thick. Eliza wondered if it was like cell phone service—the signal was stronger the closer you were to the receiver towers. Maybe being back in New York brought it out in full force.

"Did he tell you we're doing the opening?" Hildy said.

"No." David glanced at his watch. He had not looked at Eliza again since that first moment—much to her relief.

"Well, it was nice seeing you," Hildy said with a wave. "We'll see you next Friday."

"Go," Eliza murmured. "Just go."

"Bye now." Hildy waved again and finally inched the car forward.

"A little faster?" Eliza prodded. When they were finally a distance away, Eliza exhaled audibly. "Oh, brother."

"See what I mean?" Hildy said. "Stuck up. Did you see how he wouldn't even look at me when I was talking to him? I don't know how Teddy turned out so good. Their parents must have spent all their charm school money on him."

Eliza was still processing the information. "That's David Walsh? He's who we're working for next week?"

"Not that you'd know it—can't be bothered to meet with me. I'm sure he didn't have a meeting yesterday. Look at him —it's nearly eleven o'clock and he's still out getting coffee for himself. Why doesn't he buy coffee at Walsh's? Is he too good for his own store?"

While Hildy continued her rant, Eliza imagined what it would be like to work for the man. *"No, I said non-fat,"* and it was the way he said it that bothered her: short, clipped, irritated. She hadn't come to the opposite end of the country just to be mistreated by some New York suburb richie.

"Hildy, I'd be happy to help you cook for next Friday, but I'd really prefer not serving."

"What? Why not? Come on—you know we always have fun together."

"I know, but...I really don't like doing it. It's embarrassing —I'm terrible at it."

"You're wonderful. I couldn't do it without you. It'll be over before you know it. Come on—I'm not taking no."

"That's the guy," Eliza explained. "The one whose dog Daisy tried to kill."

Hildy gave a hearty laugh. "Good for her!"

"Hildy, I'm serious." But soon Eliza, too, cracked a smile. "I really don't like him."

"So you'll stick your finger in his mashed potatoes. Don't worry about it. Trust me, this gala is the kind of thing you're going to want to write about some day. I wouldn't let you miss it if you paid me."

"I have the feeling David Walsh may be my Lucy Greaves."

"Don't worry, honey," Hildy assured her. "He won't bother us—Teddy won't let him. We've got that boy wrapped around our fingers."

5

The next morning, Eliza walked down to the Jackson house. Carolyn Jackson answered the door and motioned Eliza inside.

"Yes...okay..." She pinched the phone between her cheek and shoulder and scribbled on a napkin. "Okay, I'll do that. Thanks a lot." She hung up and rolled her eyes. "Girls' Club. I'm co-leader this year, and I swear I've never worked this hard."

Eliza followed Carolyn upstairs to the living room. The layout was similar to Hildy's house: all the primary living areas upstairs, the laundry and family room downstairs.

"What can I get you?"

"Coffee would be nice," Eliza answered. Her hair was still wet from her post-walk shower.

Carolyn's kitchen was long and narrow, with a half wall and shutters separating it from the living room. The shutters were open.

"Go ahead and sit in the living room. As you can see, I've got a project going on the table."

Eliza fingered the layers of fleece in various colors and patterns stacked on the corner of the dining room table. In the center of the table was a thick plastic sheet for measuring and cutting fabric. A yard of pink fleece with a gray and blue paw print pattern lay on top of the cutting sheet.

"We're making blankets," Carolyn explained. "In Girls' Club. Have you ever seen these?" She brought Eliza a mug of coffee. "Whoops, cream or sugar?"

"A little milk, please."

Carolyn doubled back to the refrigerator. "They're no-sew blankets. You put two pieces of fleece together, cut half a square off the corners, then cut strips along all the sides. Then all the girls have to do is tie knots. It's the greatest project I've ever seen. I wish they'd had it when I was a girl. I've already made about five of them for our house."

"Are these for you, too?"

"No, we're donating them to a children's shelter for Easter," Carolyn said. "My co-leader and I split them up, so I only have to cut twenty pairs. *Only*," she added for emphasis. "It's killing me. My hand keeps seizing up."

"Want some help?" Eliza offered. "I don't mind working while we talk."

"That would be great. Except I don't want you to think I got you over here as cheap labor."

Eliza laughed. "I'm sure you didn't. Really, I'd be happy to. I like to keep my hands busy."

They sat at opposite ends of the table. "You can use the

cutting sheet if you want, or just estimate it. You want the strips about an inch wide, and about four inches long." Carolyn demonstrated. "Just pick a print and then a solid color you think would look good with it, lay them on top of each other, and start cutting."

Eliza chose a burgundy print with dogs on it, and a plain navy for the back.

"You're going to want to make one for yourself," Carolyn said, "I swear."

"I might like this one."

"We need all these for the girls, but next time I go for fleece I'll pick up a little extra."

Eliza smiled. She already liked this woman. She appreciated people who were naturally generous. Jamey had been that way, too.

"So," Carolyn said, "tell me everything you feel like telling. I promise I'll only pass it on to most of the neighbors."

Eliza furnished her with a brief history of her life.

"Jeez, you were only twenty-nine? That must have been awful." There was no mistaking the pity on Carolyn's face.

Eliza had had her fill of pity. "It was hard," she agreed, "but I've managed."

"Yeah, I guess you would, but—"

"So that's me," Eliza said. "What about you?"

Carolyn paused in her cutting. "Short, sweet. Married my high school sweetheart when we were twenty, got my degree in nursing, had Katie, work part-time now, that's about it."

"Is it wrong to ask how old you are?"

Carolyn laughed. "I hope not, because I would have asked you if you hadn't already said. I'm thirty-five. So's Will."

"Oh, so he probably didn't know Jamey that well."

"We both knew him from just around, but yeah, we were a few years ahead."

Eliza cut a few more strips before adding, "I like to hear about him, you know?"

"Sure, I understand."

"I mean, he told me a lot, but I still like to hear what other people remember about him."

As long as I'm the one asking the questions, Eliza thought. She hadn't told Carolyn she was writing a book. People tended to get nervous when they thought they might be quoted. Eliza just wanted background—a sense of what people thought of Jamey before she met him.

"Well, here's one," Carolyn said. "This one was pretty famous. Did you ever hear about the pigeon?"

"No."

"He shot a pigeon with an arrow."

"He did?"

"Yeah. He was probably about nine or ten. Nobody knew it was him at first, but there was a picture of the bird in the paper, and someone knew Jamey had been playing around with a bow and arrow, so they ratted him out."

"He never told me that."

Carolyn pointed her scissors at Eliza. "That's because he was a criminal, and he didn't want you to know. See? You think you know somebody." Carolyn smiled.

"He really did that?"

"Ask his mom."

"I will," Eliza said. "My husband the delinquent."

"So is it hard?" Carolyn asked her. "I mean...still?"

Eliza stalled while she took a sip of cold coffee. "Some days. It never really goes away, you know? But most of the time I don't think about it. I keep pretty busy."

Lies, lies, lies, Eliza thought. *You think about him all the time.*

"You think you'll ever...you know, get married? Is that awful to ask?"

"It's not awful," Eliza said, "but I doubt I ever will."

"Why? You're still young. And pretty."

Eliza scrunched up her face. "I'm an old hag, as Hildy likes to say."

"Not about you!"

"Not yet, but I'm getting there."

Carolyn pointed her scissors again. "Don't say that. It's a good thing you met me. I won't stand for talk like that."

"All right, maybe not a hag yet—"

"I bet I can find a nice guy for you within a month," Carolyn said.

"No, thanks."

"I'm serious! I'll ask Will."

"No," Eliza said firmly. "I'm serious, too. I'm not looking for anyone."

"But you could still have children!" Carolyn said. "You're young enough."

Eliza wanted to kick herself. She was usually so careful about this, but she'd let the conversation get away from her. These were the topics—remarriage, children, getting on with her life—that always hit her hard. People thought they were being helpful—she knew that. But she also knew they had no idea how much they hurt her. At least she didn't erupt into tears every time it came up anymore. In the first year she felt like she cried all the time.

"Please, Carolyn," she said, "I don't mean to be rude, but I can't talk about this anymore."

"Okay, sure. I'm sorry. I didn't mean—"

"I know. It's okay, but let's just talk about something else now, all right? Tell me about Katie."

"How was it?" Hildy asked.

"Very nice. You should have come."

"You need friends of your own. You should be able to complain about your bitchy old mother-in-law without me around to stop it."

"Never happen."

"You've only lived with me a few weeks." Hildy pointed to a page in her recipe file. "What do you think? Think Teddy would like these?"

Eliza reviewed the recipe. "Looks good, but I thought you'd already decided on the menu. Those foods we took over..."

Hildy waved her hand. "Those were just samples. That was the easy stuff. I want to trot out something really good."

"I think he really liked those horseradish potatoes. I did, too."

"I'll keep those. I'm talking about something...spectacular. Something to shove in that David Walsh's face."

"Why?" Eliza said, surprised at how forcefully Hildy had said it. "Did something happen?"

"That little—you know what he did?" Hildy asked. "He had his *assistant* call me this morning. Didn't even have the guts to do it himself. And the message is *'they've decided to go another way'*" she mimicked, "on the salmon."

"So? What does that mean?"

"He must have tasted some of what we brought Teddy the other night and decided he didn't like it. Or maybe it isn't *fancy* enough. Either way, I'm out a dish." Hildy scoffed in disgust.

Eliza plopped into the seat across from her at the kitchen table. "How come no one ever told me about the pigeon incident?"

"The pigeon?" It took Hildy a moment to understand what Eliza was asking, but then she roared with recognition. "Oh, the pigeon! What a little monster that boy was, wasn't he?"

"So it's true?"

"Of course it's true! He wouldn't ever admit it, but I know it was him. Ronny took his bow away after that."

"Why did he shoot it?"

"Who knows?" Hildy said. "Maybe he didn't think he could hit it. Jamey was always doing stuff like that—getting some idea about something he'd like to try, then doing it without thinking about whether it could work."

Hildy looked at Eliza over the top of her half-glasses. "Like you, if you want to know."

"Me?"

"Sure," Hildy said. "Why do you think he married you so lickety split?"

"Because...he loved me?" Eliza said it in a way that she

hoped was a warning to her mother-in-law. If there were some other story—something bad—Eliza didn't want to know it. She had her own memories of their rapid courtship, and she wanted to preserve them the way they were.

"He got an idea about you," Hildy said. "Thought you'd be the perfect girl for him. So he went for it—you know Jamey."

Eliza nodded slowly. "Is that it?"

"Why did he jump out of that airplane once?" his mother asked. "Why did he climb all those crazy mountains? He was always doing such dangerous things."

"But you know he never worried about that," Eliza said. "He was just having fun." She wished he had worried more. Maybe he'd still be alive.

"He thought they were worth the risk," Hildy said.

"Yes."

"Honey, he felt the same way about you."

6

"Well, don't you look nice?"

"I'm thinking of pants instead."

"Not on your life," Hildy said. "My assistant has to look classy."

Eliza stood in front of the hall mirror, surveying her costume for the gala. She wore a gray wool dress with a collar that came to her chin and a hem that fell to her calves. It was her Modest Widow dress, the one she wore to fancy occasions where there might be single men on the move. She had bought it for her friend Amy's wedding, and worn it only once since then.

"A little make up?" Hildy proposed.

"I'm just there to serve potatoes."

"You should wear your contacts."

Eliza narrowed her eyes. "Why? What are you trying?"

"Nothing. It's just that Teddy will be there—"

"I'm sure he'll have a date."

"He probably will, since you never called him."

"I wasn't supposed to call him."

"You could have," Hildy said. "I have his number."

Eliza sighed. "Stop, all right? I'm doing this as a favor, remember? Don't make me regret it—or worse, refuse you from now on."

Hildy held up her hands. "All right, all right, I'm just saying.... Anyway, you look beautiful, even without your makeup and your hair all hidden like that."

"Food workers should tie back their hair."

"Yeah, but even a ponytail looks better on you. A bun is so…"

Eliza placed her hands on her hips. "Do you want me or not?"

Hildy chuckled. "Yes, dear, I want you." She slapped her daughter-in-law's behind. "Now go get your coat."

They drove to the Walsh's Fine Foods in Monarch.

"Good heavens," Eliza said when she laid eyes on the monstrosity.

"I know. You should see some of their other stores—this one's only a medium."

It was a little after four o'clock, and although the store didn't officially open until six, the parking lot was already a quarter full.

"Other workers," Hildy guessed. "They must have a hundred of them working tonight."

Eliza followed Hildy into the store, into the "shopping experience" Ted Walsh had promised.

Just inside the door, where the shopping carts would normally be, was a row of folding tables covered with floor-length white tablecloths.

"Look at that," Hildy muttered, nudging her chin toward the other caterers already setting up. "They must have all got here early. Didn't Teddy say four o'clock?"

"Yes, but—"

"There he is." Hildy waved. "Hi, Teddy!"

He turned and smiled in acknowledgment, then continued his conversation with a small cluster of workers. After a few minutes he broke away and strode toward Hildy and Eliza.

"Now be nice," Hildy whispered.

"I'm always—"

"Ladies." Ted favored Eliza with that charming half-smile of his.

"So where do you want us?" Hildy asked. She searched for whatever prime real estate might be left. "Is there somewhere else in the store?"

"No, I want you right up here," Ted said, "where everyone will pass you. How are you, Eliza?"

"Fine," she said. "Hildy, I'll start bringing things in..."

"I'll get someone to help you," Ted said. He motioned to one of the men he'd been talking to. "Steve, this is Hildy and Eliza Shepherd. They're my stars tonight. Give them whatever they need."

"Well," Hildy said, raising her eyebrows at Eliza. "Isn't that nice?"

"Whatever you need," Ted repeated. "That food you brought me was perfect."

"Your brother didn't think so," Hildy huffed.

"He only likes things with ketchup," Ted said. "Steve'll

take care of you. I'll see you both later. I've got to get back to work."

Hildy seemed happy to have someone new to boss around. "Bring a cart out to my car," she told Steve. "And be careful you don't drop anything."

Once they were set up, with burners warming for the potatoes and all the other food ready to set out on trays, Hildy finally seemed to relax.

"Now," she told Eliza, looking around to make sure no one could hear. "I want you to smile at people tonight. Don't be yourself."

"Thanks a lot!"

"You know it's true. Sometimes you try to act like you're not really there, but it's not fair to people. You're new in town, and they want to get to know you."

"No one in Monarch is ever going to see me."

"You don't know that. Monarch isn't that far from Careyville, and you've already run into at least one person you know."

"Who? David Walsh? I'd hardly say I know him."

"The point is—"

"The point is," Eliza interrupted, "you want me to smile. Fine. I can do that."

"Not just smile," Hildy corrected. "Be *nice* to people. Friendly. Act like you like them."

Eliza groaned. "I'll do my best."

Hildy patted her hand. "I need better than that."

"You know, some people might say you're a little mean to your favorite daughter-in-law."

"That's because I know what's best for you."

"Oh, you do?" Eliza said with a laugh.

"I do, and here he comes now."

"So, all ready?" Ted asked. Sweat beaded his temples. He glanced around at the various tables. "Everything all right?"

"I think so," Hildy answered. "How are you? Nervous?"

Ted grimaced theatrically and pulled his collar away from his throat. "Just a little."

"How many of these have you done?" Hildy asked.

"This is my fourth. David used to be in charge of all the openings, but we're trying to split up the work more evenly."

"Oh, so he won't be here?" Eliza asked hopefully.

"No, he'll be here, the bastard, pretending to enjoy himself while I sweat it out."

At six o'clock the staff unlocked the doors and ushered a surprising number of people inside.

"Wow, not much to do on a Friday night," Eliza said.

"Are you kidding?" Hildy said. "This is big stuff. Wait till you see how some of the people dress—like they're going to a symphony or something."

Eliza saw immediately that it was true. Women in high heels and elegant dresses and long fur or wool coats. Men in sports jackets.

"I'm surprised there isn't a chamber group set up in here."

"Teddy told me they thought about that," Hildy answered. "Not a chamber group, but a few violins wandering around. But Davey did that before, and Teddy wanted something different."

"So what—fireworks?"

"You'll see," Hildy answered with a mysterious smile.

Shoppers wandered through the store, sampling the food

and wine offered at every aisle. From where their table was positioned, Eliza and Hildy could see only some of the selection: champagne in glasses the guests could keep, engraved with the Walsh's logo; cheese cut from enormous blocks; red and white wine; cigars; desserts in every shade of chocolate.

"I'm going to need a break," Hildy warned. "That mousse over there is calling me."

"Don't you dare leave me," Eliza said as she spooned out more mashed potatoes into someone's empty champagne glass. "I thought Ted said glass was too dangerous."

"Guess he bought a few brooms. Here you go, ma'am. Enjoy."

Hildy cast a devilish glare at her daughter-in-law. "You're not smiling."

Eliza did. "My face gets tired," she said through clenched teeth.

"Maybe you should practice smiling an hour a day instead of walking all the time." Hildy demonstrated her own smile to the next customer in line. "Enjoying yourself? Here you are, enjoy."

Enjoy, enjoy, enjoy, Eliza practiced mouthing. When she lifted her head to tend to the next customer, her smile immediately evaporated.

"Davey!" Hildy said. "I want you to try some of this. I made it special."

Eliza thought he seemed confused—either because he wasn't expecting personal attention, or because he forgot who Hildy was. His eyes flitted to Eliza, who quickly looked away. David hesitated before shifting to Hildy's side of the table.

"Give me your glass," Hildy ordered. "Try these potatoes first—horseradish."

"Yes, I already t-tried—"

"Wait, and these," she said, spooning four mushrooms onto a cocktail plate.

"Yes, thank you."

"And wait," she said, holding up her finger. "Just for you, because I remembered how much you like it…"

Hildy bent down and opened a small plastic container whose contents had not yet been set out. "Close your eyes…"

David's face grew even sterner. "I'm not going to—"

"You'll like it, Davey—I promise," Hildy coaxed.

Irritated, David Walsh closed his eyes. The woman in line behind him snickered. David's eyes flew open and he turned to her. "D-do you think that helps?"

The woman shrugged one shoulder. Her ornate scarf slipped just a bit. Chandelier earrings sparkled beneath her short black hair. "Take your time, *Davey*, but the rest of us would like a turn."

David faced Hildy once more and closed his eyes. "Now, please hurry."

Eliza dearly wished her mother-in-law did not feel it necessary to torture this unwilling and sour-faced man. "Yes," she agreed, "let's hurry."

"Open up…"

David opened his mouth just enough to allow the merest taste of what Hildy held out on a plastic fork. He swilled it around on his tongue and opened his eyes.

And against all odds, he smiled.

"Yes, Mrs. Shepherd, you're right."

Hildy nodded in satisfaction. "I made a whole batch just for you. Come by on your way out and I'll send some home."

The woman behind him poked him in the back. "What is it, Davey?"

Eliza thought for a fleeting moment the man had blushed. Impossible.

"N-nothing. I have to go find Ted. I'll meet you back in liquor."

The woman stared after him, obviously displeased with his reaction to her teasing. Quickly she shifted gears and went about trying to charm Hildy.

"Tell me, what was that?" she asked. "It looked sort of like—"

Hildy held her finger to her lips. "Old secret. Sorry, can't tell you."

The woman turned to Eliza. "Crafty, isn't she? Maybe you'll tell me."

"I have no idea."

The woman smiled as if she practiced smiling an hour every day. "I'll take some of the mushrooms, please. No pota- toes—they make you fat."

"They make you fat," Hildy muttered under her breath as soon as the woman was gone. She spooned an extra large helping into the next person's glass. "Potatoes are good for you." She clucked to herself a few more minutes while continuing to serve her customers. Finally she cooled down enough to switch topics. "Did you hear that? Davey still has a little of his old stutter."

"He stutters?" Eliza whispered through her most profes- sional server smile.

"He's much better. It used to be so bad you'd think he'd never get through a sentence."

"I didn't even hear it."

"Maybe you wouldn't if you didn't know. Back again?" she asked a young woman in line. "Good for you! Potatoes'll keep your hair shiny."

"How's it going?" Ted asked. He looked considerably more relaxed than the last time Eliza had seen him. The glass in his hand might have had something to do with it.

"Fine. Perfect," Hildy reported. She checked her watch. "How much longer do you figure?"

Ted, too, consulted his watch. "Maybe another hour. They're still coming."

It was true. Even now, past nine o'clock, a steady stream of finely-dressed customers continued to enter the store.

Eliza remained amazed. "What are all these people doing here on a Friday night?"

"I told you," Ted said, "it's a shopping and dining experience. This isn't just a grocery store, Lizzy—"

Eliza winced at the familiarity. Only her family and Hildy called her that. Even Jamey had only called her "Liz," or "El."

Ted leaned over the table. Eliza automatically took half a step back. She could smell the alcohol on his breath.

"I'm telling you," Ted whispered, "this store is going to be the biggest seller yet—much bigger than any of David's."

"I see," Eliza said, "so it's a competition?"

"No," Ted answered, "it's all in the family, of course. But it never hurts to beat my big brother at something, does it? Especially if it benefits us both?"

"Of course not," Hildy answered with a wink. "I promise to only shop here, even though the one in Careyville is much closer. That's Davey's, isn't it?"

"Well, technically they're *all* all of ours, right? But yeah, that one's David's."

"I'll drive up here," Hildy promised. "For whatever good it does you. I appreciate you giving me the chance to work here tonight. I'd like to start planning some classes here as soon as you're ready."

"Right...classes." Ted shifted his attention back to Eliza. "Do you teach those, too?"

"No, I write, remember?" Never much of a drinker herself, Eliza always felt a little prim when it came to alcohol. She could tolerate a little bit of drunkenness, but not much more. And Ted Walsh seemed to be bordering on much more. It surprised her that he would jeopardize his responsibility for the evening, but maybe he had had a few drinks to calm his nerves, and had just forgotten when to stop.

"Should I add more potatoes?" Eliza asked Hildy, trying to redirect the conversation.

"I don't know, do you think we'll see that many more people tonight, Teddy?"

"I hope so!" he said. "Bring out everything you've got. If they don't eat it, I will."

When Ted finally wandered off, Eliza had her first opportunity to quiz her mother-in-law. The stream of customers in front of them had temporarily stopped.

"All right, what was it?" Eliza asked.

"What was what?"

"You know. I saw what you fed David Walsh—it wasn't the recipe you showed me."

Hildy smiled. "Some memories never die."

"Such as?"

"Aren't there some foods you loved when you were a little girl, and you still love today?"

"Of course."

"Probably things your mother made you, right?"

"Yes, so what was it?"

Hildy retrieved the mystery container and popped open an edge.

"Brownies?"

"Not just brownies," Hildy said. "Special—" Her eyes shifted upward as she tried to recall the full title. "Special Super-Duper Delicious Amazing Remarkable Peanut Butter and Chocolate Chunk Brownies with Marshmallow Frosting."

"Oh, my gosh, that sounds disgusting."

Hildy laughed. "I know, it does, doesn't it? But the boys used to love them."

"Who? What boys?"

"Jamey and the neighbor boys, including Teddy and Davey Walsh. I bet he hasn't thought of those in years." Hildy patted another small container. "I made a separate batch for Teddy. I'm going to surprise him."

"Wait a minute, Teddy and Davey—David—were neighbors of yours?"

"Sort of. Their parents owned that house on the other

side of the fields where you take Daisy. In fact, those are their old fields—six of them, I think. They sold them to the state a few years ago when they made the lake into a state park."

"So that's all Walsh land—the trails—all of it?"

"Everything from the hill down to the lake."

"Do the parents still live there?"

"Their mother's a widow. She moved to Monarch a few years ago, probably to be closer to Suzy. Davey owns the old house now."

It was nearly midnight before Hildy agreed to pack everything away. Eliza's feet throbbed. Her back ached from standing so long.

The jazz band Ted had hired to get people dancing was finally packing up, too. The band members wandered among the remaining tables, searching for any leftovers.

"I just realized we didn't get to eat anything," Hildy said, watching them. "I really wanted to try that mousse."

"Want me to see if they have any left?"

"Sure. That's sweet of you."

Eliza spoke to the chocolate mousse woman and carried back two plastic cups filled to the brim. The woman had even crowned each serving with a mountain of whipped cream.

Eliza retrieved a tablecloth from one of the cleared tables and spread it on the floor. Then she and Hildy sat with their backs against the wall, enjoying a midnight picnic of chocolate.

Ted found them on the floor, savoring the last of their cups. He plopped onto the tablecloth beside Eliza. He laid his head on her shoulder. "I'm whipped."

She politely pushed him off. Clearly he had continued to sample his store's wine after they last saw him. "You're not driving home like this, you know."

Ted smiled at Eliza. "Oh, you care?"

Hildy brightened. "Good idea. We'll take you home."

Eliza wasn't anxious to spend any more time with the drunken Ted, but she also wasn't about to let him endanger himself or others on the road. He had no way of knowing, she thought to herself, but he'd fallen down several notches in her estimation that night: gone from charming to reckless. She expected him to act more professional—mature—at the grand opening of his own store.

Ted rested his head on Eliza's shoulder once more, and she removed it once again. She stood and pretended there was still more cleaning to do.

"I almost forgot," Hildy said. "I have something for you." She pulled one of the plastic containers from the stack beside her. "Remember these?"

Ted smiled when he saw the brownies. "Not the whole thing? Everything?"

"Peanut butter, marshmallows, everything," Hildy confirmed.

"Mrs. S., you slay me. You have my heart." He took a bite and savored it. He held out the remainder of the brownie to Eliza. "Have you tried these?"

"No, thanks, I'm not a big fan of marshmallows."

Ted stood. "You have to try it." He pressed the brownie

toward Eliza's mouth. She turned just in time to feel the sticky marshmallow against her cheek.

Ted laughed. "I'm sorry!" He used the end of his sleeve to wipe it off.

"It's okay," Eliza said irritably. She caught Ted's wrist. "Please stop. I'll do it myself."

Ted widened his eyes at Hildy. "Ooh, touchy, isn't she?"

Eliza glanced up and saw David Walsh standing in a nearby aisle, watching. As soon as she caught his eye he turned around.

"We should go," Eliza said. "Ted, we're giving you a ride."

"Okay," he said. He held out his wrists as if for handcuffs. "I'll go quietly."

Eliza ignored him. She put on her coat and loaded Hildy's equipment and containers onto two carts. "Here," she told Ted, "you push that one." She was tired of babying him. She wanted nothing more to do with him.

Once everything—including Ted—was loaded into Hildy's car, Eliza had a flash of guilt.

"Hold on." A promise was a promise.

She opened the back of Hildy's car and took out the container she had deliberately left on top. Pulling her coat close around her to fight off the wind, Eliza hurried back into the store.

She found David in the back, checking inventory against a list.

"Here," Eliza said, handing him the plastic container. "From Hildy."

David briefly met Eliza's eyes, then accepted the brownies with a nod.

"Th—" He paused, swallowed. "Thank her."

"I will."

Eliza turned and strode back the way she came. Maybe David Walsh was cold and surly, but at least he wasn't drunk.

Ted chatted merrily the whole way to his house, recounting the evening's highlights. Eliza glared out the window. When they pulled up in front of his house, Hildy handed him the container of brownies she'd kept in the front seat, and thanked him again for letting her cater the event. "I'll call you Monday about classes. I'd like to start them right away."

"Call me," he agreed. "Call me," he told Eliza as well.

"Good night," she said coldly.

Ted exited the back seat, slammed the door, and tapped on Eliza's window. Reluctantly she lowered it.

"You looked beautiful tonight," he said as he leaned forward and kissed her cheek. "I think I love you." He straightened and waved to them both.

"Ass," Eliza muttered as they drove away.

"He was nervous about tonight," Hildy said. "You saw that. He's not usually like that."

"How do you know? You haven't seen him in years."

"I know how he was when I met with him last week. And I know how he was when we came to his house. You saw—wasn't he different then?"

"Maybe he just hadn't hit the bottle yet."

"Give the boy some credit," Hildy said. "He's a very successful young man. So what if he gets a little high-spirited now and then?"

"I've been around a lot of drunks, Hildy. The guys on the

outdoor circuit are famous for it. Jamey didn't drink—he didn't have to. He was funny and charming as he was."

"Teddy is funny and charming, too. I think you make him nervous."

"Oh, now *I'm* the one who made him nervous? First it was the store—"

Hildy pulled to the side of the street and turned to her daughter-in-law. "Lizzy, did you not hear the man tell you he loves you?"

Eliza laughed. "He was drunk!"

"A man can say what's in his heart much more easily if he's had a few."

"If I believed every drunk guy who told me I was beautiful or he wanted to marry me or he loved me..." Eliza sighed. "Just give it up, Hildy. You're not going to find a new husband for me among the famous men of Syracuse."

Hildy shrugged. "I'm just saying, he's normally a very nice man. He's always been a sweetheart. And did you notice he didn't have a date tonight?"

"I understand why."

"Do you? It's because he wanted to flirt with you."

"No, it's because no one would have him."

Hildy huffed as she resumed her drive back home. "No one would have him—do you understand how much money that family has?"

"It doesn't make up for bad manners—you've said so yourself. That arrogant David, and Ted stumbling all over the place. Unless their sister has any manners, I'd say it skipped a whole generation."

"No, their parents are pretty awful," Hildy confessed.

"Sibylla Walsh is a horror. And that husband, rest in peace, was as rude as they come."

"See?"

They rode in exhausted silence the rest of the way home. As they carried the leftover food up the stairs, Hildy tried one more time.

"You should call him in the morning to make sure he's all right."

"I'm not doing that."

"Even if it means the difference between your mother-in-law starving and being able to make a living?"

Eliza groaned. "It shouldn't depend on me."

"But it wouldn't hurt for you to be nice to him, would it?"

"You are an evil, conniving woman," Eliza said. "I'm not talking about this anymore."

Hildy sank into one of the kitchen chairs. "Oof. I'm too old to stay up so late."

"Me, too." Eliza dropped into the chair across from her.

Hildy lifted her weary eyes to Eliza's. "Honey, I wouldn't say this if I didn't mean it: You're too hard sometimes. You don't give in. You're a lovely girl, but sometimes it's hard for people to see it because you can be so hard."

Eliza swallowed her answer. Her mother-in-law had hit a nerve she might not have known Eliza had.

It was something Jamey had worked on all the years of their marriage. Because Hildy was right: Eliza could be hard. Closed off to new people and new experiences. It was a matter of safety—something she'd always thought she needed to survive.

But Jamey had gently coaxed her from her cocoon. Pulled

her out of the comfort of her routines. Shown her a world and a way of living she never could have imagined for herself.

And then the moment he died, she'd retreated from it so quickly. Pulled back. Closed in. Facing Jamey's mother now, Eliza wondered if maybe she really did need some sort of outside intervention. Something to keep her from completely closing again.

She sighed deeply. "Hildy, I need you to understand: I don't want a boyfriend. I'm being honest with you—I really can't bear it if you're going to push me at anyone. Do you understand?"

"Not a boyfriend," Hildy agreed. "So how about a friend?"

"I've met a friend—Carolyn Jackson."

"Another friend, then," Hildy said. "Give him another chance. You'll see what he's really like."

Eliza closed her tired eyes. "If I call him..."

"Just to ask how he's feeling. Tell him how nice his opening was."

"Fine." Eliza rose from her chair and headed down the hall for bed.

"Thanks for all your help tonight, honey."

"You are sincerely welcome," Eliza answered, "and I hope I won't have to do it again for a long time."

SHE WAITED until ten o'clock the next morning to place the call.

"Hello, Ted? It's Eliza. Shepherd."

"I know which Eliza. How are you?"

"Fine. I wondered...how you were?"

"You mean other than this jackass headache of mine? Oh, fine. Listen, I'm going to be out that way this afternoon. Can I stop by and bang my head against your wall?"

Eliza smiled despite herself. "Why would you want to do that?"

"To prove what a jackass I am. I can't believe I slobbered all over you last night. Thankfully I can only remember parts of it, but please feel free to shoot me now."

"You were nervous."

"Got that right. A beautiful woman like you—"

"No," Eliza cut him off, "I mean about the opening."

"Ah, that was nothing—a few snacks, a little wine, some glad-handing—I've seen it all before. Can I take you to dinner?"

"No."

"Not even if I give myself a huge lump on my head from banging it?"

"Especially not."

"Eliza, I'm being serious here. I'd like to take you out."

Eliza closed her eyes and knocked the phone against her forehead a few times. Then she put the phone back to her ear and said, "Look, I don't mean to hurt your feelings—"

"Then don't," Ted insisted. "Look, it's just dinner. I swear I'll mind my manners, and if you have a terrible time you never have to speak to me again."

"That's an attractive offer—the last part."

"And I won't try to get by with giving you free food from Walsh's. I'll take you out for a proper meal."

Eliza weighed her options and her fears carefully. "I

really need you to understand that I don't date—anyone. I don't want to—ever."

"Ever?"

In the silence that followed, Eliza took the time to replay what she had just said. How must that sound to a normal human being?

"I'm not...ready."

"Okay, fair enough," Ted said. "We'll go out to dinner just this once and it will be fine—I promise. If you hate it, you never have to do it again."

Even if he meant if lightly, the promise actually mattered to Eliza.

"I need to tell you right now," she said. "I don't want you to kiss me."

"Okay, then, I won't."

"You have to swear it to me. I'm serious, Ted—there can't be any of that."

"You make an attractive offer yourself," Ted joked, "but I promise I'll be good." In a more serious tone he repeated, "Really, Eliza, I promise."

"No place fancy," she said. "I'm done wearing a dress for a while."

"No fancy. Check. I know just the place. See you at seven."

"Tonight?"

"Tonight."

"Wait, I—"

"Nothing fancy. Bye."

Eliza held on to the phone even after she heard the click.

Coward, she thought of him, *hanging up before I could refuse.*

Liar, she thought of herself, *you weren't going to refuse, were you?*

7

Eliza tried on four outfits before settling on a lavender sweater, black jeans, and black boots.

"Put on makeup," Hildy urged.

Eliza turned from the mirror. "Do you know how insulting that is?" she asked good-naturedly. "You're telling me I'm ugly without it."

"No one would ever call my Lizzy ugly. I just think you could use some color."

"I'm sure I'll be blushing enough on my own. I have no idea what to say to this man for a whole evening."

Hildy chuckled. "I like seeing you like this. I missed out on all those mother-daughter things like proms."

"What, you mean Jamey didn't try on everything in his closet before a date?"

"I think he picked whatever didn't smell too bad. I refused to do his laundry after he was fifteen, so he usually didn't have many clothes to choose from."

"Well, by the time he got to me, I can assure you he was fully informed about the washer. So good job on your part."

"Thank you. Now, what're you going to do about your hair?" Hildy ran her fingers through Eliza's ponytail. "you're not going to wear it like that."

Eliza gave her best imitation of an annoyed teenager. "Mother..."

Hildy smiled. "I'm just saying—"

"I'm going to feel weird enough on this date without having to wear my hair some different way. Let me take it one step at a time, all right?"

"Can you at least put it over one shoulder?"

"No. It stays as it is."

Hildy sighed. "Will you wear a necklace if I pick one out?"

"Maybe."

Eliza surveyed her work. She compromised on the makeup issue by adding a smear of cola-flavored lip gloss. It gave her lips a light brown tint.

"Here." Hildy handed her a simple gold chain. "That's not too much, is it?"

"No, but I don't usually wear jewelry. I think I'll go without."

"Speaking of which..." Hildy pointed to Eliza's left hand. "Believe me, honey, I appreciate how much you loved my son, but the fact is he's gone. If you keep wearing your wedding ring..."

Eliza closed her other hand around it protectively. "The ring stays. That's non-negotiable."

"For how long?" Hildy asked softly.

"I don't know. I don't want to talk about it right now." Eliza glanced at her watch. "Is it normal to be on time? I hope not."

"In my day a boy had to be prompt or the girl's parents would think he was a heel. I don't know how they do it anymore. Now he can probably show up a month later and a girl will still go out with him."

"It's shocking the lack of manners," Eliza teased, knowing how seriously Hildy took the subject.

"It really is."

At 7:06 by the living room clock, Ted Walsh rang the doorbell.

Hildy hugged her daughter-in-law. "Have a good time, honey—I mean it."

Eliza forced a smile. "I'll try."

Hildy pointed at her. "No, *do*." She waited at the top of the stairs while Eliza opened the front door.

In his black knit shirt, charcoal wool slacks, and a brown suede jacket, Ted looked so handsome and dapper and...masculine. He had gotten a haircut since she last saw him—short on the sides, still thick on top. He wore his wire-frame glasses again, although Eliza realized he hadn't worn them at the opening. She wore her glasses, too—one step at a time.

Eliza felt her body tremble with nerves. She squeaked out a hi.

Luckily, Hildy diverted his attention. "Hi, Teddy," she called from up above.

"Hello, Mrs. Shepherd. I promise to have her back by midnight."

"Way before midnight, if you don't mind," Eliza said.

"We'll see—I might run out of gas."

"Have a good time," Hildy called.

"Okay, thanks."

"We will," Ted promised.

Eliza waited until she had closed the door behind them before telling Ted, "I was serious, what I said before. You have to understand this is a scary thing for me. I have to be able to trust you."

Ted held up his right hand. "I promise. Nothing funny. But you have to promise me something, too."

"What?"

"That you'll let yourself have a good time tonight if that's how it goes. I don't want you spending the whole night feeling guilty or nervous or whatever this is."

"I can't help being nervous. I barely know you."

"That's how this works," Ted answered. "Look, if it makes you feel any better, I've been a little nervous around you, too. I think maybe that's why I drank about five times what I should have the other night."

"Somehow I think you had bigger issues on your mind."

"A few," he said, "but you were definitely one of them."

The news didn't relax her in the least. "Okay, let's say this," she said. "I intend to have a good time tonight. How's that?"

"Good enough."

Ted offered her his arm. The sleeve of his jacket felt warm and soft against her hand. Eliza willed herself to relax. *Nothing's going to happen.*

"By the way," Ted said, "you're not one of those women who's afraid to eat on a date, are you?"

"Not that I recall," she said with a slight smile.

"Good, because I won't stand for it," he said. "Not where I'm taking you. I expect you to eat at least as much as I do." Ted opened the passenger door of his SUV and Eliza slid onto the leather seat.

"I don't know if I can compete," she said once he joined her. "Hildy tells me you're a big eater."

Ted patted his stomach. "I have to work out about fourteen hours a day just to keep it all off."

"Impressive."

"Yeah, the ladies tell me I'm a fairly fine specimen."

"How nice for you," Eliza answered, finally finding the rhythm of his sarcasm.

"There's a website, if you want to add your testimonial at the end of the night."

"So, you're kind of a jerk, aren't you?"

He flashed her a smile. "See? We're getting to know each other already."

Zeiger's was half an hour away on the freeway. Tucked behind a few industrial-looking warehouses, the restaurant looked quaint and unassuming from the front.

"German food?"

"Yeah, I hope that's okay," Ted said.

"Sounds great."

Ted escorted her inside. The young woman acting as hostess broke into a smile. "Teddy!" She emerged from behind her podium to give him a hug.

"This is Eliza. Eliza, Denise."

"Hi. Hold on," she told Ted. "I'll go get him."

A minute later a short, stout man emerged from the kitchen and surrounded Ted in a bone-cracking hug.

"This is Eliza," Ted gasped. "Eliza, my uncle Herbert."

Eliza smiled. "Well, that's a surprise. Nice to meet you."

Uncle Herbert clasped Eliza's hand in his own meaty one. His German accent was unmistakable. "The surprise is mine. Usually I'm not good enough for Teddy's girlfriends."

"Oh, I'm not—"

"She's not—we're just friends, Uncle Herbert. You shouldn't say things like that."

"Why not?" he said.

"Because it embarrasses people."

"*Ach*, you're not embarrassed, are you, Miss?"

"Yes," Eliza answered.

Uncle Herbert frowned. "Teddy, not you."

"Horrified. Can we sit down now?" Ted caught Eliza's eye and winked.

"You like German food?" Uncle Herbert asked as he led them to a booth in the back.

"I'm not sure I've really had any."

"Not sure? You would be sure. Here, sit here. Is Teddy treating you nice?"

"So far."

"If he says anything wrong, you tell me. I'll call you a taxi."

Eliza smiled. "Thanks. Good to know."

"This is why I don't bring people here," Ted said. "He's crazy."

Uncle Herbert pushed Ted aside and crammed his bulk

onto the red leather seat beside him. He interlaced his fingers on top of the table and fixed his eyes on Eliza. "How do you know Teddy?"

"Uncle—"

Uncle Herbert held up his hand. "If she doesn't want to answer she won't, correct?"

"Correct," Eliza said. "I met him last week when my mother-in-law brought some food for him to sample."

"Your mother-in-law? Are you married?"

"Uncle Herb—"

"Was," Eliza said. "He died."

Uncle Herbert seemed strangely affected by the news. He reached across the table as if to clasp Eliza's hand, but at the last moment withdrew and settled both hands into his lap. "My wife—Freida—she died, too."

Eliza had always hated the response "I'm sorry" when she told people about Jamey. Sorry for what? It wasn't as if any them had pushed him off that cliff. But those words were so automatic, she almost said them to Uncle Herbert. She stopped herself in time, and said instead, "I see."

"When did your husband—"

"Uncle Herbert," Ted interrupted, "do you mind? I brought Eliza here to have a good time—with me." He nudged the old man in the ribs. "If you want to talk to her, you ask her out next time."

Eliza smiled apologetically at Uncle Herbert, but she was grateful Ted had interfered. The last thing she wanted to do on her first time out with a man in two years was to spend the evening talking about Jamey.

And yet, between bites of her enormous open-faced

Reuben sandwich with steaming red cabbage and melted Swiss cheese on top, and between sips of dark beer out of a stein, Eliza found herself questioning Ted about her late husband:

"How old was he when you knew him?"

"What did he like to do?"

"Who were his friends?"

Ted tolerated the inquisition fairly well, Eliza thought, and even seemed to encourage it at first. "Let's get it out on the table," he had said in the beginning, "since Uncle Herbert brought it up."

"I'd rather not."

"Come on, Eliza, we might as well."

But after an hour of reminiscing, Ted finally called an end to it. "Well, as much as I've enjoyed talking about Jamey all night—"

"Oh Ted, I'm sorry. I didn't mean...I guess I got a little carried away."

"It's okay. My turn to pick a topic. Want another beer?"

Eliza peered into her stein. "I'm only half way." She noticed Ted had finished his, but not ordered another.

"You ate quite a lot," Ted said.

Eliza cocked her head. "That's good, right?"

"It's excellent. We'll have you porky in no time." Ted relaxed back against the booth. He gazed at Eliza and smiled. "I like the way you look tonight."

Eliza adjusted her glasses and averted her eyes. Talking about Jamey had been easier.

"So," she said, clearing her throat, "tell me about your family. Who is Uncle Herbert related to?"

"He's my mother's older brother. They came over together with their parents."

"Does your mother have an accent?"

"It's gotten less over the years, but when I was growing up it was like living in Berlin."

"And you have a sister? How old is she?"

Ted consulted the ceiling. "Let's see...probably thirty-four now. David's thirty-five, I'm thirty-two—"

"So a year older than Jamey."

"Yep."

"Ever married?" Eliza asked.

"Once. She was a two-headed dragon disguised as a princess."

"The usual story."

"But absolutely true in my case," Ted said. "The Discovery Channel came out and took pictures."

"How long were you married?"

"Four tortuous years. Let's go back to talking about Jamey."

"Your sister's married?"

"Very. With two boys, and don't ask me how old they are."

"Babies, or older?" Eliza asked.

"Oh, definitely walking and talking—one of them might even go to high school. I don't really keep track of that."

"Don't you get along?"

"With my sister? Sure. And her husband and the nephews —all one big happy family."

"Are you being sarcastic?"

Ted laughed. "No. I really do love my family—all of them. Even David."

"So you two are partners?"

"It's actually a family business. My parents and David and Sue and I all own shares. My dad died a few years ago, and now David and I run it."

"Sue never wanted to?"

"Nah, she's too smart. She got an engineering degree, worked at that for a few years, then took off for a while after the kids were born. Now she teaches high school math."

"Never one of my best subjects," Eliza confessed.

"Not mine, either."

"So what were you?" she asked. "In school, I mean."

"Prom king—can't you tell?"

"Of course. I always hated guys like you."

"Why?" Ted asked. "The world needs bubbled-headed beauties as much as it needs brains."

"Somehow I doubt you're a bubble head."

"No, you need to examine our family tree. David is the brain, Suzy is the über-brain, Teddy is the screw-up."

"How have you screwed up?"

"Oh, let's see...got a girl pregnant in high school, wrecked my first three cars, partied my way out of one college and had to start all over again—"

"Wow."

"Oh, it gets better," he said. "Married the first girl I thought I actually loved, let her clean me out in the divorce, had to start all over by going into the family business..."

"So you weren't going to go into it to begin with?"

"No," Ted scoffed. "That's David's world. He worked for

my dad from the time he was twelve. He's always had that store in his veins. It probably kills him to have to share it with me." Ted chuckled and shook his head.

"You two don't get along?" Eliza asked.

"No, we do, it's just...we're pretty different."

"I've noticed."

"I like David," Ted said, "but he's...different."

"Different how?"

"Now I feel like we're back to talking about Jamey," Ted said. "So far I can't say I've done much to woo you."

"This wasn't a wooing date."

"How do you know?" Ted asked. "Maybe that was my whole plan."

"Then it was destined to fail. I am unwooable."

Ted leaned forward, that look of mischief in his eyes again. "A challenge."

"No," Eliza said, flustered. "Just being honest."

"You think there's nothing I can do to make you like me?"

"I do like you," she said, "but not in that way."

Ted's mouth curved into that half-smile. "Oh, Miss Eliza, what way is that?"

"Romantically."

"I'm happy to hear you say it out loud. That's always the first step."

"You got a girl pregnant?"

Ted slouched back into his seat. "You're going to bring that up again? Yeah. I was a total turd."

"What happened?"

"Her parents talked her into an abortion. Which was a relief. I don't know what I would have done."

"How old were you?" Eliza said.

"Fifteen."

"What happened to her?"

"She hated me," he said. "We had to see each other at school for three more years, then finally she went away to college. I was such a jerk."

"And when did you get married?"

"When I was twenty-three. Listen, I'm convinced it's this booth. We can't have any pleasant conversation as long as we keep sitting here. Let's go someplace else."

"You're leaving?" their host asked as they headed toward the door.

"Yes, Uncle Herb."

"It was delicious," Eliza said.

"But you should stay!"

"Eliza needs some ice cream," Ted told him.

"I do?" she asked.

"You do." Ted lifted her hand and threaded it through his arm. "All part of my plan to fatten you up."

As they walked to the car, Eliza checked her watch. "Oh my gosh, it's already eleven o'clock."

"Good. We have another hour before Hildy calls the cops on me."

"No, really," Eliza said, "I have to get home. It's late. I'm not used to hours like this."

Ted opened the passenger door, but before Eliza could get in, he lazily leaned against it.

"You look very beautiful tonight."

Eliza cleared her throat and crossed her arms over her chest. "Thank you."

"This hasn't been so bad, has it?"

"No," she admitted, "it hasn't."

He nodded. The soft brown eyes behind his glasses met hers and refused to look away.

Eliza held his gaze for as long as she could. Then she stared down at her boots.

"Eliza..."

She glanced up. In the yellow glow of the parking lot lights, she could see his seductive smile.

"No," she answered quietly.

"Why?"

"Because you promised."

"It was a bad promise," he said.

"I trusted you."

"You can still trust me."

She tried to meet his gaze again, but a cold kind of panic swept through her. She could feel the blood freezing inside her veins. Her body shivered in response.

"Cold?" He took a step forward and reached out toward her.

Eliza stepped back.

This time she forced herself to look at him.

He waited a moment, then asked, "Are you sure?"

No.

"Yes."

"Not even one kiss?" he said, smiling in that sleepy way. "Just this once?"

She didn't trust her voice. Eliza shook her head.

Ted shrugged and stepped aside. "I'm a man of my word. Come on, I'll take you home."

When he settled into the driver's seat, he turned to face her again.

"There's one thing I forgot to tell you," he said. "About Jamey."

Eliza's throat felt tight. "What?"

Ted started the ignition. "He always got the best girls."

8

———————

Eliza awoke the next morning to renewed signs of spring. The last traces of snow had finally melted, and the daffodils in Hildy's front yard seemed safe again.

"Come on, Daisy. Long walk."

They stepped out into the bright morning sunlight and headed in the opposite direction of their usual route, past Carolyn Jackson's house this time, toward the woods at the east end of the street.

Eliza knew that the fields on top of the hill would be beautiful this morning, but they were too exposed. She felt like she needed to hide.

She hadn't slept well. The scene at Hildy's door hung over her.

"Good night," Ted said, and waited.

Eliza hesitated, then offered him her hand. In a clearly business-like way.

"Thanks," she said. "I really enjoyed it."

"Me, too," he said, holding her hand longer than he should have. "Except for this part."

"Sorry," she said, and meant it.

Ted let go of her hand, nodded once, and turned.

She watched him walk to his car.

He's never calling me again.

Good. That was the point, wasn't it?

Not really sure whether she slept at all, Eliza gave up trying at four in the morning. She wrapped Jamey's old flannel robe around her and padded into the kitchen to make coffee. Then she curled up on the couch with a sleepy dog and her journal, and poured out all of her fears.

He's too good looking. He's too wild. He'll expect too much. I can't do it.

She paused to sip more coffee and stroke Daisy's comforting ears. The dog snuggled closer and gave an enthusiastic snore.

He reminds me of Jamey, Eliza wrote to herself. *That can't be good. But he's not like Jamey, and that's not good either.*

Eliza groaned at the contradiction. "Hopeless," she whispered to the dog.

Now the two of them walked along the spongy trail of the forest, Daisy manic over the new smells, Eliza still journaling in her head.

"Daisy, quit." Eliza tugged the terrier away from the remains of a squirrel. Daisy lunged forward again and continued to examine the corpse.

"Stop!" Eliza dragged the dog back onto the trail. "Can't we just enjoy a nice quiet walk?"

In the next second she knew the answer was no.

"Bear!"

The black Lab came bounding toward them, with David running behind. Eliza tightened her grip on Daisy's leash just as the terrier launched her attack.

"Daisy, no!"

But the Lab wasn't intimidated. He barked and growled in response, ears up, tail wagging furiously. He dropped his forelegs and stuck his rear into the air, clearly believing the whole thing was play.

Daisy was deadly serious, as always. She kept up her assault as far as the leash would allow her.

David caught up with them and grabbed the Lab's collar. "Bear, sit."

The dog did, but only for an instant. Then he was on his feet again, circling Daisy, barking and egging her on.

Eliza sighed. "Look, she's crazy. This isn't going to stop. You should just keep going."

Instead David pulled his dog to a spot a few feet away and once again ordered him to sit. Bear did, but his body quivered, obviously ready to break the command and dive back into battle at any moment.

David had to shout over Daisy's barking. "You went out with my brother last night."

"Great, was that on his website?"

"What?"

"Nothing. You should probably go. She's never going to shut up."

Still he stood there. Even though he didn't seem to have anything else to say.

"I thought you ran up on the hill," Eliza tried.

"Some days. I usually go through the woods once or twice a week."

My good luck.

Remarkably, Daisy was starting to settle down. Now she just yipped in between bouts of trying to catch her breath.

"Okay," David told his dog, and the Lab immediately released. He came toward Daisy, but this time the terrier didn't lunge so much as strain. Soon the dogs were nose to nose, sniffing each other's faces before moving to parts further down the body.

"Wow, she's...okay," Eliza said.

"S-sometimes..." David paused and swallowed. "Some-times you just have to let them get used to each other."

"I guess I've never gotten that far with her," Eliza confessed. "She's such a psycho I just try to get her away."

The dogs were now doing a sort of leaping, spinning dance with each other, Bear getting tangled up in Daisy's leash. But Eliza didn't dare let go of it. Daisy could go off again at any minute.

Instead she let the dogs pull her forward down the trail. And David walked with them.

"So," Eliza said, feeling that at least one of them should make small talk, "how did you like the opening?"

"It was fine."

"The food?"

"Good." David reached down to pick up a stick. He threw it for Bear and Daisy strained to follow. "How's your wrist?"

"My wrist?" It took her a moment to remember the kick David had delivered to it the week before. "Oh, it's fine." She rotated it to show him. "No permanent damage."

He nodded. The Lab trotted back with the stick and David threw it again.

"How old is B—"

"Do you cook?" David asked her at the same time.

"Do I...cook?" Eliza repeated. "You mean the food Hildy brought to the opening? No, that was all her. I can cook, but not like that. I'm more...basic."

David nodded. They continued to walk along the path, Daisy relatively calm now, the Lab manically retrieving the stick. After a few minutes of silence Eliza felt like she should say something more, but she didn't know what.

Finally David spoke. "You write."

"Yes."

"I've...read some of it."

Eliza turned to look at him. "You have?"

David nodded.

And...? Eliza couldn't tell from his tone what he thought of it. But she knew it wasn't polite to ask.

She decided to switch topics. "Hildy tells me you live in your parents' old house."

"Yes."

"Where, exactly?"

"Over the hill, toward the lake, then down to the left."

"By yourself?" she asked, and immediately regretted it. What business was it of hers?

"Yes. You met my Uncle Herbert last night?"

Eliza halted. "Seriously, where are you getting all this information?"

"I talked to Ted this morning."

"He's awfully chatty."

"Did you like my uncle's restaurant?"

"Yes, very much."

"We're thinking of setting up an area in one of our stores for him."

"That sounds like a good idea." But Eliza couldn't help wondering, *Why are you talking to me?*

"Goodbye," David said abruptly.

"Oh, okay. See you."

David whistled for Bear and the two resumed their run.

When they were safely a distance away, Eliza paused and knelt beside her dog. "I don't understand these people," she whispered to her confidante. "Can you explain them to me?"

Daisy licked her hand.

"I thought so. You're useless." Eliza straightened and took in her surroundings. Somehow she had lost the urge to walk the legs off the terrier that morning. She turned and headed back toward Careybrook Lane.

"Something came for you," Hildy sang down the stairs as Eliza came through the door.

"What?"

"Come see."

Hildy beamed as she pointed toward the kitchen.

Sitting on the counter was a vase overflowing with cheerful-looking white daisies—Eliza's favorite flower.

Hildy chuckled. "You think he got those because of Daisy?"

"I doubt it." Eliza approached the flowers feeling every bit as nervous as if Ted himself stood there holding them. She read the card.

"Not bad for a first date. Let's try again."

Eliza bit her lower lip.

"What's it say?"

"You know what it says—you already opened it."

"You can't blame an old woman for being curious."

"It's called nosy. And I like how you're an old woman only when you think it excuses some bad behavior of yours."

Hildy chuckled. "He likes you."

"Well, good for him."

"Lizzy—"

Eliza faced her mother-in-law. "I've decided not to see him again."

"Why? I thought you liked him. He certainly likes you."

"I'm not ready."

"He's not proposing—it's just a date."

"I'm not ready," Eliza repeated. "Just leave it alone." She

passed her mother-in-law and headed down the hall to her bedroom.

"You'll never guess who delivered them," Hildy called after her. "Funny thing."

Eliza paused. "Funny how?"

"You think the florists work on Sunday?" Hildy taunted.

Eliza retraced her steps and stood before her smug mother-in-law. "All right, out with it."

"It was Davey Walsh."

"What?"

"That's right."

"Why would he deliver them?"

Hildy shrugged. "He said he was passing by."

"Jogging, carrying a vase of daisies."

"No, in his car—it's across the street."

"Why would he have flowers from Ted?"

"He said he was at the store this morning—the one in Careyville—when Teddy called in the order. Instead of sending a delivery boy, Davey decided to bring them himself since he was coming right by here."

"Why would he do that?"

"That's what I thought," Hildy said. "When I saw him at the door holding flowers, I thought for a minute my Lizzy had two suitors."

ELIZA SLAPPED her brain back to attention. She needed to work. She had a new essay due for her newspaper column in a few days, and had no idea what she was going to write.

She syndicated her newspaper columns herself. She and

Jamey had figured out how. Instead of going through a service, Eliza contacted each and every potential newspaper on her own, pitching herself, her background, and the kind of "lifestyle" pieces she would write.

The list of newspaper clients had grown slowly. First just a handful, then twenty, and now around eighty-five. But to sign up that many, she'd sent queries to hundreds and hundreds more. She'd gotten used to rejection, but it still was never fun.

A few thousand dollars here, a few thousand there, and over the course of a year Eliza made a reasonable wage from her writing. It had been nice to get the advance from the publisher for the book about Jamey—she hardly ever saw that many zeros all in one check.

But writing books took a long time, and a sustained effort, and right now the short essays she wrote for newspapers and magazines suited her attention span perfectly. She could write a draft in a few hours, spend another hour or so editing, and be done in the space of a day.

That was if she had an idea for it to begin with. If not, she sometimes spent hours and days researching, waiting for an idea to spark.

This was one of those times. Eliza felt completely at a loss for some topic her readers might like.

She booted up her laptop and sorted through some of her usual sources of inspiration: quotes from philosophers, poets, adventurers. But nothing spoke to her. All she kept hearing was a vague whisper in her ear, telling her to *"Run."*

So that's what she wrote.

Run. Even when we think something might be good for us, we still run from it if it means change. Why is that? Is it some prehistoric instinct? Did the cave people who lived by the creed "same ole, same ole" live longer than the thrill-seekers?

Nah, Eliza thought, *try again.* She often had to write her way through many false starts before finally finding the rhythm of a piece.

Why, she rehearsed on the keys of her laptop, *do we run from what might be good for us? Are we so sure that the way we've always done things is the best possible way to get along? What's wrong with trying something new every day—driving a different route, eating something besides our standard peanut butter and jelly—*

"Ugh," Eliza groaned out loud. "You suck."

She folded the laptop closed and took her restless mind out into the back yard.

Hildy knelt at the edge of the garden on a piece of sheepskin she had found in the salvage bin at the fabric store. She dug in the dirt and planted another pansy from the flat of flowers at her side.

Eliza didn't bother offering to help. Her lack of gardening skills was legendary. She either overwatered or underwatered, never weeded, wanted the plants to just fend for themselves and look pretty. She was always shocked when something she had planted over the summer died from a winter freeze. She'd see houses all along her street with sheets and pillow cases draped over the plants, but it never registered that she should do that, too. It was nature—wasn't it supposed to take care of itself?

Eliza plopped into one of the plastic chairs beneath the porch and watched her mother-in-law enjoy herself.

"Want something to drink?" she asked.

"No," Hildy answered. "I'm fine."

Eliza wanted to talk: about the date, about the flowers, about her strange conversation with David, everything. But suddenly Hildy seemed like the wrong choice.

"I think I'll walk down and see if Carolyn is home."

"Have fun."

Eliza changed into shorts and a long-sleeved T-shirt and made her way down the street.

Katie answered the door. "Where's Daisy?"

"At home asleep. She had a big morning. What are you up to?"

Katie admitted her to the house. "My mom and I are making up baskets for Mother's Day."

"Mother's Day? Is that here already?"

"In a few weeks," Katie said. "You'd better send your mom some flowers."

"I'd better," Eliza agreed.

"Thank goodness," Carolyn as soon as she saw Eliza coming up the stairs. "Another pair of hands."

"Put me to work," Eliza said. "I'm bored out of my mind today."

The dining room table had been cleared of fleece, and in its place were stacks of colorful baskets, several bags of ribbons and colored tissue paper, and an assortment of candy and school supplies.

"We're making these for the women's shelter," Katie explained. "The moms get the chocolate and the kids get the stupid stuff."

"Katie!"

Katie rolled her eyes at her mother. "It's true. I'd rather have chocolate."

She grabbed a piece and unwrapped it just to prove her point.

Carolyn reached toward her and slapped at the air. "Stop eating our inventory."

Katie grinned and handed some of the chocolate to Eliza.

Eliza surveyed the room, from the cluttered dining room table to the wall hangings and the other furnishings.

"Do all you Syracuse women do all this superwoman stuff?"

"What superwoman stuff?" Carolyn asked.

Eliza swept her hand across the room. "All these crafts. Those afghans over there. Those fleece blankets you made. Hildy must sew about three or four quilts a year—they're hanging all over the house and piled on the beds. And she gardens, and cooks—I barely know how to do anything but brush my own hair."

"It's just something you learn," Carolyn said. "My mother taught me, I'm teaching Katie—"

"Your mom never taught you stuff like this?" Katie asked.

"She and I are more into movies," Eliza said. "Sometimes we'll see three or four in a weekend. And she does cook—I've learned a lot of that from her."

"You should come to Girls' Club," Katie offered. "We learn all kinds of stuff."

Carolyn smiled. "Not a bad idea. Next week they're learning to make paper from scratch."

"From scratch?" Eliza said. "I could probably use that in my profession."

"You should come give a talk to the girls sometime," Carolyn said. "Talk about being a writer."

"Maybe I will. What do you think, Katie?"

She nodded, distracted by the refinements of her task. She repositioned the pencils and the chocolate in her basket until they looked perfect.

Carolyn said, "You can come any week if you want to help. We meet Friday nights."

A good excuse for being busy Friday nights, Eliza thought. "Maybe I will."

"But you'll have to work much faster than that," Carolyn observed. Eliza was just wrapping up her first basket, while Carolyn had already moved on to her fifth in the same amount of time. "We run our crafts like a chain gang."

As she was leaving the Jackson house, Eliza met Carolyn's husband Will just coming in from basketball with his friends. His shirt was stained with sweat. He wiped his palm on his equally damp shorts before shaking Eliza's hand.

"I knew your husband," Will said. "Went to school with him."

"Were you friends?"

"Sure. He lived just up the street."

"I might have to quiz you about him sometime."

"Any time," Will said. "He was a great guy—sorry you lost him."

"Me, too. Nice meeting you."

The afternoon breeze felt cool against her bare legs. Eliza ambled back up the street, in no hurry to get back to her work. The Mother's Day basket break had done nothing to stir up ideas for her column. She felt as hopelessly blocked as before.

"Teddy called," Hildy announced as soon as Eliza came in.

"Great."

"He had a nice time last night."

"So everyone keeps telling me."

"I invited him for dinner," Hildy said.

"You didn't!"

Hildy clicked her tongue. "If you're not going to be nice to that boy, I will."

"He's not a boy, and don't you think that should be my decision?"

"I told him I want to talk business tonight. I need to set up some classes."

"I've already seen him two nights in a row," Eliza said. "Don't you think this is a little much?"

"We're making friends."

"*You* are," Eliza corrected. *I'm staying in my room.*

"I thought we'd make that pasta—the one you like? With the sausage?"

"Fine. Whatever."

"Lizzy, are you going to act like that all night?"

"Probably."

"Because if you are, I'll cancel."

"Good. Cancel."

Hildy sighed. She patted the chair beside her. She marked the place in the cookbook in front of her and closed the cover. "Honey, what's wrong?"

Eliza almost held a hand against her heart, that question hurt it so much. *I miss your boy. I want him back. I want to be kissed. I want to be loved. I miss being loved by Jamey.*

"It's just too much right now," Eliza said instead. "The move, getting settled in..."

Hildy reached over and stroked Eliza's hair. "Honey, I'm sorry. I guess I forgot how it must be for you. I'm used to this place—for me it's coming home. If you don't want me to have him over tonight I won't. We'll make it another night."

Eliza chewed her thumbnail. Suddenly all the fight had gone out of her. "Either or," she said glumly. "I guess it doesn't really matter." *Nothing's going to happen.*

Hildy brightened. "Good. Because I have some ideas for the first class I want to teach. Look here..."

Eliza looked without seeing. She eyed the daisies still sitting on the kitchen counter. She thought again how strange it was that Ted had sent them after such a disastrous date, and that his brother had delivered them. She thought about her awkward conversation with David Walsh in the woods and about the merits of her first date. And she wondered—not for the first time—whether she was the worst kind of coward for refusing to let another man into her life.

Hildy removed her half-glasses and peered at her daughter-in-law. "You aren't listening."

"Everything you cook is wonderful," Eliza answered. "Ted will love it no matter what."

Hildy studied her silently for a moment, then reached for Eliza's hand and held it between her own. "My girl. When are you going to stop being so sad? I miss him, too, but we have to go on."

Eliza's heart felt leaden.

Never, she thought.

"Soon," was what she said.

9

———

Eliza opened the front door to admit their guest. Ted shook her hand. "There," he said. "We got that out of the way."

"Very funny."

"Did you like the flowers?"

"No. Everyone hates daisies. Hildy, your date is here."

Some time between the afternoon and that evening, Eliza had developed a new attitude toward Hildy's matchmaking and Ted Walsh's attentions: She just wouldn't care. They were free to do as they liked, and so was she.

Eliza reached for her coat inside the front hall closet. "See you in a while."

Ted's smile faded. "Where are you going?"

Hildy called from the kitchen, "She's pretending she doesn't like us. Won't she be sorry when she finds out how much fun we had?"

"You're not serious," Ted said.

Eliza smiled pleasantly. "Have a good time."

"When are you coming back?"

"In a while. You two go ahead and take care of business—I don't want to get in your way."

Ted's eyes narrowed. Eliza noticed he wasn't wearing his glasses. "It won't work, you know."

"What?" she asked innocently.

"Trying to hide from me. I know where you live."

"Apparently. See you." And with that she made her escape.

As she started up Hildy's car, Eliza smiled to herself. She felt good. Satisfied. On top of things again. She'd taken a positive action on her own behalf, instead of just flailing around feeling uncertain.

Eliza dined on pineapple fried rice and mixed vegetables in a Thai mango sauce at Careyville's only Asian restaurant. The food was better than she had hoped, and she liked the look of the rest of the menu. It might be a good place for takeout on those nights when neither she nor Hildy felt like cooking. Eliza's usual fallback was a peanut butter and jelly sandwich, but she was willing to sacrifice that for something spicy and delicious instead.

She brought her blue legal pad and a pen and sat puzzling over what her column should say. Usually by Sunday night she had at least an idea for the next week's work, but tonight her thoughts were too scattered. She knew if she forced it, any piece she wrote would sound bad. So instead she pretended she was under no pressure and had so many ideas she couldn't decide which to tackle first.

If she were truly desperate by Tuesday, she could always

pull something from her Extras file, where she stored columns she had written in a fit of creativity, but never used yet.

"Everything all right?" her waitress asked. She wore low-riding jeans and a red T-shirt with the restaurant's logo in gold.

"Yes. Wonderful."

"Sure you don't want to try one of our Asian beers? They'd go really good with that."

"No, thanks." Eliza's capacity for alcohol had weakened over the years. Just a few sips usually sent her straight to bed, and left her with a pounding headache in the morning.

Satisfied at last with the prodigious amount of food she had managed to stuff in, Eliza paid her bill and left. She checked her watch: eight-thirty. Time for bed after two nights of too little sleep. No doubt Ted would still be at the house, but maybe she could plead exhaustion and slip past both of them.

If Ted was offended by what Eliza had done, he didn't show it. In fact, he acted as though Hildy were the most delightful dinner companion he could imagine. Their laughter greeted Eliza at the door and carried her up the stairs.

Hildy batted Ted's arm. "You're awful!"

Ted shrugged and didn't deny it. "Have fun?" he asked Eliza.

"Lots." She held up her notepad. "Work, you know."

"Oh, can I see?" he asked.

"No. I don't show it ahead of time. You'll have to buy the issue just like everybody else."

"Teddy has a surprise for you," Hildy practically sang.

Great. Eliza pasted on a smile. "Oh?"

"I'll tell you later," Ted said. "Maybe you can walk me out." He stood, stretched, and thanked Hildy for the meal. "I haven't eaten so well in...years, probably."

"I'm sure that's not true," Hildy said, obviously relishing the compliment. "You must go to some really good restaurants."

"Nope," Ted said. "My uncle's is pretty good, but other than that..."

Hildy beamed.

Eliza resisted the urge to roll her eyes. The two of them looked too cozy. "Well, I'm off to bed," she announced.

"Wait," Ted said. "I really am leaving. Mind walking me out?"

Manners took over. "Sure." Eliza waited while Ted praised Hildy's cooking a few more times, and Hildy pretended not to believe him.

"I'll get you those schedules," Hildy said in parting.

"Great. We'll work something out."

Hildy caught her daughter-in-law's eye and smiled. Apparently the dinner had been a success.

Eliza led Ted down the stairs and outside. She stood with her arms wrapped across her chest and pretended it was because she was cold.

Ted moved closer to her than she liked, but Eliza forced herself to stand her ground. She would not appear afraid.

"I have a strategy, you know," Ted said.

"Oh?" Eliza answered. "What's that?"

"To be as much in your way as possible."

Eliza's teeth mildly chattered. She knew it was from her nerves, not the weather.

"Why do you want to do that?" she asked. "You don't even know me."

"But that's the point—I'd like to."

"I'm sure there are lots of other women who'd be thrilled to go out with you."

"That's true," Ted said without any attempt at modesty. "But maybe I'm not interested in them."

"You'll survive," she said. "What would you have done if I hadn't moved here?"

"Suffered." Ted moved closer as if to kiss her, then caught himself—or caught the look on Eliza's face—and backed away.

"Look," she said, dropping any pretense of being tough. "I need to not see you for a while. I'm sorry, but the truth is, this is all too much for me right now." *Stop shaking.*

"All right," Ted said, "how long?"

"Weeks. Maybe months."

"No good," he answered. "We have an appointment this Thursday."

"An appointment? For what?"

"I might have another newspaper for you."

"What?" Eliza heard it, but didn't entirely understand.

"I got you an interview," Ted said. "We're meeting with the editor of the *Syracuse Tribune* this Thursday at eleven."

Eliza stood there stunned for a moment, unsure what to say. Yes, having her column picked up by a newspaper as large as the *Tribune* would definitely help her finances—and help her convince other major newspapers to give her column a try.

But Eliza wasn't expecting—and wasn't sure she wanted —an opportunity like this to come through Ted Walsh. She wasn't sure what kind of obligation she might feel toward him. Or what he might expect.

Something Ted said nibbled at her brain. "Did you say *'we're'* meeting with him?"

"Well, Walsh's does give them an awful lot of advertising," Ted said. "They know me pretty well."

"I see." Eliza wasn't sure how she felt about that. But she was sure that Ted Walsh had just gained the upper hand in the last few minutes, and she wasn't very comfortable with it.

"I'll call you," Ted told her, then got into his car and drove away before she could disagree.

Eliza stood in the darkened driveway, still hugging her arms across her chest. *What just happened?*

You got played, that's what, she told herself. *He figured out what you wanted, and he got it for you.*

But that's nice, isn't it?

Is it? a part of her shot back. *You just finished telling him you didn't want to see him for a while—a long while—and instead he manipulated you not only into spending more time with him, but also being in his debt.*

Wow, Eliza thought, *he's good.*

And she wasn't so sure that was good.

But one thing had come from all that: the idea for her next column. As she walked back into the house and mounted the stairs, the opening paragraphs were already writing themselves in her brain:

I met a self-defense instructor once who said people who refuse to hear your "no" are trying to control you. To bully you. It might be your spouse, your mother, your in-laws, a friend. Or it might be an attacker testing the waters to see how vulnerable you are.

In any case, the solution is to practice. You have to say "no" more times than "yes" for a while until you finally feel comfortable with it coming out of your mouth. You have to learn to say it and mean it, and to expect others to listen to you and honor your wishes.

Which is all my way of confessing that I've lost my edge somewhere along the way, and it's time I got it back.

10

"Cut it all off," Eliza said.

"Really?" Delia the hair stylist slid her second and third finger across a section of hair parallel with Eliza's chin.

"Okay, maybe not that short. How about another inch?"

Delia slid her fingers down. "Like this?"

"Perfect. I guess."

"Because once I take it off—"

"I understand. Do it." Eliza closed her eyes, but thought better of it. Wasn't this part of the plan—to embrace change, to charge head-first into it? Change on her terms, of course, instead of everyone else's.

She had written a different column that morning than the one she imagined the night before. That column—the *"No"* column—would have to wait two weeks, she decided. First she needed to lay the groundwork for a more ambitious plan.

She had awoken with it clawing at her brain, and by six-thirty that morning had pounded it out and e-mailed it two days ahead of deadline.

Have you ever hidden out so long, she wrote, *that you begin to wonder how you ever did half the things you used to? You know, for example, that you used to be able to make friends easily (maybe not since grade school, but at least there was a time). You used to be able to make decisions—peanut butter and jelly today or baloney? You used to like experimenting with your life. And remember when you used to get excited over surprises, instead of avoiding them?*

I put forth this challenge to myself and to you: Do something different today. It doesn't have to be huge, like quitting your job or disappearing into the wilderness without leaving a note. No, let's just agree to try something small. Today I am getting a haircut—not the kind of action that normally will get you on the front page, but for me, it's different. I've worn my hair the same length in the same style for at least ten years. All right, there was that brief stint of getting it permed, but basically it's always looked the same, which is fine since I don't normally think too much about trivialities like how I look. I prefer to save all my brain power for solving world problems and memorizing song lyrics.

So here's our action plan: Choose just one thing, but you have to do it today. Drive a different route home from work. Drink a different flavor of coffee. When you take a shower tonight wash your left leg first instead of your right. Do you understand IT DOESN'T MATTER what insignificant thing it is? What matters is that you decided to be the driver of your life today

Eliza surprised herself by smiling at the first dramatic snip of the scissors.

"You okay?" Delia asked. "A lot of people get freaked out right now."

"I'm fine. I like it. Keep going."

Forty-five minutes later Eliza rose from Delia's chair feeling the weight of what was missing. She pocketed her ponytail holder and slipped a generous tip into Delia's cup.

Delia smiled. "You look fantastic."

Eliza put her glasses back on.

Delia assessed her. "Hmm...you looked better without them."

"One step at a time."

"You could get green contacts and really bring out the color of your eyes."

"I'd look like an alien."

"Suit yourself." Delia brushed a few stray hairs from Eliza's shoulders. "A little lipstick could be nice, too."

"Did my mother-in-law put you up to this?"

"I sell Wisdom Cosmetics on the side," Delia said. "Take this catalog. I keep most things in stock at my house, so if you call me I can bring it here the next day."

"I'll keep it in mind."

Eliza exited the salon and went next door to the small grocery store where she continued to make her purchases. Hildy might have promised to patronize only the Monarch Walsh's from now on, but that was her business. Eliza felt the thrill of rebellion as she walked down the cramped aisles of the tiny store, viewing its limited and inferior selections, knowing what Ted Walsh would say if he saw her.

It wasn't that she disliked him, she thought to herself, it was that she didn't want him telling her what to do. Same for Hildy. It was time, Eliza knew, that she seized control of her own choices. She had been in Careyville for a month now, and it was time to start living in the place with the knowledge she would be there a while.

It was Eliza's turn to cook dinner. She bought the makings for her special lasagna—as special as any recipe from the back of the lasagna noodle package might be—as well as a bag of prewashed lettuce, and assorted vegetables to cut up on top. Although Hildy could cook gourmet when she wanted to, both she and Eliza preferred simpler meals for just the two of them. When it was Hildy's turn, she often brought home a quart of Walsh's soup along with a loaf of fresh bread from their bakery, and made a salad to go with it.

Before returning to her car Eliza stopped at the espresso counter on the other side of the grocery store. *Drink a different flavor of coffee*, she reminded herself, and ordered a mocha instead of her standard house blend.

So far so good, she thought. But this was the easy stuff.

She waited until after lunch to phone Ted Walsh.

"Hi, gorgeous."

"Don't say that."

"Okay, I'll add that to the list."

"Ted, I appreciate you setting up that interview at the *Tribune*. I really do."

"Good. My pleasure. You're not going to try to back out."

"No, but I'd like to go alone. I've done it before, you know."

"I know, but I thought it might be easier—"

"Like I said, I really appreciate the gesture, but I'll take it from here." Worried she might be coming across as too rude, she said again, "But I appreciate it."

"I heard you. Okay, no problem. The point is to get you another newspaper, right? So I've done my part, and now you can do yours."

"Thanks. I—"

"Really appreciate it. I know."

On Thursday morning Eliza rose before dark, ran the little legs off of Daisy, then put her mind to the task of deciding what to wear and what to say.

Do one thing different.

In the past, she had pitched her column to new editors either over the phone or by e-mail. They usually wanted to see three or four of her most recent columns, so Eliza kept a file of her favorites and continually updated them.

She had decided to bring three columns from the past year to her meeting with Leo Pagnozzi, Managing Editor of the *Syracuse Tribune*. She knew nothing about his tastes, so she chose one each from her three basic topics: world issues (in this case funding and lack thereof for the AIDS crisis in Africa), family issues (the piece on her mother's breast cancer scare and the reactions among different friends and family), and personal growth (this week's column).

Hildy appraised her outfit. "Oh, that's very nice. I like the jacket."

"It's my Eliza Shepherd, Ace Reporter look. I thought a newspaper guy might like it."

She wore black dress pants and a matching jacket that tapered at the waist. The collar of her white cotton blouse lay crisply against the black lapel. She wore black loafers she had taken the time to shine. On her wrist she wore the one piece of jewelry, other than her wedding ring, that Jamey had ever given her. It was a hard gold bracelet she snapped closed like a handcuff. On top was a row of pearls and diamonds that had once been a broach. Jamey had found it at an antique jewelry store and given it to Eliza on their first anniversary.

"You look lovely," Hildy said. "Truly lovely."

Eliza retreated to her room and removed the entire outfit. One decision down, two more to go.

She closed herself in the bathroom, removed her glasses,

and popped in her contacts. The last time she had worn them was for a yoga class back in Henderson. She had discovered during a class before that that her glasses slipped off every time she did an inversion pose.

Eliza blinked her contacts into focus.

"On, or off?" she asked herself. She turned her face from one side to the other, and decided to take the next step before deciding.

She removed her makeup bag from under the sink, and began what had once been a familiar routine. Everything was old, much of it dried up or crusted away. She wished she had thought of looking in there the day before so she could have ordered something from Delia. She would have to make do.

She applied a thin layer of foundation, patted on a little powder, and swiped the blush brush up high on her cheekbones. So far, not too frightening, she decided, so she continued.

She drew a line beneath her eyes with a thin navy pencil. The green of her irises immediately intensified. She drew another line on her top lid, then muted that one with a swipe of brown shadow. Finally she curled her eyelashes and brushed on two layers of mascara from a nearly dried up tube.

"Make up—yes or no?" she asked herself.

In the spirit of her column, she could not refuse to take this risk. So the answer was yes.

Which also informed her third choice—contacts, yes.

Eliza returned to her bedroom to dress again, and emerged looking much like the woman she had been two years ago. The black pant suit had come along only with the Widow's Wardrobe, but other than that—and the hair that now brushed against her neck and fell to her shoulders instead of to the middle of her back—she looked like someone she once used to know very well.

"Oh, Lizzy," was all Hildy could say, but it was enough. Eliza hoped that if she couldn't bring herself back from the inside out, she might be able to do it in reverse. Perhaps if she started looking like the old Eliza again, she would remember how to act like her, and some day to feel like her once more.

"Lipstick," Hildy reminded her before Eliza headed down the stairs.

Eliza returned to the bathroom and smeared a thin layer of dark red across her lips, blotted it, then added her cola-flavored lip gloss on top to keep her lips from feeling too dry during an interview in which her mouth surely would.

"Wish me luck."

"You don't need it," Hildy assured her. "You're brilliant."

THE PHOTOS on Leo Pagnozzi's wall confirmed what anyone would know from looking at him: that he had been a wrestler in his former life. He was nearly neckless, with a broad chest and slightly broader belly, forearms as unrealistic as an action figure's, and fingers that might have been as thick as hot dogs.

"It's a little soft, don't you think?" Leo Pagnozzi asked after reading her column about her mother. "I got a lot of men reading my paper."

Eliza smiled politely. "I assume women, too."

"Look," said Pagnozzi, handing back her file, "maybe later."

Eliza had heard "no" many times before. She was used to second tries. "All right, when shall I check back with you?"

"Huh?"

"You said maybe later, so when would be a good time...?"

"Look, I don't mean to hurt your feelings." Pagnozzi scratched his nubby fingernails against his opposite palm. He turned both hands up plaintively. "We're not your market."

"The *Tribune,* or Syracuse?" She smiled pleasantly. There was nothing to gain from arguing with the man.

"Maybe one of the town newspapers would be better," Pagnozzi suggested.

"All right, can you give me a few names?" She pulled out her pen. "I'm new here."

Obviously irritated, but no doubt remembering she was a friend of one of his biggest advertisers, Pagnozzi rattled off a few names. "You're living in Careyville? There's a paper there—a weekly. Guy's Frank Sawyer. Monarch has a weekly, guy's Marty Plank." He listed five more small newspapers in the surrounding area. "That'll get you started."

Pagnozzi stood, signaling the interview was over. It had lasted all of ten minutes.

Eliza offered her hand. Once more Pagnozzi only took the fingertips. Eliza hated men like that—ones who pretended women were too fragile to shake a man's whole hand.

"Thank you so much for your time, Mr. Pagnozzi."

"Yeah, sure. So, Teddy got you all set up?"

"Excuse me?"

"You're his new girlfriend, right?"

Eliza reddened. "No, I've just met him."

Pagnozzi grinned. "He's a smooth one."

Eliza's voice deadened. "I'm sure he is. Again, thank you." She spun toward the door before Pagnozzi could say any more, but she was half a beat too slow.

"Watch out for him," Pagnozzi advised with a chuckle. "He's an animal."

Eliza smiled coldly. "Thanks for the advice."

She waited until she was clear of the building before muttering everything she really thought. She hated that kind of men's club behavior—the back-slapping, whiskey-swilling camaraderie of men joking about their conquests. Eliza had no intention of adding her name to some list.

Ted Walsh was just a friend—someone she owed some gratitude toward now, even though the lead had turned into nothing. She would do the polite thing and square her account with a thank you card, and leave it at that.

Eliza sat in her car for several minutes, drumming her fingers against the steering wheel. Now that the steam was starting to clear from her ears, she realized the meeting hadn't been a complete waste. Not if she made good use of the information Pagnozzi had given her.

She pulled out her phone and looked up the number for the Careyville weekly. She was still dressed the part, she figured, so she might as well make the most of it.

"Hi, is this Mr. Sawyer?"

"Yes," the gruff voice answered.

"My name is Eliza Shepherd. I'm a nationally-syndicated columnist and freelance writer—"

Frank Sawyer chuckled. "Afraid you got the wrong place. We don't pay squat."

"I've just moved to Careyville," Eliza continued. "I'd like to talk with you about carrying my column in your newspaper."

"Maybe you didn't hear me—"

"I did, sir, but right now it doesn't matter to me. I'd still like to talk with you. I'm leaving an appointment now, and can be there in half an hour if you tell me where you are."

"You'll be disappointed."

"Maybe, but you won't."

"How'd it go?" Ted asked when he phoned that afternoon.

"I'm too girly for your friend Pagnozzi."

"He said that?"

"We arm wrestled for it, and I didn't get the job."

"Want me to call him?"

"No," Eliza said, "I'm on to bigger things. I have to go."

"Wait—"

Eliza held her hand over the mouthpiece. "What, Hildy?" she said to the dog. "Okay, I'll be right there. Ted, I have to go."

"Let me talk to Hildy."

"Can't. She's busy right now," Eliza lied. Her mother-in-law was nowhere to be found.

"I want to ask her something."

"She'll have to call you back."

"When can I see you again?" he asked. "I still owe you an ice cream."

"What, Hildy? Sorry, Ted, I have to go. Hildy needs something. I'll talk to you later. Bye!"

Eliza hung up, ignoring the sound of his voice still coming through the receiver.

When Hildy did arrive an hour or so later, Eliza reported the day's failure and success in quick, unemotional details, and she passed along Ted's message.

"Good," Hildy said. "I called him earlier. I had a question."

While Hildy returned Ted's call, Eliza retreated to her room to read. She always felt relaxed and leisurely on a day when she had already sent out her column. She had nothing more to do for the next week or so than read and think and develop her next ideas.

And she'd actually convinced Frank Sawyer to give her column a try. That felt like a feat all by itself.

Hildy knocked on her bedroom door. Eliza had changed out of her suit as soon as she returned home and had washed off all her makeup. She was wearing her glasses again, too—the transformation from ambitious professional writer back to quiet bookworm was complete.

Hildy sat on the edge of Eliza's bed. "What're you reading?"

"King Lear."

"Hm. We've been invited somewhere."

"By?"

"Teddy."

"You go," Eliza said. "I'm staying home."

"But it's a good one."

"I'm off the meat market right now. Afraid I won't be going on any dates."

"Why do you have to say it like that?" Hildy asked. "Teddy's a nice man."

Eliza shrugged.

"Did he do something?" Hildy asked. "Something you didn't want?"

"No, he's been perfectly gentlemanly," Eliza answered, thinking of Pagnozzi's smirk and the *"Watch out for him. He's an animal."* "I just don't feel like seeing him for a while."

"He got you that nice interview—even if the man didn't know quality."

"I've already written Ted a thank you card. See? It's over there."

Hildy patted Eliza's leg. "Just hear me out. For me."

Eliza rolled her eyes. "Yes, mother-in-law, dear."

"Easter. We're invited."

"We're already going to Carolyn Jackson's."

"That's for brunch. This is for dinner."

"Have a lovely time."

"It's going to be at Sibylla Walsh's house—the mother's. Wouldn't you like to see that?"

Eliza kept her eyes on her paperback. She had reread the line, "And thou, his yokefellow of equity," four times since Hildy came in. "Sorry, but I have no interest in that at all."

"Come on, Lizzy, it might be fun. Or maybe not fun, but at least interesting, don't you think? I've never been inside any of the Walshes' houses except Teddy's. I never got invited when the Walshes lived so close."

"That's a very sad story," Eliza said, "and I can see why

you'd like to go now, and I wish you nothing but happiness with your new friends."

"You sound awful."

Eliza laughed and set down the play. "Why? Because I'm not falling all over myself to be Ted Walsh's new girlfriend, or to see his mother's house? I'd rather hear about it from you—you always do a place like that justice."

"Are you mad at Teddy for something?"

"Only for giving me the full-court press when I've made it clear I don't want that."

"The full what?"

"It's basketball. The point is, he's pursuing me awfully hard, and I have no idea why."

"Because you're beautiful and smart and fun and kind…I can think of lots of reasons."

"You've known me a decade. He's known me a few weeks."

"People fall in love—"

"Love! So now it's love?"

"I'm just saying—"

Eliza leaned forward and clasped her mother-in-law's hands with more force than she intended. She loosened her grip to restore Hildy's circulation.

"I don't know how else to say this," Eliza told her, "so I'm just going to say it: I don't want a boyfriend. I don't want Ted Walsh for a boyfriend. He's moving too fast, and it makes me uncomfortable. So I told him last Sunday, and I'm telling you now, I don't want to see him for a while."

Having gotten some of it out, Eliza let go of Hildy's hands and slumped back against her headboard.

"Look," she said, "I'm sure he's a nice man, and I know you like being friends with him. You should go ahead and do that—I absolutely don't want to interfere. But Hildy, you have to understand: Jamey's dying was the worst thing that's ever happened in my life. It's not the kind of thing you get over—at least not the kind of thing *I* get over. I might never fall in love again, and that's okay with me. I already had the best. You gave me the man who was the best."

Hildy stared at her for a moment, then her face crumpled in grief.

Taking Eliza completely by surprise.

Hildy rarely cried. At her husband's funeral, she maintained a kind of sad dignity, brushing away her few tears and holding her gaze steady.

Even at the funeral of her only child, she didn't wail the way Eliza did. Eliza's grief had been so raw and bottomless that day, she thought she'd never climb back out. Hildy had held her hand—hard, so hard Eliza's fingers felt sore and swollen for days afterward—and stared straight ahead while Jamey's friends got up one after another to memorialize the man they couldn't believe was gone.

"Best friend I ever had..."

"Luckiest bastard I ever saw..."

"Saved my ass on that climb up the Thumb..."

"Damn it, Jamey—" Then a wrenching sob from the sunburned, scraggly-haired, wiry-muscled climber who had flown a day and a half from Australia just to say goodbye to a friend he expected to meet up with later that year. *"You screwed up, bro. You were supposed to outlive all of us. Remember? That's what we said.*

"Sorry, Eliza," he added, pausing to release another room-shaking sob. *"We thought he was immortal. Guess we got it wrong."*

Eliza's heart had wanted to burst. Wanted to go up in flames and burn itself to ash. She couldn't feel any more—couldn't bear it. But the pain just went on and on.

So to see Hildy cry now—when she'd forced herself to stay so controlled at Jamey's funeral, saving all her tears for the hearse ride home when it was just her and Ron and Eliza—it was such a shock it took Eliza a moment to realize it was really happening.

"Hildy! It's all right. What's going on?" Eliza gathered her mother-in-law in her arms and held on to her tightly.

"I've been so lonely!" Hildy cried. "And I worry about you. You can't live like this, Lizzy—I can't, either. We have to get on with our lives. I have to be with people. I can't keep thinking about Ron all the time and missing him so much."

"But...you hardly ever talk about him."

"What's there to say? I loved him every day, and now I don't have any part of him anymore. I can't stand it sometimes."

"Shhh, shhh..." Eliza stroked her mother-in-law's back. "I'm sorry. I didn't know."

"And seeing you like this," Hildy sniffled, "it only makes me feel worse."

"Seeing me like what?"

"So closed off. So afraid of men."

"I'm not afraid—"

"Yes, you are," she said. "Teddy's a nice boy. There are lots of nice boys. I don't want you to be alone the rest of your life, Lizzy. It isn't right. I want you to be happy. To have children some day."

"But I don't want—"

"Yes, you do," Hildy cut her off. "I know you did. I kept telling Jamey he had to stop messing around with all his climbing and traveling and everything else he did—"

"It was his work, Hildy."

"You know what I mean. He could have been home more. He should have been raising a family. You deserved children, Lizzy—I kept telling him that."

Eliza's throat hurt. "I don't want to talk about it," she said. She'd been calm up until that point, but now Hildy was pressing on an open wound. Of course Eliza had wanted Jamey's child—lots of them. But even one, just to have a piece of him now. She'd imagined it more times than she'd ever dare admit: what a son would have looked like, the sound of their daughter's laugh. Fantasies Eliza knew were far too dangerous to ever think about again.

"If you'd just do this one thing for me," Hildy said. She sat up again and pulled a tissue from the box beside Eliza's bed. She blew her nose and grabbed another tissue to blot her eyes.

"What one thing?" Eliza asked, watching her mother-in-law to make sure she seemed all right again.

"Come with me to Easter," Hildy said. "Please."

Eliza sighed. "Why? Why is it so important that I come? I don't understand this whole obsession of yours. Why does it have to be Ted Walsh?"

"Because what if he could make you happy?" Hildy said,

gazing at her daughter-in-law with red, puffy eyes. "Why can't you give him a chance?"

Learn to say no, Eliza recited to herself. *Learn to say no.*

"If he's the right one, then he'll still be there when I'm ready for him."

"But what if he meets someone else?" Hildy argued.

"Then he wasn't right for me."

"You don't believe that nonsense, do you? Sometimes people just can't wait. They have to settle for someone else— the wrong person."

"But what if *he's* the wrong person?" Eliza countered. "What if I already know he's not for me?"

"Do you?"

"I don't know...maybe."

"See? You don't know either way because you're too scared to find out."

Eliza squeezed her eyes shut for a moment. She hated to give in, but she also hated to be stubborn just for stubbornness's sake. It was a quality Jamey used to point out to her, and she'd worked hard to fix it.

"If I go," Eliza said, opening her eyes again, "will you let me decide about him for myself?"

"Of course."

"I mean none of this matchmaking and hinting or any of that. I get to decide, independently, whether or not I ever want to go out with him again."

"That sounds fair."

Then why can't I decide that right now and say no and mean it?

"I'm only doing this for you."

"I understand," Hildy said. "Thank you."

"If you say anything at this dinner to embarrass me—"

"I promise I won't."

Eliza scowled at her mother-in-law. "Has this all been a trick?"

Hildy laughed hoarsely. She blew her nose again. "Lizzy, I love you. I want you to be happy."

Eliza sighed. "All right. One more try. But you have to leave it completely up to me—got it?"

"Yes."

Eliza hugged her mother-in-law. "I love you too. Please don't ever cry like that again. I can't take it."

"I promise I'll only cry at your wedding."

"Hildy—"

Hildy pantomimed locking her lips. "I swear I'll be good."

"I have to get back to King Lear," Eliza replied wearily. "At least that was a normal family."

12

"You won't be sorry," Ted whispered to Eliza as he admitted them to the house Easter evening. "My mother is worth the price of admission."

Brunch at the Jacksons' that morning had been noisy and fun. Katie and her friends raced around the yard searching for hidden Easter eggs, while a collection of neighbors and friends of the Jacksons sat around eating homemade cupcakes and an assortment of potluck dishes the families had brought. Eliza and Hildy contributed puff pastries filled with chorizo. Eliza noticed most of the guests seemed to take a taste, then set the pastry aside.

"Too spicy," Hildy murmured as they saw yet another person repeat the same action. "We should have just brought mac and cheese."

Carolyn introduced Hildy and Eliza around. It turned out Hildy knew several of the neighbors, some of whom, like

Will Jackson, now lived in the homes previously owned by their parents.

"You think Jamey would have ever moved back here?" Hildy asked her daughter-in-law when they stood momentarily alone.

"Sorry, but I doubt it," Eliza said. "He couldn't stand the winters."

"He spent a month in Antarctica!"

"I know, I can't explain it, " Eliza said, "but somehow that was different."

Carolyn Jackson joined them. "So, what time's the big party?"

Eliza groaned. "Don't remind me. I'm nervous just thinking about it."

"Why are you nervous?" Hildy asked. "They're just people like this."

Carolyn and Eliza exchanged an amused glance.

"The Walshes are not like this," Carolyn said. "I guarantee it."

"How are they different?" Hildy challenged.

"For one thing," Carolyn answered, "all their forks and knives will match."

Hildy snorted dismissively. "I can hold my head high at Sibylla Walsh's house any day. I have nothing to be embarrassed about, and neither do you, Lizzy."

"I'm not embarrassed, just…"

"Reluctant," Carolyn offered.

"Shy," Eliza elaborated.

Hildy linked her arm through Eliza's. "My Lizzy will shine. Don't you worry."

Now, entering Sibylla Walsh's museum-like mansion, Eliza felt every bit as small and awkward as she worried she would.

The house was as excessively tasteful as any Eliza had ever seen. Everything was magazine-quality, from the Oriental rugs to the dark red velvet sofa and chairs to the heavy, dark antique furniture masterfully cluttering the enormous living room.

"When's the next tour?" Eliza muttered courageously to her mother-in-law.

Hildy's whispers were always too loud. "Can you believe it?"

Ted heard it and smiled. "Let's make the rounds," he said cheerfully, and escorted both women into the fray.

There were about thirty people in the room—easily as many as at the Jacksons' much smaller house that morning—but the effect of this group was completely different. As Eliza stepped forward to meet them, she immediately understood that nothing she could do that evening would ever come close to meeting their standards.

The women all looked perfect. They wore what should be worn. Eliza felt underdressed in her version of a festive Easter outfit: black skirt, black flats, and a silky peach top she'd bought specifically for the occasion.

For good luck she'd worn the bracelet Jamey gave her, but clearly even that couldn't save her outfit. Normally Eliza felt no need to impress anyone with her wardrobe—she dressed for comfort and practicality, not fashion—but walking into Sibylla Walsh's living room, facing this particular gathering of strangers, made Eliza wish she'd tried a lot harder to find the best of everything she owned.

Among the group, Eliza recognized the woman who had waited in line behind David Walsh at the grand opening of the store. She, thought Eliza, looked right in this place.

She wore her short-cropped black hair smartly styled so it swept upward, drawing attention to her blue eyes and fine high cheeks. She was elegant in her long red dress, belted at the waist to emphasize her slim—"boyish," Hildy called it later—figure.

Ted introduced her as Livia Keane. She had a handshake as firm as Katie Jackson's. "Hi, nice to see you again."

"Yeah, you too." *Yeah, you too.* Eliza winced internally at her own lack of polish. This was why, she reminded herself, she didn't mingle with people like the Walshes or the Keanes. No matter how confident she might feel in most situations, somehow being around classy people made her feel like a troll.

"And this," Ted continued, escorting the Shepherds to a throne-like wing chair in the corner of the room, "is my mother, Sibylla Walsh."

"Nice to meet you," Eliza said. "Thank you for inviting us."

"Hello, dear, welcome."

Eliza could hear the faint touch of a German accent. The matriarch did not get up, but extended her hand horizontally as if expecting Eliza to kiss it. As it was, Eliza felt an impulse to curtsey. She doubted Mrs. Walsh would object.

The woman nodded to her other guest. "Hilda."

"Hi, Sibylla, how are you?" Hildy said. "You look good."

"And you," Mrs. Walsh said without a hint of sincerity.

Someone was waving to them from across the room. Eliza smiled in relief. It was Mrs. Walsh's brother, Herbert.

"How are you?" he shouted. "Good to see you!"

Eliza gave a small wave in return and resisted the urge to shout back. Wouldn't Mrs. Walsh love that?

Ted continued to lead the widows Shepherd around the room. David Walsh nodded curtly as they passed and returned to his conversation.

Ted stopped in front of a pleasant-looking woman with short curly brown hair. She wore a simple, pastel blue dress and comfortable-looking shoes, and offered the first genuinely friendly smile Eliza had witnessed from any of the women since she'd entered the room.

"This is my sister, Sue."

"Hi, Eliza, it's nice to finally meet you."

"You, too."

"Suzy, how are you?" Hildy asked, giving the woman a hug—a gesture, Eliza noted, which had not been offered to Sibylla Walsh. "You look wonderful."

"Thanks, Mrs. Shepherd. You're the one who looks great."

"Call me Hildy—we're all grown up now. I hear you're a teacher?"

"Yep. High school math." Sue laughed and rolled her eyes. "Hard to believe I have the nerves for it, huh?"

"I bet you're great," Hildy said. "You were always so smart."

"Thanks, but believe me, some days not smart enough. I don't think you've ever met my boys. Danny?" Sue motioned for the teenager closest to her to join them. The boy greeted them shyly and shook both women's hands. "And that's Mike over there," Sue said, pointing. "The one talking to my husband and David."

Mike was as tall as his uncle David, with an expression equally as serious.

"How old are they?" Hildy asked.

"Mike will be eighteen this summer. Danny's fourteen."

Ted pinned his nephew's arms behind his back. "Dan the Man. When's your mom going to let me take you driving? Don't you think it's about time?"

"Never," Sue answered. "I happen to love my son. So, Eliza, how do you like Careyville—it's nice, isn't it?"

"Very. I like it a lot."

"I miss it," Sue said. "Monarch's a little too...what would you say, Teddy?"

"Up-tight?"

"Maybe," Sue said. "I think I should have bought Mom and Dad's house instead of letting David get it."

"Then Mom wouldn't have moved," Ted said. "She'd still be living in there with you."

"Good point," Sue said with a laugh. "Never mind." For the Shepherds' benefit, she added, "It's not that I don't love my mother..."

"Sure, Suzy," her brother said. "I'm telling her what you said."

Eliza liked listening to the two of them together. It reminded her of how she and her brothers still teased each other after all these years.

"Careful, Teddy," Sue said, "or I'll let Eliza in on a few of your secrets."

"I already told her everything."

"*Everything?*"

Ted grinned. He wrapped his arm around his sister's shoulder, pulled her close, and kissed her on her cheek. "You keep my secrets, I'll keep yours. Hey, Danny, did your mom ever tell you about her tattoo?"

Sue elbowed her younger brother. "He's not so bad," she told Eliza. "Just don't believe a thing he says."

"Would you like some wine?" Ted asked them. "Dan, I know you will."

The boy grinned and cast a guilty look toward his mother.

Sue ignored it. "I'll take some red."

"That sounds good," Hildy agreed.

"Water for me," Eliza said.

"You sure?" Ted asked. "You might need it tonight."

"I think I need my wits more," Eliza answered. "Water will do."

"Danny, come with me," Ted said. "I'll teach you how to make a martini."

The boy snickered. Sue shook her head.

Soon Livia Keane joined the trio of women. "It's a shame you didn't cater the dinner tonight," she told Hildy. "I loved what you made for the opening."

"It's nice to be a guest instead," Hildy answered politely.

"Did you ever taste her potatoes?" Livia asked Sue.

"No."

"Neither did you," Hildy pointed out. "Remember? You said they were too fattening."

"They looked delicious," Livia continued smoothly. "Everyone raved about them."

"You should try them some time," Hildy said. "It wouldn't hurt your figure."

"Oh, but a little here, a little there..." Livia patted her completely flat stomach. She cast her gaze around the room. Eliza guessed she was already bored, and searching for better conversation than theirs.

"Well..." Livia said, training an expert smile on the three of them.

"Nice to see you again," Hildy said flatly. Then she turned her back on Livia and resumed her conversation with Sue. "What's your husband doing these days?"

As Livia wandered off, Eliza couldn't help smiling to herself about Hildy's behavior toward the woman. Why was she so cold? Was it just because Livia had insulted her potatoes? Knowing Hildy, that was as good a reason as any.

Ted and his nephew returned with the drinks, and their small group made small talk until finally Sibylla Walsh announced that dinner was served. Ted offered his arm to both his dates, but only Hildy accepted. Eliza saw a better prospect walking toward her.

"Reuben sandwiches?" she whispered to Uncle Herbert as the two of them merged into the dining room with the rest.

"I wish," he said. "My sister never lets me cater."

Eliza paused at the threshold a moment, taking the place in. The dining room was at least half the size of Hildy's entire second floor. Gold-trimmed white dishes gleamed bright on a dark mahogany table that could have seated many more than the thirty Easter guests. Family portraits hanging along the north and south walls gave Eliza the feeling that many eyes would be checking her table manners that night.

"Can I sit by you?" Eliza asked Uncle Herbert. "Or do you already have a date?"

He pointed to the place cards. "Sorry, *Liebchen*. No such luck."

Eliza searched for her name. Much to her surprise—and horror—she'd be spending the meal sitting between Livia Keane and the grand matron herself.

As Eliza ate the opening course—a bland corn chowder she saw her mother-in-law taste, then set aside—she wondered cynically whether the only reason Sibylla Walsh had placed Eliza next to her was so that Eliza could feel the full force of being ignored. From her position at the head of the table, Mrs. Walsh either stared straight ahead in silence or occasionally turned to Sue, who sat on her other side. Never once in the first half hour did Mrs. Walsh deign to speak to Eliza.

For her part, Livia Keane had much to say: about the quality of the caterers ("I could have told Sibylla not to hire them. I used them once, and never again."), the backgrounds and quality of some of the guests ("He's with GM. I don't know what she does, but I'm guessing it isn't fashion. I'm just kidding—she seems very nice."), and her own work as Director of Marketing for the Walsh stores ("I increased sales by fifteen percent last year. That's when David finally had to look up from his spreadsheet and notice me. Didn't you?").

Livia looked right at David as she made this last comment, but he appeared not to hear. Or, thought Eliza, he was practicing his mother's art of ignoring people.

"How long have the two of you been together?" Eliza asked Livia. Even if she didn't particularly care for the woman, Eliza was always curious to hear about people's relationships.

"Since New Year's," Livia said. "No one can resist a brainy woman in red, can he, David?" She gave him a playful nudge.

"What?" he asked irritably. His eyes flitted past Livia to Eliza. He nodded to her again as if he had only just noticed she was at his mother's party.

"Eliza was asking how we met," Livia said.

"Oh." Apparently he had nothing more to add, because he turned back to his nephew Mike and resumed their conversation.

"He's a brilliant businessman," Livia said, smiling in her smooth way, "but as you can see, not a very social creature." She leaned toward Eliza and added conspiratorially, "He's definitely a work in progress."

Although David Walsh was definitely not one of her favorite people, Eliza couldn't help resenting Livia's comment on his behalf. *A work in progress?* Eliza knew women like that—ones who viewed men as fixer-uppers, waiting to be molded into something more "acceptable." Eliza preferred people with a come-as-you-are attitude. She could at least meet a standard like that. And she knew Jamey used to feel the same way.

She didn't have many choices for conversation, but she was tired of the one with Livia. Instead, Eliza turned toward her hostess.

"This is delicious, Mrs. Walsh."

The woman slowly turned to face her. "Hm? What?"

"I said the dinner—delicious. The soup, the crab cakes..."

"I didn't make them," Mrs. Walsh informed her.

"I understand," Eliza said, blushing. She wished she'd never opened her mouth. But now she was in it. "They're still...good."

"Hm." Mrs. Walsh turned to Sue and reminded her not to eat with her elbows on the table. Sue dutifully removed hers, and Eliza did the same, wondering if the remark had really been intended for her. Eliza and Sue exchanged guilty smiles.

As the meal wore on, Eliza felt more and more the divide between the climates at the table. To the south were all the fun people—Hildy, Ted, Sue, Danny, Uncle Herbert, and a collection of other laughing, joking guests.

To the north were David Walsh, Livia Keane, Eliza, and a dozen others suffering under the same cloud of civility and dullness. Eliza wondered what could account for the difference in the two ends of the table. She decided there must be toxic waste buried beneath the chairs on her side, playing havoc with all of their nervous systems.

Eliza gave up trying to talk to either of the women on each side, and instead gazed idly across the table.

Into the waiting eyes of Ted Walsh.

He offered her that half-cocked smile of his and a sympathetic shrug. Eliza couldn't help smiling back and subtly rolling her eyes. At least someone understood.

It wasn't until the end of the main course—duck in a sauce so weak Eliza knew Hildy must be howling inside—that Mrs. Walsh turned to Eliza to engage in the least civilized of all conversations.

"So, I understand your husband died quite suddenly."

Eliza froze. The buzz of conversation seemed to fade away, and Eliza imagined all ears had rotated toward her.

"Yes, he did," she said simply.

"Jamey was always a wild boy."

"You knew him?"

"No. My sons did."

Eliza considered what she should say next, and decided it was best to say nothing. She went back to eating food she didn't want.

"How did he die, exactly?" Sibylla Walsh persisted.

"Mother—" Ted warned.

Eliza smiled politely. "I'd rather not talk about it, thank you." She knew every eye in the room, including the ones in the portraits, must have been trained on her at that moment as she chewed a tasteless bite of duck.

Sue laid her hand on her mother's wrist. She leaned over and whispered something.

The old woman shook her off. "I'd like to get to know Teddy's new girlfriend."

Eliza felt the heat rush to her face. "I'm not his—"

"It was a climbing accident," the nephew, Danny, offered up. "Remember, Grandma? I told you that."

"What kind of accident?" Sibylla Walsh asked.

Eliza's stomach felt hard as granite. She couldn't eat another bite. She couldn't look at her hostess, either. Clearly Mrs. Walsh understood that Eliza didn't want this spotlight, but just as clearly, the woman didn't care. She intended to keep shining the light right in Eliza's face.

"Remember?" Danny tried again. "He fell while he was climbing. A bolt broke off the mountain."

Eliza stared at the boy. "How did you—"

"I read that article you wrote about it. In *Outside Adventure*? Uncle David still has—"

Both David and his sister jumped in to cut him off. "Danny—"

The boy looked at his mother. "What? I was just going to say—"

"That's enough," Sue said. "Mother, can we talk about something else? I'm sure Eliza would like that."

Mrs. Walsh directed her next cruel question at Sue. "I've always wondered why wives let their husbands do such dangerous things. Do they want them to be killed?"

"Mother!" three voices sang out.

Eliza jolted to her feet. She knew she should say something, but her lips seemed frozen shut.

"That's a wicked thing to say," Hildy snapped. "You have no right!"

Mrs. Walsh pretended to be perplexed by the reaction around the table. "One wants to know these things. I meant no offense, I'm sure."

"I'm sure," Hildy repeated sourly. "Lizzy, you sit down and enjoy your meal."

Eliza continued to stand. She knew everyone was

watching her, but for the moment she couldn't do anything but stare at her accuser.

"Of course I didn't want him to die," she told Mrs. Walsh. "That's a terrible thing to say." She felt the tears coming, and fought as hard as she ever had in her life to keep them from running out.

Mrs. Walsh smiled wanly. "I'm certainly sorry if I offended you, dear. I had no idea you'd be so sensitive."

Sue glowered at her mother.

"Come on, boys," Ted said, breaking the tension. "Let's bus the table."

His nephews rose and began clearing the table. Over Sibylla Walsh's protests—"Sit! Sit! I'm paying people for that!"—Eliza joined them.

When she was safely in the kitchen, Eliza sank against the counter. Her hands shook with unspent rage and humiliation. She understood now that impulse someone could feel to throw dishes against a wall. Or to shoot a hole in the ceiling with a shotgun.

Ted stood beside her and wrapped his arm around her waist. "I'm so, so sorry," he said. He pulled her hip up against his and kissed her on the cheek. Eliza felt too numb to resist.

"I don't know why she did that," he said. "No, I do know —it's because she's an evil, bitter, heartless, bi—" He glanced over at his eavesdropping nephews. "Not that we don't love her, right, boys?"

"Right, Uncle Ted."

"Get back to work, swabbies. Eliza and I are talking."

He drew her off to the side of the kitchen, into a corner where no one could hear.

The caterers bustled around the room, scraping dishes, packaging leftovers, and putting the finishing touches on a dessert tray to rival anything Eliza had seen at the Walsh's opening. At least this, she thought, would impress her mother-in-law.

Ted stood close enough to her she could feel the warmth radiating from his body. "If I had any idea she'd do that," he said, "I swear I never would have asked you here."

Eliza nodded. She could still feel the tears trapped and ready to escape. She swallowed hard to force them back.

"So," Ted asked, "is this almost better than having a root canal?"

Eliza laughed, despite the feeling that her heart at that moment looked like raw meat. "That was pretty rough."

"I'm really sorry. I don't know what else to say. We've tried to have her knocked off, but she keeps getting away." Ted reached down for Eliza's hand, and cupped it between both of his. "You're cold."

Eliza gently pulled away. She stood up straight and tried to compose herself. "So," she said, hoping she sounded normal, "your sister's nice."

"Yeah, we're all nice, except for—you know."

"Right."

Ted reached forward and sifted the ends of her hair through his fingers. "I meant to tell you, you look beautiful tonight. I like your hair this way." He gazed warmly into her eyes and bent forward as if to kiss her.

Eliza gently held him off. "Please. Don't."

He sighed and let his shoulders slump. "You're never going to forgive me for tonight."

"Probably not," she said in a tone that let him know she already had.

Eliza noticed the nephews watching with intense curiosity. "Show's over, boys," she said as she brushed past Ted. "I think it's time I went home."

"Had about all the fun you can take, huh?" Ted asked.

"Just about."

"So does this seal it once and for all? My mother is a shrew, so you never want to see me again?"

"You're mother isn't a shrew," Eliza lied politely. "She's just nosy—a lot of people are. I'm highly exotic, didn't you know? Young widows always are. We're so...tragic."

A movement behind Ted caught her attention. In that moment of distraction, Ted laid his hand against Eliza's hip, pulled her toward him, and kissed her softly on the lips. Eliza stepped back in surprise.

"I know what I promised," Ted said, "but you just seemed to deserve a kiss right now. Besides, you're never going to see me again, so what do I have to lose?"

Eliza gazed into eyes that were unmistakably kind. And unmistakably inviting. She needed the first part, but the second had her pulse racing.

Why was she so resistant? she asked herself. Why make up these rules about what she could and couldn't do? Here was a nice man, friendly and warm, someone who was obviously interested in her. Why wouldn't she allow herself to be comforted? To have companionship? To stop insisting on being alone?

Because you had a nice man once, and once was enough.

Because you're terrified.

Because you're a fraud, pretending you can inspire other people to take risks when you can barely do it yourself.

D, all of the above.

"I have to go," Eliza choked. She cleared her throat and tried again. "I'm sorry."

Ted studied her face a moment longer. "Can I call you?"

Eliza nodded. She didn't trust her voice.

"So tonight wasn't a complete disaster?"

"Oh, it was."

Ted reached for her hand, and this time Eliza decided not to resist. She could let him touch her that much—the world wouldn't crumble.

She dreaded re-entering the dining room, but Ted stayed at her side and made her apologies for her. "Terrible headache, maybe food poisoning—you all understand."

Eliza smiled despite herself. She forced herself to remember the forms of polite society. "Thank you for inviting me, Mrs. Walsh. You have a lovely home."

Sibylla Walsh extended her hand. Eliza considered kissing it, just to see a smile on the old woman's face. Instead she shook the limp hand and repeated her thanks.

Livia Keane whispered, "I'll call you."

Eliza agreed without enthusiasm. What did Livia Keane have to say to her?

Safely outside the doors of Sibylla Walsh's house, Hildy said, "I could have strangled that woman with my bare hands."

"Next time," Eliza promised.

"Did you see Teddy's face? He looked ready to tackle her."

Eliza sighed. "I need a hot bath. Let's go home."

As they drove out of Monarch, Eliza replayed the whole evening. What a nightmare, she thought. She never should have agreed to go.

"At least the sister is nice," she said out loud.

"Suzy's a lovely girl," Hildy agreed. "Kind as they come."

"Ted can be kind himself," Eliza added.

Hildy glanced over at her. "So, does that mean you like him a little better now?"

"I don't know, maybe." Eliza was beginning to believe Ted's lie to the group—she really did feel a headache coming on. "I guess he isn't so bad, in comparison."

"In comparison?" Hildy snorted. "To who? That mother?" She turned onto the road to Careyville. "You like him," she said to Eliza. "I told you."

"Just a little," Eliza conceded.

"We'll start with a little, build up to a lot."

"Easy there," Eliza warned. "One step at a time. I've had a rough night."

Hildy let her look out the window in peace for a few moments before asking, "So, did he kiss you?"

"What?"

"When you were alone."

"Maybe," Eliza said. "It's none of your business."

"Then he did."

"No."

"If he didn't you would have said so."

"Then I'm saying," Eliza told her. "He didn't." She paused and added, "If he did, it's still none of your business."

Hildy laughed her deep, throaty laugh. She reached over and patted Eliza's leg. "Have I ever told you how happy I am you came to stay with me? It's like having a sister."

Eliza smiled, despite the horrible evening. She gazed out the window at the approaching signs: Careyville Cleaners, Careyville Community Church, *The Careyville Independent*.

It wasn't Henderson, any of it. These weren't her people, her stores, her haunts. Eliza leaned back and closed her eyes, and replayed one particular scene from the night.

It was when she was in the kitchen with Ted. The nephews were behind him, watching, grinning while their Uncle Ted worked his magic on yet another woman.

David had entered just then, carrying a few plates. He stopped, a look of—what? Disgust? Disapproval?—on his face. Ted had leaned forward and kissed Eliza, and David's expression had darkened even more. He turned and left the room.

What was wrong with all of them? Eliza wondered. With her, with Sibylla Walsh, with David Walsh, with any of them? Why couldn't two people find each other and decide it was all right to feel good when they were together? Why couldn't Eliza decide once and for all to get on with her life as it was, instead of wishing she still had what was gone?

"I'll try," Eliza said to herself and to Hildy.

"You will?"

"Yes. I'll try and see."

"That's my girl. I'm proud of you."

Why couldn't Hildy have stopped there?

"And," she added, "Jamey would be proud, too. I know he would."

The tears she'd fought so hard to keep back found their

way into her eyes. Eliza rolled down the window to feel fresh air against her face. To feel the life rushing past her. To feel something new, instead of more of this constant old.

Will it ever be easy? she wondered. *Can I ever feel happy the way I used to?*

Maybe not easy, she told herself, but wasn't it at least time to make a start?

13

"Hey, Frank."

Frank Sawyer, editor of *The Careyville Independent* glanced up from his computer screen. He was a lean seventy-five-year-old with a head full of fading red hair. "Liza, dear, how are you?" He didn't wait for her answer, but went back to work.

It was nearing the end of June, and over the past two months Eliza had become accustomed to Frank's particular quirks, including the fact that he hated reading her submissions electronically, and always preferred that she deliver them in person. In part, Eliza guessed, because he enjoyed the company every few weeks.

She slipped her two pages onto Frank's desk and came around the other side to read what he was writing.

"Oh, that's not good," she said.

The old man grinned. "You bet it is."

"I guess the libel laws in New York are pretty lax?"

"It's the Op-Ed page—I can say whatever I want."

Eliza sank onto Frank's ancient leather couch and waited for a break in his tirade. When he finally finished, he leaned back in his chair and considered the only columnist *The Careyville Independent* had ever had.

"So, how's tricks?"

"Tricks are good," Eliza replied. "Did you go to the game?"

"I did. Seven-zip. My grandson's a wonder."

"I thought they didn't keep score at that age."

"*I* keep score."

"I was thinking of checking out a lacrosse game myself," Eliza said. "Suzy Walsh invited me. Do you think I'll like it?"

"Never seen one?" Frank asked. "Don't you Nevada kids play?"

"No, we're more soccer and basketball."

"Suzy's a good girl," Frank said. "You tell her I said so."

"I hope you mean it, because I actually will."

"So," Frank asked, "how's that boyfriend of yours?"

"Not my boyfriend." Eliza knew from previous experience that a sure way of deflecting Frank's attention from her own love life was to redirect it to his. "When are you going to ask Hildy out?"

Frank scowled. "That woman'd eat me alive and you know it."

"How can you say that? She's the sweetest person I know."

"Then you pal around with some real killers. Hey, tell me what you think. I want to sponsor some big event for Fourth of July. Got any ideas?"

"Yeah, first make some money so you can afford it."

"Sales are picking up," Frank said. "It must be all the women buying it for your column."

"Men read my column, too."

Frank snorted. "Sure."

Eliza pointed at him. "You know, that's just how Leo Pagnozzi acted."

"Except Pagnozzi didn't see you were golden—I did."

"I'm going to write a column just for men next time," Eliza said. "You'll see."

"Give it a try. Doesn't hurt me."

Eliza stood. "Oh well, on to my next thing."

"Which is?"

"I told you—going to my first lacrosse game."

"Let me give you a hint," Frank said. "You're gonna want to stay well back from the mothers."

"Why?"

"Vicious. Some of the dads can be pretty bad, too, but watch the moms. I think there might be a column there."

"I need to write things people in Henderson and Anchorage and Alamosa can all understand," Eliza said. "I don't think they play lacrosse in Anchorage."

"Yeah, but think of some of those sled-racing moms. I'll bet they're no better—'Run over his foot!' You'll see—vicious. So, will Teddy be at the game?"

"I happen to know Hildy is free this Friday," Eliza said in response, "if you wanted to call her."

Frank waved her off. "I haven't lived this long from playing with bears."

Eliza pretended to whip out a notepad and pen. "Another famous Frank Sawyer saying? Let me get that one down."

"You let him hold your hand at least?"

"Who? Ted? Sure, he can hold my hand any time."

Frank shook his head. "You gotta be careful there."

"Careful how?"

"Man's gonna want what he wants sooner or later."

"Not really something I want to discuss with you, Frank."

The editor shrugged. "Just some friendly advice."

"Thanks." Eliza pointed to the column on Frank's desk. "I like that one. People are going to like it."

"They always do. Like I said—you're golden."

"Oh, jeez!" Sue winced.

The woman next to her was more explicit. "Poke him! Poke him with your stick!"

Eliza glanced at the mother from the corner of her eye. Before the game started she had seemed so...normal.

"Aww! Come on!" The woman rose to her feet and jabbed her fist into the air. "Come on, Robby, hit him!"

"Well," Eliza murmured.

"I know," Sue whispered back. "It gets really bad."

Eliza sank lower into the lawn chair Sue had brought for her and studied the players from beneath the brim of her hat. She studied, too, one of the adults standing on the opposite side of the field clapping his hands and shouting to the kids on Danny's team.

"You didn't tell me David was the coach."

"Surprised?"

"Very." Eliza caught herself. "I mean, I didn't think he'd have the time for something like that."

"He makes time. He's really pretty good with the boys."

"He just seems so..."

Sue turned to her and smiled. "Yes? So..."

"I know he's your brother, but you have to have noticed he's not very...friendly."

"He's a little shy, I admit."

Shy? Eliza thought. *More like hostile.* "Does he ever say more than two words to anyone, or is it just me?"

"He's not as outgoing as Ted. But he's really a sweet man, once you get to know him."

Eliza thought of her many interactions with David Walsh over the past few months, from their run-ins on her walks with Daisy to his stern, almost disdainful treatment of her the few times they'd seen each other socially since the disastrous Easter dinner. "Sweet" was not a word she would pin on him.

"David's not that comfortable with people," Sue explained. "And Ted seems to cover that for all of us."

"You're pretty outgoing."

"Yeah, but I'm different," Sue said.

"That's what Ted says about David."

"I guess we're all three different, then. Must be why we get along." Sue broke off to stand and cheer for Danny as he raced down the field toward the goal. He passed the ball with a flick of his wrist, then accepted it again, catching it smoothly inside the net of his lacrosse stick.

"That looks really hard," Eliza said.

"It's impossible. You should try it. I can't seem to get my eyes and hands to work together."

At the half, Danny plopped onto the grass beside his mother. His face was red with exertion. "Hi, Eliza."

"Hey. Looking really good out there. Some nice passes."

"Thanks." He pawed through his mother's tote bag.

"Ooh, don't touch anything," Sue warned, "you're sweaty." She handed Danny a sports drink and a granola bar.

"Did you see twenty-two?" Danny asked his mother. "He fouled me twice, and the ref didn't call it." While mother and son analyzed the game so far, Eliza stole a look at the team's coach.

David spoke animatedly to two of his players, gesturing toward the field, then drawing plays on the grass. He didn't seem angry, and the boys didn't respond as if he were, but something about his expression always made him seem so severe and unapproachable. Such a contrast between him and his brother. Eliza still couldn't get over it.

Danny ran back to join his team for the second half. Sue and Eliza settled back into their chairs and pulled their hats low against the glare of the sun.

"So," Sue asked, "has Teddy asked you to the lake yet?"

"No, what lake?"

"Our family has a place up in the Adirondacks, right off one of the lakes. John and the boys and I are going up next weekend. I told Ted to ask you."

"That sounds nice. I'd like to." Eliza watched the game a few minutes more before asking casually, "Um, not to be too...prudish, but what would the sleeping arrangements be?"

Sue took her eyes off the game to give her full attention to a topic far more interesting. "So that's how it is? I'm shocked."

Eliza flushed. "It's just that—"

"I'm just teasing you," Sue said. "No need to explain—it's none of my business. I'm just a little surprised, knowing Teddy. But really—I don't want to know. The answer is there are plenty of bedrooms for all of us. Four on the top floor, two on the bottom, and two couches in the living room."

"Wow. Pretty big place."

"It was great having it growing up. We had some huge parties there when we were in high school."

"Did your parents know?"

"Unfortunately, yes."

After the game Eliza had yet another opportunity to be disappointed by David Walsh's manners.

"Great job," she told him.

He nodded in response.

"How long have you coached?"

"I don't know—hey, Sean! Don't forget your cleats!" He jogged away from Eliza to reunite the boy with his shoes.

"Nice talking to you, too," she mumbled.

Sue caught the exchange. "You need to keep in mind he doesn't really know how to talk to women. That was pretty good for him."

"I don't know what I ever did to him—no, on second thought, I do. I almost let Hildy's dog eat Bear."

"Oh, that would do it," Sue said. "I once scolded Bear for chewing the strap off my purse when I wasn't looking, and

David gave me a ten-minute lecture about 'there are no bad dogs, only bad owners.' And apparently bad sisters."

"But the two of you get along?"

Sue smiled. "David's great. He's been a great big brother. And a great uncle to my boys."

Eliza shook her head.

"What?" Sue asked.

"Nothing, it's just...I mean, I'm sure he's as nice as Ted—"

"Nicer," Sue said. "You just have to get to know him."

Hard to believe, Eliza thought as she watched David drive away without saying goodbye to his sister or anyone else.

14

"Don't forget your bathing suit," Hildy said.

"I know." Eliza was nervous enough packing for the trip without her mother-in-law evaluating everything she put in her bag.

"Not those sandals—take the blue ones."

"Do you mind?" Eliza said.

"I'm just saying—"

"This isn't a fashion show."

"Will Livia Keane be there?" Hildy asked.

"No."

"Okay, then wear what you want."

Eliza paused in her packing. "Why should that make any difference?"

"Because I don't want that woman criticizing you in front of Ted," Hildy said. "I know she'd do it."

"Why do you have it in for her?"

"Because I know lots of women just like her," Hildy said.

"Snooty east coast girls who think they invented how to dress and act." She shook her head in disgust. "Never could stand a girl like that."

"Why should I care what she thinks about me anyway? I'm not trying to impress her."

"But who needs to hear it?" Hildy argued. "'*Oh, you're wearing that?*' Drives me crazy."

Eliza smiled. She loved hearing new items added to the collection of things that rubbed Hildy wrong. Her mother-in-law could be such a generous, forgiving person in so many respects, but a few specific things always set her off: bad cooking, bad manners, snobby rich people, and now, apparently, snooty east coast girls.

Eliza searched her dresser for her two nicest pairs of underwear and threw them onto the bed. Then she added a modest nightgown and robe.

Hildy eyed the nightgown. "Where you going to sleep?"

"In one of the bedrooms."

"Alone?"

"Who are you—Frank Sawyer? You're about as nosy. That's how I know you'd be perfect for each other."

"That old buzzard. Don't change the subject."

"Oh, that's right, because my personal life is fair game, but yours isn't?"

"What do I need another old man for? I already took care of one."

"That's a nice way to talk about Ron."

"Honey, you know what I mean. I loved that man to the bottom of his toes, but those last few years were hard labor. Why would I want to take care of another one?"

"Because maybe he'd take care of you," Eliza said. "Besides, can't you be the least bit romantic? Think of the good parts—having someone to go to the movies with, going out to dinner—"

"What, you're going to stop doing all those things with me?"

Eliza scowled. "So it's okay for you to force me to go out with Ted, but I'm not allowed to fix you up with Frank."

"Force you? I didn't know you were suffering. Seems to me you got good and googly-eyed over Teddy all by yourself."

"Don't change the subject. You, madam, are a bossy old cow. And you can dish it out but you can't take it."

"So sue me. What time is he picking you up?"

Eliza checked her watch. "Soon."

"Are you nervous?"

"Of course."

"Are you going to let him get to second base?"

"Mind your own business," Eliza said. "Go get your own boyfriend."

Hildy reached for her daughter-in-law's hand, and pulled her down beside her. Eliza sat on the bed with her hands between her legs, prepared for the motherly lecture she suspected was coming.

"It's okay," Hildy began.

"I know."

"You're not doing anything wrong."

Eliza sighed. "I know."

"If you like him, he likes you…" Hildy shrugged. "Things can happen."

Eliza tried to stand, but Hildy caught her wrist. Eliza chuckled. "What? Can I go?"

"Not until you promise me."

"Promise what?"

"That you'll let yourself have a good time."

Eliza raised her right hand. "I do solemnly swear I will laugh once a day."

"You know what I mean."

"I'm sure I do." Eliza gave her mother-in-law a peck on the cheek. "You'll be okay for a few days without me?"

"Yeah, me and Frank are going to whoop it up."

"Not really?"

Hildy slapped Eliza on the rear. "Go have fun, young lady. I want to hear all about it."

TED STOOD at the door wearing shorts and a black knit shirt with "Walsh's Fine Foods" stitched in yellow above the chest. He pushed his sunglasses down his nose and motioned with his eyes toward the SUV behind him. "Sorry, but we have company."

Eliza peered past Ted's shoulder to the two waiting passengers.

"Livia heard about it, and they sort of...invited themselves."

Eliza punched him gamely in the shoulder. "It'll be fun. Don't worry."

"Fun? With David?"

"Be nice."

"He'll probably make me go over the books while we're

there." He lowered his voice in imitation of his brother: "'The Delmar store isn't looking so good. They lost a penny last month. We need to analyze costs. Put down that beer—boot up the spreadsheet.'"

Eliza followed him to the vehicle, determined to be cheerful. "Hi, guys. Oh, Bear's coming? Hi, boy. How are you?"

The dog lifted his head from David's lap and thumped his tail against Livia's thighs in greeting.

"Of course—can't forget the dog!" Livia said with a forced smile as she pushed the dog further toward David. She brushed away the smear of dirt Bear had left on her red and white-striped sundress.

Eliza took note of the rest of her ensemble: high-heeled sandals, a white straw hat, full makeup, nails that looked fresh from the salon.

David wore khaki slacks, brown loafers, and a blue button down shirt. Together the two of them looked like what they were: a wealthy couple on their way to his summer house.

Eliza could see Livia scrutinizing her outfit in return: the backpacking pants with zip-off legs—so handy for converting them to shorts so she could wade across rivers; a long-sleeved light blue shirt made of sun-protective fabric; light hiking shoes; and a wide-brimmed cotton hat for keeping the sun off her face.

"Afraid you might accidentally get a tan?" Livia asked.

"When you grow up in Nevada," Eliza replied, "you learn to hide from the sun."

Livia tilted back her straw hat. "Not me. I plan on lying on the dock for hours."

*Skin cancer, premature aging...*Eliza nodded politely and kept her Public Service Announcement to herself.

"I want to point out, Livia," Ted said, slamming down the rear door, "that Eliza only brought one bag. At least some women know how to pack."

Livia waved her soft, manicured hand. "Some of us know how to make a good impression," she told Ted. "Not that you don't, Eliza, of course. Just a *different* impression."

In the front seat, Ted flicked his hand against Eliza's leg. She caught his fingers and squeezed. She didn't dare catch his eye.

"Okay!" Ted said merrily. "Won't this be fun?"

THE TWO-HOUR DRIVE from Syracuse to the mountains was a feast of green for Eliza's desert-trained eyes. She had grown up in the brown, baked landscape of Nevada, where residents boasted of the "dry heat" and where having a lawn was an indulgence—or a sin, depending on a person's attitude about water conservation.

Here in upstate New York, shamelessly lush front lawns gave way to farmlands lined with alfalfa, to the cool pine trees, rivers, and lakes of the Adirondack mountains. Eliza rested her head against her seat and gazed out the window, drinking in the scenery while trying to tune out Livia's endless chatter.

"I imagine there'll be some concerts up there, won't there, David?" she asked. "I should have looked that up before we came. Do you know if there's anything going on this weekend?"

"No."

"Not that hanging around with your sister and the kids and the dog won't be *fascinating*, but maybe we'd all like to get out for a little break. Would you like that, Eliza?"

"Sure."

"So, David," Ted said, "you ready for some fishing?"

"If I have time. I brought some work."

"I told him no work on this trip," Livia said. She reached over to pat his thigh, and had to settle for patting the dog instead. Bear wagged against her dress in gratitude. "We're going to relax. I had tons of work I could have brought—the new TV spots need a desperate overhaul—but I deliberately left it all behind. Tuesday will be soon enough, right, honey?"

David ignored her and looked out the window. Bear's tail continued to thump while David scratched the Lab behind the ear.

Eliza wondered about David and Livia's relationship. From what she'd seen, Livia did all the pursuing, all the talking, all the touching. David didn't recoil, but he didn't seem to encourage any of it, either. He was the most passive participant in a couple Eliza had ever seen.

She wondered how she and Ted appeared to other people. Ted was affectionate, holding her hand, putting his arm over her shoulder or around her waist, occasionally kissing her on the cheek, but so far that—and one or two kisses Eliza had made sure stopped too soon—had been the extent of their physical relationship. Eliza was clear about her boundaries. She had broached the subject at the first sign that things were moving too quickly.

"Do you mind if we talk about something out loud?" she asked one night before getting out of Ted's car at the end of a date. She felt safer talking to him in the dark, where he couldn't see how nervous she was.

"Okay, sure."

She had rehearsed it, planned it, but now that the moment was here she dreaded saying what she knew she had to. Couldn't she send him an e-mail instead? Slip a note under his door?

"It's about...sleeping together."

"Ah."

"And I just have to ask," she blundered on before she lost her nerve, "I need you to...keep being patient."

"Hmm."

Eliza studied his profile. Was he annoyed? Tired of this high-maintenance woman?

She took a breath and bravely continued. "Look, I understand you're probably used to..."

"Sex?"

"Right."

"It's true," Ted said, "I am."

"And I understand, if this is too...weird for you."

Ted leaned against his car door and looked at her. "You mean reliving my teenage fantasies about whether I'll ever get to sleep with a girl I have a crush on? Yeah, it is a little weird."

"I'm sorry. Maybe...maybe we shouldn't go out any more. Maybe this is too hard."

"Eliza...hold on. Come here." Ted met her halfway and wrapped his arm around her shoulder. "Can you at least pretend to relax?"

Eliza's teeth chattered. She was not cold.

"Tell me something," Ted said. "Tell me the truth. Will you ever be ready?"

Eliza's skin warmed with embarrassment. "I-I think so. I really do." She waited a second, then added, "Eventually."

Ted reached for her hand and stroked his thumb across her knuckles. It was a touch Eliza knew, and one that always seemed to travel straight from her hand to her core. Her breathing grew shallow, her cheeks hot.

"How 'eventually'?" Ted asked. "This year? Five years? Tomorrow night?"

"Not...tomorrow. But maybe soon."

"Soon." Ted stroked her fingers. "Okay, soon..."

He kissed her on the cheek. "Look at me." When she did, Ted brushed his lips against hers, softly, chastely. Maddeningly.

"I guess soon will have to be good enough," Ted whispered. "Until then I can wait."

Eliza nodded slowly, as if she had been drugged. "But you can't keep kissing me like that," she murmured sleepily. "I have no will power."

"Good. I'm counting on it."

That had been a month ago, and although they hadn't spoken of it since then, Eliza knew it was always in the air. It was in the way he looked at her sometimes, his eyes narrowing seductively as he studied her face, her eyes, her mouth. It was in the way he stroked her back when they hugged goodnight, and the light touch of his thumb against her palm when they held hands. It could send jolts of electricity through her limbs, and make her palms sweat and her mouth go dry.

But it still wasn't enough to overcome that essential fear of one day making love to someone other than the love of her life. She had been old-fashioned when she met Jamey, and still was. She had to believe—to *know*—that the man she shared her body with loved her with all of his heart, and that she loved him in return. So far, as much as she liked Ted, she couldn't claim she felt love.

Maybe liking someone—a strong like—was as much as she'd ever feel toward any man, Eliza thought. Maybe love was out of the question anymore.

"...then when Suzy said you were all coming up here," Livia was saying, "I finally convinced David it was time to show me the infamous Walsh summer camp. I told him he doesn't have to work every weekend—the stores won't fold just because he isn't there to keep his eye on them every minute."

Eliza decided it was time to seize control of the conversation and give her ears a break from Livia's voice.

"What do you usually do up here?" she asked Ted.

"Fish, kayak, lounge in the hammock—all your gentleman's sports."

"Where do you kayak?"

"On the lake. There are some islands out in the middle that are fun to cruise around. Or I can find you some white water, if you're interested."

"No thanks. It's been too long. I wouldn't really trust myself in rapids."

"What's the hardest you did?" Ted asked.

"Class five."

"Oh, tough girl, huh?"

"More like tricked. Jamey didn't tell me until we were already through them."

The subject died there. Eliza could feel everyone's discomfort as they rode along in silence.

Can't you keep your big mouth shut? Eliza thought. *People don't always want to hear about your dead husband.*

The problem was, so much of her life—all of it since she was eighteen—bore Jamey's fingerprints. She could hardly tell an interesting story that didn't include him.

A voice came from the back, and for once it wasn't Livia's. "On the S-Salmon."

Eliza turned. David quickly looked out the side window again, as if he hadn't spoken.

"Yes," she said, "how did you know?"

"What salmon?" Livia asked. "I suppose you fish, too?"

"No, the Salmon River in Idaho," Eliza said. "It's where we did the rapids. Seriously, David, how did you know?"

"It was a good article," he mumbled without looking at her.

Eliza turned back to face the front. Once again, she felt how little she understood David Walsh.

Livia must have felt the same way, because she couldn't leave the subject alone. "You read some article about it? When?"

When David didn't answer right away, Eliza jumped in to

help. She felt embarrassed for him—maybe even a little protective—even though she wasn't sure why. "It must have been about five years ago. We did a whole backpacking and rafting tour of the state. I wrote several articles about it."

"And you read one of them? How sweet," Livia said, her tone conveying just the opposite.

Now it was Ted's turn to join in. "Yeah, Davey's read quite a bit of Eliza's stuff, haven't you, Davey?"

Eliza turned just enough to see the elder brother shrug. He kept his eyes focused out the window.

Eliza had had enough of the strained, puzzling conversation. "That's nice. Thank you," she told David, then turned to Ted. "I meant to ask you, are there any antique stores up here? I'd love to look around."

"Loads of them, I'm sure," Livia answered. "What else would all us city girls do up here? We're not all Class Five sportswomen like you." She reached forward to pat Eliza on the shoulder. "Let's have a date tomorrow. I've been looking for hooks for my bathroom. If you think Teddy can spare you."

The sign above the porch said *Camp Walsh*. Behind it rose two stories of a stunning wood and glass house, mounted on top of a layer of large gray and white stone. It looked like every lake house Eliza had ever admired in an architecture or decorating magazine. And she was about to walk into one.

Bear had vaulted from the car as soon as David opened the back door, and was now racing toward the water. Livia stood and slapped the black hair from her sundress. She pushed her sunglasses up into her hair and gazed at the house in front of them.

"Not too shabby, Walshes," she said.

"This is just the servants' quarters," Ted answered.

Sue and her husband and their two boys were already relaxing on the porch, sprawled out in the wide Adirondack chairs, contentedly sipping iced tea and sodas.

"Help yourself," Sue told the arriving guests. "This place

is completely self-serve. I'm on strike all weekend long."

"She's been telling us that since we got here," her oldest, Mike, complained. "Can you make her stop?"

"I will not stop," Sue said. "Do you understand that I have spent the last month cooped up with a hundred and fifty wild savages, trying to teach them advanced algebra when all they wanted was for me to shut up and let them text or listen to their music until it was finally time for summer vacation? As if every teacher in that place wasn't dying to get rid of them! And the only thing—I mean the *only* thing—that kept me going was knowing I'd be sitting right here, right now, enjoying a delicious raspberry tea, waiting for my husband and sons and brothers to wait on me hand and foot."

"Nice fantasy, Sue," Ted said. "Hate to burst your bubble."

She pointed at her little brother. "Listen here, mister. I busted my butt doing all the shopping these past few nights so I could stock this place with everything we might possibly need for the next three days. But I am *done* now—done. I have served my last meal until I get home, and I'll be damned if anyone here even dares to ask me to lift a finger."

"See?" Mike appealed to his uncles.

"It's how she gets," Ted answered. "That's why we don't let her come up here too often."

"My *life* doesn't let me come up here too often," Sue corrected him. "But now I'm going to savor every single second."

"So let me get this straight," Ted said. "This is our vacation, too, but we're not supposed to enjoy it—only you are."

"Enjoy it as much as you want," his sister answered. She tipped her head back, closed her eyes, and rested her legs on footstool in front of her. "But I'm expecting three delicious meals a day out of all of you—and not just burgers on the grill. I mean something *good*—and you might as well get started with lunch. I'm starving."

Eliza wasn't sure whether to laugh or be concerned. This was a side of Sue she hadn't seen. Eliza widened her eyes at Ted, who answered her with a wink.

"I can help," Eliza said. "Just tell me where my room is, and I'll drop my bag off and come back."

"Don't you dare," Sue said, her eyes flying open again. She snapped her fingers at her little brother. "Ted, you take her bags up. She's in the lavender room. David, Livia's in the rose. You two," she said, pointing to Eliza and Livia, "are our guests. You come sit over here with me. The men can take care of everything else."

"Sounds heavenly," Livia said, immediately taking her up on her offer. She settled into one of the chairs near Sue and stretched her feet out onto the porch railing. "David, I'd love some tea."

Eliza stole a look at David to see his reaction. In fact, she'd been secretly watching him on and off ever since they got out of the car. She wondered if he would be as cold and closed off on vacation, around his family, as he was every other time she saw him.

True to form, he hadn't said a word so far, but Eliza did notice him smiling several times while his sister went off on her tirade. So maybe there was a personality inside there after all, Eliza thought. It would be interesting to see if any more of it might sneak out over the next few days.

For now, he hoisted his own bag and two of Livia's three.

"Where am I?" he asked Sue.

"You and your wet dog, if he ever comes back, are in the blue room downstairs, next to the boys."

David nodded and disappeared into the house.

"Where am I, sister dear?" Ted asked.

"Upstairs," she said. "White room. Hurry back. I wasn't kidding about being hungry. I'd like some chips and salsa, pronto. Wedge of lime on the side."

"Now, are we supposed to cut the lime lengthwise or widthwise?" Sue's husband, John, asked. "I wouldn't want any of us to get into trouble."

"It's a good thing I'm here," Ted told his brother-in-law. "Your wife is seriously out of hand. I'll have to set her straight right away."

"Just try it," Sue warned him. "I'm not above embarrassing you in front of your girlfriend."

Eliza smiled a little more nervously than she meant to. Sue must have noticed.

"Come on, Eliza, sit. Relax. This place is beautiful. You'll love it here. These will be the best three days of your whole summer."

NOT A BAD START, Eliza thought. Not only did the men produce a generous spread of chips, salsa, crackers, cheese, grapes, olives, and assorted nuts, they also managed to come up with a few ideas for the dinners they'd make over the next two nights. Even Danny and Mike would have roles as prep cooks, assigned all the peeling and knife work so their elders could concentrate on being chefs.

"We can trust you with the knives, can't we?" Ted asked his younger nephew.

"Come on," Danny answered. "You know my ninja skills." He pretended to throw an imaginary knife at one of the wooden porch beams. He gave it the sound effect of *thwick*, and said, "Deadly."

"That's what I'm afraid of," Ted said. "Your uncle David once sliced a man's ear off. Coordination only runs on one side of the family."

"Mine," Sue said.

"And mine," Ted added. He picked up one of the grapes, positioned it between his thumb and third finger, then expertly flicked it in a perfect arc that landed on his brother's lap. "See? First time."

David didn't bother looking up from his phone, but merely brushed the grape aside.

Eliza couldn't figure the two of them out. For the past hour or so, she'd watched Ted try to bait his older brother over and over. David rarely even acknowledged it. He was like a water buffalo ignoring the fly buzzing in and out of his nose.

Which seemed to make Ted try all the harder.

"Whatcha working on there, Davey?" he asked, throwing another grape. "Don't suppose you noticed your entire family—well, the good parts—are here right now. And you have a lady friend—did you notice that? I noticed," Ted added, giving Livia the once-over. "Nice legs, Keane."

"Thank you, Mr. Walsh. Please include that on my performance review."

Eliza and Sue exchanged a glance. Sue rolled her eyes.

"I have a lady friend here, too," Ted said, pushing out of his chair. "Come on, Shepherd, I heard you're a kayaker."

Eliza raised an eyebrow. "Yes..."

"Time to put some boats in the water. What do you say we paddle out to an island?"

Eliza smiled. It had been years—probably three, if she remembered right—since she'd been in a kayak. The last time was with Jamey on the Salt River. Just the thought of moving her arms like that again made her muscles itch in anticipation. "I'd actually...love that."

"I love what you love," Ted answered. "Let's do it."

"Can I go?" Danny asked.

"No," Ted answered immediately.

"Me, too," Mike said. "Come on, Uncle Ted."

Ted sighed. "Fine. Everybody who wants to ruin my romantic kayaking date with Eliza, raise your hand."

The two nephews and their father raised theirs.

And a few seconds later, so did David.

Livia let out a tinkling laugh. Then she raised her hand, too.

Ted looked around in disgust. "Have any of you ever heard of taking a hint?"

"Do you have that many kayaks for everybody?" Eliza asked him.

"Unfortunately, yes."

Livia surveyed Eliza's outfit. "Aren't you going to change?" While the men retrieved kayaks from the boathouse, Livia disappeared into her room—the rose room, as Sue had called it—and emerged twenty minutes later wearing a tight red tank top, short khaki shorts, and black leather flip flops.

Eliza still wore what she'd dressed in that morning. Her backpacking pants and sun shirt were perfect for water sports—she'd worn them on dozens of excursions. The only change she made was trading her hiking shoes for a pair of sturdy Teva sandals. "I'll be fine," Eliza said.

Livia had also freshened up her blush and lipstick, Eliza noticed. Eliza had merely smeared on more sunscreen.

"Ready?" Livia asked, threading her arm inside Eliza's. "We girls'll stick together. You'll coach me if I need it, won't you? I'd hate to have to ask the men for anything."

"Sure," Eliza answered, wondering when Livia had decided the two of them were so chummy. "Have you ever kayaked before?"

"No," Livia scoffed, releasing Eliza and trotting nimbly down the stairs. "But honestly, how hard can it be?"

It was a beautiful afternoon on the water. Eliza had forgotten how free she could feel, gliding along under the power of her own arms, feeling the craft slipping through the waves. There was a slight headwind—not enough to be annoying, but just enough to stir up a few whitecaps and make the effort more of a challenge.

Eliza glanced to her left. She'd have preferred being alone on the lake, but that wasn't what she signed up for. This was a group activity, and unfortunately, she was saddled with one particular member of the group.

"You boys go on ahead," Livia had told Ted and the others. "Eliza and I are going to practice."

"You sure?" Ted asked. "Maybe David should teach you. Then Eliza and I can—"

"No," Livia insisted, "it'll be just us girls for a while, but then we'll catch up. Then I'll race you all back to camp. Sound good?"

Sound bad, Eliza thought, but she wanted to be a good sport. So she, too, had agreed that the men should go on ahead, and she and Livia would catch up when they could.

Having been alone with her now for the past half hour, Eliza realized Livia was smart not to let David teach her—he wouldn't have liked her very much after the lesson.

"You're drifting again," Eliza called out helpfully. "You need a more even stroke on each side."

"I know that," Livia snapped. "I'm doing that. There's something wrong with this paddle."

Of course there is, Eliza thought. *It couldn't possibly be you.*

"Well, try again," she said. "Try to get into a rhythm. Watch me: Stro-o-o-ke, stro-o-o-ke, keep your movements nice and smooth..."

Livia cursed and lifted her paddle out of the water. She rested it on top of the kayak. "Let's forget it," she said. "They're too far ahead of us anyway."

They could see the men in the distance, past all the houses lining the shore, and finally out in the open water, heading toward the island. From the look of it, three of them seemed to be racing. Ted and the two nephews, Eliza guessed.

"Let's go back," Livia said. "Nice glass of wine on the

porch, maybe lay out on the dock…"

Eliza forced herself to smile. "Sure, if that's what you want. I'll take you back. Watch me and I'll show you how to turn—"

"I know how to turn," Livia said. "It's not that hard."

"Suit yourself," Eliza muttered as she paddled out ahead.

THIS IS NICER ANYWAY, she thought later. Out on the lake all alone. It might take her an hour to reach the island. A whole hour, all by herself.

Bliss.

She studied the houses as she paddled past. Some of them as grand as the Walshes', some of them very small and modest.

Jamey and I would have liked one like that, she thought, seeing a little white cottage with shutters painted yellow. *Or that one.* Green roof, blue wooden sides, a little flower garden in front. *Not that one, or that*—the fancier mansions that tried too hard to look like cabins. *That one. That has Jamey and me written all over it.*

Eliza sighed. What was the point? The point was she did this sort of thing all the time: What would Jamey have said to so-and-so? What would he have thought of this column or that? What would he have said that night after they were snug in the lavender room and they could whisper privately about some of the people on this trip? *"If there were some kind of nuclear explosion, and Livia Keane and I were the last two people on Earth, I'd have to say, 'I'm sorry, the population dies here.' Because there's no way I'd ever—"*

And then Eliza would have to shush him before he went off on some colorful explanation of how he wouldn't be doing *that* with *this* no matter what Livia tried. And the two of them would agree they didn't understand a woman like that—"How does she even survive in this world?"—and then Jamey Shepherd would kiss his wife and tuck a loose strand of her hair behind her ear, and he'd tell her how much he loved her and how lucky he was, and *"Come on, we'll be quiet,"* and then his warm touch and his hot mouth and his expert hands—

"Search party," shouted a voice in the distance.

Eliza looked up. She could see two kayaks coming toward her. Ted and one of the nephews—Danny, she thought.

"Come on, Liz, we'll be quiet."

"Shh."

"Everybody's probably passed out anyway. Did you see how fast that tequila went? Come on, El, I dare you."

"Ooh, you dare me, huh?"

"Knew that would get your shirt off."

"You think you know me, huh."

"'Course I do. But isn't it nice that someone who knows you so well loves you so much?"

Yes, Jamey. That was nice—so very nice. Every single day.

She had time. If she stopped paddling, just drifted there, they wouldn't reach her for a while. Eliza closed her eyes and replayed the scene one more time. Start to finish, first line to last, and the slow, quiet lovemaking that followed.

"Come on, El, I dare you."

I could never say no to you.

16

Eliza read a quiz in a magazine once about how to tell if you're an extrovert or an introvert. The test was whether you draw energy from being around other people, or feel depleted by them afterward.

Eliza was definitely feeling depleted.

It started with the gamesmanship before the game. Sue and her boys had recruited most of the group—excluding John, who had a baseball game to watch on the enormous flat-screen TV, and David, who said he had work to do—to play one of the games they'd brought along. It involved categories of drawing, acting, singing, and word play. Something Eliza thought she might actually enjoy.

The six of them divided into two teams: Ted and the nephews against Sue, Eliza, and Livia.

"I have to warn you," Livia told the men, "I'm unbeatable."

"Sorry to hear that, Keane," Ted answered, "'cause so am I. Looks like you've finally met your match."

Livia laughed. "Maybe I have."

Sue gave Eliza a look.

"Enough trash talk," Sue said. "Come on, ladies. Let's grind these boys into the dust."

An hour into it, Eliza had already had enough.

"Ha! Wrong!" Livia shouted at Mike. She showed him the card. "Next!"

Eliza's head hurt. She had brought a book with her—a collection of prize-winning short stories—and she longed to be up in the quiet of her room, reading instead of listening to this.

"Watch me, watch me," Livia told Sue and Eliza. She started pantomiming the secret word.

"Uh...chopping something?" Sue guessed.

Livia shook her head.

"Poking...hitting..."

Livia frowned.

"Knife—stabbing with a knife?"

Livia groaned and shook her head harder.

When time was up, she shouted, "Downtown!"

"How is that downtown?" Sue wanted to know.

"Dooowwwn," Livia said, demonstrating again by jabbing her hand downward. "You couldn't even get to the town part."

Sue looked at Eliza. "Sorry. I'm usually good at this game."

"Not your fault," Eliza mumbled.

Ted reached for her knee under the table and gave it a

squeeze. Then he left his hand there and stroked it lightly against her thigh.

She gently removed it.

Eliza had had this feeling the whole night: that she didn't belong there. That she was watching it from outside. There she was, in this gorgeous, fantasy lake house, and all she wanted to do was go home and sit on Hildy's couch and eat cold pasta with her mother-in-law. Get up in the morning and drink her coffee alone. Spend the day without someone constantly trying to charm her, touch her, make her laugh, win her over. Spend her day without someone being so interested in her.

There had to be something wrong with that picture. Eliza knew in her heart it wasn't normal.

But she also knew there was something wrong with sitting there in that room with a family that wasn't hers, forcing her smiles, pretending she was having a great time. She wasn't. And she wasn't sure how much longer she could keep it up.

Before they could move on to another round in the game, Eliza leaned over and whispered to Ted, "Can I talk to you?"

Ted turned to his teammates. "Break, gentleman. Our opponent wants to concede."

"I doubt it," Sue said. "But I wouldn't mind a break, either. Anyone want anything else to drink?"

"I thought you weren't serving us," Ted said.

"I wasn't talking to you."

Ted smirked at his big sister, then followed Eliza to the door. The two of them stepped out onto the porch.

"It's still light," Eliza observed. "I keep forgetting how far north we are." She could see David out on the dock, sitting with his legs over the edge, watching his dog play in the water.

Ted tipped back his beer and drained it. Then he leaned against the nearest post. "So, what's up?"

"I just wanted to say I'm sorry. I'm afraid I'm not going to be very good company on this trip."

"Starting when?" Ted asked. "'Cause you're a barrel of laughs right now."

He met her gaze. And didn't crack a smile.

"I'm sorry," Eliza said again.

"So what am I supposed to do?" Ted asked.

"I don't know," she answered quietly.

"I don't know, either. I can't make you have fun, Eliza. Just like I can't make you like me. I've tried—"

"I do like you."

"Not enough," Ted said. "And I'm sick of trying."

He flipped his empty beer bottle into the air and caught it by the neck on the way down. "You let me know if you change your mind," he told her. "Until then I have a game to go win."

He went back inside the house and shut the door. Eliza stood on the porch alone.

She could feel her body shaking. That annoying, shivery reaction, like when her teeth chattered for no reasonable reason. Part of her wanted to go back inside, ask Ted to talk to her more, mend this and sort it out.

The other part of her felt relief.

She was acting like she was fourteen. No exaggeration, she thought, since she remembered very well having exactly this kind of physical reaction at her first high school dance. A boy two grades older—someone she'd never seen or talked to before—came straight toward her within minutes after she entered the room and told her he'd been waiting for her to show up.

"Do I...know you?" Her body felt cold and stiff. Her jaw felt so tight it had been hard to get the words out. She could feel the strange shivering start.

"I'm Troy," he said, looking offended that she didn't remember.

"Oh." She glanced around, hoping to see any of her friends. Some escape. But she couldn't find anyone.

"So you gonna dance with me?"

"Uh..." She could feel a layer of cold sweat spring up all over her body. "No, I'm supposed to meet someone. I...I have to go find my friend."

"I'll help you look," Troy said.

"No, that's okay. I have to go."

Then she'd fled into the crowd, hoping no one saw her and no one followed. She felt like a wild animal, cornered.

That was the closest she came to dating in high school.

Which was why Jamey Shepherd had been such a revelation. Someone who spoke to her on her first day of college and didn't make her want to shiver or panic or escape. Someone who picked her out and let her know there was no hurry, but he wasn't going away.

The Labrador splashed into the water. Eliza made her choice. Better a silent man and his wet dog than more games with the loud crowd inside.

And she made another choice: To leave as soon as she could.

"Do you mind if I sit here? We don't have to talk."

David hesitated. "That's f...fine."

Eliza lowered herself onto the dock. The wood felt rough and damp against the back of her legs. She drew up her knees and leaned against the closest post.

She could see the dog out in the water. He seemed content just to paddle by himself, without someone throwing him a ball or a stick. Self-contained, Eliza thought. A perfect dog for David Walsh.

"I think your brother's tired of me."

David didn't answer right away. He waited a few beats before saying, "Why?"

"I don't think I'm fun enough."

David paused again, then nodded.

"Livia seems fun," Eliza said.

David didn't answer.

"Right," Eliza mumbled under her breath. *I said I wouldn't talk.*

She hugged her knees into her chest and rested her head on top of them. She closed her eyes and listened to the sounds around the lake.

When her back started to ache from sitting that way, she lay back flat against the dock and let her legs dangle over the edge.

Eliza gazed up at the sky, now dark enough she could see a light sprinkling of stars.

"Can I ask you something?" she asked David.

"Yes."

She felt bolder now that she wasn't looking at him. "In the car today, what you said about my trip down the Salmon —how did you remember that?"

A slight pause, then, "I told you. I r-read it."

"But that was five years ago. How could you remember?"

"I just do."

She swung her legs back and forth for several quiet minutes. She heard Bear emerge from the water again and shake himself. "That's enough, boy," David told him softly. "Let's go in."

"Oh," Eliza said, sitting up. "You're leaving?"

"It's late," David said. He stood and then offered her his hand. She held up her arm and he helped pull her to her feet.

Eliza brushed off the back of her shorts. "Thanks for letting me sit out here. It was too loud in there."

They walked along the dock, Bear tracking them from below. When they joined him again on solid land, David bent down to give the dog a few sturdy pats to his side.

"Can I be honest with you?" Eliza asked. *Why am I telling him this? It's not as if he cares.* But she knew she just needed to say it to someone, and someone who wouldn't ask her a lot of questions seemed like a good choice.

David waited and looked at her. Eliza took a breath and continued.

"I think it was a mistake coming up here. I think...I feel like an intruder on your family's time. I don't feel like I belong here."

"You're not intruding," David answered. "You were invited."

"But I don't..." Eliza sighed. "I know this is probably too personal, and you probably don't care, but I'm going to tell you anyway." She laughed at her own nervousness, and at the fact that was still going to tell him, despite that. "I don't think your brother and I are destined to be together. Which makes it kind of awkward for me to be here. I think he was hoping for...something more."

"You can leave whenever you want."

He said it simply, not in a petulant way—*"Fine! Then you can leave!"*—but in a very matter-of-fact, easy tone.

"Not really," Eliza said. "I rode with all of you, remember?"

"I can drive you home tomorrow."

"But..." Eliza studied his face in the dark. Was he serious? Was he mad? "Won't people be angry with me? Won't your sister?"

"Why?" David said. "You can do whatever you want."

"I can't ask you to drive me."

"You didn't," he said. "I offered."

"I don't want to ruin your weekend."

"I didn't want to come here, either."

The confession surprised her. "Then why did you?"

"Livia wanted to."

"Oh. Right," Eliza said, comprehension dawning. "Then of course you can't leave. But thank you anyway."

"Livia can stay if she wants," he said. "It doesn't matter."

"No, David, I'm really sorry I bothered you. Never mind."

Eliza took off toward the house, feeling embarrassed and

foolish. It was nice of David to take pity on her, but obviously she was acting like a child. *"Take me home! I don't like it here!"* She had signed up for this trip, and she could tough it out. It wasn't like the place or the people were awful. She was just being difficult. Self-indulgent and insecure and melodramatic. So what if she wanted to go hide in her room and read a book and fall asleep? She could act like a grown-up and go be sociable with the other grown-ups and stop behaving as if the world revolved around her.

"She's back!" Livia said as Eliza walked through the door. "Not that we needed you—Sue and I are trouncing the competition. But if you want to bask in our reflected glory..."

Eliza plastered on a smile. "Good job, you two. Sue, can I get you anything? Livia? Anybody?"

"I'll take another rum and Coke," Livia answered, holding out her glass. "Teddy, something for the losers?"

Ted glanced up at Eliza, then held out his empty bottle of beer. "Time for some tequila," he said. "Last cupboard on the left. And bartender, don't be shy."

It was after midnight when Eliza finally dragged up the stairs. Sue was cleaning up—despite her speech at the beginning of the day—and her husband had gone to bed hours before. Ted and the nephews had moved on to a card game. Livia sat drinking and watching.

"I'll see you in the morning," Eliza said, patting Ted on the shoulder.

"Yeah, see you," he answered, not looking up. He

slammed another card onto the table. "You're going to owe me your college fund, Mikey."

"Me, too," Danny said, slapping his own card on top. "You really suck at this."

Mike gave his own cards a cool appraisal, then calmly fanned them out in front of him.

"Damn it!" Danny shouted.

"Settle down," Sue warned from the kitchen.

"I'm dealing," Danny said, scooping up the cards.

Ted leaned back and stretched. Eliza still stood behind him, waiting.

Waiting for what? she wondered. She wasn't sure.

His attention? His approval? His forgiveness?

"Okay, so good night," she said again.

"'Night," Ted answered.

"Coffee's here," Sue said, pointing to the coffee maker. "Supplies are up here. John'll probably be up before you and he can make it, but just in case."

"Okay, thanks."

Eliza walked across the room to the staircase and started going up.

"Good night," Livia called after her. "Remember, shopping tomorrow!"

"Shopping. Right." With Livia. The weekend was getting better by the minute.

She stopped at the first room at the top of the stairs and turned on the light. The room certainly was lavender: lavender walls, white bedspread with lavender flowers, matching white and lavender curtains. But she didn't mind it. It was overly feminine and fussy, but it felt right as a guest room in a fancy, professionally-decorated lake house. She could easily see this room in a magazine spread. *"The lavender room, with its sunny windows and soft, inviting bed."*

Soft and inviting it was. Eliza quickly brushed her teeth in the bathroom two doors down, then returned to change into her nightgown. Then she slid between the cold, soft sheets and fell asleep within minutes.

And woke a few hours later to the unmistakable sounds of sex.

17

Of course he didn't make any noise, Eliza thought. Why should David be any different during sex?

Livia, on the other hand: giggling, moaning, and at one point—thankfully, only one—crying out. Then Livia shushing herself and giggling again. *Save me,* Eliza thought.

She tried blocking it out with a pillow over her head, but that muffled only some of the sound. There was still the rhythmic pounding of the headboard against the wall—such a classically embarrassing touch when you were staying at someone else's house. Whenever Eliza and Jamey stayed with friends, he made fun of her for lying on the bed first thing and making it bounce and shift. If there were even a hint of squeak or knocking, she'd tackle the problem like a sound engineer until she had moved, padded, or otherwise fixed the bed.

And if she couldn't, they'd be making love on the floor.

"No one cares," Jamey would tell her, but Eliza cared. "We're married. It's legal. It's required."

"It's personal," was how Eliza always explained it, and Jamey let her continue stuffing T-shirts behind headboards and testing for sound if they moved horizontally instead of vertically.

Apparently Livia Keane played from a different rule book.

As did David.

In the morning, all it took was one look at Sue to realize she'd had an even rougher night.

"Morning," Eliza muttered.

Sue couldn't even answer. She just selected the biggest mug she could find in the cupboard and poured coffee up to its rim. She stood in her robe, leaning against the counter, drinking dark roast with the kind of grim concentration of a climber who knows she used up all her strength on that last pitch, and she still has four more impossible ones to go.

When Livia came down, about an hour later, Sue unceremoniously got up from the dining table and took her third refill of coffee outside. Eliza admired her lack of pretense. She wished she had gotten up and run out with her.

"Where is everybody?" Livia asked cheerfully. She'd showered, styled her hair, and put on a fresh layer of makeup. She wore black yoga pants and a loose white blouse open over a lacy red camisole.

Eliza wore shorts and a T-shirt.

"I don't know," she answered with a yawn. "I've only seen Sue."

"Coffee?" Livia said, spying the machine. "Mm, good."

Eliza felt torn: On the one hand, she wanted to go sit on the porch with Sue, if that's where she was, and stare out at the water in silence. On the other hand, she felt some obligation to Sue—just a matter of pure, human kindness—to keep this woman away from her until Sue had rejoined the land of the living. It was a sacrifice Eliza hated to make, but she knew she had to do it.

But she could do it on her own terms, she decided. Take a lesson from Livia's lover, and not feel compelled to speak, just because she was spoken to.

Livia started in right away. "So, ready to head into town? I thought we'd try that store we saw when we turned off the highway. It looks like one of those places that has everything —tools to linens. And there were all those antique shops— you said you wanted to look at antiques, right? Then maybe we can find someplace decent to have lunch, although I doubt they have anything good up here..."

Eliza tried to tune her out as she droned on. But she'd never acquired the talent for *not* listening. Sometimes on trips, she and Jamey would be stuck with a guide or a fellow hiker or climber who could not...shut...up. Eliza would always be the one stuck nodding and "hmm"-ing and "oh, is that right?" while Jamey read a book or slept. He never felt that insane compulsion to be polite and attentive if he didn't really want to. Eliza scolded him all the time for making her do all the heavy lifting in a conversation.

"Why do you have to do it?" Jamey would ask her. "Who appointed you?"

"But they're talking to me," she'd say. "What am I supposed to do, just get up and leave?"

"Do whatever you have to. You're not doing these people any favors by letting them think they're interesting. People have to learn how to tell stories. If they're boring, they need to know that."

Eliza would always give up. Jamey just didn't understand. And besides, he didn't have to listen as long as Eliza was around. People would just keep yammering at her.

"...still think it's worth looking for a concert or some kind of show tonight. I didn't even see a movie theatre—did you? I don't know what people do out here in the woods."

Have loud raucous sex all night.

"I have to use the bathroom," Eliza said.

She escaped up the stairs. She pulled her travel kit out of her bag and headed for the bathroom. A shower sounded good. Something long and solitary and quiet.

The door was locked.

"Just a minute," came Ted's voice from inside.

"Oh. Don't worry—I'll just wait in my room."

The door swung open. "It's fine," Ted said. "I'm done." His hair was wet and he smelled like aftershave. "Good morning." He leaned forward and kissed her on the cheek.

"Hi." Eliza wondered if he'd heard his brother and Livia next door. The bathroom was between their two rooms, but if Eliza could hear them from the end of the hall, surely Ted had, too.

"So," she said, "interesting night, huh?"

Ted smiled. "Interesting."

"What are you doing today? Livia wants me to go shopping, but I think I'd rather poke out my own eyeballs."

"You should go," Ted said. "You might have fun."

"Oh. Okay." Eliza backed away as he brushed past her. "So...what are you going to do?"

"I don't know, I'll figure something out," he said. Then he headed down the stairs.

Eliza shut herself in the bathroom. It was still steamy from Ted's shower. The window high on the wall was open, but very little air circulated through.

She stood under the warm water, then adjusted the faucet to make it colder. A day on the lake might be nice. Maybe she could take one of the kayaks out again, and this time paddle all the way out to that island. Bring her bathing suit and take a swim. But the key was: alone.

Or maybe with Ted. If he suggested it.

But definitely not shopping with Livia.

Learn to say no. Once again, not living up to her own column. If people knew how little she practiced what she preached, they'd stop reading her and move on to someone who wasn't such a fraud.

But by the time she got back downstairs, ready to take a stand, the matter had already been taken care of for her.

"We're leaving," David Walsh said. "Do you still want a ride?"

18

It was the reverse of how they'd driven up there: David and Livia in front, Eliza in the back with Bear stretched out along the seat, his head in her lap. If only there had been a divider between the seats, Eliza thought, like a limo. She could have ridden in perfect contentment with just the scenery passing by her window and the sound of a big black dog snoring on her lap.

It seemed impossible, but Livia was even chattier on the ride home than she had been on the ride up. Luckily, most of it was marketing related—her new ideas for various campaigns for the Walsh's stores—so Eliza really could practice what Jamey tried to teach her, tuning people out, treating their voices like white noise.

Except every now and then, Livia would try to involve her.

"Eliza, which would you rather see in an ad: a mother and her daughter shopping for food, a mother and her two kids—maybe a toddler and a baby—or a single woman, like you, dressed for work, maybe shopping for fresh produce?"

Before Eliza could answer, Livia rolled on.

"I think you'll always bring in the single shopper," she told David. "You're a neighborhood store, they can get everything they want there, and maybe they'll meet somebody in front of the seafood counter, you know how people think, it's the same reason they pay four dollars for a cup of coffee they could make at home, because they're not meeting Mr. or Ms. Right in their kitchen every morning—but the family dollar, that's what we need to fight for. Because let's face it, Walsh's is boutique when it comes to most of your prices, and moms can get detergent a lot of places more cheaply..."

Eliza curled forward and whispered in Bear's ear, "I'm going to jump out of this car right now. Are you with me?"

When they finally reached Careyville, Eliza knew she only had to hold on a few more minutes. But still, Livia continued her monologue. Eliza couldn't remember David chiming in even once.

When the SUV pulled up in front of Hildy's house, Eliza unbuckled her seat belt, gave the dog a quick kiss on the head, and leapt out of the car. Livia rolled down her window to say goodbye.

"It's been fun. I'll call you," she said.

Why? Eliza wanted to answer.

She met David at the back of the car, where he separated Eliza's one bag from the pile of Livia's.

"I'm sorry," he said.

"For what?"

He motioned his head toward the front of the car.

Eliza narrowed her eyes. Was he really apologizing for his girlfriend?

"Thank you for the ride. This weekend has been..."

David nodded and lowered the back hatch.

He got back into the car and pulled away. Eliza could hear Livia already talking again.

"I'm home!" she called as she came in downstairs. Daisy barked and ran down to meet her. "Miss me?" she asked the dog.

"Uh-oh, there's a story there," Hildy called from upstairs.

"There is," Eliza answered, "but I'm not really sure I understand it."

"Well, come up here and tell it," Hildy said. "I thought I'd have to wait at least one more day for something juicy."

"You know what I think," Hildy said when Eliza had told her everything she knew. "I think there was some hanky-panky."

"Of course there was hanky-panky—I already told you that. Sue and I both heard it."

"But you think it was Livia and David."

"Right," Eliza said.

"I think it was Livia and *Teddy*."

"No." Eliza thought about it for a second. "No. I don't think so. I think that would have been—" She looked into her mother-in-law's smug, knowing face. "Do you really think so?"

"Put it together," Hildy said. "They're drinking, you've

told Teddy he isn't getting anywhere, David doesn't seem that interested in her—nature takes its course. You said the two of them were flirting."

"Maybe," Eliza corrected. "They were both joking around with each other. That doesn't necessarily mean anything."

"He told her she has nice legs. She said he'd met his match."

"Actually, I think he said she'd met hers."

"Details," Hildy said, flicking her hand. "And then while you're in the shower this morning, the four of them have it out."

"What four?"

"Suzy and her brothers and that woman."

"Sue wouldn't do that."

"Wouldn't she?" Hildy said. "That Suzy is a pistol when she wants to be. Maybe not as much as when I knew her, but even when she was a little girl, she could give those brothers a real talking-to."

"So you think she confronted Ted and Livia, right in front of David?"

"Why not?" Hildy said. "She doesn't owe that Livia anything. And why should she keep Teddy's secret if it's going to hurt Davey? She always liked Davey better—I could tell. And Suzy can get on her high horse. She's not going to stand for one brother messing around with the other one's girl."

"Huh." Eliza propped her elbows on the table and rested her chin in her hand. "I have no idea if you're right, but that is pretty juicy."

"And you know what else I noticed?"

"What?"

"You don't seem very upset."

Eliza sat up straight and put her hands back in her lap. "Oh."

"Yeah, 'oh.' Want to tell me what that's about? I thought you liked him."

"I guess not that much."

"I guess not," Hildy said. "So that's worth knowing."

It was. Eliza thought about it for a moment more, and realized it was true: She didn't actually care. She could pretend to feel hurt or angry or betrayed, but that's all it would be: pretend. The truth was Ted could sleep with Livia or whomever else he wanted to. It had nothing to do with Eliza—she would never be in his bed.

"What I don't understand," Hildy said, "is why Davey gave that woman a ride home. Or why she left in the first place. If she's with Teddy now, why didn't she stay and whoop it up with him all weekend? Or why didn't Teddy come back with her?"

"I don't know, Detective, you tell me."

"I'll tell you why: She's scared for her job, for one thing— that's why she was yammering about work all the way home. She slept with her boss's brother."

"They're both her bosses," Eliza pointed out.

Hildy dismissed it. "Davey has the power. Everybody knows that."

"Then why did David give her a ride home? Why didn't Ted?"

"Because I think Teddy doesn't really like her—maybe it was just some drunken fling—but then Suzy threw Livia out anyway, and Davey's a gentleman and said he'd drive her home. Or else he's a wimp and he doesn't care that his brother just slept with his girlfriend."

"I doubt he's a wimp," Eliza said. "You just said he holds the power. But there is one other possibility, you know."

"What's that?"

"That you're completely, a hundred percent wrong, and none of that ever happened. It was David in there with Livia, and Ted had nothing to do with it."

Hildy shrugged. "I like my way better. You think about it and you'll see. Hanky-panky last night, family fireworks this morning, and you were just an innocent bystander."

"Unless Ted only ended up with Livia because he thinks I rejected him. In which case I'm an accessory."

"If that boy had any guts, he'd keep trying with you. He wouldn't let some skinny girl with loose morals trick him into bed."

"I doubt that she tricked him," Eliza said, "*if* that's what happened—and didn't we both just agree that I don't want him to keep trying? Plus, I think the truth is Livia is a much better match for him. You should see the two of them together."

"Then who's the match for you—David?"

"No," Eliza said, letting out a sigh. "Neither of them—no one. My match was Jamey. I couldn't stop thinking about him yesterday. I think about him all the time."

"Honey—"

"No, Hildy, it's time to face it. Some people have just one person who was right for them in their whole lives. That person was Jamey. And it's okay. I had eleven perfect years with him. Some people don't even get that."

"Lizzy..."

"No. It's time we really have this discussion," Eliza said. "Because I'm tired of feeling like I'm sneaking around every time I think of him. I don't want to feel like I'm disappointing you just because I haven't gotten on with my life. I have gotten on with my life—this is it.

"It's one where I miss your boy every day. Where I think about conversations we had, and places we went, and all the dangerous, incredible things we did together. That's a good life for me, Hildy. If I can't have him anymore, I want to at least feel free to think about him twenty-four hours a day if I want to. And I don't want to lie anymore and pretend I'm not.

"No," Eliza said forcefully, pointing at her mother-in-law's face. "Do *not* cry again—I can't take it. It means I can't ever be honest with you."

"But it's just so sad," Hildy answered, her voice thick. "I know Jamey wouldn't want that for you."

"Then he should have been more careful," Eliza said, fighting back her own emotions. "Because he doesn't have a say in this anymore."

"So that's it?" Hildy said. "For the rest of your life?"

"Till death do me part."

"That isn't how the vow goes."

"It's how it goes with me."

19

Ninety-five degrees, ninety percent humidity.

Or was it ninety degrees, ninety-five percent humidity?

Whichever way, Eliza thought, it was hell, and she couldn't imagine why people lived there voluntarily.

Every time she stepped out of the shower, she felt just as wet as when she'd been in. Hildy's house didn't have central air conditioning, just a unit stuck in the kitchen window, so Eliza bought them three more fans, including a small one she carried with her from room to room.

Still, the heat was oppressive. No, not the heat, Eliza thought—Henderson routinely saw July temperatures over 110 degrees—it was the energy-sapping, soul-destroying humidity that made her want to book her return ticket now and retreat to the desert where at least it was a dry heat. People joked about that, but Eliza could feel how much it truly mattered.

She hadn't been able to write for days. She couldn't think. All she could do was be moist and miserable.

"Complaining doesn't help," Hildy told her. "You need to take your mind off it. Want to go to a movie? They usually keep it freezing in there."

"No, I have work to do," Eliza said. She could hear how cranky she sounded. She really did need to improve her mood or Hildy was going to buy the return plane ticket for her. "I have a column due tomorrow, and I can't think of anything to write."

"I thought you had backups," Hildy said.

"I do. But I looked through them yesterday and they're all terrible. I don't know why I ever thought I could write."

"You need to take a cold shower."

"I need to win the lottery so I can buy this house some air conditioning."

"Then go buy a lottery ticket," Hildy said.

"Maybe I will."

SHE AWOKE at four the next morning with an idea. Writing sometimes worked that way for Eliza, and she was always grateful. She'd learned to capture it right away, because if she fell asleep again, so many of the best words would be lost. So she got up, made coffee, and pounded out the column on her laptop while the words were still fresh.

Fake it till you make it. We've all heard that before, right? Imagine some better version of yourself—smarter, richer, more confident, loved—and then start pretending you already are that person. Eventually, so the theory goes, you forget that you're pretending and you actually become who you want to be.

But there's another kind of pretending: pretending that you aren't who you really know you are. You're shy. You're angry. You don't really like other people. You don't really like this job. You're bad at something you pretend you're good at. I'll bet if I asked you to be honest with yourself, you could make a list of at least ten of those things right now: 10 WAYS IN WHICH I AM A FRAUD.

Here's number one on my list: I've been lying to all of you. I'm not really over Jamey. I don't write about him anymore because I think it will depress you, but he's all I really want to talk about. And you know what's crazy about that? I'm supposed to write a whole book about him, and I can't seem to get past the first page. The page that starts out:

"Jamey used to play this game at people's birthday parties. He made everyone go around the table and say something we liked about the birthday person, and something we didn't like—and it had to be the same thing. So, 'I like that Allison is spontaneous, because it makes it fun to be around her. I don't like that Allison is spontaneous, because it makes it impossible to plan things with her.' Things like that.

"One year on my birthday, when it was Jamey's turn, he said, 'I like that Eliza loves me despite all my faults. I don't like that Eliza loves me despite all my faults.'

"We waited, and finally I had to remind him: 'You have to give a reason for both.'

"'Okay, I like that Eliza loves me despite all my faults because it makes me feel secure. I don't like that Eliza loves me despite all my faults because it makes me feel responsible.'"

"People weren't sure whether to laugh or not. Because sometimes Jamey could be deadly serious when you thought he was joking around.

"'Responsible how?' I asked him.

"He thought about it, then said, 'I feel like if I go, you'll never be happy again. Because you'll forgive me. And maybe you shouldn't.'

"Everyone got very quiet, and Jamey made some joke to break up the tension, but he knew I wasn't finished with him. He knew I'd pester him the minute we were alone.

"'What did you mean by that?'

"'That I love you. Happy Birthday.'

"'No, Jamey, what did you mean by that?'

"He tucked my hair behind my ear, the way he always did. 'If I die, I die. And I won't be sorry. I've had a great life. Mainly because of you.'"

"I waited. Finally I said, 'So that's all? That's what you meant? What was that thing about forgiveness?'

"'I don't know, El. I was just talking. Come on. It's bedtime. Happy Birthday.'"

"Why do I remember every word?

"Because it was my twenty-ninth birthday.

"And my husband Jamey Shepherd died the following week."

"Come on, Daisy." It was light out now, sometime after six. Eliza had had three cups of coffee already and felt jittery and weak.

She wasn't sure about that column—not at all. It might be

too personal. It might be too soon. It might be something she should never say out loud.

She felt the same way about the book.

Every month that went by was a month closer to her deadline, and she still hadn't written more than the introduction. She hadn't tried to interview any of Jamey's friends. She hadn't made any notes, or gone through their old columns or any of their old magazine articles. What was the point? She remembered everything, and didn't want to know any more. Even stories from his boyhood—like shooting the pigeon with an arrow—she thought she'd want to know, but she didn't. She just wanted to keep him as he was, encased in glass, something she could take out and polish and look at any time she liked.

And he was really no one else's business.

You're messed up, she told herself as she stood and arched her back. *Encased in glass? Secret? Jamey lived in the public eye— that was his work. It's why you still have any work at all. People read you only because you were his wife. You had adventures to write about only because he took you along. Item number two on your fraud list: I am no one without Jamey.*

Ugh. Stop it. Please. It's the heat. Shut up and go do something normal.

"Come on, Daisy," she called again. "Let's go for a walk in the sauna."

The sweat actually felt good. Like she was purging her body of its worst, most vicious thoughts. The clammier her clothes became, the more sweat that slid down her back, the cleaner she felt. It really was like a sauna, drawing out all the toxins, purifying her so she could start again fresh.

They had crested the hill a little while ago, and taken the trail to the right. They would end in the woods, Eliza thought, where it was at least shady, if not cool, but she'd take the longer route to get there, to really build the sweat. She needed to come back in a better mood, for once, and stop biting Hildy's head off. It wasn't her fault she owned a house with no air conditioning in a place where no humans should really be expected to live. Well, maybe it was, but there was nothing Eliza could do about it now. She needed to figure out a way to adapt. It was only for this one summer, then she could go back to a heat her body understood.

She'd been so preoccupied with thoughts of Jamey, the column, the heat, the house, Eliza didn't realize at first what was happening.

"Come on," she said, pulling the dog. "Leave it."

But Daisy wasn't dragging the leash because she'd found something irresistible to sniff. She was dragging because she was sick.

The dog's sides heaved as she tried to vomit, but only a cloudy phlegm came out. Then Daisy's eyes rolled, and she toppled onto her side, convulsing.

"Oh my God, oh my God, oh my God—"

Daisy panted and seized. Eliza knelt in horror beside her as the little dog began to die.

20

Eliza stood back up and frantically looked around. If she could leave Daisy in the shade somewhere, run back to the house for some water—

No, she should carry Daisy back *now*. Find a vet. Take her to an emergency pet clinic.

She won't make it. She's dying. You've killed this dog, you selfish, crazy—

In the distance she saw movement. A runner, about to turn onto a different trail.

A runner she recognized.

"David! David!"

He halted where he was, saw her, changed course.

"Come on, Daisy, it's okay. You're okay, you're okay!"

The dog continued to heave and pant. Her eyes were white slits behind her eyelids.

"What's wrong?" David stood flooded in sweat, huge

drops of it melting off his body. Bear came up a few steps behind, panting.

"I pushed her too hard. She overheated. We're not used to humidity like this." Eliza's hand flew to her mouth. "Oh my God, David, if I've killed Hildy's dog—"

"You haven't killed anybody," he said. He scooped up Daisy and took off at a run. "Come on—I'm down the hill."

ELIZA FOLLOWED as fast as she could, but the sauna sapped her of her breath. She slowed to a walk, keeping sight of David and the two dogs in the distance. She followed them down the hill, and then along a trail toward the left. Finally she saw his house up ahead.

She picked up her pace again, and arrived just as David swung open a gate and disappeared behind it. She heard a splash. She ran through the same gate to find David and the two dogs in the water.

He cradled Daisy, gently dipping her in the swimming pool while he scooped up handfuls of water to pour along her scalp. Bear paddled nearby, lapping up water as he swam.

"Here," David said. "You hold her. I'll call the vet."

Eliza pulled off her shoes and socks, took her keys and phone out of her pocket, and jumped into the water. As David handed her the limp dog, she could see he was still fully dressed, down to his shoes. He took them off once he climbed out, then pulled keys out of his pocket and unlocked his door.

"I'll be right back," he said. "Don't worry."

Eliza nodded. She felt frozen, useless. "Come on, Daisy," she whispered. "Come on, sweetie. Please be all right."

The dog's eyes remained closed. Her breath came out in shallow pants.

Please don't let me kill this dog.

When David returned, he carried an armful of towels. "The vet says take her out, gently. Don't move her too much. Let her cool down inside."

Eliza nodded. She swallowed hard. David knelt at the side of the pool, one of the towels laid across his arms. "Hand her to me. That's good. She'll be fine."

He sounded so calm. So sure. Eliza slowly transferred Daisy to his arms, then remained in the pool, just watching.

David covered the dog and very gently dried her. Then he carried her toward the house.

"Towel's there," he told Eliza. "Come in when you're ready."

Eliza nodded. It was all she could do.

SHE FOUND David in the kitchen, kneeling next to a dog bed on the floor. Bear stood nearby, panting and curious.

"Should I...get some water?" Eliza asked. Her voice shook.

"Not yet," David said. "She's too weak to swallow right now."

Eliza sank to her knees on the polished oak floor. Absently, she noticed she was still wet. But so was Bear, and David didn't seem to mind the water pooling underneath him. Eliza let herself drip.

Minutes went by, with just the sound of both dogs'

breathing. Daisy was taking deeper breaths now, which Eliza felt was an improvement. But she was afraid to ask David what he thought. In case he might tell her the truth.

Finally he looked up. "Are you all right?"

Eliza nodded. And forced herself to answer, "Yes."

"You can get her some water now," he said. "Bear's bowl is over there. For when she's ready."

Eliza felt grateful for something to do. Her legs felt stiff as she stood. She walked over to where David had pointed and picked up the bowl. Her hand trembled. She closed her eyes and took a breath. Then she carried the bowl to the sink.

She had to know: "Is she going to be all right?"

"I think so," David said. "Yes."

Eliza bent over the sink and let out a sob. Just one, before she was able to stop it. She clamped her mouth closed, held a hand over it for extra security, and with her other hand shut off the faucet.

She picked up the bowl and turned. David was standing there.

"Eliza."

She stepped into him and pressed her face against his damp shirt. "Oh, God," she murmured, and then the tears came, more of them than she could possibly hold back.

David took the bowl from her, set it on the counter, and then wrapped her in his arms.

"You'll be all right," he told her. "I promise. Don't worry, Eliza, you're fine."

Not *the dog is fine* or *Daisy is fine* or *don't worry, your dog will live.*

David was right: Those weren't the words she needed to hear.

"Shh, Eliza, you're all right...don't worry, you'll be fine."

She stood there and let him hold her while she cried out all of the tension of the morning.

21

He smelled clean, and like chlorine. Eliza breathed him in once more before she finally pulled away.

A small puddle had formed beneath them. "I need to go get a towel," Eliza said, twisting her face toward her shoulder so she could wipe her nose against her short sleeve. "I'm ruining your floor."

David squeezed her arm, then let her go. "I'll check on Daisy."

Eliza took her time out by the pool. She dried her hair and clothes on one of the plush towels David had left on the deck, then she put her socks and shoes back on. She picked up her phone, but realized her pocket was still too wet to put it back inside.

Besides, she should probably make a call.

"Hi."

"Everything okay?" Hildy asked. "You've been gone a long time."

Eliza cleared her throat. The mature thing—the brave thing—would have been to tell the truth. She wasn't feeling very brave.

"We ran into David Walsh. I'm over here at his house."

"You don't say," Hildy answered. It was hard to miss the implication in her voice.

"We're just..." Eliza cleared her throat again. "I asked him to show me around. He has a pool, too. Daisy and I might take a swim."

Coward. Liar. Dog killer.

"So, um...we'll be along," Eliza said. "In a while."

"Take your time," Hildy said, chuckling. "You kids have fun. Be home before dark. Or don't."

"Ha, ha," Eliza answered, feeling anything but merry. "I'll see you in a while."

David waited in the doorway out to the pool while Eliza finished her call. "Did you tell her?"

Eliza shook her head guiltily.

David smiled. "I wouldn't have, either."

DAISY SLEPT. Eliza sat on the floor beside the dog bed—Bear's dog bed, which he'd graciously relinquished while he slept on a rug a few feet away—listening to her breathing, resting her hand against Daisy's chest every few minutes to make sure her heartbeat felt the way she remembered it.

"Would you like some coffee?" David offered. "Or water?"

"Water, please," Eliza said. "Thank you."

She accepted the glass from him, then held on to his

wrist. She looked up, feeling just as cowardly as she had when she'd spoken to Hildy.

But this time she forced herself to be brave.

"Thank you."

"You're welcome."

"Not just for the water."

"I know."

"And I don't mean...about Daisy."

"I know."

"So...thanks."

She let go of his wrist and scooted back against the wall to sit more comfortably while she rehydrated. She didn't realize how dry-mouthed she was. She hadn't drunk anything since before they left the house that morning.

"What time is it?"

David looked at the clock above her. "About ten-thirty."

"Oh, David, I'm sorry—I should let you get to work."

"Don't worry about it."

"No, I've taken up your whole morning—" She started to get up, but then realized there was no point. She wasn't going anywhere without the dog, and she wasn't about to rouse Daisy yet. She wanted that dog to sleep until she could wake up healthy again. However long it might take.

David joined her on the floor. He'd changed out of his wet clothes into dry shorts and a T-shirt. Now he offered Eliza the same. "At least a T-shirt," he said, when she refused. "You might be here a while."

Eliza tugged at her shirt. "It's almost dry. I don't want to put you out."

"I have more than one T-shirt."

"Actually," she said, "I could use something else. The only thing I've had this morning is coffee, and I think with the stress...I could use a banana or something if you have it."

David pushed off the wall. "I can do better than that."

He loaded plates and utensils onto a tray, then carried it over to her by the wall. He positioned himself next to her on the floor, and handed her one of the plates.

On top of the omelet was a layer of melted cheese and single slices of mushroom, tomato, and avocado. "That's so you know what's inside it," he told her. "Old restaurant trick."

She didn't trust herself to speak. He was being so nice. More than nice—heroic. To save her dog *and* cook her a delicious meal. It was laughably unreal. If she felt like laughing.

She took her first bite, then another. The omelet was perfect: fluffy, seasoned just right, with oozing melted cheese and lightly sautéed mushrooms. He must have added the tomato and avocado later, Eliza guessed, because both were slightly colder and fresher-tasting, making it perfect for the summer.

"David..." She savored another bite. "This is..." She turned to smile at him. Then on impulse, she kissed his cheek. "Thank you. I'm going to be saying that every time I see you: thank you."

They ate the remainder of their brunch in silence. Eliza glanced over at Daisy every few minutes—she couldn't help herself. But the dog seemed to be sleeping naturally now.

"Will she ever wake up?"

"Eventually," David answered.

"How will I know...if she's all right?"

"I think you know it now. She's still alive. Her breathing is normal. When she wakes up she should be very thirsty. The vet said not to let her drink too much at a time, or she'll vomit."

Eliza took a deep breath and released it. "Okay. She's going to be all right—I'm just going to have to believe that."

"Are you still hungry? Do you need anything else?"

"Well, actually, I do."

It had occurred to Eliza that at some point her mother-in-law was going to expect a full report. Not about Daisy—Eliza still wasn't sure whether or when she was going to confess that—but about the interior of David's house.

"Hildy is sort of...nosy about other people's houses," Eliza explained. "She really wanted to see what your mother's was like."

"What did she think?" David asked.

"She liked it."

"What did she think?" David asked again.

"That it was pretentious and overdecorated."

He laughed. "What would she think of mine?"

So far Eliza hadn't paid it much attention. Her limited line of sight had been trained on Daisy's chest. But now that she felt she could relax a little more, she took the time to gaze around the kitchen.

"It's nice," she said. "Hildy would think it was masculine.

She'd like the black stove and black refrigerator against the cherry cupboards. She'd think that was very distinguished." She remembered Ted had a similar kitchen—same kind of wood, same colored appliances—but his had felt wrong somehow. Unused, cold. Something that might be there just for show.

David's, on the other hand, was clearly a kitchen that got used. It felt worn in, comfortable, real.

Maybe more like the man who owned it, Eliza thought, than she understood before.

David set the dishes back on the tray. Then he stood up and offered Eliza his hand. "Want the full tour?"

"Guess I'd better," she said.

SHE NOTICED he hadn't stuttered once. Or hesitated in that way she assumed was his strategy for avoiding a stutter—the way he'd pause, reset his mouth, start again.

But he also didn't say much. More, maybe, than he ever had with her, but still not that kind of careless banter his brother was so skilled at. David wasn't trying to be charming, as far as she could tell. He was just being a good host.

The downstairs was divided into three main rooms, or two, really: the kitchen and living room, which occupied one continuous space, separated only by their different furnishings; and a large room off of the hallway that held exercise equipment.

The living room was Eliza's favorite: two of the walls made up of multiple windows, one wall looking out on the pool, the other onto a garden. He had a long leather couch, a shorter one upholstered in some sort of soft brown fabric, and several upholstered chairs in complementary colors. There were books stacked on the floor beside one of the chairs, and a pair of shoes lying in front of another. He obviously wasn't a neat freak, Eliza thought, even though the whole house generally looked clean. Clean, but lived in. The sort of place where you wouldn't be afraid to drip pool water on the kitchen floor.

The exercise room housed a treadmill, an elliptical trainer, and several weight machines. There were also a few benches, one flat, the other on an incline, with barbells racked over both.

"Do you use this?" Eliza asked, pointing to the room. "I mean, not that you don't look like you do..." She stumbled over her words. "You look...good, obviously. What I mean is that sometimes people get all this stuff and then only use it for a little while."

She felt the heat on her cheeks. Somehow in the last few hours she'd forgotten how to talk.

"I use it every day," David said. "I don't like going to a gym."

"Oh. Why? If you don't mind me asking."

"Too many people."

"Oh. Sure."

He studied her face for a moment, then smiled. "Eliza, are you nervous?"

"Yes. Very."

"Why?"

"I don't know why. I just feel...self-conscious right now, if you must know. Can you just pretend you don't notice?"

"I'm usually very nervous around you," he said. "For some reason I'm all right right now."

"Great," Eliza said. "Any time you want to switch back..."

He smiled again, then continued with the tour. "Downstairs bathroom—make sure you go in there so you can report to Hildy."

Eliza turned on the light and stuck her head inside. "Nice. She'd like the black and white tile. Very classic."

"The black towels?" he asked.

"Manly, which she already thinks you are. What did she say? 'Everyone knows he has the power.'"

"'The power.' Good. I always liked Mrs. Shepherd."

"I think she liked you, too," Eliza said. "At least when you were younger. She thinks you're a little stuck up now—you wouldn't meet with her when we first came to town, and I think you had your assistant call her instead of calling her yourself. Very bad form."

"You're less nervous."

"I'm getting there. Don't draw attention to it. Let me just work on it."

"Satisfied with the downstairs?"

"I think I can describe it."

"Ready for upstairs?"

"I suppose so. How do I sound now?"

"Nervous again."

"Damn it," Eliza said.

She knew what it was: She was feeling slightly giddy. She had food in her stomach now, her dog was going to live—and she'd broken the ice with this stranger who had been nice enough to let her bawl all over his shirt. Now that the worst of the crisis seemed to be over, Eliza felt foolish for how distraught she'd been. And David had seen it. It was like knowing someone has seen you naked, Eliza thought. It was hard to act too dignified after that.

"This is my office, which used to be two guest rooms, but I don't want guests, so I tore out the wall."

"You really are anti-social, aren't you?"

"Yes."

"And you don't seem...sorry about that."

"No."

"Hold on, let me snoop a little," Eliza said. "Hildy will want some details."

She walked around the expansive room, noticing the black bookcases, the black wooden desk and matching chair, the dark burgundy rugs, the black credenza with a framed photo of Bear.

"You like your dog," Eliza observed.

"A present from my nephews."

"The dog or the picture?"

"The picture."

"I notice you don't have any photographs of people."

"No."

"Because then they might think they could stay in your guest room?"

"Right."

"But there is no guest room, so they'd be disappointed. Very smart. Don't get people's hopes up."

"You're not nervous," David said.

"Not right now. Are you?"

"Some."

"Good. The personality transfer is almost complete."

"I like it when you talk to me," he said.

"I like it when you do, too," she said, smiling. "It's kind of a shock, to tell you the truth."

"Why?" he asked.

"I always think of you as Silent Man. I always think you're angry at me for something. Or annoyed."

"I'm never angry at you."

"You were when Daisy attacked your dog."

"That's different," David said. "Bear is defenseless. He looks big, but he doesn't know how to fight. Other dogs bully him all the time."

"That makes me sad," Eliza said. "I love that dog. He's great. I loved that he slept on my lap the whole way home."

David shook his head.

"What?" Eliza said.

"Family weekend at the lake."

"Hm. Yeah," she said. "It was...interesting."

David led Eliza from the office, back into the hall. "Another bathroom, please inspect."

"You're not nervous," she said.

"Not right now."

"I'll bet I can make you nervous," Eliza said.

David leaned against the wall. "Why would you want to do that?"

She looked down at her feet, considering whether she wanted to broach the topic. But she wanted to know. For more than one reason.

"Are you still seeing Livia?" she asked.

David stood looking at her silently for so long, Eliza wasn't sure he would answer.

Finally he said, "No."

"Since the lake trip?"

"Right."

"Is there a reason?" she asked.

"Yes."

"Do you want to tell me?"

"No," he said. "Not unless I have to."

"You don't have to," she answered.

"Would Hildy like these towels?"

"No," Eliza answered truthfully. "She thinks white towels are always a poor choice. They show all the dirt and have to be washed too often. So points off for white."

"I'll replace them right away."

"Then I won't have to report them."

SHE KNEW IT WAS COMING. Of course she knew. He was an adult, human male, and obviously slept in a bed. But she avoided knowing as long as she could.

"Any other rooms?" she asked. "Den, second office, file room?"

"No, just the one."

"I don't have to see that," Eliza said. "I can make something up."

"Nervous?"

"Very," she said.

"Then we'll just stand here until you're ready."

David casually leaned back against the wall. And kept his

eyes on Eliza's face. She tried looking away at first, but then realized she felt much braver gazing back at him.

They stood that way for several minutes, not speaking, just waiting.

Finally Eliza said, "You have no idea what you're getting into."

"I could say the same to you."

"I am...a mess sometimes. This morning, for example. Even before I almost killed Hildy's dog."

"What if I don't care?"

Eliza broke his gaze and looked down. "Okay, now I'm really nervous."

He reached out and lifted her chin. "Eliza, what if I don't care? What if you can say anything, or do anything, and I won't care?"

"What do you mean?" she asked. Her voice felt thin. She could feel her mouth trembling, and knew David must feel it, too.

"I'll wait until you're ready," he said, letting his hand fall back to his side. Then he crossed his arms in front of his chest and relaxed again against the wall.

Eliza laughed. "So you're just going to stand there? And wait?"

"Yes."

She drew in a breath and slowly let it out. Then reached for his hand. "All right, then, come show me."

22

The bedroom was full of light. The same long, broad windows as down in the living room, again filling up two connecting walls and meeting in the corner.

The room had very little furniture: a king-sized bed with a black wooden frame, much like the furniture in his office; two matching bedside tables on either side; a dark brown love seat beneath one of the windows; a black bookcase against one of the solid walls.

Eliza stood just inside the doorway. David stood beside her, not touching, but close enough that she could feel him.

"This is really pretty."

"Thank you," he said.

"I like the windows."

"Thank you," he said.

"And the bedding—Hildy would approve." A dark, wine-colored paisley, with solid dark green pillows.

"No hurry," David said.

"Oh, God." She reached for his hand and gave it a single squeeze. Then she let go and turned to face him.

Keeping her eyes on his, she reached down and pulled her shirt over her torso. She lost sight of him in that brief moment it took for her the shirt to clear her head, but then she kept on looking him in the eyes. His gaze didn't shift from hers, even when she pulled her sports bra up and over her head. He didn't touch her. He just waited.

She wrapped her arms around his neck and pressed her body against his. "Would you kiss me already?"

"Gladly," he said.

And then it was the strangest sensation, Eliza thought: as if they had skipped years of courtship, years of awkward conversation and missed signals and misunderstandings and makeups; as if they'd grown up together, knew everything about each other from the time they were young, and one day had simply turned to each other and began what was obviously the next step. David kissed her like he already knew her, understood what she liked, how she liked it, touched her breasts as if he'd touched them hundreds of times before and wasn't just discovering them in that sunlit room for the first time on a day when she'd unexpectedly needed his help.

Like he'd been waiting for this all along, and had no doubt it would one day happen.

Eliza slipped her hands beneath his T-shirt and pulled it over his head. David swiftly removed her shorts. She undid the snap on his, pulled down the zipper, and pushed shorts and underwear down his legs.

The two of them stood naked, still looking at each other's

faces, then David lifted her just enough to clear the floor and carried her to the bed.

Eliza pulled him down with her. She hadn't broken contact since their first kiss, and she wasn't about to. She knew if she let him get too far away, even inches, both of them might have the chance to think, and this wasn't a time for thought. This was a time for pure physical pleasure. No Jamey, no heartache, no past, no fears. She wasn't afraid of David. He didn't seem afraid of her.

He explored her body with his hands, with his mouth. Eliza closed her eyes and let herself feel. He had a way of pausing just where she would have wanted him to, then moving on exactly when he should.

He was hard, and she liked the feeling of it against her leg. It felt natural, real, not a memory of lovemaking she had once had, but a man in the flesh, kissing her, teasing her, cupping her breasts, stroking her thigh, sliding his fingers where she was wet, pressing them where she never thought a man would touch her again.

Abruptly, he got up.

"No," Eliza said, reaching to pull him back down.

"Wait." He crawled toward one of the bedside tables and pulled open its single drawer. He brought out a short string of connected condoms.

She waited while he tore open the package, slipped one on. But even then, it took too long. Too much time away. She needed him against her, inside her, not leaving her.

"David, hurry—"

One more move, and then he was back where she

wanted, sliding between her thighs, body pressed against hers, the two of them joined the way she had wanted for years, she thought, even before she met him. Maybe he had been waiting all along for her to turn to him and open and take him in where he belonged. Eliza wrapped her arms around him harder, pulled him in deeper, kissed him and moved with him and found the way they both fit together, no space between them, her body like a puzzle piece lost and now slipped back into place.

Then they heard a sound.

Eliza jerked her head up. David was still inside her, but he paused so they could both listen.

Eliza pushed him away. "It's Daisy—"

She bolted from the bed, picked up David's T-shirt from the floor, and held it in front of her as she went tearing down the stairs.

Daisy stood in the kitchen, retching. The liquid was clear this time, just water, and Eliza could see why: The dog had obviously woken up thirsty and tried to drink half the water in Bear's bowl. But she was standing. Awake. Alive.

"You should take her outside," David said from behind them. Eliza turned and found him naked, still partially erect, and for some reason that felt fine to her, correct, normal and perfectly expected. "Carry her out to the garden," he said. "Let her try to walk."

Eliza picked up the dog, still managing to keep David's T-shirt draped in front of her. She hadn't had time to put it on, but she didn't want to stand there without it. The top of it flopped over Daisy as Eliza carried the dog across the living room to the door David unlocked. She set Daisy on the short slab of concrete that led to stone steps across the grass. Daisy sniffed the edge of the lawn, then toddled out further, toward some bushes. Then she squatted and watered them for an unusually long time.

Eliza stood at the window beside the door, monitoring the dog. David stood behind her, gently stroking her hips and the curve of her behind. His hands moved upward, sliding beneath the T-shirt she held with a single fist. Eliza could still feel him hard against her. The whole sensation made her laugh.

"What?" he asked.

"This has to be the strangest foreplay I've ever seen. You stroking my breasts while I'm watching a dog pee."

"We can do whatever we want," he answered.

Eliza liked that answer. She closed her eyes for a moment and just enjoyed the sensation of what he was doing. Then finally Daisy was ready to come back in.

The dog's nails clicked against the wood floor as she made her way across the living room. She didn't go far: She found a chair that she liked, leapt up onto it, then curled in on herself with a sigh.

"Let's stay down here," Eliza said.

"I'll go get the supplies."

David bounded back up the stairs, still taking too long, as far as Eliza was concerned. He returned with a longer string of condoms.

"Now, go back to where you were," Eliza told him, padding across the floor to stand by the garden window. She let the T-shirt drop. "I kind of liked that."

He followed, and stood behind her, this time closer, cupping her breasts in his hands. She parted her legs. "Do it that way," she said, her voice low and breathy. She bent over to help him find his way. He pulled on another condom and gently entered her again. Eliza braced herself against the window.

He was perfect, she thought. This was perfect. Why hadn't she known he was here? She laid one hand on top of his over her breast and moved together with him, wanting it faster, harder, wanting it done already so she could find him some other way, climb on top of him, or pull him toward her at the sink, or make love to him in the shower, or back upstairs on that wide, cool bed.

Eliza cried out with surprise as she felt her body release. She had hoped for it but not expected it. It took several tries with Jamey. She hadn't known how to get there, what she was supposed to feel. It had been a revelation when the two of them finally got it.

But now she knew. And her body throbbed with it as David plunged in deeper and found his own release. He held her around the waist and they both breathed hard. Eliza pushed back against him, kept him there as long as she could, savoring the sensation of him inside her.

She waited until his breathing slowed down.

Then, "Five more," she said. "Can you do that?"

"Over what space of time?"

"As long as you need, but I'm not leaving until we're done."

"I need to make a few calls."

"Me, too," Eliza said. Or at least one.

"Are you happy?" David asked her.

"So happy right now, you wouldn't believe it."

He turned her around so he could kiss her. She laced her fingers behind his neck and kissed him harder. She pressed her body into his.

Eventually they broke away, and David bent down to retrieve his shirt. "Here, you probably want this."

"I do," Eliza said, not feeling self-conscious at all about wanting to be covered. She tugged David's T-shirt over her head. It rested against the top of her thighs.

"Need anything else?" he asked.

"Not right now. Thank you."

She smiled at him, an easy, satiated smile.

He kissed her lightly and turned around. "I'll see you in a while."

David took the stairs more slowly this time while Eliza watched him go. He was stockier than Jamey, more filled out, not thin and wiry like a climber. He had light body hair instead of Jamey's dark. He was a grown man, Eliza thought, not a teenager she'd grown older with, a man who had died in his twenties. David was another category entirely. As if Eliza had skipped a stage of her adulthood, and restarted it a few years ahead. She hadn't met the men in between, the ones who were thirty, thirty-one. The ones who were still too inexperienced, too immature, who couldn't understand why she felt so much older, how death could make a person feel removed, isolated, too ancient for someone who had never had anything tragic happen to him.

Eliza sat down next to Daisy in the chair. Repositioned the dog so her head rested against Eliza's thigh.

She gently scratched behind the dog's ear. And waited patiently for David to return and show her what he could do next.

23

It turned out three times was enough. Or at least all they could manage.

Around dinner time, Eliza suddenly snapped awake.

"My column."

"What about it?"

"I was supposed to e-mail it to everybody by noon." She draped her arm lazily above her head. "Although right now I can't seem to care about that."

David took advantage of her nipple.

"We can't really stay in bed all day and all night, can we?" she asked.

"I have food enough for a few days. Then I'll have to go into the store."

"Did they miss you at work today?"

"I'll go in tomorrow," David said. "People can manage on their own."

"Are you always like this about your business?"

"It's a special time," he said. "I'm on vacation."

Eliza propped herself up on one elbow. "How long to you think this can last?"

"As long as we want," he answered.

"You don't seem very..."

"Nervous?" he asked.

"Worried," she said.

"I'm not."

She looked into his eyes. He gazed back at her and smiled. "Eliza, I meant what I said before: We can do whatever we want. I'm available for this any time, any day. All you have to do is come over."

It seemed so...secretive. And so easy. Like a boy telling a neighborhood girl to climb in through his window.

"So I could come over tomorrow?" Eliza asked.

"Or tonight," David said. "Midnight. Or you don't ever have to leave."

Eliza rolled onto her back. "I need to at least check in with Hildy. Let her see that I'm alive. And I should probably tell her about Daisy."

"Will you tell her about me?" David asked.

"I don't think so."

"Afraid?" he said.

"No, just..." She leaned up and looked at him again. "Have you ever had something all to yourself, and you don't even want to talk about it because that would mean you have to share it?" She shook her head. "I'm sure that doesn't make any sense."

"I do know," he said. He stroked a finger down her shoulder, then kissed her parted lips. "This house is yours. My time is yours. My body...is obviously yours."

"Good. I like your body. I like the things you do with it."

"Which things?"

"New things. I don't know..." She lifted both arms above her head. "Surprise me."

Four times was enough.

"I can't go back to Hildy's smelling like sex."

"So you'd rather smell like you just took a shower?"

Eliza sighed. "I see your point. What time is it?"

"Eight-thirty."

"Can you take us home?"

"Sure."

"Daisy hasn't eaten all day."

"I should have fed you both dinner," David said.

"I prefer how you used your time."

"When you're dressed," he said. "I want to show you something."

She found him downstairs, standing by door leading out to the pool. He pointed to the box on the wall next to it.

"This is my alarm. Here's the code." He pressed four numbers in succession. Then he handed her a key. "I meant what I said. You can come over any time. The cleaning lady comes on Thursdays from noon to four, but other than her, no one is ever here. Except Bear and me."

"What if you're not here?" Eliza asked.

"Then make yourself at home."

"What if you are here?" she asked, smiling.

"Then lucky me."

Daisy had moved from the chair back to the dog bed in the kitchen. Now, at signs that they were leaving, she stretched and then gave her body a shake.

"Thank you," Eliza said. "For Daisy. And for..." She kissed him lightly at first, then deeper. They spent several minutes like that, propped against the wall.

"Okay, then," Eliza said, shaking her head the way Daisy had shaken her fur. "Head, cleared. Body, exhausted."

"Do you want some food to take home?" David asked. "I want to make sure you keep your strength up."

"Don't worry," Eliza said. "I'm in training now. I'll eat something nutritious, get a good night's sleep, and come back for another round."

"Tomorrow?"

"I don't see how I can stay away," she said. "You've pretty much made that impossible."

David nodded. "Come on, Bear. Let's take these ladies home."

Eliza let herself into the house, knowing Hildy was probably waiting to pounce.

But when she climbed up the stairs, she found her mother-in-law sitting in a chair in the living room, working out menus for her class.

Hildy looked at her over her half-glasses.

"Nice day?"

"Very nice."

"Hungry?"

"Uh-huh."

"I left you some spaghetti," Hildy said. "And a nice green salad. Was Davey nice?"

"Very."

"That's nice." Hildy flipped over a sheet of paper and went to work on the next.

Eliza stood watching. And waited for her mother-in-law to break.

Hildy didn't look up again, but she smiled.

"He's a nice boy, then, that Davey Walsh?"

"He said he always liked you."

"What did you tell him?" Hildy asked.

"That he shouldn't have let his assistant call you."

"He shouldn't have."

"I told him," Eliza said.

"Good."

Hildy hummed a little tune.

"I'm going to feed Daisy and warm up the spaghetti. Thank you for saving me some."

"Any time you want to talk..." Hildy said.

"You'll be the first to know."

Hildy took off her glasses and looked Eliza squarely in the eyes. "I'm happy for you, honey."

"Don't say anything more—"

Hildy held up her hand. "Won't say a word."

Eliza waited for it.

"Except—"

"Hildy..."

The old woman smiled. "Still waters run deep. It's the quiet ones who always turn out the best."

"Okay, thanks," Eliza said. "I'm going to the kitchen now."

"Lizzy?" Hildy called out a few moments later.

"What?"

"Are you seeing him again?"

"I'm sure."

"Want some advice?"

"No."

Eliza had to admire her mother-in-law's restraint. She waited until Eliza was seated at the table and eating before she finished her sentence.

"You need to be careful with that man."

"Why?" Eliza said. "He's nice. He's not going to hurt me."

"No, but I know what he was like as a boy," Hildy said, "and you could hurt him. I'd hate to see that happen."

Eliza swallowed a bite of pasta. Her throat felt narrower than before. "Thanks a lot."

"Not on purpose," Hildy said, "but maybe if you're not careful."

"I'm not going to hurt him," Eliza answered defensively.

"Good. That's all I wanted to say."

Eliza turned on her laptop.

She opened the column she'd written that morning.

She moved it into a different file. *Save As: Documents/Extras/Fraud.*

Then she returned to the list of other documents in the Extras file.

She reread one, then a second, then made her choice. She

reformatted it, saved it, and attached it to the e-mail she sent to all of the editors of her newspaper clients.

Then she printed out a hard copy for Frank Sawyer of *The Careyville Independent.* She'd deliver it in person, as usual, and give him the chance to brag about his grandson, but this time she wouldn't let him pry anything out of her about her love life.

She'd meant what she said to David: This was private. Just hers and his alone. It was like writing, she thought: Sometimes if you talk about an idea too much, you take all the heat out of it. You don't ever end up writing it because it feels old now, familiar, like you've already heard it too many times before. So the only way to feel excited again is to move on to the next new idea.

She didn't want that to happen with David. She wanted to keep all the heat right where it was, bottled up and protected in that vast house of his.

Eliza took a shower, sorry, almost, to wash away the effects of the day. *There's always tomorrow,* she thought, *and the next day, and the next...*As many as she wanted, according to David. She knew people got tired of each other—even she and Jamey were sometimes happy for his separate trips—but she'd enjoy David as long as this affair of theirs—or whatever it was—lasted. And then...then she'd deal with the "then" when it happened.

Eliza almost didn't mind the humidity this time as she stepped back out of the shower. David's house was so cold with air conditioning, at one point she'd cuddled up to him like it was winter.

She slipped into her robe and returned to her bedroom.

Then automatically reached into her dresser and pulled out her summer pajamas: a pair of Jamey's boxer shorts and one of his long T-shirts. She put them on and was about to get into bed when she caught sight of herself in the mirror.

She stood there for a moment, staring at her reflection, then opened her dresser again. This time she pulled out one of her own T-shirts and a loose pair of underwear. She changed into them and folded the set of Jamey's clothes back into the drawer.

Then she added one more thing. She stood there for a long time trying to decide whether to do it. But it didn't feel right, otherwise. She couldn't do what she'd done with David—what she intended to do again and again—still wearing her wedding ring on her finger.

She gently twisted it off. And stowed it at the back of her underwear drawer.

Eliza slid between the sheets of her bed. Daisy waited until she was in position, then hopped up beside Eliza and settled into her regular spot.

Eliza turned out her bedside light, and lay staring at the dark ceiling.

Wondering how early was too early to go back to David's.

SHE TRIED to time it so she'd be there just as he got back from his run. Even though he'd told her to make herself at home, she felt odd being in the house too long, not knowing where to sit, not wanting him to catch her in some room where she might have given in to some impulse to snoop.

Eliza unlocked the gate to the pool area and stood for a moment remembering the scene from yesterday: David bathing the dog in cool water, complete disregard for his clothes. Eliza felt a little ashamed of herself for having taken the time to remove her shoes and take out her phone—

"Did your phone get wet?" she asked him when he entered through the gate fifteen minutes later.

"Yes."

"Is it ruined?" she asked.

"Yes."

"David! Why didn't you say something?"

"It doesn't matter. My assistant ordered a replacement. It'll be here today."

He stripped off shirt, his shoes, socks, and his shorts, and dived naked into the pool.

"I have an early meeting," he told her when he resurfaced.

"Oh." Eliza tried not to show her disappointment.

David smiled. "Are you coming in?"

LIKE A LOVESICK TEENAGER, Eliza thought as she exited David's car. *No, not lovesick, sexsick.*

I'm okay with that.

David rolled down the passenger window. "I'll be home around six."

"Is that an invitation?"

"You have an open invitation," he said. "I already told you that."

"Would you like me to cook something?" Eliza asked. "In return for the omelets?"

"I'm not keeping score," he said, "but yes. Whatever you want."

A car slowed as it passed them. Carolyn and Katie Jackson both waved. Eliza saw Carolyn look to see who was behind the wheel of the car in front of Hildy's house. David was still turned toward the passenger side, talking to Eliza, so she wondered if Carolyn got a good look.

Do I care?

Yes, I care.

People are going to find out.

Not yet.

Why do you care?

Because this is special.

You think you're the only two people who have ever had sex?

No, Eliza continued to reason with herself, *of course not. But this is different.*

Why?

Because David is different. He's private. He's shy.

Does David want to keep it secret?

I don't know.

You're allowed to make love to someone, you know. You're not betraying Jamey—

"Eliza?"

"Hm?" She realized he'd been talking. She hadn't heard a word.

"Are you all right?"

"Absolutely."

"So I'll see you tonight? I have to go."

"I'll see you tonight."

He rolled the window back up and continued on down

the street. As soon as he turned the corner, Eliza went inside the house.

Daisy barked and raced down the stairs. Eliza had let her out into the back yard that morning, but hadn't taken her on a walk.

She knelt beside the dog, whispering so that Hildy wouldn't hear. "It's too hot. I'll take you out tomorrow, but we're only going on short walks from now on. No more death walks for the rest of the summer, all right?"

Daisy panted. It was a normal sound, not at all like the day before.

If not for the death walk, Eliza thought, *none of this would have happened with David.*

Would it? Eventually? Eliza used to wonder that about Jamey: What if either one of them had ended up in a different freshman English class? Would they still have met somehow? When? That year, two years later—when? Or would they both have found other people, and some other woman would have been Jamey Shepherd's wife, and maybe she would have convinced him not to go that day, and he'd still be alive. And Eliza would probably never know, and never care...

For want of a nail, the shoe was lost. For want of a shoe, the horse was lost.

For want of a heat-stroked dog, David Walsh was lost. For want of David Walsh, Eliza Shepherd was...

Lost?

Yes, she supposed, in a way.

And what was she now?

Different, she thought. *Happy,* she was willing to admit.

Willing, period. And that was a change.

It reminded her of the column she'd written months ago, back when she'd first moved there, and the most daring thing she could think of was to go cut her hair.

I put forth this challenge to myself and you: Do something different today.... You and I are going to wake up and be involved in our lives again.... Creativity will blossom. Joy might even creep in.

Was this joy? Eliza wondered. Or just sex?

"We can do whatever we want." David said.

Including, Eliza thought, not overthinking it.

24

"Will she ring the doorbell?" Eliza asked about the cleaning lady.

"No, she has her own key."

Eliza groaned. "All right, then. We need to get up."

It was just after noon on Thursday, their ninth day together, and Eliza and David had stretched out their time in bed as long as possible. David had arranged his schedule that morning to work from home. Which meant phone calls, e-mails, Eliza. E-mails, phone calls, Eliza.

They dressed again, and Eliza insisted on making the bed.

"She'll redo it," David said, but Eliza didn't care.

Downstairs, Eliza looked nervously out the windows. "Which door will she come in?"

"The pool door, same as you," David answered. "What are you so worried about?"

"She'll see me."

"And?"

"And...she'll say something."

"I doubt it," he answered, "but so what if she does?"

"So I'll be embarrassed."

"Why?"

The man was maddening.

"Because...we've been in bed all morning."

"Eliza, I really don't understand the problem."

And she wasn't sure she could explain it.

"I just feel..."

"Ashamed?" he asked.

"No! I feel..."

And just then, Teina made her entrance.

"Hi, David. Hello," she greeted Eliza.

"Teina, this is Eliza. Eliza, Teina."

"Hi," Eliza said, wishing she hadn't wasted the last few minutes talking. She could have been up on the path behind the house by now, walking in searing, oppressive heat. That sounded much more pleasant.

"Well, bye," she said to them both, and aimed herself toward the pool.

"Eliza, I'll give you a ride."

"No, that's okay—"

"*Eliza.*" David turned to Teina, exchanged a few words with her, then told his dog and the cleaning woman good-bye. Then he followed Eliza outside where she stood waiting in the shade.

"May I give you a ride now?" he asked. "Please?"

He seemed amused, but Eliza glanced back inside the

house just the same. She could see Teina already setting up her supplies.

"I guess I should deal with this," Eliza said.

"I guess you should," he answered.

"Are we public, or are we not?" she asked.

"What do you want?"

"I'm...not sure."

"Well, you think about it while I drive you home and save you from heat stroke."

She still didn't have an answer for him by the time he dropped her off.

"Will I see you tonight?"

"Uh-huh." She said it without conviction.

"Are you worried?"

"Yes."

"About what?" he asked. He shifted the car into park, and let the air conditioning continue to blast.

"I'm afraid she's going to say something to someone."

"And then it will be in the papers and on TV and everyone will know we're lovers—is that the problem?" David asked.

Lovers. It sounded so...

"It wouldn't be in the papers, would it?" How Frank Sawyer would love to have that scoop.

"Eliza, I was joking. I doubt anyone would care."

"What about your family?" Eliza countered. "Sue, your mother—"

"Sue likes you."

"Your mother doesn't."

"I'm not sure that's true," David said, "and I don't care anyway. My mother isn't making love to you."

"What about...Ted?"

"Were you lovers?"

"No."

"Then what are you worried about?"

It kept coming back to that: *What are you worried about?*

"Eliza, do you want to be with me or not?"

"Yes! Of course I do—David, you don't even have to ask me that."

"Good. And I want to be with you. So who cares what anyone thinks? We can do whatever we want. I only care what you think."

He kissed her, and she returned the kiss. Knowing that a part of her cringed at the thought of anyone seeing.

What is your <u>problem</u>?

"Then I'll see you tonight. I'll cook. And Eliza?"

"Yes?"

"This time, why don't you spend the night?"

"You had a visitor," Hildy said.

Eliza froze. Her first and only thought was that it had been Ted. Although why would he bother? They hadn't spoken in weeks—not since the lake.

"A visitor?" Eliza repeated, feeling a cold dread. "Who?"

"That little girl up the street—the Jackson girl."

"Oh. Katie." Eliza could feel the breath relax again in her lungs. "What did she want?"

"To invite you to some girls' event—she'll tell you all about. She said come down and see her when you're free."

Hildy studied Eliza's face. "Something happen?"

Eliza sank into the chair across the table from her mother-in-law. "Psychoanalysis, please."

"Shoot," Hildy answered.

Eliza described everything that had just happened, from meeting the cleaning woman to her conversation with David in the car.

"Easy," Hildy said. "Guilt."

"About Jamey?"

"About a lot of things," Hildy answered. "Jamey, Teddy, that Livia woman—"

"I don't care about her."

"Would you feel bad if she really loved Davey, and you stole him away from her?"

"Well...yes. I suppose. But I don't think it was like that. She fooled around on him, remember?"

"Oh, so I was right!" Hildy cackled. "He told you that? Davey?"

"Mm, not exactly. But I think you might be right."

"Of course I'm right," Hildy said, "and I'm right about this. You're a nice girl, Lizzy. You don't like to hurt people's feelings. You want everybody to be happy before you can be happy yourself."

Eliza took a few grapes out of the bowl between them and sat back to consider Hildy's theory. Did she feel guilty about Ted? She was pretty sure she didn't feel bad about Livia—that was too extreme. But Ted? Maybe. He had tried awfully hard, over several months, and all it took was one morning for his brother to get her into bed.

One morning and a heroic, life-saving effort. And a display of patience that made Eliza want to rip the clothes right off him.

"And there's Jamey," Hildy reminded her. "Think that's part of it?"

"Probably."

Hildy reached across the kitchen table and patted her daughter-in-law's ringless hand. If she'd noticed the change, she hadn't mentioned it.

"It'll pass," Hildy said. "You just have to get used to someone new. Does he make you happy?"

"Yes."

"Then let him make you happy," Hildy said. "Take your foot off the brake. Jamey's dead two years. I promise he doesn't mind. He wants you to live your life."

Before Eliza could argue, Hildy went on. "Hate to tell you, honey, but if the situation was reversed, Jamey would have found somebody else by now—I know he would. You know it, too. And you know what? I would have told him, 'Good for you—Lizzy would have wanted that.' And I wouldn't be wrong, would I?"

"No," Eliza answered quietly.

"So...problem solved?"

"I don't know," Eliza answered. "I have to think about it. You're probably right—about all of it. I just have to...feel it."

· · ·

After lunch, Eliza walked down the street to visit the Jacksons. Katie answered the door.

"Guess what?"

"What?" Eliza asked.

"We're going climbing tomorrow!"

"Climbing? What kind of climbing?"

Carolyn Jackson appeared at the door. "The girls voted to take climbing lessons this summer at the gym. Their first class is tomorrow night. We thought you might like to come."

"Um...that's really sweet of you..."

"Mom says you used to be a climber," Katie said.

"I was. But I don't do that anymore."

"But you could still show us how," Katie said.

"I'm sure they have instructors who can do that—"

"The girls were hoping..." Carolyn turned to her daughter. "Katie, why don't you go get the brochure? You can show Eliza. That might give her a better idea."

Katie took off up the stairs, while meanwhile Carolyn Jackson lowered her voice.

"It's a self-esteem thing," she said. "Girls' Club is really big on finding women in the community that girls can model themselves after. We've had other women speakers come in all year—a firefighter, a products engineer—I'll tell you the whole list later, it's pretty impressive. So when I was telling Katie last night that you used to climb..."

"It was a long time ago," Eliza said. "I really...don't want to do that anymore."

"You wouldn't have to do any of the climbing," Carolyn said. "Just be there for the girls to look at." She laughed.

"Honestly, I think that's the most important part—the girls just stare at these women the whole time they're talking, and don't seem to hear a word they say. They're looking at their clothes, their hair, their *teeth*—one of Katie's classmates is obsessed with people's teeth—"

"Here," Katie said, handing Eliza the brochure. She pointed to the picture on front. "Look at that—doesn't that look cool?"

"It does." The photo showed gray concrete walls studded with colorful handholds and footholds.

"Have you ever climbed someplace like that?" Katie asked.

"Sure," Eliza said. "Lots of times."

"Is it hard?"

"Sometimes. Some of the routes are really hard. You have to stretch or let go and throw yourself upward to catch the next hold."

Katie looked up at her mother, obviously nervous.

"But those are the advanced routes," Eliza hurried to say. "You can work up to them. In the beginning you'll learn all about the knots, and how to make sure you're safe, and how to belay someone else—that's holding on to their rope from down below so you can stop them if they start to fall..."

"Oh," Katie said, looking less enthusiastic by the moment.

Eliza put her arm around the girl. "I'm making it sound harder than it is. It's fun—you'll have a great time. See," she said to Carolyn, "this is why I shouldn't come."

"No, you have to come!" Katie said. "You'd be so great!"

"I...I think I'm going to pass," Eliza said. "But you can tell me all about it. I really want to hear."

"Are you sure?" Carolyn asked. "It's just for about an hour."

"Please?" Katie tried again.

"I'll...think about it, okay?"

"It's tomorrow at six," Carolyn said. "You can keep the brochure—directions are on the back."

"Okay. I'll let you know." Eliza started to turn away, when Carolyn stopped her.

"I'll walk with you," she said.

"It's a hundred and eighty degrees out."

"Just for a minute," Carolyn said.

The two of them strolled down the driveway onto the sidewalk. The trees along the lane offered some shade, Eliza noticed, but not enough. She stuck her hat back on, even though it made her head sweat.

"So who was he?" Carolyn asked. "The man in the car last week?"

Eliza sighed. "I should have known that was coming. What took you so long?"

"I've been working split shifts," Carolyn said. "This is my first chance to bug you. So. Is it anyone I know? Or are you going to say it's none of my business, in which case I'll be crushed?"

It's none of your business.

Eliza made a decision, then and there.

"David Walsh."

"Really?" Carolyn said. "I didn't recognize his car. I guess I've never seen him in the neighborhood. He must take Florence Street to get out onto Highbridge."

Eliza waited an extra moment. "That's all you're going to

say?"

"Why? He's a really nice guy," Carolyn said. "Will and I went to school with him. He had that terrible stutter, poor guy. Kids made it really miserable for him. I don't think he has it anymore though, does he?"

"No, he got rid of it," Eliza said, relief spreading through her body. What had she expected Carolyn to say? *No! That's scandalous!"*

But Eliza knew suddenly what her problem had been—why she'd been so shy about telling people. It wasn't because she felt guilty. She'd have to let Hildy know her theory had been wrong—

"So how did Ted take it?" Carolyn asked.

"What? Oh, I don't think he knows."

"Well, that's going to be a good one," Carolyn said with a laugh. "Love to be a fly on the wall there."

"What do you mean?" Eliza asked.

"Those two have been at each other's throats since they were kids. They compete for *everything.* Teddy was one of the ones who made school so hard for David. He had to be the *most* popular, have the *most* friends—"

"Who, Ted?"

"Of course Ted," Carolyn said. "David hardly talked to anyone. I'm not even sure if he had any friends, to be honest. He started working for their dad when he was pretty young, and just sort of disappeared from the whole school social scene. Next thing I knew he was running the business, no surprise." Carolyn shook her head. "It probably killed him when Teddy just showed up and their dad gave him a piece of it. It was all David's show, but now here's Teddy again."

Eliza stood in the heat, dripping sweat, transfixed by the story. They were standing in front of Hildy's house by now, but she couldn't tear herself away to go inside.

"So you think they're still like that?" Eliza asked. "Because I've been around them both, and they don't seem to hate each other that much. Not that they particularly like each other—"

"Well, we're all older now, aren't we?" Carolyn said. "Although I'm thirty-five, just like David, and sometimes at family dinners my older brother and I act like we're still seven and ten. He just has to push the right buttons."

"So you think it's going to be a problem that I dated both of them?"

Carolyn laughed. "What do you think?"

Eliza set up the fan directly in front of her bed and sat there for the next few hours, thinking.

She wasn't ready to tell Hildy any of it. She still wasn't sure she understood.

As the time grew closer to evening, Eliza wondered what she was going to do. What she was going to say. Whether she should say anything at all.

Not to Hildy, but to David.

Eliza packed a bag full of overnight essentials. She added a sleep outfit, then took it out again. That was part of her epiphany when she was talking to Carolyn: the *why* of why she felt so insecure telling anyone about her and David. Eventually she pared down what she was bringing to what could fit in her larger purse.

"I may not be back until morning," Eliza told her mother-in-law. "Are you going to be okay here by yourself?"

"Daisy and I will get by," Hildy answered. "You have fun."

Eliza hesitated before going down the stairs. "Do you think David and Ted hate each other?"

"Hate? That's a strong word," Hildy said. "You saw them at that Easter dinner, same as I did. They didn't act like they hated each other. Not lovey-dovey, but decent."

Eliza nodded. "See you in the morning. Call me if you need anything."

Hildy smiled. "All I need is for you to have fun."

SHE COULD HAVE CALLED David for a ride, or asked Hildy to drive her there. But Eliza wanted the walk. Even in the awful, stifling heat, her mind seemed to do its best thinking when her body was doing something monotonous like walking.

By the time she reached David's, she'd made a decision.

And as soon as she saw him there in the kitchen, leaning over steaming pots on the stove, then turning when he heard her come in, and smiling in a way she couldn't imagine as anything but warm and kind and genuine, she changed her mind again.

"Hi." She molded her body against his and gave him the kind of kiss she'd given him that morning, and the morning before, and the mornings and nights before that. Just nine days together, and she felt as easy and comfortable with him as she had after years with Jamey. Effortless. Natural. Right.

Which was part of the problem, she'd come to realize

that afternoon—part of the reason why she felt so shy about letting the world know.

It was too easy. Too fast. Too right.

It was like the feeling she had sometimes when she was rappelling. Standing on the edge of a cliff, feet braced against the rock, her body supported by a harness around her waist and thighs.

There was always that moment when she didn't want to lean back, didn't want to kick off, to feel her body falling through the air. She had to believe in the rope and the anchor, trust that they would hold her, but there was always that space of time in freefall when she couldn't actually be sure.

And as Jamey had proven, she was right not to believe.

But sometimes, if the day was just right, and the air felt pure, and Eliza knew she was strong and ready, she could kick off and actually enjoy it. Close her eyes and take pleasure in the fall. Savor those few seconds of weightlessness before the rope tensed and her feet touched rock again.

It felt like that with David. Like the freefall on a perfect day. And that, Eliza realized, was why she'd been fighting it.

It was all too easy: Too easy to forget Jamey. Too easy to fall for someone else. After two years of grieving, it was as though it had all been wiped away in a single day. Eliza felt happy again. Alive. *In lo—*

Eliza stopped herself. She needed to be more careful than that.

"Can that wait?" she asked.

David turned off all the burners. "If not, we'll order pizza."

25

He was still dressed in his work clothes, the khaki pants and white button-down, a slight scent of sweat on his shirt that Eliza didn't mind. He smelled different from Jamey. He tasted different.

Eliza knew that sex wasn't love. She knew there was a difference between the heart and the body. A person could feel excited by someone, hungry for them, but that was just the animal side of being human. It allowed cave people to start populating the earth.

She unbuttoned and unzipped and stripped David down to his skin. Every time he tried to remove her clothes, she told him to wait. She wanted to see him first, to really look at him in the light, touch him when it was only him, and not let him distract her with his mouth and hands.

He was hard already, and she liked that. Just the thought of what she might do was enough for him.

"Come here," she said. She took him by the hand and led

him toward the exercise room. They'd been in there once before, after the initial tour, and she'd liked the way they used the equipment.

She led him to one of the weight benches and told him to lie down. His legs draped on either side, bracing him against the floor.

Eliza straddled the bench, sitting close to him, not touching.

She'd left the light on. Not something she normally did with Jamey, although they'd made love plenty of times in the open air, in daylight, in a tent or in the grass, on the bank of some natural pool where they'd dipped at the end of a long day to wash off the dirt and sweat.

Eliza didn't mind the light, but she'd always preferred the dark. She was a virgin when Jamey met her, and she worried those first few months whether she was doing it right, whether the expression on her face looked right, whether Jamey wished she had more experience. In the dark, she could let go a little more, let her body simply respond. Even years later, if they'd begun with the lights on, Jamey would sometimes get up and turn them off again.

"Now let's see you really cut loose, El. I want the neighbors to call and complain."

She felt different with David. From the very start. Once she dropped the T-shirt she'd been modestly holding, and they made love against the garden window, something clicked in her, a switch was flipped. *We can do whatever we want.* Magical words. Backed up by a man who really did do what he wanted, lived the way he was comfortable, expected Eliza to do the same.

She trailed her fingers up his bare thigh. Stopped before she got where he wanted. David moaned. He sat up and tried again to pull off her shirt. When that didn't work, he shifted his groin closer to hers.

Eliza scooted back further on the bench. "If you try anything, I'll only make you wait longer."

David promptly lay flat again.

She liked the blond hair on his legs. The way it grew lighter, and softer, the higher up she explored on his thighs. Jamey's was so dark and thick. "If we ever have a girl," Eliza had told him, "she'll probably have to start shaving her legs when she's five."

"I had a mustache in junior high," he told her.

"Then pray you have a son."

Eliza stroked David's calves. He didn't moan this time, but she didn't care. She was feeling them for her, not for him.

"You're really sturdy," she told him. "I like that."

"Thank you, but can you hurry up?" He reached for her hand, tried to move it to a better position.

Eliza took off her shirt. That ought to distract him for a while. She left on her black bra—the closest thing to sexy lingerie she owned—and let him stare at her erect nipples through the lace while she continued to admire his body.

His chest and arms were muscular, but not too. He wasn't one of those men who spent hours every day standing in front of a mirror watching himself pump dumbbells. He had a modest collection of weights in there, just enough to keep a person occupied a few hours a week. David hadn't worked out once while she'd been with him, but Eliza imagined it was because she'd been sapping him of all his strength. He'd certainly done that for her.

She reached back and undid the clasp on her bra. Let the fabric fall to the floor.

"Happy?" she asked.

"Oh, yes."

He reached out both hands for her, but she pushed them away. "Hold still."

She got up off the bench and moved around to the side. She bent over his mouth. She teased his lips just lightly with her tongue, then glided forward until her breast hovered above him. She closed her eyes as he teased her in return, hands at his side, just using his mouth.

"Ohh...okay, that's enough."

He protested as she stood back up, but she silenced him by shimmying out of her shorts. She left the matching black lace panties on. She hardly ever wore them. Not the least bit practical.

This time when she straddled the bench, she moved close enough to touch. She leaned back and pressed against him, let him feel her through the thin cloth. To know how wet she was, how near he was to entering her, but still she made him wait.

"David?"

"Hm?" His eyes seemed glazed, his breath shallow, his mind both a million miles away and intensely focused on her breasts and the particular torture she was practicing between his thighs.

"David?"

"Yes?"

"Are you ready?"

"Yes."

"Are you sure?"

"Eliza!"

"Then touch me."

He managed to salvage the dinner. Or at least enough of it that they could sit upstairs on his bed eating sautéed mushrooms and shallots over Walsh's Select Organic Spinach Pasta.

Eliza set her bowl down on one of the bedside tables and leaned back and patted her stomach. David reached under the Walsh's Fine Foods T-shirt of his that she wore and stroked her bare belly.

"I told someone about you today," she said. "See? I'm going public."

"Who was it?"

"Carolyn Jackson. She said she knows you."

"She does know me. She used to be Carolyn Ryder."

David's hand made wider circles now, still stroking Eliza's belly, but also venturing higher.

"What did she say?" he asked.

"That you're very nice. Which I agreed with. Mm, that's very nice. Be careful, I just ate."

He set aside his bowl, too, and stretched out beside Eliza. She closed her eyes while he continued to lightly stroke her body.

"She said something...else," Eliza said. A cold clamminess erupted on her skin, signaling she was about to do something dangerous. She had felt it so many times on expeditions with Jamey—that warning that she was about to go where she shouldn't.

"Come on, Liz, you've got this," Jamey would coax her, and inevitably she'd come out on the other side of some experience feeling proud that she'd mastered her fear.

Eliza controlled her breath. With David's hand now concentrating on her chest, he'd feel it if she started breathing too hard.

"What did she say?" David prompted her when too much time had gone by.

Eliza tried to make her voice sound light. "She said you and your brother were notoriously at each other's throats when you were kids."

David's hand paused. He said, "Hm," and then went on stroking.

"And she said..." The pulse of cold along her nerves was stronger now, centered on the back of her neck, and Eliza knew it was her body's way of trying to stop her, but her mouth continued anyway. She had thought about it too much that afternoon, and didn't know where else to go for the answer.

She sat up and took David's wandering hand between hers. She stretched out his fingers and slipped her own between the joints.

"I'm only going to ask you this," she said, "because I don't want there to be any lingering doubts between us." She couldn't meet his eye, but continued looking down at their joined hands. "Carolyn said...you and Ted are always competing. Would you say that's true?"

"No."

She looked up and met his gaze. "You wouldn't say that?"

"No."

"Oh." She had expected him to admit at least that much. Now she didn't know how else to move forward.

"It d-depends on what you mean," David added. "Ted may compete with me. I don't compete with him."

Eliza noticed the slight stutter. She was making him nervous—she didn't want that. She shouldn't have brought it up in the first place.

David let go of her hand. He got up from the bed and began gathering their used dishes. He wore just a pair of loose shorts, and as he bent over her to retrieve her bowl, Eliza trailed her hand down his bare chest.

"David, I'm sorry. I'm sure it's a sensitive subject—"

"Do you know why I asked you that today?" he said.

"Asked me what?"

"Whether you and my brother had been lovers."

Again the cold chill on her neck. "I assumed you wanted to know."

"I wanted to know it from *y-you*," he said.

"Why?"

"Because I believe you."

"Did Ted say something different?" Eliza asked.

"Ted n...never changes. If he thinks I want something, he tries to take it away."

David carried the stack of dishes from the bedroom down the stairs. Eliza stayed where she was, digesting what he'd just said.

She took her time going downstairs. She didn't want to

sound angry. She wanted a calm, rational—truthful—discussion.

Because more hinged on this than David knew. If she was wrong about him—wrong about any of it—she needed to know now. Before she fell any further. Before her rope slipped and the anchor broke and she ended up smashed against the rocks.

"Did Ted sleep with Livia?"

David continued loading the dishes in his dishwasher and appeared not to hear.

"David."

He slammed the dishwasher closed. He turned to her. "Why are we discussing this?"

"Because I'm trying to understand."

"They have nothing to do with us."

"I hope that's true," Eliza said.

"Wh..." David paused, took a breath. "Why do you say that?"

"Because I'd hate to think I'm part of some sick game you and your brother are playing."

David seemed genuinely confused. "What sick game?"

"He steals your girlfriend, you steal his."

David's face reddened. "Is that what you think?"

"No, I wouldn't have, but now I'm asking you. Look me in the eye and tell me that's not what happened."

"That's not what happened," he said without hesitation, glaring at her. "Y...you have it all wrong."

"Then tell me," Eliza said. "Explain it to me. Why am I here?"

The question hung in the air for too long.

Finally David asked, "Why *are* you here, Eliza? Don't you want to be?"

"If it's real," she answered. "If I'm here because it happened by accident. Not if it's some sort of plan of yours."

"It's not a plan," he said wearily. "It was your dog."

Eliza slumped against the nearest wall, feeling just as weary. She looked at the man in front of her, wondering why she was so ready to believe the worst.

"I need to take Bear out," he said.

"Oh, okay."

He slipped on a pair of shoes set beside the back door, and took Bear's leash off a hook. The dog immediately leapt to his feet and joined David.

"Do you want me to come?" Eliza asked.

"No, I won't be very long."

Eliza nodded.

David and the dog went out past the pool, and Eliza could hear the gate slam shut behind them.

What had just happened?

She had touched a nerve, obviously, one that she should have understood from Carolyn Jackson would have been better left alone.

But wasn't I right to ask? Eliza consoled herself. *Wouldn't I have been wondering otherwise?*

Maybe, but maybe you shouldn't have been wondering that in the first place. Do you really think David would seduce you—spend all his time with you day and night—treat you with the kind of kindness and tenderness that's had you falling for him in the first place—if this wasn't real? If he didn't really want you?

Eliza straightened up off the wall and went to the sink to

finish cleaning up. David had already done it all. There was nothing left for her to do.

Eliza wandered into the living room and curled up on the soft brown couch. She stared out the window into the darkness beyond, wondering what she should say when he returned.

She had worried about the rope failing, the anchor breaking?

Something was broken, all right. And she was the one who broke it.

26

Eliza spent the night, but they were restless hours. Curling against David, wrapping her arms around him, then the two of them shifting positions and him doing the same to her. It might have felt natural, easy, but for the fact that she knew he wasn't sleeping. She knew because she wasn't, either.

In the morning she found him bleary-eyed, sitting behind the computer at his desk. He had a large mug of coffee beside him, and a large black dog lying at his feet.

"How long have you been up?" Eliza asked, yawning. She had finally fallen asleep some time in the early hours, after she'd already reconciled herself to the fact that sleep would never come.

"A while," he said. "Do you want some coffee?"

"I'll make it," she said, motioning for him to stay. He went back to typing on his computer.

She fixed herself an equally large mug of coffee, and

brought it into the living room. She sat in what she considered the Daisy chair, and leaned back and closed her eyes.

Restart. Rewind. Repair.

Rather than sit there and wait for him, not knowing if he would even come, Eliza got up from the chair and climbed the stairs again.

She entered his office and came over to stand beside him. He wrapped an arm around her waist, gave her a quick squeeze, then went back to work.

"Everything okay?" she asked.

"Everything's fine."

"I mean...with us."

"Everything's fine," he repeated.

"Listen, I'm sorry about last night—"

"I told you," he said, not looking up from his computer, "we can do this as long as we want. If we don't want to do it, we won't."

"Do you...not want to do it?"

"I didn't say that. Look," he said, pausing in his typing to give her his full attention, "can we talk about this later? Something's come up, and I need to deal with it before I go in."

"Oh. Sure." Eliza backed away from the desk. "Did you want me to go walk Bear?"

"We already went," David said. "But thanks."

There wasn't anything about his tone that she could put her finger on, but there was a coldness, a dismissal in what he said that made her know things had changed. The man who had been so open and free with her was now closed.

Eliza realized she could continue to stand there, bothering him, or she could go.

And go with her dignity intact.

"Okay, well, I'll see you," she said.

Say tonight. Say that you'll see me tonight.

"See you," he answered.

Eliza's eyes burned as she turned from the room and left.

"Come on, Daisy, let's go for a walk." It was early in the morning still, not desperately hot, so Eliza felt safe taking the dog the short distance up to the park.

She let Daisy pick the pace, sniff whatever she wanted to sniff, pull her in whatever direction the dog wanted.

If only she hadn't talked to Carolyn the day before, Eliza thought. If only she hadn't brought it up to David. *For want of a nail...* She'd still be at his house, probably making love to him right now. His work would have waited. She would have given him a reason for it to wait.

"So is that it?" she asked the dog. "Nine days, and it's over? I guess ten, if we want to count today."

Daisy scratched at a wrapper she found under a bush. Eliza let her have her way.

When they'd made the full circle around the park, Eliza paused at the water fountain and cupped her hand under the stream. Then she poured the water over Daisy's head. The dog shook it off immediately. "Not taking any chances," Eliza told her.

She hadn't said anything to Hildy yet, but maybe it was

time. Including confessing to her how the whole affair had started, with Eliza almost killing her dog.

Hildy would know what to do. Eliza was counting on it.

"Leave him alone," Hildy said.

"For how long?"

"Men are different. They like to go off in the cave and sulk about things for a while. So let him sulk—you didn't do anything wrong."

Eliza brightened at the news. "You really don't think so?"

"No! You heard some rumor that made you think you might be some man's toy, and you stuck up for yourself. I don't see anything wrong with that. He should respect you for that."

"But I think I hurt his feelings."

"He'll get over it."

Eliza shook her head in wonder. "Weren't you the one who said I had to be careful with him? That I might hurt him?"

"He's a big boy," Hildy said. "And you're worth it. He should come around saying he's sorry."

"I don't need him to say he's sorry," Eliza said. "I just want things to be all right with us again."

"Give him time," Hildy said. "Let him alone. If he feels about you the way he should feel about you by now, he won't last for long."

"How should he feel about me?"

"Same way you do about him. You don't even have to say it."

Eliza sighed. "What if he doesn't feel that way?"

"Then he's a fool and has no business in your life."

"It's all very easy for you to say," Eliza told her.

"I had a husband for fifty years and a son for twenty-nine. If I don't know a few things about men by now, I'm a slow learner."

"ALL RIGHT," Eliza told Carolyn Jackson, "I'll go."

"I'll tell Katie!" she said. "She'll be so excited."

"I'll see you tonight. But I'm just there to show off my teeth."

Carolyn laughed. "And your clothes—don't forget the clothes. Wear something that tells the girls you're some brave climber and adventurer—I'm telling you, they'll really love that."

"I'll see if I have any of my brave climber and adventurer clothes left," Eliza said. "I may have thrown them all out."

"It's good you're coming," Carolyn said. "Thanks a lot."

Leave him alone, Eliza thought. *Let him miss me.*

"See you tonight."

THE CLIMBING GYM was in an industrial district, next to a warehouse that held uncut slabs of granite to be turned into people's countertops.

Eliza had done her best with the outfit: khaki-colored hiking pants with cargo pockets, a black tank top, her black boots. She pulled back her shoulder-length hair into a tight ponytail. She hoped she looked like an explorer. Or at least like these 10-year-old girls' image of one.

The climbing gym where she and Jamey used to practice back in Henderson was only a third the size of this one. The walls here seemed much higher, too. Someone could spend weeks in this place and never have to repeat the same route.

The building was packed. But Katie's group stood out. They were the only people wearing matching yellow T-shirts that said *Girls Rock* on them. Eliza wouldn't be surprised if Carolyn and her co-leader had made those T-shirts themselves, especially for the occasion.

The girls were clustered around a male instructor who was having a hard time getting them to focus. He'd given them all strands of rope so they could practice the essential knots.

"Okay, so this one is called a Figure Eight," he said. "Can anyone tell me why?"

"Because it looks like an eight?" one of the girls said. Then she rolled her eyes as if to say, *"Duh."*

"Eliza!" Carolyn motioned for her to join them. "This is Marsha, my co-leader." The two women shook hands. "And this is Blake," Carolyn said. "He's our instructor tonight. Eliza used to be a climber. Have you ever heard of Jamey Shepherd?"

"No..." Blake said.

"It's okay," Eliza rushed to say. "Don't worry about it. I don't really climb anymore. I'm just here to observe."

"And to set a good example," Carolyn said loudly. "Girls, this is Eliza Shepherd. She's a famous climber."

"No, Carolyn," Eliza mumbled. "Please stop saying that."

Carolyn brushed away the objection. "They don't know any different," she mumbled back. "I could say you're a famous astronaut and they won't remember your name tomorrow. But they will remember the outfit—nice job."

Eliza was wishing very much she hadn't come. "I'm just going to stand back over here. Let Blake do his job." She motioned for him to continue.

"Great! Okay, ladies," he said, "who wants to learn how to make a Bowline, the king of knots?"

"When can we try some of those?" one of the girls asked, pointing to the colorful handholds on the wall in front of her.

"Soon," Blake said. "Really soon. But you girls have to pay attention."

It was going to be a long hour, Eliza thought.

WHEN it finally came time to fit the girls in harnesses and climbing shoes, Eliza could see they were excited again.

"I'm telling you," Carolyn said, keeping her voice low, "it's because it's clothes. I don't mean to be sexist, but these girls really fit the stereotype—even Katie. Will and I have never been into fashion—as you can see," she said, pointing out what she was wearing, "but they must all get it from each other at school. Katie came home one day obsessed with pink and sparkles, and she's been lost to us ever since."

"I want that one!" one of the girls said, pointing to a harness that had purple flowers along its straps.

"See?" Carolyn said.

. . .

IT HAD SEEMED SO SIMPLE. Just a quick demonstration, standing with both feet safely on the ground.

"I can't get it," Katie said, tugging at the loops around her thighs. "It feels weird. Eliza, will you come help me?"

She had Katie step out of the harness so she could make a few adjustments to the straps, then step into it again.

"See?" Eliza said. "You want the waist strap here, and the thigh straps to fit right about here."

"You put it on," Katie said. "Let me see."

"I think it's too small," Eliza said.

"Please? Can you just try?"

Eliza glanced at her watch. She'd already been there an hour and a half. Carolyn told her the whole meeting usually went two hours, but that was when they were in people's homes, with snacks and activities to fill the time. Carolyn and Marsha had assumed the girls would get tired of the gym after an hour—especially without the snacks. So far, they were wrong.

Eliza lengthened the straps of the harness again, and set it on the floor.

"So you want to step into it like this," she said, "then pull it up and fasten it here."

Eliza felt a change in the temperature.

That cold clamminess she'd experienced at David's the night before was back, but much more severe. It broke out on her face, a sheen of cold sweat, and sprang out of the pores on her back.

Her ears began to buzz. Eliza shut her eyes. She opened them again because she'd felt herself sway.

"Eliza?" Carolyn said, steadying her by the arm. "What's wrong? My God, you're white as a ghost."

Eliza sank to her knees and dropped her head. She felt dizzy, nauseated, weak.

"Stay with the girls," Carolyn told Marsha. "I'm taking her outside."

She helped Eliza to her feet and rushed her outside, no doubt worried Eliza was about to vomit.

The warm, steamy air felt sickening to Eliza, but being inside the climbing gym was worse. Being inside that harness, feeling it touching her legs, the memory of it, the memory of all of it, sent Eliza to her knees again.

"What's wrong?" Carolyn asked. "Tell me what's wrong!"

"It's...Jamey," Eliza said, hearing the sob before she could stop it. "It's just Jamey. It's always Jamey. I can't ever get away."

She fought to control herself: This wasn't what she did anymore. She didn't fall apart like this. She didn't have the nightmares or the panic attacks or any of the other tortures of the first months after he died.

"I'm so sorry!" Carolyn said. "I never should have asked you. God, I'm such an idiot! I should have known this would be too hard."

"*I* didn't know," Eliza said, pulling up the bottom of her tank top to wipe the sweat and tears from her face. She reached over and squeezed Carolyn's wrist. "It's okay. I don't know what happened in there. It was just...so fast."

She continued kneeling in the parking lot, breathing in gulps of the hot, fetid air. What was she doing there? Why had she even come? This wasn't her life anymore. And this was exactly why.

Eliza slowly rose to her feet. "I think I need to go home now."

"I'll give you a ride. I don't think you should drive. Just wait, and I'll go tell Marsha."

"No," Eliza said, "you should go back inside. You need to be with the girls. I'll be fine. Let me just sit in my car for a while."

"Can I call someone for you?" Carolyn asked. "Do you want me to call David?"

"No," Eliza blurted out. "He's...busy tonight. And don't call Hildy—I have her car, so she can't pick me up anyway. I don't want her to worry.

"I'll tell you what," Eliza said, seeing the concern on Carolyn's face. "I'll sit out here for a while, and if I feel better, I'll drive home. If I don't, I'll ride home with you and Katie. I can pick up the car tomorrow."

"Are you sure?" Carolyn asked.

Eliza nodded. "I'll be fine. You go back in."

Alone again, Eliza sat on the curb and rested her head in her hands.

I'm a mess, she had told David that day, before she ever let him touch her.

"What if I don't care?"

Oh, you care, Eliza thought. Just one wrong move and he was already out the door.

Maybe he had the right idea.

"How long you going for?" Hildy asked, watching Eliza pack.

"Just a few weeks. You'll be all right, won't you?"

"Sure, honey, I'll be fine."

Eliza tried to sound upbeat. "It's just that I haven't seen everybody in a long time, and it would be good to just check in. Get away for a little while. Clear my head."

"Sure, honey," Hildy said. "You do that. You're entitled."

Eliza could take her lightest bag. All she needed were a few pairs of shorts, some underwear, her sandals, and a few T-shirts. She still had drawers and a closet full of clothes at home. She was only bringing her favorites.

She zipped up her carry-on.

"They gouge you on the price?" Hildy asked.

"Not too badly," Eliza said. "Just the change fee on my ticket and some price difference."

Hildy nodded. "That's good."

They both knew there was an unspoken question hanging in the air.

So Hildy spoke it.

"You sure you don't want to call him?"

"Nope."

"Just to tell him you're going?"

"I'll be back before he even notices," Eliza said. She'd lost her upbeat tone. "I'm leaving him alone, just like you said."

"Yeah, but I didn't mean like this, just sneaking off—"

"I'm not sneaking," Eliza said. "I'm just...going. Just for a little while. Like you said, let him miss me. Or let him...not. I'd rather know where we stand. And I need the break right now. Last night was...bad."

Hildy nodded. Eliza had told her all about it.

Eliza looked at the clock. "We need to go." She'd found the first flight out, leaving around nine-thirty that morning. She had nine hours of travel ahead of her. But then she'd be sleeping in her own bed.

"You sure you don't want to think about it one more day?" Hildy asked.

"I thought about it all night," Eliza said. "I still haven't been to sleep. Come on, Hildy, we need to go."

Eliza sat on the plane, staring out the window. She liked the window seats because she could prop her head against them with a jacket or a T-shirt as cushion and maybe catch a little bit of sleep.

Jamey could sleep anywhere: on sheer rock walls, hanging from a portaledge; at high altitude where falling asleep felt like running out of oxygen, and so people jerked themselves awake; on tiny airplanes, on large ones; in the car minutes after Eliza had taken over the driving. He slept deeply and peacefully, and then once he was awake again, he was on.

But Eliza felt strung out right now. She always needed her sleep. She'd gotten by with so little of it over the past week and half, and now it was catching up to her.

Her seatmate fished in the bag at her feet and accidentally bumped Eliza. "Oh, sorry."

Eliza smiled briefly, then let her face go slack again. She went back to staring out the window, anxious for the plane to get going. She had some crazy idea—no doubt brought on by her sleep-deprived brain—that David might suddenly show up, out on the tarmac below, waving his arms and shouting for her to stay.

Never happen, the rational part of her knew.

I know. But what if? Would I run off the plane? Jump into his arms? Live happily ever after?

The flight attendant closed the forward door.

Eliza reached down and twisted the ring on her left hand. She hadn't wanted to leave it behind. It had seemed like a natural thing to bring, just like her favorite navy blue T-shirt and enough underwear to last her a full week without having to do laundry. And it made more sense to wear it through the security checkpoint than leave it in her pocket, where it might set off the alarm, or worse, put it in the tray and then accidentally forget it. So she'd slipped it over her finger once Hildy hugged her and walked away, and now Eliza was glad to feel it again on her finger.

They were finally speeding down the runway, and in another moment, climbing. Eliza closed her eyes and leaned back against the seat.

Please miss me, she thought. *Please want me. Don't let this be all.*

She twisted the ring once more, and then tugged it from her finger. She slipped it back into her pocket.

"Marriage troubles, huh?" said the woman next to her. "Don't I know."

Eliza peeked open one eye to find the woman nodding and obviously gearing up for good long cross-country chat.

"He's dead," Eliza said simply. Then she closed her eyes again.

"Oh...I'm so sorry," the woman said.

"It's okay," Eliza said automatically. "But now I need to sleep. I'm exhausted. Please don't let anyone wake me."

"Sure," the woman said. "Sure."

Eliza knew she had recruited an ally. The woman would keep people from offering her peanuts or pretzels or water. Eliza bundled her extra T-shirt against the window, then draped its end over her eyes. Please let me sleep, she thought. She felt sick with it: the exhaustion, the emotion, all of it.

She needed to rest, that was all. Just a few weeks. Then she'd come back and sort it all out. Go back to that climbing gym, maybe. Prove to herself she could do it. Start over with David. Restart, rewind, repair.

A two-week vacation, then she'd return to her normal life.

Or what passed for it anymore.

28

E liza sat at her desk, staring alternately at her laptop screen and the patch of dirt outside her window. She kept meaning to buy flowers of some kind, just to have some color out there, but right now it was low on her list.

She'd been struggling with the column for the past few hours. She still had two days to complete it, but she hated waiting until the last minute. She wrote better when she could put something on paper, then walk away from it for a while. Let better phrases come to her while she was out running or in the shower. Let the piece mature.

Eliza got up and went into the kitchen. It was just a few short steps away in the two-bedroom house she and Jamey had bought a few years before. Hildy and Ron helped them with the down payment, and one of Jamey's book advances had added to the pot—enough so that Eliza could make the mortgage payments now without too much stress every month.

She'd considered renting it out while she was away, but decided eight or nine months wasn't a long enough lease to make it worth packing up her belongings and putting them in storage. So the house had gathered dust, but otherwise had stood waiting, ready for her return.

Eliza drank a glass of water and stared out the window. September in Henderson was still remarkably hot. But it was the dry, roasting heat her skin and hair loved—not that moist, basting heat of the east coast. Here she could go outside with her hair wet and find it dry half an hour later. She had cut it again so all she had to do was run her fingers through its short length and give it a slight fluff. Practical. Easy. Different.

She waited until midmorning before phoning her mother.

"Movie today?"

"Of course," Joyce said.

Eliza looked on-line while her mother consulted the paper. They found a science fiction thriller playing at noon. Neither of them particularly liked science fiction, but it didn't matter—it was a movie.

When it was time, Eliza packed up two peanut butter and jelly sandwiches, and drove the few blocks to pick up her mother. It was one of the reasons Jamey and Eliza had bought that house: First, they could afford it, and second, it was within walking distance of several members of their family. Hildy and Ron lived two streets away, Joyce and her husband just on the other side of a major street, and Eliza's older brother in the neighborhood beyond that. Her younger brother lived further away in Summerlin, a suburb of Las Vegas.

"How's Hildy?" Joyce asked as she settled into the car.

"She's fine." Eliza called to check on her every few days. "Walsh's just published the schedule for her new fall classes, and she said people have already started signing up."

"Good for her."

A brief silence followed. Eliza knew one of two possible questions would follow next.

"No, she hasn't run into David," Eliza said, "and no, she didn't ask me when I'm coming back."

"Just wondering."

"I know."

"Have you thought more about—"

"No," Eliza said. "Hildy's doing fine right now. I like being home. Stop trying to get rid of me."

Joyce smiled. "Stay as long as you want. I had you first, you know. Here." She handed Eliza a fistful of hard butterscotch candies.

"Thanks. Your sandwich is in my bag."

THE MOVIE WAS loud and overly complicated and obviously intended to set up a sequel. It was just the kind of distraction Eliza needed. Her mind had played with the column a little more, and she paused outside the theater to make a few notes on her phone.

As soon as she turned it on, she saw that she had missed a call from Hildy. Eliza returned the call as she and her mother walked to the car.

Hildy answered the phone with, "Lizzy, I'm fine."

"Okay…" It was an unusual way to start the conversation, Eliza thought, especially since they'd just spoken the day before.

"It was just a little accident," Hildy said. "I'm not hurt that bad."

ELIZA SAT on the edge of Jamey's and her bed and stared into the open closet. She tried to remember exactly what clothes she had brought with her on the first trip and left up at Hildy's. A few sweaters, a fleece-lined pair of pants, a scarf and a fleece hat—she'd ended up wearing all of those during the lingering, snowy cold of Careybrook's early spring. Now she wondered if she should bring more.

There was no doubt now that she'd be staying through December. Maybe even longer, depending on how quickly Hildy healed. Her doctor said it would take at least two months before the cast came off, and then there would be rehab after that.

"What an idiot," Hildy complained as she told Eliza the whole story.

"Hildy, it could have happened to anyone. It wasn't your fault."

"I'm not saying it's my fault!" she answered. "*He's* the idiot for rear-ending me! It's illegal to talk on the phone while you're driving here, you know. Only idiots would try to text. What was so important? 'Coming home. Just have to hit this old lady first. See you soon.'"

Eliza stifled a laugh. "Hildy, I'm so sorry this happened to you. I'm coming back right away. I'll be there in just two days. Can you wait that long?"

"I'll manage."

"I'm sure Carolyn Jackson would drive you anyplace you need," Eliza said. "Or she can bring you food. Do you want me to call her?"

"No, honey, that's nice of you. I'll be fine. But I don't mind you coming back."

Eliza winced when she saw the cast. It covered Hildy's right arm from the knuckles up to the elbow. Worse yet were the various bruises on Hildy's face from when the airbag had deployed.

"Oh, Hildy," she said, hugging her mother-in-law hard. Hildy patted her with her good arm. "And Daisy—yes, I see you, girl. Try to settle down."

The dog yipped and barked and frantically tried to jump closer to Eliza's face. Eliza bent down to give the dog her proper dose of attention. Then she stood back up and looked around the upper floor.

"Place hasn't fallen apart."

"As if it would," Hildy said. "You were only gone two months."

"But I suppose you'd like a live-in maid now," Eliza said. "And a cook, and a chauffeur, and a dog-walker..." She did her best to sound cheerful and light. She doubted she was fooling either of them.

In the beginning, as she'd packed to leave Hildy's house in July, she'd been able to push away the guilt. She'd already done so much, Eliza reasoned—more than most daughters-in-law would probably do—and Hildy could get along without her for a while. Eliza would come back. It was only a few weeks. Then she could return refreshed and ready again.

The fact was, two weeks hadn't been enough. Once she was home, Eliza realized how desperately she'd missed it. And how uncomplicated it was. Hildy seemed to be doing fine. There wasn't any harm.

But always in the back of her mind, Eliza had dreaded a call just like this: *Your mother-in-law is sick. She fell. She had a stroke. We found her dead...*She didn't used to feel so responsible when Ron was alive. Somehow just his being there in the house with Hildy, even if he wasn't competent anymore, made Eliza feel like she could leave the two of them alone. If something happened, she could be there right away. But nothing was going to happen.

But ever since Ron had died, Eliza knew she was carrying the burden for two. Jamey would have wanted to take care of his mother, to look after her. Maybe he never would have moved back with her to Careyville, but he would have watched over her in some way, visited her often, maybe insisted she come stay with Eliza and him during the winters.

And Eliza would have said yes, of course. She loved Hildy as much as she loved her own mother. It's just that her mother...didn't need her like this. Not yet, anyway. Joyce was a dozen years younger—Jamey had been a late baby for Ron and Hildy. And seeing Hildy like this now, so battered and bruised, Eliza realized she'd been selfish for leaving the poor woman alone.

"I brought you some soup," Eliza said, taking a grocery bag into the kitchen. "And a big, fat, decadent cookie from that place in the Syracuse airport."

"Let me start with the cookie," Hildy said. "I can eat that with my fingers."

Eliza understood the comment as soon as she tried to help Hildy with her soup. The spoon jerked and jittered as Hildy fought to maneuver it with her non-dominant hand.

Finally they both gave up. "Got anything else?" Hildy asked.

"Bread, turkey. I can make you a sandwich."

"That and a cup of tea and I'll stop bothering you for the night."

ELIZA ZIPPED open her suitcase and unloaded clothes to the closet and drawers. The room felt so familiar—she hadn't really been away that long. When she returned to Jamey's and her house, she felt like she'd been gone for a century. Everything looked old and abandoned. It took her days before she felt right in there again.

But this, she knew: the blue bedspread, the blue and white quilt hanging on the wall, the white lamp beside the bed, the shaggy white rug in the middle of the room. She had written some of her columns in here, and some of them out in the living room, or at the kitchen table, looking out on the yard. This house was fine for her, Eliza thought. She could live here until December, and even a little longer if Hildy needed.

But then, Eliza had already decided, she was going to suggest a change. The two of them needed a better, more permanent solution. Some sort of exchange program, where Eliza lived with Hildy part of the year, and Hildy lived with her the other. Two single women with two houses at their disposal should be able to come to some sort of workable arrangement.

It was just a matter of deciding which side of the country had the better weather for each season of the year. So far, Eliza was already planning on never spending another sticky, steamy summer in Careyville again.

And if as a result of her plan she occasionally had to run into David Walsh throughout various parts of the year, then so be it. He had been part of the reason she'd so selfishly run away, and it was something she felt ashamed of. It was time she grew up. Took care of her responsibilities. Remembered why she'd come to Careyville in the first place.

It wasn't to get involved with a man. That part of her life was over.

29

Eliza cruised the aisles of the small grocery store near Hildy's house. She looked for anything that didn't require a knife, fork, or spoon. They were eating picnic style, Eliza had announced, no utensils allowed, until Hildy had the use of her hand back. Maybe the doctor would have wanted Hildy to try harder, but Hildy and Eliza both agreed, "Forget it."

Eliza bought pita bread, hummus spread, lettuce, tomatoes, cucumbers, and avocados to make what she and Hildy were calling Salad in a Sandwich. It was something Hildy could eat with one hand without requiring a lot of coordination. Eliza also bought regular bread, peanut butter and jam, tuna, cheese, and lunch meats. She only hoped she wasn't compromising an almost 70-year-old woman's health by keeping her alive on sandwiches for a few months.

"Remember, it's apple season!" a banner in front of the produce section announced, so Eliza stocked up on some of those, too. Then she checked out, loaded her bags in the back of the rental car the other driver's insurance was paying for, and drove on to her next destination.

She hadn't been in the bookstore for months. After her first visit there back when she'd first arrived, Eliza made a point of returning every few weeks. It was a way of easing into a new, unfamiliar life, hiding out among the familiar territory of bookshelves. Now Eliza returned to it simply to have a cup of good coffee and to do a little research.

And to rest.

Eliza had to admit that taking care of her mother-in-law was hard. It wasn't that Hildy had a bad attitude—she didn't. But some days her arm hurt, which made her cranky, and all days having the cast was inconvenient. It made it difficult for her to shower, to use the bathroom, to find a comfortable position in which to sleep. She was used to driving herself wherever she needed to go, cooking what she wanted to eat, never having to ask Eliza or anyone else to do those things for her.

"I want to go over to his house and throw a rock through his window," Hildy had said that morning of the driver who rear-ended her. "I bet he sleeps like a baby."

"No, I'm sure he lies awake feeling guilty for what he did," Eliza answered. "He just hasn't worked up the courage to send you flowers yet. They're coming—we'll just keep waiting."

"Speaking of flowers," Hildy said.

Eliza looked at her from the corner of her eye.

"Remember when Davey brought you those daisies?"

"They were from Ted."

"I think you should call him up. Davey, I mean. Let him know you're back."

"No, thank you."

"I think you've left him alone for long enough," Hildy said. "He's stewed on it, got it out of his system. Bet he misses you."

"Hildy, just drop it."

"Did I give you bad advice before?" She seemed genuinely dismayed. "Maybe you shouldn't have listened to me. You should have gone over there and talked it out—"

"*Hildy*," Eliza cautioned her. "Let it go. We're not having this discussion now or ever. I came back for you, not for David."

She meant to stop there, not to think the next few thoughts—and certainly not to say them. But her mouth continued moving.

"He could have called me. He didn't. He could have written to me. He didn't. You know how people are around here—he's probably known I was back since last week. You didn't give me bad advice—you were right. If he felt anything toward me except basic animal lust, he would have done something to keep me around. I'm sure I was a good time, until I wasn't. So that's that. Just *leave* it."

Daisy's ears pricked up. She'd heard that command before.

Eliza let out a breath. Suddenly the house felt too small. She cleared her throat and tried to sound pleasant.

"I need to go shopping," she said. "Would you like a tuna in your salad sandwich tonight?"

"Sounds great," Hildy said, sounding equally, forcefully pleasant. "Thank you."

Eliza smiled, then escaped to the car.

SHE BROWSED through the magazine aisle at the bookstore, picking out the current issues of every magazine that had ever bought her work. It was time to start pitching articles again. Magazines paid so much better than newspapers: Even the short quiz Eliza wrote for *Adventure Girl* at the beginning of the year earned her more than she'd made the past month from two rounds of her newspaper column.

But that wasn't the only problem.

Eliza had been dipping into her Extras file more and more to come up with essays for her biweekly column. The truth was, she worried she was running out of things to say.

It was easy to try to inspire people, Eliza thought, when you were trying to inspire yourself. *Say no. Be braver. Make a change. Write your book.* So much of what she suggested to her readers were actually suggestions to herself.

But lately she was out of those ideas. Back in Henderson, she'd refined her life: *Call your mom and go to a movie. Read another Shakespeare. Go the farmer's market on Sunday. Make yourself a real dinner instead of having just salad and pretzels every night. Stop thinking about him.*

There was nothing there to inspire anyone.

"HIYA, GORGEOUS," Frank Sawyer said, "what happened to your hair?"

"I assume that means you like it."

"Hair's hair. You're a sight for sore eyes."

Eliza sank onto the newspaperman's ancient leather couch. She thought of the first time she'd visited *The Careyville Independent*, dressed in her black pantsuit and crisp white shirt. Now she wore jeans and Jamey's old UNLV sweatshirt. She imagined she made a different impression.

"So where you been, golden girl?"

"Here and there," she said casually.

"Mostly there. Too long," Frank added. "Glad you're back."

Eliza sighed. She flipped sideways along the length of Frank's couch and stretched her feet out over the edge. She draped her arm over her eyes.

"That's what you came for?" Frank said. "Take a nap on my couch?"

"I came for advice," she said. "Then I might take a nap."

"Two words," Frank told her after she had poured out her most personal feelings about the work she'd been doing—and not doing—for the past two years. "Burned. Out," he said. "See it all the time."

"Have you ever been burned. Out?" she asked, parroting the way Frank said it.

"Sure, plenty of times," he said. "But I kept going. Know why?"

"No."

"Two words: Wife, child."

Eliza sat up again, but still slouched into the soft couch. "I think I've lost it, Frank."

He shrugged. "I like what you write. I'll still keep publishing you."

"Would you ever tell me if you think something I've written is garbage?"

"Sure I would."

She straightened up with interest. "Would you really? You're not just saying that?"

"Shepherd," Frank said. "I've been in this business a long time. I've written plenty of garbage myself. But when I've written something worth a Pulitzer, I know it. Maybe no one else knows it, but I do. And that's what keeps me doing it. The hope that after I write a hundred pieces of garbage, I'll write one shiny diamond I can stick on top. That's what I saw when I read your stuff: a shiny diamond. So you just keep writing, and I'll tell you when you've lost it."

Eliza smiled with genuine relief. "I'm trusting you, Frank."

"Turn in your next column on time and I'll tell you if it stinks."

He hadn't asked her about her love life, Eliza realized. She'd felt so tired and defeated when she got to Frank's office, she'd forgotten to even worry about it.

He used to ask her about Ted all the time. She hadn't been with David long enough, she supposed, for Frank to hear about it.

As Eliza drove home, she thought about what he'd said.

She knew what he meant about feeling proud about something you'd written, even if no one saw that it was good but
you. She'd felt that way many times, usually about articles
she and Jamey had written together. They played off each
other so well, raised each other's game. They made good
money in those days—enough to finance Jamey's endless
hunt for adventure.

But she also knew what it felt like to write garbage. And
no matter what Frank said, Eliza knew she was slipping. She
needed to try harder. Go back to some of the tricks that had
helped her in the past: Reading more. Getting out more.
Interacting with people so she had someone else's stories to
tell besides just her own. People were tired of hearing about
Eliza Shepherd—*she* was tired of it. She needed fresh
material.

As Eliza turned into the neighborhood, she couldn't help
looking toward David's house. She couldn't see it from the
road, but she could see one of the streets he might have
taken if he'd been leaving just now.

Pathetic, she thought. *Just like at the bookstore.*

She'd sat in the bookstore café, drinking coffee and
paging through magazines, and only half her mind had been
on her job.

The other half had been on him.

She kept glancing at the door, even though she didn't
want to, imagining him walking in the way he had after
she'd first met him, after they'd had that run-in over the
dogs. She'd tried to hide from him then. Would she do that
now? Slip down in her chair, hold a magazine over her face,
and hope he simply passed by?

Or would she acknowledge him, nod to him, even put out her hand as he came over and say, "It's nice to see you again"?

Would he even come over? Or would he take one look at her and turn around and leave? He was capable of it—she'd seen him do it before. He never seemed to mind what people might think.

She'd spent nearly an hour in that condition, trying to focus on her research, watching the door, taking notes from a masthead, watching the door.... It was maddening. Stupid. Painful.

She returned all the magazines to the rack without buying a single one. She was there to figure out how to make more money, not to spend it. She tossed her coffee cup in the trash and pushed out through the door he might have come in. On another day. In another life.

Her car had found its way into *The Careyville Independent* parking lot without her really planning to go there. But she wasn't ready to see Hildy again, when she was feeling so low and insecure. That house had enough misery in it at the moment without Eliza dragging any more inside. She'd planned on just a quick visit with Frank, a chance to say, "Hi, I'm back," and it had turned into a therapy session. But he didn't seem to mind. And maybe, Eliza thought, it had helped.

She'd start getting out again—right away. Go visit Carolyn and Katie, see what the Girls' Club was up to. There might be a column there. Maybe go apple picking—she'd seen an advertisement for a U-Pik-It farm in the pile of papers on Frank's desk. Maybe write something seasonal, something that would appeal to readers in Careyville and Anchorage and Henderson.

Where *was* he? Eliza caught herself thinking. She was bound to run into him. And then what? What would she say?

Might as well get it over with, Eliza thought. Right away. Put herself where she knew he'd find her. And then get all the ugliness out of the way at once.

The weather was cool enough. It was time to start walking Daisy again. Up along the hill.

30

Definitely *here in the fall,* Eliza thought. She could see her breath as she and Daisy made their way up the hill at the end of the street. She had noticed the maples before—they'd already starting turning before she arrived back—but for some reason this morning they seemed especially red, especially vibrant. When she and Hildy worked out their bicoastal life—something Eliza still hadn't mentioned to her mother-in-law, but would soon, she thought—she'd definitely want to be back here by late September, early October. Be in position to watch the birches turn yellow, the maples turn red. Henderson had one color during every season: brown. She could understand now why people might endure a summer up here if this was their reward at the end.

Her heart beat too fast. She paused along the path and took a breath. She might see him this morning, she might not. She tried not to overplan it. She wanted to sound natural. *"Oh, hi... Okay, see you..."* She hoped she could pull it off. She hoped she could get it over with and not have to go through this tomorrow, too, or even worse, for the next few days.

Eliza unzipped the top of her jacket. She wasn't as cold as she'd been leaving the house. The day should warm up nicely, she thought, and if she could just get over this one, awkward obstacle, she and Daisy could come up here every morning and enjoy long walks again before Eliza started her day.

She had other things to think about, not just David. When she'd returned home from shopping yesterday and from visiting Frank, she found Hildy just finishing a phone call.

"Okay, thanks, hon. I'll let you know."

She hung up the receiver and looked at Eliza. Smiling in her most conciliatory way.

"That was the girl at Walsh's," Hildy said.

"Oh?" Eliza tried to seem unconcerned as she unpacked the groceries.

"Good news: She said there are already twenty-two people signed up for my October fifth class."

"Twenty-two, wow," Eliza said, trying to sound cheerful. But something about Hildy's tone made her suspicious. "That's great. Congratulations."

"It's great if I could teach it."

Eliza turned to see Hildy holding up her cast. "I can't chop anything with this. I can't do it left-handed. I could probably stir things, but..."

Hildy paused and gave Eliza an innocent look.

"Maybe Walsh's could give you an assistant," Eliza said. "Maybe whoever just called."

"Or maybe you could be my assistant."

Eliza briefly closed her eyes. Then she looked into her mother-in-law's expectant face. "Hildy, I'd rather not."

"It's just one night every few weeks."

"I know, but it's Ted's store..."

"He's never there," Hildy said. "It's at night, and he's gone by then."

"Couldn't you find someone else?"

"I could, but I'd rather not," she said, echoing Eliza's words. "Come on, honey, you know I hate to ask. You're already doing so much for me..."

Get out more, Eliza reminded herself. *Be among people. Develop new material.*

Stop trying to avoid the Walshes—you're here now, and you're going to be here for a while.

"We'll try one class, all right?" Eliza said. "See how it goes."

"Thank you, Lizzy."

"I'm going to go throw a rock through that guy's window tonight. Want to come?"

SHE SAW him in the distance, working his way up the power line trail, his big black dog running at his side.

Ready, steady...

She saw him see her. Should she wave? Just keep walking? Keep walking.

Eliza put her head down and made the terrier pick up the

pace. She wanted to appear purposeful, busy, not just a woman out ambling with her dog.

She glanced up to check David's progress. They were within shouting distance now. Another minute or so and he'd reach her.

"Hi," she practiced. "Hello..."

He reached a fork in the trails and turned. He continued running right, parallel to her. Their paths would never intersect.

Bastard! Eliza thought. *If you think I'm going through this again tomorrow, you're crazy.*

"David! Hello." Her voice sounded stern and commanding. She liked that.

David slowed, halted, turned around.

Eliza stood and waited, not saying anything more. Phrases bounced around in her head: *I know you saw me. Let's be adult about this. I'm back for a while, so we might as well get used to it—*

Daisy started to growl.

Eliza tugged lightly on the leash. "It's Bear. You know him."

But as David and the dog came closer, Daisy's hackles rose.

"Daisy! Don't be a lunatic. For once."

Now she was barking, lunging, carrying on the way she had the first time she saw them, and the second and third. It was as though David had never saved her life, she had never slept in Bear's bed or David's, never curled up on David's chair.

The dog howled as the two of them came closer. Eliza tried to control her.

"I'm sorry," she called over the noise. "She's still crazy."

David nodded and kept his distance. Bear whined and wagged his tail, ready to play.

Finally Eliza had to admit defeat. "Come on, Daisy, we're going this way." She jerked the dog around and dragged her in the opposite direction. She glanced back to say goodbye, but David and Bear had already resumed running.

Her shoulders slumped. "Thanks a lot." But another few steps and she realized the sentiment was right: "Thanks a lot," she repeated to the dog. "Maybe that was the right way to handle it."

"Well, I saw him," she reported to Hildy when they returned.

"What did he say?"

"Nothing."

"Nothing?"

"Not even a syllable," Eliza said. "But you'll be happy to know your dog is as deranged as ever."

Hildy considered for a moment, then said, "He's embarrassed."

"I don't care if he's embarrassed or not," Eliza answered. "He's rude, he's strange, and I'm not going to worry about him anymore."

"That's good," Hildy said, although her expression said otherwise.

"What?" Eliza asked, knowing something was coming anyway.

"I don't understand him."

"Join the club. I'm taking a shower. I'll fix you breakfast when I get out."

SHE SCRUBBED her hair and tried not to think.

He looked tired. But he still looked good. That face she had touched, the eyes she had looked into, a mouth she had seen smile, a mouth she had kissed, tongue, lips—

She pulled her fingers through her hair and rinsed out the conditioner. What was she doing today? Visiting Carolyn Jackson. Paying Hildy's bills. Cleaning the bathroom. Changing the sheets. Reading.

Why wouldn't he look at me? She kept waiting to meet his eye, but he always seemed to be looking just to the side of her face. Was this how it was going to be from now on? Complete silence whenever they met, that disturbing coldness, when she had been more intimate with him in some ways than she had ever been with Jamey?

Had it all just been about sex? A brief, intense affair that couldn't survive even one uncomfortable conversation? What kind of man behaved like that? Eliza wondered. Was he that immature? That unstable? She had read him all wrong. And that bothered her almost as much as everything else.

She dried off and dressed in her robe. And took a moment behind the closed door of her bedroom to reassess what she thought she knew.

She thought she had been falling in love. There was no point pretending otherwise—at least not to herself. She never had to reveal it to anyone else, not even Hildy, no matter how curious the woman might be. This was Eliza's secret, and it was her lesson alone. She'd been foolish. Confused. Too easily seduced.

He felt nothing for her—that much was clear now. A man who had missed her over the past two months would have looked her in the eye, searched her face for some kind of sign that she cared for him, made even a minimal attempt to speak.

It was so easy to break your own heart, Eliza thought. No, not break it, but at least bruise it. Batter it. You just have to open it too fast and let the wrong person in. Start believing the fantasies your own mind invents. There was probably a column in that, but she wasn't going to write it. This chapter of her life was closed. Writing about it would only seal it in her memory.

They were ten days she'd rather forget.

Carolyn Jackson looked pained when she opened the door. "I knew you were back. I've been afraid to come see you."

"Why?"

"Why? That horrible night. I never should have made you go—"

"You didn't 'make' me," Eliza said. "It wasn't your fault. I used to get that way sometimes right after Jamey died. Something would remind me, and suddenly I'd be on the floor. It just hasn't happened for a while. But it wasn't your fault—really, Carolyn. So please stop worrying about it."

"But I never should have pressured you—"

"It's done," Eliza said. "Over. Now come on. I came over here hoping for some arts and crafts."

"We weren't going to do this for another few days," Carolyn said, "but since you're here."

She had Katie help her spread out newspapers over the table.

"Are you a good carver?" Katie asked.

"I have no idea," Eliza said.

They hoisted three engorged pumpkins onto the table, then Carolyn gave them their weapons: a book full of stencils, and a container full of knives.

"You know the rules," Carolyn said.

"No stabbing, no slicing, no bleeding," Katie recited. She turned to Eliza. "We're not allowed to have to go to the emergency room."

"Seems fair," Eliza said.

"So cut *slowly*," Carolyn reminded her daughter. "Carefully."

Katie rolled her eyes. "Mom, I've done this a million times before."

"Well then maybe I was talking to Eliza."

. . .

She felt better walking home. A few hours of laughter and hard physical labor trying to wrestle with a difficult pumpkin, and Eliza could almost forget the morning.

She returned to the house and found Hildy and Daisy on the couch with Hildy's recipes spread out all around.

"I'm trying to find ones you can do," she told Eliza.

"I do know how to cook."

"Yeah, but some of these are really tricky," Hildy said. "I don't want you to get discouraged."

Eliza laughed. "I'm not trying to become a master chef. I'm just there to chop a few onions for you and stir a pot."

"And you have to be nice," Hildy said. "You have to smile —remember? People are there to have a good time. They drink a little wine, watch me make them food..."

"I thought they were supposed to be learning to cook."

"Some of them," Hildy said. "But a lot of them just come for the cheap food and booze. Doesn't matter to me—I get paid either way, and Teddy gets people into the store."

Eliza narrowed her eyes. "You're sure he won't be there? Because I've enjoyed just about enough of the Walsh boys for a while."

Hildy waved her hand dismissively. "You'll never see him. We'll be in and out before he even remembers we were there. You'll see—it'll be an easy night."

"An easy night," Eliza thought later, didn't really describe it.

31

Eliza wheeled Hildy's cart into the store. It was five-thirty, and class wouldn't begin for another hour.

"I'm over there," Hildy said, pointing to the left side of the store. "Out in the space between the deli and the sushi bar."

Eliza had fought her on the outfit.

"I'm not pretending to be a caterer tonight."

"You'll look more professional," Hildy argued.

Eliza had been just about say no when Hildy added, "You'll blend in. Nobody notices the staff. You'll be practically invisible. Which I know you want."

"All right, all right."

So now she wore her white button-down shirt and a simple black skirt. Black flats to round out the boring look. She left her hair loose, since it was short enough now to only come to her chin.

She found a table where Hildy had indicated, draped in a

thick white cotton tablecloth that reached all the way to the floor. Eliza unloaded the electric burners, the soup pot, sauté pan, and various other cooking equipment, then lined up Hildy's spices.

"Go get the shrimp and scallops," Hildy directed. "They're supposed to be set aside at the meat counter. And then get a couple of green peppers and a head of garlic, three onions, some celery—"

"Can I have a list?"

Hildy handed her one of the recipe sheets she'd be giving the class. "And don't be long, because you need to start chopping."

"This is a lot of fun for me so far," Eliza said. "So glad I volunteered."

"And remember to smile," Hildy said. She demonstrated. "Everyone notices a surly assistant. If you want to blend in..."

Eliza muttered to herself as she headed off toward the meat counter. She actually didn't mind helping Hildy, and didn't mind getting out of the house with her for a change instead of making yet another dinner-worthy sandwich and eating it in front of the television. But it wouldn't be good to let Hildy know that. She didn't want her mother-in-law to think this was a permanent arrangement. Eliza would happily resign as assistant as soon as Hildy had the use of her arm again.

"Well," she heard a woman's voice say.

Eliza looked up from her ingredient list to see Livia standing in her way.

And behind her, David.

Eliza felt sick.

"I heard you were back. How are you?" Livia smiled and kissed Eliza on the cheek. "I love your hair." Livia ran a hand through the ends of her own. "Short hair looks so much better on women over thirty."

Eliza's eyes flicked toward David. She caught him looking back before he quickly glanced away.

"So what are you doing?" Livia asked. She laughed as she surveyed Eliza's costume. "I know what you're doing tonight —I saw it on the schedule—but I mean in general. If you're free, we should get together some time next week. Have coffee. Catch up."

Eliza felt completely, utterly confused. By the entire situation. Was David back with Livia? Why was Livia still trying to be her friend?

Eliza stumbled over her words. "I...I have to get this shopping done." She held up the recipe sheet. "I'm...I've got to go."

"All right, but I really am going to call you," Livia said. "I think I still have your number." She turned to David. "Or you can give it to me."

His face turned as red as the maples. Eliza was happy to see it. At least he had the decency to be ashamed, or if not ashamed, at least embarrassed.

Once again, he hadn't said a word. Eliza felt a perverse pleasure in forcing him to answer her now.

"How are you, David?"

He nodded.

"I thought this was Ted's store."

"David supervises all the locations," Livia informed her.

"Uh-huh." Eliza felt her strength returning with every

moment that went by. She looked directly at David, forcing him to see her. She wondered if her own face was red. If so, it was with anger, not embarrassment.

"I enjoyed our chat the other morning," she said.

"When was that?" Livia asked.

Eliza ignored her. "It was nice to catch up," she told David. "Find out what we've both been doing the past few months."

Now she turned to Livia. "But I can see you've been well—both of you. I have to go now, but it was great talking to you both. See you later."

"I'm going to come to one of Hildy's classes," Livia said as Eliza walked away.

"You do that," Eliza answered, not turning around. She'd spent every last bit of energy on that conversation, and had nothing left to spare.

She stood at the meat counter, waiting for them to bring Hildy's seafood, and felt her heart pounding as if she'd just climbed a mountain peak. She closed her eyes and tried to steady herself. She forced herself to breathe.

When she turned around, David was there. Alone. Now it was Eliza's turn to avoid looking him in the eye.

"She works for me," he said.

"Don't...say anything." She closed her eyes for a moment, then slowly opened them and gazed into David's. "I can't take it."

She clutched the packages to her chest and walked away from him. Wondered if he would follow, hoped to heaven he wouldn't.

"El...iza."

She kept on walking. If she turned now, he'd see her. Know the effect he had.

Eliza waited until she reached the end of the store before changing course and heading for the produce. She glanced back quickly to make sure it was safe, then lifted the cuff of her sleeve to her face. She hadn't cried for any man since Jamey, and she wasn't going to start again. Especially not over something like this. Jamey was a true tragedy. David was...

Different.

And free to do whatever he liked.

Eliza felt drugged for the rest of the night. She smiled, because it didn't matter anymore. She didn't need a personality of her own. She was satisfied turning it over to Hildy, to the crowd of increasingly-tipsy men and women, to the store, to the Walshes—take it all.

But when Hildy and Eliza finally closed themselves back in the car, Eliza let the flood overtake her.

She sat in the front seat, sobbing against the steering wheel, while Hildy tried to console her and find out what was wrong.

It passed like a storm. Eliza cried in one great burst, then found herself laughing five minutes later.

"I'm such an idiot!" she told Hildy. "I'm the stupidest person I've ever met! I can't believe I ever thought..." She let just one more sob escape, then stifled it with her hand. "I ever thought he might love me."

"Was it David?" Hildy said gently. "Did you see him?"

"Didn't you?"

"No, honey."

Eliza wiped her nose on her sleeve. "He was there with *Livia*." She said it like she was ten—Katie Jackson would have been proud.

"I'm sorry, honey. I'm so sorry."

Eliza shook her head and started the car. "What a nightmare."

They drove several blocks before Hildy said, "Thank you for tonight. You were a great help. I couldn't have done it without you."

"It was just the shock, you know?"

"I know, honey."

And in the back of her mind she thought, *This is Jamey's mother. I'm crying over a man. I'm crying because a man hurt me. Boo-hoo—at least he didn't die. I'm such a fool. I'm a child. I was right to leave. I wish I'd never come back.*

"Lizzy?"

"What."

"It might not mean what you think."

"I don't care. And I'm sure it does, Hildy. That man has...needs, shall we say. I'm sure he didn't last a week before he took up with Livia again."

Hildy paused for a moment. Then, "It doesn't mean he never felt something for you."

"It doesn't matter," Eliza said. "I learned my lesson. Now I know. I won't ever be shocked again."

They rode the rest of the way in silence. Eliza helped Hildy out of the car and into the house. Then she went back to unload the equipment.

The night was cold—maybe colder than any since she had returned. She wore just a thin jacket over her white blouse, and it barely warmed her arms. She zipped it all the way to the collar, then leaned back against Hildy's car, studying the moon and the stars.

The way he had looked at her...

Not just shame, but maybe regret. Just a small touch of regret.

Maybe if he had known she'd be coming back, he would have waited the two months. Eliza doubted it, but she was willing to imagine. Just for this moment. Just for the sake of argument.

He would have waited and welcomed her back. Taken her into his arms and into his bed the very first night. Picked up where they'd left off, and made her fall even harder for him.

That was the problem, Eliza thought. The inevitable *what if* of that fantasy of hers. She might not have known—not for a long time. She might have come back to him and believed he was the right second man for her. She would have lied to herself—let him lie to her. When all along she was dispos- able. *"We can do this as long as we want."* And when he didn't want her anymore, there she would be, that much deeper in, that much further up the cliff. No safety, just her foolish belief that he would hold her, no matter what.

And that's when he'd cut the rope.

32

"What do you want to do for your birthday?" Eliza asked.

"Saw this cast off," Hildy answered.

"Besides that. Should I throw you a party?"

"And invite who?" Hildy said.

"I don't know, Frank Sawyer maybe..."

Hildy scowled. She'd been doing that a lot more lately. Eliza knew the woman was on her last nerve, having to be dependent for so long. It didn't suit Hildy's personality. But there wasn't much they could do about it. At her appointment the day before, the doctor confirmed it would be at least four more weeks before he could take the cast off.

Even after that, Hildy would still need about a month of rehab before the doctor would sign off on her driving. Hildy took the news hard.

"I'm not an old lady!" she'd complained to Eliza on the

way home. "But I feel like one with you having to take me everywhere."

"Just pretend you're rich," Eliza said. "It has nothing to do with your age. I thought fancy New Yorkers have drivers take them everywhere."

"Not in a piece of crap car," Hildy pointed out. She'd gotten it back from the shop, finally, and both she and Eliza agreed they preferred the rental car. Even with the rear damage fixed, the frame made strange, creaking noises, and seemed ready to fall apart any minute.

Now Eliza did her best to cheer up her mother-in-law.

"Let's have a party where everyone has to eat with one arm tied behind their backs—and it has to be their good arm. Then we'll serve Chinese food and make everyone eat with chopsticks."

Hildy cracked the slightest of smiles.

"I think it'll be good for you to see people spilling food all over their chests," Eliza said. "Then we can criticize their table manners."

"Just a quiet dinner at home, Lizzy. It's just another birthday."

"It's your seventieth birthday, and you and I have had enough quiet dinners at home to last us forever. I'm throwing you a little party, so you might as well be happy about it."

"Can I consult on the guest list?" Hildy asked.

"Yes, as long as no one's last name begins with W."

· · ·

Eliza didn't recognize the phone number displayed on her screen.

"Hello?"

"Hi, Lizzy, it's Livia."

Lizzy?

"Let's grab coffee this morning. I just finished my meeting early, and I don't have to be across town until ten. You're on my way—I'm driving toward you right now. So get dressed and I'll be there in ten minutes. See you!"

She hung up before Eliza could slip in a word.

Eliza stared at her silent phone.

"Who was that?"

"Livia Keane."

Hildy made a face. "What did *she* want?"

"To be best friends, apparently. She's picking me up for coffee."

"When?"

"Right now."

"You're not going, are you?"

It was a reasonable question. Eliza had absolutely no interest in being Livia's friend, and in fact, found the woman repulsive.

"No," Eliza said. "You're right. I'm not going. I'd rather clean out your basement."

"Good," Hildy said, "it needs it."

Eliza carried their breakfast dishes to the sink.

"You know why she wants to, don't you?" Hildy asked.

"No idea."

"Keep your friends close and your enemies closer."

"I'm not her enemy," Eliza said. "I just don't like her."

The doorbell rang. Daisy barked as if burglars had just broken in.

"There's something fishy," Hildy said as Eliza headed down the stairs.

"Maybe so," Eliza said, "but we'll never know. I'm sending her away."

Eliza replayed the whole scenario in her head afterward, trying to understand how it happened.

It was because Livia was so *disarming*.

"I wish I could dress like that," Livia said, embracing Eliza and pressing a cool cheek against hers. "You always look so comfortable. I have to wear these." She tugged up the hem of her slim black pants and showed Eliza the chunky high heel of her boot. "You probably never had to deal with corporate life. I love the clothes sometimes, but sometimes I'd rather leave the house in sweats and a big shirt and tell people, 'This is what you get,' like you do. So," she asked, "are you ready?"

"Uh...no, actually. I have some work around here that I need to do for Hildy."

"No! Come on," Livia said, "I'm dying for a girls' date. I've just been meeting with four fat farmers—hm, that's a nice slogan—and I'm sure the minute I left they all grabbed their crotches and spit out their *chaw*. I need girl energy—female energy. And four shots of espresso. Come on, Lizzy, there's a little café in the village, no one will see you. You don't even have to comb your hair. Let's go right *now*."

In the coffee shop, Livia paid for Eliza's drink, waving

away any objection. "I'm sure I make five times what you do," she said with a friendly laugh. "You go ahead and sit down."

Eliza watched while Livia placed their order, complimenting the barista on her hair. "Is that naturally curly? Ugh. You know we straight-haired girls hate you." Livia laughed. "But then you probably hate us, too." When the barista agreed, Livia stuffed an extra large tip in her jar. Then she carried the two to-go cups to the table.

Livia pulled the lid off her own, closed her eyes and drank deeply. While Eliza watched the performance. It really was a performance—all of it, Eliza thought. From the costumes Livia wore—today it was black wool pants, black boots, a black knit turtleneck, and a hip-length red wool jacket—to the way she made sure her voice carried throughout a room. No wonder men like Ted and David noticed her. It would be impossible not to.

"So, are you working on something?" Livia asked her.

"Uh, sort of. I'm always basically working."

"Me, too," she said, sighing. "I live and breathe the job. That's why I need to grab these times whenever I can." She reached over and squeezed Eliza's hand. "I need this, don't you?"

Like a daily blow to the head.

"So, how did that class go the other night?" Livia asked. "It looked like a nice turnout."

"Oh, yeah, it was." Eliza's stomach tightened. She hoped Livia wouldn't say any more about that night.

"Ted is very happy, you know," she went on. "Those classes have been a success. Tell Hildy she's very popular.

Ted is always looking at the numbers."

Eliza nodded. She wasn't sure how to respond.

"So," Livia began again. "Let's just clear the air."

Oh, please, Eliza thought, *let's not.*

"I know about you and David. He told me all about it."

Eliza could feel the color drain from her face.

"Those Walsh boys are..." Livia drew in a deep breath and shivered as if shaking off her feathers. "Well, I think we both know. The point is, men move on, don't they? Much more easily than women, I think. I've always wondered about that: Is it because they're externally-driven, and we're internal? We take them into our bodies, but for them it's..." She shrugged. "Maybe more mechanical. I think it's harder on us emotionally, don't you?"

Eliza just stared at her, trying to keep her face as expressionless as possible.

"David is so..." Livia looked off to the side. "What's the word?"

Eliza didn't help her.

"*Physical*. I think that's it," Livia said. "He lives very much in his body."

From that point forward, Eliza hardly heard anything else that she said. She felt a million miles removed, staring down from above at the scene of her and that horrible woman. It was like finding herself trapped somewhere without any means of escape, and all she could do was hope she would wake up soon and know it had all been a dream.

Livia glanced at her slim gold watch. "Oh! I have to go." She had ordered the largest size coffee they had, and now threw away half of it untouched. "Thank you *so* much for coming out with me. I feel so much better already."

Eliza, on the other hand, felt as if she'd been pushed off a mountainside and landed on her back a thousand feet below. And still had to get up and drag herself out of the canyon even though every single bone in her body was broken.

"Thanks, doll," Livia said as she dropped her off. "You have saved my morning."

Eliza drifted back into the house, feeling that the whole conversation had been unreal.

When she rose up the stairs she found her mother-in-law waiting for a report.

"So, did she sleep with him?" Hildy asked.

"Which one?"

33

"Happy Birthday, Hildy," Frank Sawyer said. He handed her a cellophane-wrapped bouquet of flowers with the Walsh's Fine Foods sticker still on them. "Hope you like roses."

"Roses, Hildy, isn't that nice?" Eliza said, giving Frank an approving nod.

"How old are you?" Hildy asked him.

"Seventy-five."

"How do you like it?"

"Okay so far," he said.

"Do you feel old?"

"Older than you," he said.

Satisfied, Hildy told him, "Go ahead and stick around."

There were only six other guests in the living room: all three Jacksons; a woman named Irene, whom Hildy knew from the fabric store; and the neighbors from across the street, Mr. and Mrs. Nolan. Mr. Nolan drove a car that leaked oil in their driveway—an eyesore that Hildy always resented—but she'd forgiven him for the sake of the party and now treated both of them very cordially.

"This is Frank Sawyer," she told them. "He runs the *Independent*."

"The independent what?" Mr. Nolan, who appeared to be in sixties, asked Frank.

"*Careyville Independent*," Frank told him. "You read it, I suppose?"

"Never miss it," Mr. Nolan answered.

"Good," Frank said. "That makes one."

Katie seemed bored. Eliza went over to her, tugged on her sleeve, and motioned her into the kitchen.

"Do you know how to decorate a cake?" Eliza asked.

"Uh-huh, I'm really good at it."

"Good, because I'm horrible," Eliza said. "I bought all these supplies, but I have no idea how to use them." She showed Katie her collection of sparkles, candles, and tubes of colored frosting. "Can you do something really nice for Hildy? I think she'd really like that."

Katie tackled the assignment with fervor. "Did you make this cake?"

"I did," Eliza confessed.

"It looks good."

"Thank you. I hope it is."

Eliza heard the doorbell ring again. She wasn't expecting anyone else.

"Can you take over?" she asked Katie. "I trust you. Make it great."

"I will," Katie told her, then set seriously about her task.

Eliza sent Hildy an inquiring look on her way toward the stairs. Hildy shrugged and went back to talking to Frank. Eliza liked that the two of them had something to say to each other. She hoped they might say something together more often.

She opened the door. To be greeted by a bouquet of roses twice as big as Frank's.

Ted shifted the roses aside, drew Eliza in by the waist, and kissed her on the cheek. "Remember me?" He left his hand on her hip. She pointedly removed it.

"Are those for Hildy?"

"Of course," he said. "Who else?"

"Did she invite you?"

"Not exactly," he said, "but word travels. And since she's my favorite lady over the age of thirty-one, I thought I'd swing by and wish her Happy Birthday."

Eliza glared at him suspiciously.

"What?" he asked. "Didn't you miss me?"

"Not particularly."

"Heard my brother dumped you."

"*Ted.*" She made a move to push him back outside the door, but he chuckled and swept her into one arm again.

"Don't be so sensitive, beautiful. We all make mistakes. He made a big one. But now I'm here and it wouldn't hurt you to be friendly. We're still friends, aren't we?"

Hildy appeared at the top of the stairs. "Teddy!"

"Hello, Mrs. Shepherd," he said, doing his best imitation of a young man in a 1950s sitcom. "I heard you turned fifty today."

"I'm not afraid of my age," Hildy said.

"Okay, then, sixty," Ted said, "but that's my final guess." He flashed a smile at Eliza as he mounted the stairs.

Frank Sawyer's eyebrows nearly disappeared into his hairline. Eliza shook her head in warning. If he thought he was going to pester her about Ted later, ask her questions, wheedle some sort of juicy gossip out of her, he was dead wrong. Eliza returned to the kitchen to check on her cake decorator's progress.

"Katie! That looks fantastic!"

The girl stepped back and admired her own creation. "You like it? I put the flowers on the sides and on the top so people would get two of them on each slice."

"I can't believe it," Eliza said. "You're really good."

Carolyn Jackson came into the kitchen. "Beautiful!" she told her daughter, but she wasn't really there for that.

"What's he doing here?" she mumbled to Eliza from the side of her mouth. They could hear Ted and Will in the other room, laughing about something. "Will's thrilled—he has a little playmate. But did you invite him?"

"No," Eliza said emphatically.

"Mom, can you do that rose thing you did on the cupcakes?" Katie asked. "I can't get it right."

"Sure." Carolyn barely looked at what she was doing while she still talked to Eliza. Yet four perfect frosting roses quickly bloomed beneath her hand.

"So he just showed up?"

"Yes."

"How did he know?"

"No idea," Eliza said.

"Do you think Hildy invited him?"

"I really don't think she would," Eliza said. "She knew I wouldn't like it."

"Then what do you think he's here for?" Carolyn asked.

Eliza shook her head and glanced at Katie.

"Katie, honey," Carolyn said, "can you go tell Dad I need his cell phone? I think I left mine at home."

Katie left on her errand, and Carolyn leaned in. "Okay, so what do you think?"

"He said he heard David dumped me."

Carolyn huffed in outrage. Eliza appreciated that.

"He said I should be friendly," Eliza said.

"Friendly," Carolyn said. "Right."

Katie returned with the cell phone, which Carolyn pushed into her pocket on top of her own.

"Dad wants to know if there's any beer."

"I'm sure he does," Carolyn said.

Katie stood there, waiting for an answer.

"Yes," Eliza said, "there's beer." She opened the refrigerator to retrieve one.

"Mr. Walsh wants one, too."

Eliza and Carolyn exchanged a glance.

"So I guess he's staying," Eliza said.

"Just one beer," Carolyn told her. "That's all. Then you send him on his way."

"You act like I want him to stick around."

"No, but I've known Teddy a long time."

• • •

THE NOLANS LEFT FIRST, then Irene, and then Frank.

"Got an issue to get out," he told Hildy. "But best wishes to you—I mean it."

Hildy gave him a more relaxed smile than she'd offered all evening. "Thanks, Frank. You're not so bad. Lizzy says nice things about you."

"All true, I'm afraid," Frank said. "And I can say the same about you."

They parted with a handshake, which Eliza viewed as a success. Maybe she'd find Hildy a different dinner companion yet.

"Thanks, Eliza," Carolyn said. "Mrs. Shepherd, happy, happy birthday."

"Thanks, sweetie, you're a good girl," Hildy answered, giving Carolyn a hug and a kiss on the cheek. "And Willy, you're as handsome as ever."

"Hear that?" he said to Carolyn.

"I never said you weren't handsome," she answered. "Just a slob."

"And Katie!" Hildy said, holding the girl's face in her one good hand. "What a wonder with that cake. Thank you."

"You're welcome, Mrs. Shepherd. Thanks for inviting me. It was fun."

Eliza shot Carolyn a look showing she was impressed.

"Manners," Carolyn whispered. "We like them." She jerked her head toward the one remaining guest on the couch. "What are you going to do about him?"

"Call a taxi," Eliza muttered. Ted was six beers down, and showed it.

"Sorry," Carolyn said as Eliza walked them out. "He and

Will should never get together."

The two men had matched each other drink for drink, although Will seemed to be holding his better.

"He could have done it on his own," Eliza said. "I've seen him before." She thought of his behavior at the opening of the Monarch store. At the time he'd claimed he was nervous being around her. She wondered if he'd use that excuse again.

"Thanks for coming," Eliza told the Jacksons. "And Katie, next time I need a cake decorator, you're hired."

"What do you say?" Carolyn asked her.

"Thank you."

"Thank *you*," Eliza said, then she mouthed to Carolyn, "Manners."

She ascended the stairs again, already pulling out her phone. She searched for Careyville taxis, and found two different companies.

"You'll drive Teddy home, won't you?" Hildy asked.

Eliza pointed to the phone she held against her ear. "Already calling."

"Come on, Lizzy," Ted said. "Take me home."

"Hi, can you come pick someone up?" She gave the dispatcher their address. "What's your address, Ted?" He shook his head. "We'll give it to the driver when he gets here," Eliza told the dispatcher. Then she ended the call and looked at the two droopy people on the couch.

"Tired?" she asked her mother-in-law.

"Whipped," Hildy said.

"Not me," Ted said.

"Good, then you won't have any trouble getting down the

stairs. Let's go. The taxi'll be here in ten minutes."

Hildy gave Eliza a significant look, but Eliza shook her head. "I'm done for the evening," she said. "I need to clean up, then we're going to bed."

She went to the couch and held out her hand for Ted. He slapped his hand into hers. She pulled to help him stand up. Then he crashed into her and held onto her by the hips.

"How come David?" he mumbled. "How come not me?"

Eliza ignored the question and guided him toward the stairs.

He leaned against the banister as he slowly made his way down. "You're not going to answer?" he asked her. "Why? Aren't we friends?"

"No," Eliza said.

"Are you mad at me?"

"No."

Eliza opened the door and waited for him outside. The night was cold. She wasn't wearing a jacket.

Ted slipped his arm around her waist once more and leaned in to whisper in her ear. "I could have made you happy. You should have picked me."

Eliza extricated herself. She didn't bother answering.

"Was it Livia?" Ted asked. "Is that what made you mad?"

"I'm not mad."

"Yes, you are," Ted said. "Look at you. But you're still so beautiful."

The taxi pulled up and sat idling in the street.

"See you, Ted," Eliza said. "Thanks for bringing Hildy flowers."

Ted opened the back door of the taxi, then paused with

his arm draped over it. "You know, Jamey would have said to pick me."

"Go home, Ted." Eliza turned and stalked back to the house. And locked the door behind her.

She rose wearily up the stairs.

"Well, that was a nice party," Hildy told her. "Thanks for throwing it. Did you have fun?"

"Mostly," Eliza answered.

"What did you think about Teddy?"

"I think he plays dirty."

"What's that mean?"

Eliza didn't bother telling her what he'd said about Jamey. "He thinks David still cares whether he wins," she said instead. "Or else he thinks they're swapping girlfriends again."

Hildy patted the couch beside her. Eliza sighed and went to sit down. She rested her head against her mother-in-law's shoulder.

"Thanks for the party," Hildy said again.

"Thanks for being my favorite mother-in-law." Eliza kissed her on the cheek.

"Jamey married the right girl," Hildy told her. "I knew it the minute he brought you home."

"How did you know?" Eliza smiled at the memory of their meeting.

"You didn't put on airs," Hildy said. "You didn't pretend you were anything you weren't. You were a nice, polite girl. And you treated me with respect."

"I hope you still feel that way."

"That you're a nice, polite girl? The best," Hildy said. She patted Eliza's thigh, then pushed herself to her feet. She held up her evil cast.

"You think this means this is how the year is going to go?"

Hildy had a superstition about beginnings. She thought however she began the new year and her birthday—really any major holiday—that was how the rest of the year would unfold.

"Let's see," Eliza said. "You had a nice night with friends, Frank Sawyer brought you roses, you ate cake using a *fork* that you held in your wrong hand—"

"I am getting better at that."

"Yes, you are," Eliza said. "You have me, and I love you. You're back in your old house, and you love that. Daisy didn't bite a single person tonight—" Although Eliza wouldn't have minded if she'd bitten Ted. "—and you're generally happy, I think, aren't you?"

"Generally," Hildy agreed, "yes."

"So. The stupid cast is coming off soon, and this will all be behind us. And who knows? Maybe we'll hit the lottery and you can buy a new car. I think that would be worth looking forward to in your new birthday year."

"Seventy years old," Hildy said, shaking her head. "Can you believe it?"

"I will tell you this," Eliza said. "Ted did say one good thing tonight."

"What's that?"

"He told me his mother is only sixty, but you look ten years younger than she does."

"Ha!" Hildy answered. "That woman is sixty-three if she's

a day. Does she think people don't remember how much older they are than her?" Hildy shook her head. "But that was nice of him to say."

Eliza shrugged.

"You still don't like him, do you?" Hildy asked.

"Not much."

"Still like Davey better?"

"Good night, Hildy."

"Want to know my birthday wish for you?"

"No. Good night."

"I'd like to see you happy."

"I'm ecstatic, Hildy, good night."

Hildy smiled and turned down the hall. Eliza sank back into the couch.

Jamey would have said to pick me.

You bastard, what a low blow.

And Jamey has no say in this, Eliza thought. Jamey abandoned his post.

Jamey, Teddy, Davey—all abandoned their posts.

She patted the couch and called Daisy up beside her. The dog had been sleeping on one of the chairs, but now leapt up to Eliza's lap.

"What do you think, Daze, is this the start of a good year? At least for Hildy?"

"Yes," Eliza answered for the dog.

"Easy street from here on out? No more injuries or crises?"

Daisy licked her hand. Eliza thought later if she'd interpreted that as a yes, the dog definitely would have been wrong.

34

Eliza looked over her article for *Adventure Girl* one last time. She thought of Katie Jackson and the other girls in her group. Would they like it? Would they feel inspired?

GET THE CONFIDENCE HABIT—NOW!

You feel like such a geek sometimes—who doesn't? You're still torturing yourself over the stupid thing you said to that cute guy a few days ago. Or maybe you're dreading that speech you have to give in World Events. Stop suffering! The first step to being more confident is acting like you already are. Who says only Hollywood actresses get the cool parts? You can start acting like the bold, confident heroine of your own life story right now.

Things to practice alone:

1. Nothing spells confidence like looking people straight in the eye. If you're not used to it, it's hard! The good news is it's something you can learn with just a little practice. Start by holding up a mirror and looking yourself in the eye. Okay so far? Now start talking. Try reciting the alphabet. You can't look away until you get to Z. Did you do it? Then move on to something harder, like holding an imaginary conversation with—gulp—that cutie you've been dreaming about. Pretend you're looking him in the eye. Don't break your gaze!

2. Do you walk around with your arms crossed, back hunched, trying to hide from the world? Would a true Adventure Girl do that? Have some backbone—a straight one, that is. Pretend you're completely comfortable wherever you are. It takes practice! Start by changing how you stand around your pals. Instead of leaning against a wall or biting your nails or twirling your hair in your fingers, stand tall with your arms hanging free. Practice walking that way, too. It might feel awkward at first, but soon you'll start to feel as comfortable and confident as you look.

Eliza read through the rest of the piece. It wasn't bad, for a quick morning's work. She attached it to an e-mail to the editor of the magazine, and shut the lid to her laptop.

It was after eleven o'clock. Safe enough. The sun had burned off the morning freeze, and Eliza was anxious to feel fresh air on her face. She changed into long johns, water-resistant pants, hiking shoes, and her fleece coat, then summoned the dog.

Daisy had adapted easily to the new schedule: a quick backyard session early in the morning to relieve herself, then breakfast and a nap and sentry duty at the windows, then later, just before lunchtime, the walk.

Eliza knew she was a hypocrite. Telling girls to be confident, be bold, talk to that cute guy—when she'd done everything in her power to avoid running into David since

October . But preteen girls wouldn't understand. The rules were different when you were older.

Eliza was happy she'd worn the water-resistant pants—something she'd bought long ago for cross-country skiing. Even though there hadn't been fresh snow for several days, there were still pockets of it that she had to slush through.

As she let Daisy drag her up the hill, Eliza checked off the list in her head: article on simplifying your life for the spring cleaning issue of the over-50 women's magazine; gear review for *Outdoor Adventure*; three chapters of the book about Jamey.

It was that last one that left a knot in her stomach.

"Eliza! How are you?"

Eliza hadn't spoken to her book editor for over six months.

"How's the research going?" Christy asked her.

"It's great. It's really coming along." Eliza hated lying to people, but sometimes she had to make exceptions.

"I'd really love to see some of it," Christy said. Then she dropped the fake cheerfulness and got right down to business. "It would be good if I had something to show the publishing director by the beginning of December. Are we still on track for a March deadline?"

"Pretty close," Eliza told her, her mouth dry. "How many chapters do you need now?"

"Three would be good. Five would be even better."

"Okay, well I'm glad you called," Eliza lied. "I'll put together what I have and send it you in a few weeks."

"Wonderful," Christy said. "Everything okay there? How do you like living in my part of the world?"

"Cold, windy, wet—you people are hardy up here."

"Said the woman who once spent five weeks in a tent in Alaska. Hope that's showing up somewhere in the book."

"You'll have to wait and see," Eliza said, pressing her hand to her heart. The organ was pumping hard enough that she wondered whether Christy could hear it through the phone. "Well, back to work," she said. "Thanks for calling."

Then she'd hung up and vented with a shout. Daisy looked up in alarm. Hildy, who'd been listening to the conversation, wasn't rattled.

"How far are you?"

"Chapter one," Eliza answered. "Maybe bits of chapter two."

"Hmm."

"Yeah."

Eliza stared out the window at the blustery sky. "Guess that book isn't going to write itself."

"Probably not," Hildy said.

Eliza got up from the table and went into her bedroom. She came back with a thin manila folder—too thin. She'd barely collected any material.

"Want my advice?" Hildy asked.

Eliza blew out a breath. "Sure."

"Think about whether you really want to write this book."

"That's easy," Eliza said. "I don't. Obviously, since I haven't."

"Well, then..."

"Well, then, what?" Eliza asked. "They've already paid me for it."

"Just the down payment," Hildy reminded her. "You could always pay it back."

Considering that Eliza had set a goal for herself to pitch three articles a week to all the various magazines she had ever worked for, hoping to boost her income so she could afford all the plane tickets her new bicoastal life would require, paying back a book advance didn't make much economic sense.

"I'll write it," Eliza said. "It's good that she called. I needed the kick."

Daisy sniffed at a dead patch of grass poking out of the snow. Eliza didn't try to rush her. Three chapters in the next two or three weeks—just the thought of it made her ill.

Where had the time gone? If she thought back, month to month, she could probably reconstruct it. But the real loss had been not working on it over the summer. She had all that time to herself when she was in Henderson, and she had wasted it thinking about David.

Then there was Hildy's accident, and since then Eliza felt she was always on duty. Even with Hildy's cast off now, her arm was still weak, and Eliza still had to act as driver, cook, maid, and teaching assistant.

They had another class that night: Easy Thanksgiving Side Dishes. Roasted Brussels sprouts, sweet potato chips and cranberry salsa, sage scones. Since most of them involved baking rather than something Hildy could demonstrate on a plug-in burner, she and Eliza would be preparing the food ahead of time and reheating it in the Walsh's oven.

There had been three classes since Eliza ran into David and Livia, and she'd never seen them again. Each time she rolled Hildy's cart into the store, Eliza's throat clenched. She rehearsed what she might say, and usually came up with nothing: She'd say nothing. Let David try to initiate a conversation for once. She was tired of being the only one fumbling all the time.

She dreaded running into Livia even more than him. Ever since their coffee date, Eliza couldn't help replaying the highlights: *We're more internal. We take them into our bodies. David is so...physical.* For him to take her back after she'd slept with his brother—what kind of standards did he have? And how was it possible Eliza hadn't met them?

That's what troubled her most, she thought: the fact that he could have chosen that pretentious, preening, cheating woman over Eliza.

The fact that he could have chosen anyone over her at all.

Eliza knew what she was doing, knew she shouldn't, pretended she wasn't. But just thinking about him right then made her feel suddenly angry again. Angry enough to really want to steep in it.

It was like feeling sore after a long day of climbing or hiking, and massaging her fingers deep into her most painful spots. It hurt, but in a delicious sort of way. In part, she thought, because she knew where that hurt came from, and felt satisfied that she'd earned it.

"Come on, Daisy. Let's go look at the house."

They stood down the path from it, close enough to see his gate, far enough away that she could escape if she saw anyone around. What she really wanted to do was look into his garage. See if Livia's black Lexus was there. Really feel disgusted and angry.

Did he arrange his schedule for her the way he had with Eliza? Work from home some days so he could make love to her in between phone calls? He was so *physical*, he must have. So *external, mechanical, men move on, don't they?*

"Eliza?"

They even took Daisy by surprise. She twisted around and launched against Bear her full-throated assault.

Eliza was grateful to have something to do. "Daisy! Stop it!" She knelt down beside Hildy's dog and kept her eyes on David's shoes. They were wetter than hers were, soaked from the edges almost to the top. The bottom of his sweats were wet, too. He must have run through snow at some point. Maybe that's how he'd sneaked up on her.

She had to get out of there, tried to think of an elegant way to do it, couldn't. "Sorry to bother you," she mumbled, and pulled the barking, lunging dog back up the path.

"How are you?" David asked.

"Fine. Daisy! That's enough!"

Nothing spells confidence like looking people straight in the eye. If you're not used to it, it's hard!

Eliza tried to walk fast without looking like she was running away. *Pretend you're completely comfortable wherever you are. It takes practice!* She dragged Daisy back up the hill.

When they were far enough away, Eliza paused to catch her breath.

Stupid, stupid, stupid.

She looked back to make sure he hadn't followed.

But of course he hadn't, she thought. He'd simply caught

her in that pathetic act of spying, and was probably laughing to himself about it right now.

Laughing with Livia.

"Is she still hanging around?"

"It's not as if I encourage her."

"Women are more emotional. We take you men into our bodies..."

"Like this?"

"Just like that."

Eliza trudged on against the wind.

35

"This doesn't sound like you," Frank Sawyer said, looking up from the two-paged printout he'd just finished reading.

"In what way?" Eliza asked, biting the edge of a fingernail.

"You're so...stuck up," Frank said. "No...formal. Like you don't know us and we don't know you."

Eliza sighed and sank back against his couch. "Garbage, huh?"

"Not garbage, just not...golden."

Sitting wasn't going to do it. Eliza needed to pace. Needed to work off the nervous energy from hearing someone tell her the truth to her face.

"I'm running out of ideas, Frank."

"Take a break. You're burned out. I told you."

"But the newspapers expect something from me every two weeks."

"So you're on hiatus. Have everyone print something saying, 'Eliza Shepherd is currently on vacation. Here are some of our favorites from the past,' or something like that."

Eliza stopped. "You could do that?"

"Sure, do it all the time. You think writers really go on vacation? They never do. Even when they're away, they're still in their heads. Don't you write all the time, in your brain?"

"Used to," Eliza said.

"Will again." Frank ripped her essay in half. "Not that you couldn't have fixed it," he said, seeing the brief horror on her face, "but I don't want you to. Write to your other papers. I'm telling you, they'll understand. We all know what 'vacation' is code for. Go off and fix yourself."

Eliza let out a very tense breath. And breathed in a more relaxed one. "Thank you, Frank. You really might be the best editor I've ever met."

The man shrugged. "Been around, that's all."

"That's not all," Eliza said, "but thanks. You're really wonderful."

Frank gave a little wince.

"What?" Eliza asked.

"Maybe not so wonderful. I should probably tell you something."

Eliza didn't have a good feeling. "Okay."

"I may have brought the stray in with me."

"What does that mean?" Eliza asked.

"Ted Walsh. At Hildy's party. He saw me buying flowers at his store, and I may have said too much. When I saw him walk in..."

"Oh..." Eliza nodded. "Okay. Mystery solved."

"Sorry," Frank said. "I know you wanted the other one."

So he did know, Eliza thought. She wondered where he'd heard it.

She gave him a weak smile. "Yeah. Well. That's life."

"You go take your break," Frank told her. "You'll get it back. Counting on you, golden girl."

"Bɪᴄᴏᴀsᴛᴀʟ, ʜᴜʜ?" Hildy said. "Sounds so continental."

Eliza served her another helping of sour cream mashed potatoes. On the Thanksgiving table in front of them was just one other dish: Hildy's famous homemade cinnamon rolls, made by Eliza this year, under her mother-in-law's close supervision. Hildy had tried to make them herself, but didn't have the strength in her arm yet to roll out the dough.

They'd decided not to make a turkey. Or any of the Easy Thanksgiving Side Dishes they'd taught to an enthusiastic class.

"What do you really want?" Hildy asked her as the two of them discussed their own menu.

"Really?" Eliza said. "In my heart of hearts? If no one was going to report me to the Thanksgiving police?"

So they'd settled on the two foods she always looked forward to the most.

We can do whatever we want.

She wondered if they went to his mother's for Thanksgiving. Livia wore some perfectly elegant outfit, Mrs. Walsh seated her beside her, Mrs. Walsh actually spoke to her, since

Livia was clearly a more appropriate choice for David than Eliza would be.

"Wives shouldn't kill their husbands."

"Sibylla, I couldn't agree more."

Or maybe Sue insisted Livia not be invited. She wouldn't tell her mother why, but she'd effectively have Livia banned from any family events.

Eliza always liked Sue.

"So how would it work?" Hildy asked. "We move back and forth all year?"

"Right," Eliza said. "We decide which months we want to spend here, which in Henderson. Then we trade off between our houses."

"Sounds like a lot of work."

"I'll do everything. You don't have to worry."

"I don't know, honey…"

"Well, you think about it," Eliza said. She got up to get them both refills on their wine. It had been so long since she'd had any, she already felt the effects after just one glass.

Which was why she wanted another. She decided she liked this feeling of numbness. Liked letting her brain have a holiday for a few hours. She didn't have to think of something to write. Didn't have to think of David, maybe, if she had a little more.

"I'm an old woman," Hildy said when Eliza returned from the kitchen. "I'm not sure I'm up to flitting here and there all during the year."

"It's just one day of travel," Eliza said. "Then you'd be back in your own bedroom, in whatever house we were visiting."

"Visiting," Hildy said. "That's the problem. I like my house here. You like your house. We'd both just be visiting."

"We'd get used to it, don't you think?" Eliza asked. "Maybe it would be strange the first few times."

"I don't know," Hildy said again.

Eliza took another sip of the dark red wine. "I don't know, either, Hildy," she admitted with a sigh. "I'm making it up as I go along."

"Here's to a Happy Thanksgiving," Hildy said, raising her glass. "Wonder what the new Thanksgiving year will bring?"

"Nothing but good things, I'm sure," Eliza answered.

The ice storm struck the next day.

It began around three o'clock. Eliza had just returned from the grocery store with ingredients for a pot of chili. After their mashed potato, cinnamon roll dinner the night before, Eliza wanted to get some real food into her mother-in-law's belly, not to mention into her own. So she'd make chili and a huge tossed salad, and feel like she'd done her job.

"There's a front coming in," Hildy told her when she came upstairs. "They just did a news bulletin."

"There's something coming in," Eliza agreed. "It feels very strange out there." The sky was iron gray and the air had an odd quality to it. Eliza had been anxious to get home into the shelter of the house.

When the storm broke, it brought rain instead of snow.

"That's not good," Hildy said. "It's going to freeze."

The news reports confirmed it: glaze ice on the roads within what seemed like only ten or fifteen minutes.

"How can that happen so fast?" Eliza asked.

"Because the roads are all frozen from that last snow," Hildy said. "Everything is. So the rain hits it and freezes right away."

The news showed pictures of the freeways where cars had slid into each other or off the road. They showed pictures of post-Thanksgiving shoppers slipping and sliding on icy sidewalks.

"I've done that," Hildy observed as they watched a middle-aged woman on the TV fall hard onto her back. "Hurts like hell."

Eliza watched the reports in fascination and horror. "How do you people live like this?"

"You get used to it," Hildy said. "We don't like it, but what are you going to do?"

Move, Eliza thought, which was exactly what Jamey and his parents had done. To voluntarily come back to this...

"Better check our battery supply," Hildy said. "And candles. You never know."

"Never know what?"

"Rain hits the power lines, the lines freeze, the lines sometimes go down. Or tree branches break off and take the power lines with them."

Eliza jumped to her feet in search of candles.

She also found the three flashlights Hildy remembered having in the house, then asked if there was anything else.

"There's a generator downstairs, in the garage," Hildy told her. "Should be. Unless the last tenants took it."

Eliza looked at her blankly.

"A generator," Hildy repeated. "You know what that is."

"No...not really. I mean, it's something you use when your electricity goes out, right?"

"You never used one?"

"Never had to," Eliza said.

Within an hour, the lights went out.

Eliza shined the flashlight all along the walls of the garage, searching for the generator. She'd already been down there once, after Hildy described it, but hadn't found it then. Now she knew it was urgent. It wasn't just the lights that weren't working, it was everything electric—including the heater. The house was still warm now, but that wouldn't last if the power stayed off too long.

Eliza wasn't afraid of the cold. She'd slept in below-freezing conditions many times. Jamey liked waking up to find frost or snow on the tent—he said it made it seem like more of an adventure. Eliza preferred warm, sunny days, but she'd learned to adapt. She could put up with the cold for weeks at a time, knowing they'd always return to the sun.

But asking her 70-year-old mother-in-law to sleep in a freezing house overnight? With no hot water or hot food? Not if Eliza could help it. She continued searching, moving boxes and lawn equipment, but never found the generator.

"You're going to have to come down," Eliza said. "I'm sorry. If it's there and I'm just not seeing it..."

Hildy bundled herself in an extra coat and a blanket, and joined Eliza in the frozen garage. The space was never heated, so it gave them a taste of how the house might feel later in the night.

"You're right," Hildy said, "it's gone." There was no point in standing there cursing the former tenants. The two of them hurried back up the stairs.

Eliza ladled lukewarm chili into two bowls, glad she'd cooked it while she still had time. She and Hildy sat on the couch wrapped in blankets and quilts and ate what might be their last warm meal for a while.

The temperature in the house dropped faster than Eliza expected.

"Wish we had a fireplace," Hildy lamented. "We could burn pieces of furniture if we had to."

Eliza tucked the blankets and quilts around them again to keep any air from sneaking inside. Daisy lay burrowed between the two women. As long as no one moved, they had a warm cocoon for the moment.

It was around seven o'clock when the doorbell rang.

Eliza tucked Hildy and Daisy back in, picked up a flashlight, and quickly descended the stairs. Maybe it was a mercy call from one of the Jacksons, she thought. Maybe Carolyn had sent Will down to check on them. Maybe they had a fireplace, or surely a generator, and would take the three of them in for the night. Eliza couldn't believe she hadn't thought of it before. Somehow she'd thought of them as so isolated, when she should have asked for help hours ago. Yes, everyone was dealing with the same storm and the same outage, but not everyone lived in an old, unequipped house, or had a 70-year-old to look after.

Eliza yanked open the door. And shined her flashlight into David's face.

Too stunned to speak, she just stood there. He had to move her hand to keep from being blinded.

"I came to see if you're all right," he said. "Your lights are still out."

"The...power..." Eliza's lips didn't work. She hoped he would think it was because of the cold.

"My house has power," David said. "I came to get you. You and Hildy can come back with me if you want."

Eliza looked past him to where the rain pounded the driveway. David's car sat there idling.

Her mouth still wasn't responding. "You...have heat?"

"Heat, light, everything. Eliza, are you coming or not?"

"Yes. Yes. Coming." She still felt awkward and slow. But she remembered to ask about Daisy.

"Yes, her, too, now hurry," David said. "Before we all freeze."

Eliza watched him return to his car, unable to tear herself away from the door. He was there—how was that possible? And why? She could stand there all night and never know, or she could take him up on his offer. For Hildy's sake, she hurried back up the stairs and told her to get her toothbrush and whatever else she needed, they were leaving.

When they closed themselves into David's car, the warmth hit Eliza like she'd landed on a beach.

"This will take a while," David said. "The streets are bad."

Eliza still didn't know what to say.

"Nice place," Hildy said, appraising the living room. As advertised, David's house was warm and full of light. Eliza felt nervous, being there again, but Hildy's dog immediately broke the tension.

"Daisy! No!" She ripped the leash out of Eliza's hand and raced toward Bear. The Labrador wagged his tail and leapt while Daisy bared her teeth at him and barked.

Eliza reached for Daisy's collar and prepared to pull them apart, but then miraculously, the terrier settled down. She scratched her paws against Bear's dog bed, circled once, and plopped down on top. Bear lowered himself to the nearby rug and watched Daisy from between his front paws.

Eliza waited another moment, just to be sure, then unclipped Daisy's leash. "Okay, then," she said, straightening back up, hoping the matter had been settled once and for all.

Hildy was still inspecting the living room. "I like this place," she told David.

"Thank you, I do, too."

"So you've always lived here alone?" she asked, glancing meaningfully at Eliza.

Eliza glared at her in return.

"Except when it was my parents' house," David said. "Then we all lived here together."

"I never saw it," Hildy said. "Never got invited."

Eliza hoped she wasn't going to air out that grievance.

"I changed some things," David said. "This is different than how they had it."

"Bet your way is better," Hildy said.

"Better for me," David said. "Would you like a tour?"

Hildy grinned. "What do you think?"

Eliza waited in the living room for the two of them to return. She could hear them upstairs, Hildy laughing.

Would you like a tour?

David had said the same thing to Eliza.

Maybe he offered every woman a tour, she thought, young or old, and some tours ended the way theirs had. In bed, a brief passionate affair, then *Next tour is on Friday, ladies, see you then.*

Eliza shook her head. She didn't want to think about him that way. Not after what he'd done to come for them that night.

She saw what he had to go through to rescue them: driving rain; slick, icy streets; broken tree branches tangled in the road; detours around downed power lines. It had taken them nearly an hour to drive what normally took ten minutes.

David could easily have stayed in his nice, warm, cozy house, done some work, and gone to sleep. Instead he'd ventured out in the storm to help them.

That had to count for something.

A lot, actually, Eliza thought.

"You don't have to do this," Eliza told David as she helped him change the sheets on his bed. She forced herself not to think about who had been in those sheets last. "We can sleep downstairs on the couches," she said. "You've already done enough."

"I don't have a guest room, so it's my own fault," he said.

"No, really, David—"

"Eliza. It's fine."

The two of them looked at each other over the top of his bed.

"Thank you," Eliza said.

"You're welcome. Have you two eaten?"

"A while ago," Eliza said. "And it wasn't great."

"Would you like me to cook you something?"

"Oh, David, that would be... Yes. Thank you."

"You don't have to keep thanking me."

"I think I do," Eliza said. "We could have managed, but it would have been a very miserable night. I really appreciate what you've done. For Hildy especially."

"I told you, I always liked Mrs. Shepherd."

"I guarantee she likes you back."

David looked at Eliza with what she thought later had been a sad sort of smile. "So. Dinner," he said. "Let's go see what I have."

"You're a good cook," Hildy told David when they had finished eating his reheated chicken gumbo. She accepted a refill on her wine, and the three of them now sat in the living room.

"A lot of men think tearing the lid off a microwave dinner is cooking," Hildy said. "Your brother thinks that."

"Hildy..." Eliza warned.

"What? He knows he has a brother."

"You're right," David said. "Ted doesn't cook."

"It's too bad, because look how good you are," Hildy said. "Did Sibylla teach you that?"

David laughed. "Do you really think my mother approves of men cooking?"

Hildy shrugged. "I taught my Jamey to cook, didn't I, Lizzy? Even at eighteen he knew how to make his three basic meals."

"Spaghetti," Eliza recited, "meatloaf, and tuna noodle casserole."

"That's right," his mother said. "And that impressed you, didn't it?"

"It did," Eliza confirmed.

"And now David's impressed you, too."

Eliza shot her mother-in-law a deadly look, which the woman ignored.

"So where'd you learn?" Hildy asked.

"My uncle Herbert," David said. "He cooked for some restaurants in Syracuse before he opened his own. He let me help him on the weekends."

Eliza shook her head and smiled.

"What?" he asked.

"I feel like I hardly know anything about you."

"Well, whose fault is that?" Hildy said. "All you have to do is ask."

Eliza met David's gaze, then offered him a small shrug. "Oh, well."

He nodded. Eliza could see they both knew that time was past.

She quickly changed the subject.

"So, how long until you think they'll restore power?" she asked.

"A day or two," David said.

"Remember that ice storm in '98?" Hildy said. "Power was out for three weeks."

"Three *weeks*?" Eliza repeated in alarm.

"It doesn't usually happen," David told her. "A day or two. Three days, at most."

Three days with the three of them and two dogs sharing his house? Eliza hoped the man knew what he was doing.

"Do you need anything else?" David asked Eliza as she and Hildy prepared to go upstairs. It was late—nearly midnight —and Hildy had finally admitted she was tired. There was so much to talk about, it seemed, with Hildy and David reminiscing about kids they had known from the neighborhood, what they had grown up to be, who they'd married, where they lived now.

Eliza listened, glassy-eyed. She didn't know any of those people and didn't care. But it was interesting to hear David talk, mainly because he talked so much. Hildy had a way of drawing him out. Even though the names and events meant nothing to Eliza, she liked hearing David's voice.

He never stuttered once, she noticed. Not even a hesitation. He seemed more relaxed around Hildy than he did around his own family on the few occasions Eliza had seen them together.

While Hildy headed up the stairs, Eliza took care of letting Daisy outside. The rain had stopped for the moment, but Daisy still didn't seem anxious to leave the warm house.

"Go on," Eliza said, "make it quick." She gave the dog a nudge. Daisy reluctantly toddled out and squatted on the cold ground.

Eliza waited by the door leading out to the garden, acutely aware of the last time she had done that. If she closed her eyes, she could relive the feeling of his hands on her breasts, her butt, the curve of her hips. Him telling her, *We can do whatever we want.* Making love that first time, the revelation of it, the first man since Jamey, the second man ever in her life.

But she didn't want to relive it. Wanted—needed—to spare her mind. So she kept her eyes open and impatiently called to Daisy to hurry.

"Do you need anything else?" David asked her.

Numbly, she shook her head.

"All right, then, good night," he said.

"Good night. And David...thanks again."

"THAT MAN IS in love with you."

"Hildy, stop it," Eliza said. The door was closed, so she knew David couldn't hear them from downstairs, but still, Eliza didn't want to hear it herself.

"I can see it," Hildy said. "You could see it too, if you'd look. The way every time you say something he can't take his eyes off you? The way he watches everything you do, even if you're just moving your little pinky? I know what it looks like when a man's in love, and that man's in love."

"Hildy." Eliza steadied herself, cleared her throat. "I'm not saying there wasn't an attraction...and maybe there still is."

"Oh, there's an attraction—"

"But that's all it is," Eliza said. "He doesn't care if it's me or Livia or the next woman who crosses his path."

Hildy shook her head. "So blind you don't even know it."

"Hildy." Eliza lowered her voice to a whisper. "I made a mistake with him. And it was very hard to get over, so I don't want to make it again. Can't you understand that?"

"But what if it wasn't a mistake?"

"That's like saying, 'What if Jamey hadn't died?' He did. This is reality. It's not always fun, but it's the truth."

"You think you know everything, but you don't," Hildy said. "I know that man."

"You *knew* him," Eliza corrected. "When he was a boy. I

listened to the two of you tonight, remember? But he grew up and now he is who he is. I can't change that—all I can do is protect myself."

Hildy shook her head.

"I'm sorry," Eliza said. "I don't mean to sound like I'm angry with you—I'm not. But I can't keep talking about this. It's too hard on me. So please, let's just go to bed."

"Can I only say one more thing?"

"No. Please."

"You think a man who doesn't love you drives out in an ice storm and brings back an old lady and her dog and puts them up in his bed while he sleeps on the couch? You'd better think about why a man would do that. He didn't do it for me, Lizzy, he did it for *you*."

ELIZA LAY awake for a long time. She watched the bedside clock pass through the twelves, into the ones.

Why would a man do what he'd done? Guilt, maybe. Or yes, some innate decency—she'd grant him that, for Hildy's sake. Or maybe, if she really wanted to be cynical, he saw his chance to resurrect their affair. Go over there with the excuse of saving them, and later find a grateful Eliza in his bed.

Instead, he had a grateful Eliza, Hildy, and Daisy spread out across his mattress. If he had had a plan, this couldn't be it.

Eliza rolled onto her other side and tried again to sleep. Hildy and the dog were both snoring in different registers, at different speeds. If Eliza could just rest, she thought, shut off her mind for a while, treat the snores as white noise and let them soothe her off to sleep, maybe when she awoke in the morning the power would already be restored. She could thank David for his hospitality, gather up her small family, and quickly be on her way.

Eliza heard the deep crack of a rifle shot, then a splintering, thundering crash. Another tree branch somewhere close by had broken and fallen to the ground. The ice wouldn't melt during the night, she realized, it would only solidify and grow heavier everywhere it lay.

It was no use trying to sleep. Maybe if she got up and used the bathroom, drank a cup of water, she could come back, reset, and try again. It was worth a try. Eliza pulled back the covers and quietly slipped out of bed. She had walked that path in the dark before, from David's bed to the master bath. She closed herself inside before turning on the light.

She hadn't been in there for four months. And even though she hated herself for being curious, she couldn't help but look around. She searched for any sign of Livia: a woman's shampoo, soap, lotion, cosmetics. She even pulled open the mirror over the sink to see if Livia had left anything in there. She shut it again quickly, disgusted with herself.

But also, she had to admit, relieved. She hadn't found anything. Maybe Livia wasn't as permanent of a guest as she'd implied.

What difference does it make? Eliza scolded herself. *He can do whatever he wants.*

She wished Hildy had never opened her mouth.

Finished with her snooping, Eliza took care of what she'd come in there for. She hesitated before flushing, knowing it might wake the other people. But she did it anyway, then washed up and turned out the light.

She stood outside the bathroom, letting her eyes adjust again to the dark. She knew exactly where she was. Knew she was halfway between David's bed and his bedroom door. Just four or five steps in either direction, and she'd either be back under the blankets, or out into the hall.

Eliza stood and listened to her own breath. It sounded shallow and quick compared to Hildy and Daisy's deep, slow snores. Eliza placed a hand on her heart, feeling how her pulse had sped up, too. Afraid to consider what she was considering, she drew in a deeper breath and slowly released it to calm herself.

The power might be restored by morning. Then she could return to her normal life.

But this, right now, what was this? A few hours suspended in ice. Hours she could spend lying awake in David's bed, or awake somewhere else.

Just a few steps, Eliza thought, that's all it would take. A few steps and a decision not to care.

"Eliza, what if I don't care? What if you can say anything, or do anything, and I won't care?"

He was right, she thought. Maybe that really was the best way. Just do whatever she wanted and not care what happened next.

Eliza walked softly toward the bedroom door, pulled it

open, and stepped into the hall. She was just about to continue forward, when she realized she needed to turn back.

She twisted in place and grabbed the knob. And silently shut the door behind her.

38

Eliza descended the stairs, pausing on each step, careful not to make any noise. She even regulated her breathing, timing it so that she inhaled on one step, exhaled quietly on the next.

When she finally reached the bottom, she stopped. She listened for David. She could hear him breathing slowly and steadily, without any break in the rhythm. She peered around the wall toward the living room, and saw him stretched out beneath a blanket on the brown fabric couch. Bear slept curled up on one of the chairs.

Eliza stood there for at least a minute, trying not to breathe, wondering what to do next.

When he rose from the couch, she wasn't surprised. Nervous, anxious, uncertain, but not surprised. He carried the blanket across his shoulders and quietly crossed the room. Then he opened the blanket and folded her inside.

Her mouth was on his instantly. Hungry for him, missing

him, wanting what she couldn't have anymore, what she could take right then, wanting not to think.

She could feel him behind his flannel sleep pants, and she pulled them down off his waist. As they slid to the ground she lifted her own shirt over her head. She needed his skin against hers again, the feeling of their bodies fitting together the way they did. She ran her hands up his back, feeling the muscles there, the structure, the strength of him. Then she reached around in front and took him into her hand and continued kissing him, touching him, pressing her breasts against his chest, wanting him inside her before she lost her nerve.

He broke away only long enough to lead her to another room. She recognized the shapes in the darkness as they crossed the threshold. He closed the door behind them and threw down a mat that stood leaning on the wall. Then the two of them fell in a tangle and David covered them again with the blanket.

Eliza had teased him in this room. Straddled him on a weight bench and made him wait until she was ready.

Now it was David's turn.

She reached for him and he pinned her hand. She reached and he pinned the other. She wanted to feel his flesh, feel the weight of him, feel him inside her, but he braced his body above her, not touching, and instead used his tongue.

No! Eliza thought. He knew they couldn't make any noise. It was maddening, too much to bear. She twisted and bucked and tried to bite him. She just wanted him inside her, hard and fast and finished, but he wouldn't let her, and she couldn't stop him.

She arched her back, tried using her knees, but he wouldn't give her what she wanted. He tasted her, drove her, stripped her of any defenses, until tears took the place of sound and her face was wet with desire. She tightened her legs around him and tried pulling him into place. Then as suddenly as he had pinned her, he suddenly let her go. David got up from the mat and walked away.

Eliza rose to her elbows, ready to kick him, fight him, punish him for what he had done. But before she could launch her attack, he returned and ripped open the condom in his hand.

He rolled it over his tip, and gave her that much. Rolled it further, gave a bit more. Rolled it all the way, but still gave her so little, she jerked her hips to force him to move.

David hovered above her, barely in, barely out, driving her to the brink. Eliza dug her fingers into his shoulders and clenched her teeth to try to keep from crying out. Tears flowed freely, hot down her face, her head aching with the sounds trapped inside. Then with one shuddering breath, he plunged deep inside her, and Eliza took what she'd wanted from the start. From the moment she'd seen him at her door that night, wet and cold, so close she could taste him, she had wanted him here, flesh to flesh, repayment for all the months they'd been apart.

They rode each other the way they had learned as they'd discovered each other's bodies in the past. Eliza knew he wouldn't fail her. He understood what she needed, how she needed it, how to carry her to an eruption stronger than she ever used to allow herself before. They pressed their mouths together, hungry, urgent, and when it finally came she clenched him to her and buried her scream against his skin.

How could a man know her so well? How could he know her and not want her near? The pain returned to mix with the pleasure, and Eliza fought to hold just the one.

David panted and stayed where he was. He kissed the tears that covered her face. He kissed her breasts, her mouth again, then finally rolled to the side.

He pulled her into him by the waist, curling against her from behind, then wrapped them both in the blanket.

This was the sensation she remembered. His arms warm around her, the smell of his skin, his hair, his sweat. This was the memory she'd forgotten. She thought it was only her heart that ached at the loss. But it was her body, too. Not for the sex—she could learn to forget that, no matter how deeply she yearned for what he could do—but it was this, the time now, that her body craved the most. The hours when she could pretend she meant something more to him. When he held her like this. When they had completely given each other everything, and now lay open and undefended.

It was worth it, she thought. Feeling this again was worth it.

Even if the truth reappeared in the morning.

39

"The power's still out," David announced. He came in through the back door, dressed in rain gear and boots. Icy rain continued to fall, not so hard now, but relentless. Bear shook himself off and went to get a drink.

David stripped off his outer layer and hung the coat and rain pants on hooks. He unlaced his boots and left them by the door. Then he padded into the kitchen where Eliza and Hildy sat drinking their coffee. He rested a hand on Eliza's shoulder. Hildy met her eye.

Eliza looked back at her blankly. She wasn't ready to discuss what happened. She wasn't sure she would ever be.

"I'll make us breakfast," David said, "then Eliza, do you want to go to the house? We can pack up a few more things. I think you'll both be here another day."

Eliza nodded. She didn't look at him. Didn't trust her voice.

"You'll have to borrow some of my clothes to go over there," he told her. "We're walking."

"How can it be raining when it's so cold?" Eliza asked. She carefully picked her way across the field. "Why isn't it snowing?"

"Warmer air than the ground," David said. "It happens sometimes."

He paused and pointed to the power lines in the distance. Eliza had seen them every time she took a walk up there, and knew how they were supposed to look. Now they sagged with the weight of ice, some of the wires touching all the way to the ground. "That's the line for the neighborhood," David said. "They should be able to fix it today."

The individual power to some of the houses looked like a trickier problem. As they came down the hill onto the street below, Eliza could see the devastation. Trees everywhere had lost branches, substantial ones in many cases, and some of them had snarled in the power lines and ripped them as they fell.

Eliza understood now why it was easier to travel on foot: Branches blocked the streets, too heavy to clear by hand. Until the town sent its heavy equipment, people would be stranded on either side of the barriers. At least the people who were closer to the main road might be able to get out and go to a store. People in houses like Hildy's, deeper into the neighborhood, would have to wait until the trees were removed.

Up and down the street, she could hear what sounded like dozens of lawn mowers.

"Generators," David explained when she asked him. "The portable kind. They run on gas, so you have to leave them outside or you'll die from carbon monoxide poisoning. It's just like leaving a car running in your garage."

"Or cooking on a stove inside your tent," Eliza added.

David smiled. "I wouldn't know."

At the Nolans' house, across the street, Eliza could see two long extension cords stretching from the generator into the house. "You decide which appliances you need powered most," David explained. "Usually the refrigerator, heater, lamps, the sump pump in the basement if it's raining."

"Sump pumps, generators, ice storms—I don't know about any of those," Eliza said. "Sometimes when I hear people talk here, I feel like I grew up in a different country."

"What do you have in Nevada?"

"You know, rattlesnakes, flash floods, dust storms, monsoons, scorpions, javelina, Gila monsters—"

"Monsters," David repeated.

"Oh, yes, we're very brave."

Eliza unlocked the front door and let them both inside. The house was freezing—as cold as the unheated garage had been the night before. Eliza unzipped the coat David had lent her, and pulled off the thick pants that were too long. She stood in the entryway wearing just long john tops and bottoms, a sweatshirt, and thick socks while she waited for David to finish. Once he was down to his layer of sweat pants and a wool sweater, the two of them went upstairs.

"Oh, that poor maple," Eliza said, looking out the window to the back yard. "Hildy's going to hate that."

"But it left the power," David said, pointing to the wire running from the back of the property to the house. "So you should be all right. Yours will come on once they restore the neighborhood."

Eliza glanced around the kitchen. "I'd offer you coffee or tea if the stove worked, but..." Her voice trailed off as he came toward her.

"Which one is your bedroom?"

"You want to see?" She felt nervous again and wished that that would stop. They were just lovers, and this was a brief two- or three-day interlude when they could do what they wanted, then go. He could return to Livia, if that's what he wanted, and Eliza would return to her life.

He threaded his hand through the side of her hair, bringing it to rest on the back of her head. He kissed her softly on the cheek, the temple, the ear.

Her breath felt shallow again. She closed her eyes. He continued to kiss her gently, while she rested her arms around his waist. So different from the early hours that morning, and in some ways, more frightening. When he was tender like this, she knew she was most in danger of falling.

"Why did you come get me?" she asked softly. She opened her lips and kissed him before he could answer. She wasn't sure she wanted to hear him. It might be safer not to know.

He pulled back, still holding her, but now gazing into her face. "When I saw you outside my house the other day..."

"Oh, God—" Eliza covered her eyes with her hand. "Don't talk about that—I'm so embarrassed."

"No." He gently pulled her hand away. "When I saw you, I thought...maybe you still think about me sometimes."

All the time.

"Sometimes," Eliza agreed.

"I think about you," David said. He kissed her again, so tenderly she almost cried.

"Where's your bedroom?" he said. "Show me."

Eliza stood at Hildy's kitchen window, dressed in her robe, long johns, and socks. She longed for something warm between her hands, a mug of coffee or hot chocolate. She needed to pack clothes for her and Hildy so she and David could return to his heated house.

But another part of her was in no hurry. She worried about the outside world. Even Hildy, with her knowing looks and her questions. Anyone who could disturb what they had right now.

He came into the kitchen dressed only in the quilt that had been on Eliza's bed. He stood behind her at the window and wrapped the quilt around them both.

He kissed the back of her neck, the back of her ear, then rested his head on her shoulder. He did it all so tenderly, so reverently, the words were out of Eliza's mouth before she could stop them.

"How can you be this way with me?"

"What way?" he asked, holding her even closer.

"So...loving."

"Because I love you, Eliza."

The words hung in front of her, frozen and absolute.

"No," she answered almost breathlessly, "you don't."

"What do you mean I don't?"

"Why are you with Livia?"

"I'm...not," he said, his voice suddenly tight. "Why would you think that?"

"Because she told me."

"Then she lied."

David took Eliza gently by the shoulders and turned her to face him. "I haven't been with anybody since you. You're the only one that I want."

"Then why have we been apart?" Eliza answered impatiently. As the reality began to dawn, she wanted to grasp it as soon as possible. But it still didn't make sense.

"I thought you didn't want me," David said.

"Why would you think that?"

"You left. Without a word."

Eliza looked into his eyes, searching, convincing herself of the truth. Then she leaned forward and pressed her forehead against his chest.

"You mean we could have been together all this time?" she asked him.

"As far as I'm concerned, yes."

"I think I'm going to be sick."

Her legs felt weak, wobbly, the way they sometimes did when fear swept through her. But this wasn't fear—it was sadness, and regret. She swallowed hard against the lump that had suddenly formed in her throat.

"David, are you telling me the truth?"

"Eliza, I will love you until the day you die if that's what you want from me."

Tears began to flow down her cheeks. She didn't smile, didn't kiss him—this was much too serious for that.

Instead she pressed her wet face into his warm chest and answered, "Yes, that's what I want."

40

"Are you sure you can handle another party of hers?" Carolyn Jackson asked. "And why does she always have them on the same day that I do?"

"Well, the first one was on Easter," Eliza answered, "and there's really one choice of day. For this one, I don't know. She must be competing with you."

"Sibylla Walsh has always been jealous of my parties," Carolyn said.

"Of course she has. You think she knows how to make peppermint snowflakes?" Eliza bit down on another one.

"Seriously, though," Carolyn said, "do you feel like you're ready for her this time?"

"How could I ever be ready?"

"She's an old bat," Hildy put in.

"Yes, thank you," Eliza said. "But she's David's old bat."

"I'm ready for her," Hildy said. "Just let her try to say one thing..."

"Look!" Katie said, pointing out the window.

The Careyville fire truck drove slowly by, with a man dressed up as Santa waving from the back.

Eliza laughed. "This is not where I'm from."

Carolyn waited until she and Eliza were alone again before asking, "I mean it, Eliza. Aren't you nervous about being around all those people again? I assume Ted will be there?"

"I assume. But I have to get to used to them all sometime," Eliza said, "and it might as well be now. That terror is his mother, and Ted Walsh is his brother—nothing's going to change that."

"Guess you can't live in the bubble forever," Carolyn said.

"Believe me, I would if I could."

ELIZA SCANNED THE ROOM. She hadn't asked David if one of his mother's former guests was coming, and she didn't know what to expect.

Hildy had been doing the same thing. "No Livia," she whispered as soon as David walked away to get them drinks.

"Thank goodness," Eliza said.

"Look at who Ted's got."

Across the room, Eliza could see Ted Walsh with a new woman hanging on his arm. She was thin, blonde, pretty in a made-up, hair-styled way.

"Wonder where he got her," Hildy mumbled.

Eliza shrugged. She didn't care. "What do you think that was all about? With Livia?"

"The Walshes are rich," Hildy said. "She's an ambitious girl. Isn't hard to figure out."

Eliza smiled as David came back toward them. He handed Hildy a glass of wine, and Eliza a glass of sparkling water. She glanced at Hildy's merlot with a twinge of envy, but decided to stick to her original plan of keeping all of her wits about her.

"Shall we go say hello to my mother?" David asked.

Eliza firmed up her smile. "Love to."

"ELIZA," Sibylla Walsh said, inclining her head. "Hilda."

"You can go ahead and call me Hildy," Hildy said. "Most people do."

"Old habit," Mrs. Walsh said, smiling. "We've known each other so long."

"It's been Hildy for that long, too," Hildy said. Eliza gave her mother-in-law's arm a subtle squeeze.

Sibylla turned her attention to Eliza. "So, you're here now with a different one of my sons."

"Mother," David warned sharply. Eliza could feel her cheeks flush.

"Eliza doesn't mind me speaking frankly, do you, dear?"

"Of course not, Mrs. Walsh." Eliza and the woman locked eyes. Eliza deliberately kept her posture relaxed and gave the old bat a smile.

"I'm glad Ted introduced me to this family," Eliza said. "I wouldn't have met David otherwise. I'm very lucky I did." She squeezed his hand in reinforcement.

"You are lucky," Sibylla said with a sniff. She adjusted

herself taller against her chair. "Many women would feel fortunate to be chosen by either of my sons."

"Mother..." David tried again, but Eliza gave his hand another friendly squeeze.

"Like I said," she repeated, "I'm very lucky. But I saw your daughter over there, and I'd love to say hello. Thank you for inviting me to your party, Mrs. Walsh. You always entertain in such style."

She let go of David's hand and walked away with Hildy trailing close by her side.

"That ought to shut her up for a while," Hildy muttered.

"Let's hope so."

David caught up to them a moment later. "Sorry about that. My mother is..."

"The same," Eliza finished for him. "I didn't expect anything different."

She really had seen Sue across the room, and now headed in her direction.

"I want to talk to Mike about something," David said, spying his older nephew at the same time. "Feel safe enough with my sister? Don't mind me leaving you alone?"

"Perfectly safe," Eliza answered.

"I'm going to go find the ladies room," Hildy said. "I'll be right back."

Sue smiled as she saw Eliza approach. "Merry almost Christmas."

"Thanks, same to you."

"Are you homesick at all?" Sue asked.

"A little. Although it's nice to have Christmas in snow.

Back home we're sometimes still wearing shorts this time of year."

"Ahh, sounds heavenly," Sue said. "I might want to visit your family one winter."

"You'd be welcome," Eliza said.

They'd briefly run out of things to say. The two of them smiled at each other politely.

Then Sue said, "Can I talk to you about something?" and drew Eliza into a quiet corner.

For a moment, Eliza dreaded what might come next. Maybe Sue had her own opinion about what kind of woman would date both of her brothers. If Hildy's theory were correct, Sue certainly had an opinion about what Livia had done at the lake house. She might have some pointed words for Eliza, too.

But Sue had never been unfriendly to her, and wasn't starting now. "I just wanted to tell you how happy I am," she said. "David's a really great guy."

Eliza smiled, relieved. "I know. I agree."

She noticed Sue looking past her shoulder to check on the locations of her family. David still stood talking to Mike, and John and Danny were laughing with Uncle Herbert.

"I wanted to tell you something," Sue said quietly. "I just...think you should know."

Again, Eliza felt dread. This was it: some sort of warning or secret that stood to ruin everything.

"No, it's nothing bad," Sue said, seeing her expression. She laughed. "I shouldn't have made it sound so dramatic. It's actually very good. Very...sweet, if you know my brother."

Out of the corner of her eye, Eliza could see Hildy approaching. She shook her head very slightly, and Hildy took the hint. She casually turned and changed directions, heading toward one of the caterers to see what food Sibylla Walsh dared to serve.

"I have to ask you," Sue said. "Do you love David?"

Eliza felt shy for the briefest second, but then answered in a clear voice. "I do love him. More than I can tell you."

Sue nodded, satisfied. "He's a wonderful man—maybe one of the nicest I've ever met, and I'm not just saying that because I'm his little sister."

"You told me that before, at the lacrosse game," Eliza said. "I didn't believe you at the time. He still wasn't talking to me yet."

"But now you can see that, right?"

Eliza nodded.

Sue took a breath. "I'm not sure David would want me to tell you this, but I love my brother, and I think you should know. He's loved you for a long time, Eliza. Maybe even longer than he's willing to admit."

Eliza looked at her in confusion. "What are you talking about?"

"He met you. Maybe ten or eleven years ago. You and Jamey came here to visit his parents. You must have been...twenty?"

Eliza nodded.

"David really admired Jamey," Sue said. "From the time they were young. Jamey was always so fearless, you know?"

"Oh, I know," Eliza said.

"David had such a hard time. He didn't have many friends

and he was so shy—he hardly talked to anyone but us. But I think Jamey was always nice to him. They didn't really spend time together, since David was so much older, but he told me once that Jamey showed him how to do some crazy trick on a skateboard. David fell and practically cracked open his head, but I think he was really happy to be included. He told me he was."

Eliza's heart began to ache. For the boy who was Jamey and the boy who was David. She hadn't expected this intersection, some moment from both of their lives that might have meant something to either of them.

"When you and Jamey were up here," Sue continued, "you talked about some climbing trip you had just been on, and Jamey said he was going to try to write an article about it and sell it to a magazine."

"I remember," Eliza said. "That was the year we got started." Jamey had sold the article to a regional climbing newsletter, and other assignments followed. Soon Jamey and Eliza were both regular contributors to a variety of outdoor and sports publications. Their careers built from there.

"David followed you," Sue said. "Both of you. I think he probably read everything you wrote. He'd look for your articles every month—both of yours—and he bought Jamey's books. And yours."

Eliza nodded, finally understanding all those times when David seemed to know more about her adventures than a casual stranger should. He wasn't a casual stranger. He knew her. Or at least remembered her.

"I heard about what happened last July," Sue went on. "David told me what you said."

"What I said about what?"

"How you'd better have met by accident. He'd better not have some plan."

Eliza shook her head, confused. "I guess I remember saying that, but...I don't understand."

"He did have a plan," Sue said. "I'm not sure if he'd admit this—even to himself—but I think he probably started hoping for it the first time he ever saw you out walking Hildy's dog."

Sue gave a quick shake of her head, warning away Danny, who'd been coming toward them. Danny held out his palms as if to say, "What?" but then he turned and went back to his father.

"He's admired you for years, Eliza," Sue said. "I'm sure he had no idea you'd ever move here. And then when you did...I think a part of him started hoping that someday you'd be together. So you see, in a way he did have a plan. And after you said that...I think maybe he was worried how you'd react."

"But...he never said anything—about any of this."

"That's my brother," Sue said. "You should know that by now."

Eliza's mind reeled. None of this seemed possible. And yet, it suddenly explained something to her: why he'd seemed so shocked that first day when they met, when she stood up and he saw her face. She remembered him becoming flustered, when moments before he'd been shouting at her to control her dog.

"And then there's the Ted thing," Sue said.

Eliza's eyes widened in sudden comprehension. "'If he

thinks I want something he tries to take it.'"

"What?" Sue asked.

"Just...something David said. That night when we were fighting."

"About Ted, I assume."

Eliza nodded. Now she understood completely: Ted's initial attention, his persistence, his willingness to keep pursuing her when it was clear she wasn't giving in.

"So Ted knew David liked me?"

"We all knew," Sue said. "He's talked about you and Jamey for years. He felt like he knew both of you. He used to show my boys some of the articles you two wrote—they loved reading about your adventures. And then you wrote about Jamey dying..."

Eliza closed her eyes. It was too much. But it also explained so much.

"So Ted thought..."

"I love both my brothers," Sue said, "but Ted...well, I'm sure you've seen what he's like around David. That whole competition—I mean, look at the situation at the lake house."

"Hildy thinks you kicked her out. Livia."

"I did. I'd do it again."

Eliza and Sue both looked at each other. Then Sue nodded. "I just wanted you to understand. And to know that his feelings for you run very deep. He's not someone to treat lightly, Eliza. He's a very good man, and he deserves a very good woman. I hope that person is you."

Eliza surprised herself by hugging David's sister. "Thank you for telling me. I really appreciate it."

"Do you love my brother?" Sue asked her again.

"Sue, I thought I would never love another man for the rest of my life. I was wrong. It's David."

"What were you and my sister talking about for so long?" David asked. He stood with Eliza at the edge of the party, his hand resting comfortably in the small of her back. He occasionally stroked his thumb across her spine.

"This and that," she said. "She wanted to know if I love you."

"What did you tell her?"

"Of course."

"We don't have to stay very long," he said.

"Good. Because if you keep touching me like that, you'd better be willing to back it up."

Eliza lay with David's head on her chest, his hand resting on her belly. Idly she ran her hand over the stubble of his hair, occasionally pausing to tug a few strands. She kissed the top of his head and whispered, "I love you."

"I love you, too," he said, then burrowed his face back into her breast.

The days were dark early now—dusk around four, dead dark by six—and by morning Eliza felt as if she'd been asleep forever. Dawn came so late, she was sometimes anxious to get out of bed to try to hurry the daylight along.

She always did her best thinking and writing in the morning. She still hadn't brought her laptop over to David's. She preferred doing her work in Hildy's home while David did his own at one of the stores or his upstairs office. They had a nice arrangement, Eliza thought, both of them together all night and the mornings, then parting to their separate worlds to accomplish their own work. Only to come together again at the first sign of dark, when they could close themselves in and be alone.

"You're getting up?" David asked. "What time is it?"

"Shh, it's early. Go back to sleep."

He groaned. "Come back here."

"I need to write," Eliza said. "I'll come back in a while."

She wrapped herself in his long, green plaid flannel robe, pulled thick wool socks over her feet, and quietly stole out of the room, shutting the door behind her.

She made a quick detour into David's office and pulled a few sheets of blank paper from his printer. She selected a pen and dropped it into her pocket.

The stairs creaked under her feet. She thought of how carefully she'd descended them a few weeks before, alert for any sound, not wanting to wake David, yet wanting him awake and in her arms again as soon as possible. Now she could make as much noise as she wanted. When she reached the bottom floor she turned into the kitchen and pulled a mug from the shelf. Bear stirred on his dog bed, but didn't wake. They were all used to each other's sounds now. She knew he'd continue sleeping for at least the next hour, while she sat in the living room doing what she was about to do.

She made herself a cup of coffee, then curled up on the soft brown couch. There was a quilt lying over the back of it —one of Hildy's extras, from home—and Eliza now wrapped that over her legs. She used a book as backing for the paper.

Then she pulled out the pen and began writing the words she'd woken up with:

We all have a natural sense of self-preservation. At least the survivors among us do. Jamey used to see people messing up all the time—daredevils, idiots, drunk show-offs shouting, "Hey, check it out!" as they picked up a rattlesnake with a stick, or did handstands on the rim of cliffs. "Darwinism in action," Jamey would say. "Clearing out the gene pool." Because he assumed those people wouldn't last long. They didn't respect life.

I think people think Jamey was like that. That he took unnecessary risks and was just asking for it. I can't pretend I haven't thought that at times, too. Cursed him for going out that day, for not just staying home like any normal man and puttering around the house or watching sports on TV.

But what is a life? Aren't you supposed to use it? People accumulate clothes in their closets but don't wear them because they're saving that one for some special occasion. What if your life, all on its own, is that special occasion? You should wear what you have. You should do what you can. If you're Jamey Shepherd, you venture out into the world and explore it. You touch it and play with it. You don't hoard it and wait for some special day when you think, "Yes, I think I'll go ahead and live an interesting life today. It's time. Weather looks good. All the right people will be there. Think I'll just take this life out of the wrapper and put it on."

You fall in love with the man or woman someone is. And part of the package is loving them right up until the full expression of their lives. It might be 72 years, like my wonderful father-in-law

Ron, or it might be 29, like Jamey. It might be 35—I could lose the man I now love tomorrow.

And he might lose me. I don't know what today will bring. I could be walking somewhere and have a tree branch fall on me. Someone might be texting and hit me with their car. I could drink a bad cup of coffee and go into cardiac arrest—I don't know, and neither do you. And you can sit there afraid of that fact, or shrug, accept it, and go enjoy the day. Right up until the moment when something you didn't plan on happens, and then you deal with it, because that's how real life is.

I've been so afraid of my life. Jamey dying was just confirmation for me: Living is dangerous. Don't do it. Back off. Be safe.

But the greatest gift my husband ever gave me was taking me out into the world and letting me touch it. Bringing me up tall mountains and showing me the view. Handing me a rope and saying, "Go on, Liz, kick off. I've got you. Don't worry." I had never felt before that kind of freedom and fear and pride and courage, all wrapped up in one. Jamey meant a lot of things to a lot of people, and I know he wasn't just here for me, but he changed me—in ways deeper than I still know, or can express to you—and that was a gift I will always treasure and hold up in my heart. He made an adult out of me. He scared me and made me keep moving. And now it's time I take the next leap.

This is my last column for a while. Not because I don't enjoy it, and appreciate the connection you've brought to me over the years—I thank every one of you who ever read what I wrote or wrote to me. It matters to me that you wanted to tell me your stories. It matters that you felt touched or inspired by something I wrote, and you saw your own life in some different way. I love that we had that. Thank you.

But I'm kicking off of the wall. When Jamey first taught me rappelling, I'd stand frozen at the top of a cliff for so long, he thought we'd still be up there past dark. But he never hurried me. Never made me feel foolish for being afraid. He waited until I felt ready—not safe, I could never feel safe hanging from a rope so far off the ground, supported by only a few straps of harness—but ready. Willing. Interested in living my own life.

I have a new life now. Far away from where I grew up, in a place where the weather is unpredictable in ways I'm not used to. I'll have to learn to drive on ice. Have to learn not to suffer so much when the summers are so hot and humid I want to live in a bucket of slush. I'm doing that because I'm willing. Ready. Ready to kick off the wall.

It's called freefall, and it's frightening. But it's also living. It isn't fair to a life to keep it unused, hanging in a closet in the dark. I have been unfair to my life—maybe you have, too. I'd like you to consider that today as you pull back, resist, tell yourself no when all you yearn for is the yes.

Take care, all of you. Thank you for this friendship. I might still see you sometimes on the pages somewhere, I might not. I'm kicking out into empty space. It feels wonderful and free.

Eliza looked up from her pages. The first hints of sunlight were leaking through the windows. She was surprised David still wasn't up, but they'd had a long night. He needed as much sleep as she did. She'd just needed this more.

She fixed him a cup of coffee and carried it upstairs. She set it on the bedside table and laid her hand against his cheek. Without opening his eyes, he reached for her and pulled her back into bed with him. He kissed her and they lay like that for a while.

"David?"

"Hm?"

"I need to ask you something."

"All right. Do I have to be awake for this?"

"Yes."

He grunted and sat up. Eliza sat on the bed in front of him.

"Sue told me," she said. "About you reading my work all these years."

David didn't answer. He reached for the now lukewarm cup of coffee and took a short sip.

"Can I see?" Eliza asked.

"See what?"

"Where you keep it. What you have."

David leaned back against the pillow. He looked at her for a long time. Then he said, "If you want to."

He got up and she followed him to his office. He sat at his desk and pulled open one of the drawers. He removed a file folder, a thick one, and handed it to Eliza.

"I'm taking a shower," he said. "See you in a while."

Eliza brought the file folder back to bed. She punched the pillow into place behind her, sat with her legs crossed, and covered herself with the blankets. Then she opened it.

She laughed at the first picture. Jamey and her looking so tan and skinny and young. No, not tan, Eliza thought, at least not her. That layer on top was dirt.

Someone had taken the photo of them in the parking lot at the trailhead just after their first long trip into the wilderness. They'd climbed, backpacked, camped, and come out with the agreement to get married. The magazine had asked for a photo of the two of them to introduce their first column together. Jamey had picked that one.

Eliza took her time thumbing through the pages. She paused every now and then to read a few lines. She had to remember these weren't just her memories: David had collected all these pages over the years, and they meant something to him. She tried to imagine him, in his twenties and early thirties, reading about her and Jamey from afar. What did he get from these articles and essays? Why did he keep them?

As she worked her way through the folder, Eliza knew she would come to the end. And she knew what that end would look like. What the picture would be. Which words would appear on the page.

Finally there it was. Carefully ripped along the edges where he'd torn it from the magazine. The pages loose, not stapled like some of the other ones were, the paper still slick and fresh as if he'd only read it that morning.

Is it better to die doing what you love, or to be more careful so you can stay alive and keep doing it? Eliza didn't need to read any further. She felt like she knew it by heart.

But it was the photo. She hardly ever looked at it—why would she? She knew some people might treasure it: the last known image of a loved one, the photo taken by his own hand. She knew exactly how he'd done it. He sat on the edge of the cliff, his hard, muscular legs dangling over, and he'd held the camera high to capture a view of his feet and the drop below. It would have been a perfect shot—something he could have uploaded to various photo sites so people could license it for their own use. It might be for one of those inspirational posters that said something like *Daring*, or maybe for an outdoor magazine that didn't want to pay a photographer to spend the day climbing so he or she could get that shot. Who knows: Jamey's photos sold a lot of places. It was another small stream of income.

But Eliza never licensed this one. She let the magazine

use it this one time, and that was it. The last thing she wanted was to be flipping through a catalog some day, or be browsing through a bookstore, and suddenly see Jamey's legs hanging over the cliff where he fell. She hadn't even wanted the magazine to use it, but she knew Jamey would tell her to do it. *"Come on, El, people want to see. It's dramatic. It's shocking. I died just five minutes after that. Don't you think people will eat it up?"*

Eliza closed the file folder. She laid it on the bedside table and got up and went to the bathroom. David's shower had ended long ago, and he stood in the steam shaving.

Eliza came up behind him and wrapped her arms around his waist. She laid her cheek against his back. David rested his arm against hers. Then he went back to shaving.

"Want some more coffee?" Eliza asked him. "Hot this time?"

"Thank you," he said.

She started to leave when he asked, "Everything all right?"

"Completely," she said. "Thank you for showing me."

She crossed the bedroom toward the hall, but then turned back. She retrieved the file. She carried it back to David's office and laid it on his desk. He could keep it or not. She had seen what she wanted to see, and now she was done with it.

Bear greeted her downstairs. He stretched his forelegs long and yawned until his tongue curled. Eliza patted him on the head and began brewing another cup.

When she brought it up to David, he was already dressing. "I have a meeting," he said.

"Too bad."

"I'll come back for lunch."

"Too good."

"Would you take Bear out?" he asked. "I won't have time."

"Sure, if you think he'll let me."

David kissed her. "He'll let you."

After David left, Eliza summoned the dog and set the alarm and stepped out into the cold winter morning. They walked up the trail to David's side of the hill, then Eliza took off the leash. Bear leapt and rolled in the snow, as if he'd just seen it for the first time. He raced back and forth, tongue lolling, until Eliza laughed at what a puppy he still was. No wonder David felt protective of him. He really was just a little guy.

Eliza walked on and let the dog play until he finally returned to her side.

She had the pages in her pocket. Folded over and stuffed there so she could transcribe them on her laptop back at Hildy's.

She'd made a decision some time during the night, solidified by the column she'd just written. Rather than returning to David's with the dog, she kept on walking home.

She put Bear back on the leash before they reached the street. For such a big, powerful dog, he felt weightless compared to Daisy. He didn't pull, didn't lunge, just walked placidly at her side. She'd forgotten that was possible.

She wasn't sure how Daisy would react, but then she was sure she was. The dog screamed out a bark and rushed down the stairs and sniffed all around the Lab. Bear stood wagging his tail, waiting. And then Daisy let him pass.

The dog seemed huge in the small house. And out of place. But he sniffed around the upstairs for a while, greeted Hildy, then settled down on the floor.

"See, Daisy?" Eliza said. "That's what a good dog looks like."

Daisy stayed alert, growling low at the Lab for a few more seconds, then gave up and went back to her window.

"Hildy," Eliza said, sitting down across from her at the kitchen table. She knotted her hands on the placemat and prepared to make her pitch.

"I suppose you've bought me some Christmas presents already," Eliza said.

"I'd better," Hildy answered. "It's the twenty-third."

"Would it hurt your feelings if I said I don't want them?"

Hildy tilted her head. "No, except the one I can't take back. But I can keep one more quilt if you don't want it."

"No, I want that," Eliza said, wondering when her mother-in-law had made it. With her arm out of use since September, it had to have been over the summer. Probably while Eliza was gone.

"I have some savings," Eliza went on. "Not all of the advance, but still some of it."

Hildy's eyes softened at the edges. Eliza could see she probably guessed what Eliza was about to say.

"I was wondering if I could borrow—"

"Yes."

"It's a lot of money, Hildy." Eliza named the figure.

"You can have it," Hildy said.

"I don't want to have it, I just want to borrow it," Eliza

said. "I'd rather owe you than the publisher. I'll pay you back over the year."

"So you're not going to write it?" Hildy asked.

"I can't. It's too long ago now. I wouldn't know how to do it."

Hildy nodded. "It's good, Lizzy. I didn't want that book anyway. You and I remember what we remember. That's good enough."

Eliza got up and gave her mother-in-law a brief hug. Then she picked up her laptop and took it to Hildy's couch. Bear lifted his head as Eliza passed, then relaxed again. She could imagine him there during the days, keeping all three of them company—even Daisy—then returning with Eliza every night. It was a good life. She wanted it. She wanted it every day.

She spread out the pages she'd written that morning and began typing them into the computer. When she was finished she sent them to the wireless printer and then went to take a shower.

She dressed in jeans, a sweater, and a wool coat she'd bought the week before. It was charcoal gray, as long as her knees, and felt like nothing she would have ever bought in Henderson. She was in a foreign country now, and learning to dress the way they did. Pretty soon she'd learn what to shout at lacrosse games.

She drove to *The Careyville Independent* and handed her column to the editor. She sank into his couch and waited while he read it.

Frank looked up when he reached the end. Then he laid the pages on top of a pile of them in his in-box.

"Diamond," he said.

Eliza smiled. "Thanks, Frank. I hoped you say that."

She stood up and held out her hand. "You've been a great editor. Thanks for taking me on."

He held her hand and said, "That's not goodbye, is it?"

"Nope, I'll see you around. You can come for Christmas if you want. Hildy and I will just be sitting around drinking cocoa."

"Got my kid and grandson," Frank said, "but some other time."

"Sure," Eliza said. "Whenever you're free."

As she started to leave he said, "I thought you had David now."

"I do."

"No Christmas with him?"

"I'm sure we'll see each other at some point during the day," she said, "but no specific plans."

"Keep me posted," Frank said.

"Still nosy about my love life?"

Frank flicked the pages on top of his pile. "You said it all here, Liza. Glad it's working out."

"See you around, Frank."

"See you."

When Eliza returned from her errand, Hildy handed her a check. "You take it to the bank today," she said.

"Are you sure? I'm not in that big of a hurry—"

"Banks are probably closed tomorrow, and Christmas for sure, then it's the weekend, and before you know it it's New Year's..."

"All right. You're right." Eliza blew out a breath, then got up again. She folded the check in her pocket.

The bank was close to a Walsh's. It was the same Walsh's Eliza had driven past countless times, and always resisted going in. But it was almost lunchtime, and she had a date. It might be nice to show up with food.

She entered the store and looked around. It wasn't as new and big as Ted's store in Monarch, and that was definitely a plus. But it also wasn't as cramped and dark as the little neighborhood store where she shopped, and that was a plus, too. Maybe she could give in. Stop saying no to herself about so many little things *when all you yearn for is the yes.*

She saw him before he saw her. Talking to one of the employees, listening, nodding. Looking handsome and sure of himself. She had a crush on him, all right, Eliza thought, on top of being in love.

As she walked toward him, she watched. Wondered when he would finally see her. How his face might change with the recognition. How he would treat her when he was at work.

She got what she wanted. That moment when he looked up, smiled, softened. Stopped talking just to watch her take those last few steps.

Then he stepped forward to meet her. Wrapped an arm around her waist and gave her a soft kiss. "Did you come for me?"

"Not on purpose, but I'm here now."

"I'll be finished in a few minutes. Will you wait?"

David's worker looked on with interest. Eliza didn't care. David didn't seem to care, either, as he resumed their conversation.

Eliza pointed to her right, and David nodded. She wandered off to find their lunch. The store had a huge, separate section with prepared foods and chefs waiting to cook to order. Eliza cruised through the various selections. Then froze when she heard the woman's voice.

"Salad without the croutons, raspberry non-fat on the side. Is your hair naturally red? You know we brunettes hate you."

Eliza whirled around. She was too shocked to try to hide. But Livia hadn't seen her yet, and Eliza still had time. She ducked behind a stream of wandering shoppers and carefully made her way to the safety of a pillar. She watched while Livia finished her transaction, then carried her tray toward the store café.

Eliza felt a hand on the small of her back.

"Are you going to ask me?" David said. "I don't have any secrets from you, Eliza."

"Then why is she still here?"

"We can't just get rid of her," David said once they were in the car. "Ted slept with her. It creates problems."

"You slept with her, too."

"Only once."

Eliza scoffed. "Come on."

David continued to look at her with the same calm, open expression.

"You don't really mean that," she said.

"I do."

"When?"

"Last New Year's Eve."

"But...you dated," Eliza said. "You were still dating her when I met you—you took her to your mother's Easter party."

"Livia is...persistent," David said.

"But...you took her to the lake house, too."

"Only because I knew you would be there," David said. "When she suggested it, I agreed."

Eliza gave a small laugh, still not quite believing.

"So, the whole time I've known you..."

"Right."

"Never," Eliza said.

"Never."

She smiled. "I know this will sound strange to you, but that really, really matters."

"It doesn't sound strange," David said. "Why do you think I asked you about my brother and you?"

The two of them sat in the car, looking at each other. Smiling.

Then Eliza grew serious again. "So she's going to keep working here?"

"Not for long," David said, "but for now. I don't keep dishonest employees. Now, can we stop talking about work and move on to more important topics? How are you spending Christmas? Will you spend it with me?"

42

Eliza unwrapped her new quilt. It had a light blue background and navy blue and brick red squares. The red squares were made of velvet.

"It's beautiful, Hildy. Thank you." She reached over and hugged her mother-in-law. Then she draped the quilt around herself to begin using it right away.

She wanted to start living what she had written: *Your life on its own is a special occasion.* No more saving things for that day that might never come.

There had been snow overnight, just a light fall of it, enough to coat everything outside as if frosting it for Christmas. Eliza made a path for Daisy in the backyard so the dog wouldn't get so wet or cold.

"Merry Christmas, lunatic," Eliza told her. The dog ignored her and squatted.

When they came back in, Eliza picked up the few wrappers Hildy's and her gifts had left behind. For Eliza, there was just the quilt. For Hildy, a set of new cooking knives. They both agreed not to spend extravagantly, but just to keep things simple. Eliza preferred that—especially since she'd borrowed enough from her mother-in-law to take the place of gifts for the next twenty years.

She and Jamey always kept Christmas small, too. From the beginning, they gave each other practical gifts: a new harness, backpacking gear, items of clothing either of them knew the other wanted but wouldn't buy for themselves. There might be one special, surprise gift slipped in—a framed display from Eliza of the covers of Jamey's books; the new laptop he'd given her on their last Christmas together—but generally they kept Christmas quiet.

"What time are you going over?" Hildy asked.

"Later this afternoon. He has to make the rounds with his family."

David had shown her the gifts he bought for his mother, sister, and nephews. "Nothing for Ted?" she asked.

"We haven't exchanged gifts since we were in high school."

"That must have made for Merry Christmases in the Walsh household," she said.

"My parents were happiest if the two of us didn't speak to each other."

Eliza's jaw had dropped a little. "Really? That bad?"

David shrugged. "We were young."

Eliza thought of Ted at the lake house, pitching grapes into David's lap and constantly trying to bait him. Not to mention sleeping with who he thought was his brother's girlfriend. If that was the mature side of their relationship, Eliza could only imagine how it used to look.

"You're really not giving each other anything?" Hildy asked as Eliza loaded breakfast dishes into the dishwasher. "That seems strange."

"Why?" Eliza said. "We talked about it. We both agreed it's too much pressure. We're too new. We don't really know what to get each other yet."

"Not even a sweater or a scarf?"

"He has everything he needs," Eliza said, "and so do I. I know it sounds corny, but all I wanted for Christmas was him. Nothing can top that."

"All right, but you're starting out the new Christmas year in a pretty unfestive way," Hildy said. "That means the rest of your year? No fest."

Eliza laughed. "No fest is fine. Just give me normal. You know that."

David picked her up around four o'clock. The sky was already beginning to darken.

"How did it go?" Eliza asked.

"My sister's was nice. My mother's was...also nice."

"Do you like her?" Eliza dared to ask.

"My mother? We all like our mothers." David glanced sideways at her in the car and smiled. "Next question?"

"Can we cook something together tonight?" Eliza asked. "I don't want you to have to do it all."

"Don't you like my cooking?"

"You heard Hildy: You impress me. But I'm happy to share the work."

"It's no work," David answered. "Let me cook for you. I have something in mind."

While David made dinner, Eliza sat at his kitchen table idly discussing the day—what Sue and her family were doing over the holiday, Christmases past at the Walsh house, how Christmases had been in her own family—when suddenly Eliza noticed David squirting ketchup all over the food in the pan. She thought of Ted once saying David only liked things with ketchup. But this was something suspiciously familiar.

Eliza sprang up and came to look. Then she laughed.

"It isn't."

"It is."

"How did you know?" she asked.

"I called your mother."

"You called my—what?"

"Hildy gave me her number."

"You called my mother," Eliza said, "and asked her what my favorite dish was?"

David kissed her. "Merry Christmas." Then he went back to preparing stuffed green peppers.

On a hunch, Eliza opened his freezer. There in front was a pint of pralines and cream ice cream. She turned around, smiling. "You really are the best man." She made him stop what he was doing to give him a proper kiss. "Thank you, David. This is the sweetest."

They dined on the couch, the way Eliza liked it best. She tucked her feet under her and ate forkfuls of the soft, tender pepper, hamburger and onions, ketchup and brown sugar on top. They didn't bother with bowls, but shared ice cream out of the container.

When she had cleared away all the dishes, Eliza came back to sit next to David. "I have a gift for you," she said. "More of a story, really. Let me tell you what I've been doing the last few days."

She described her meeting with Frank Sawyer, telling him she was quitting her column. Told David about the book she had meant to write about Jamey, and about the money she'd sent back. "Hildy thought I should take care of it before the New Year," Eliza said. "Start the year off fresh."

What she didn't say was that her hand had shaken a little as she'd prepared the enclosure. She'd never written a personal check with that many zeros.

"So what does all this mean?" David asked.

"I'm moving on," she answered. "I'm closing a chapter of my life. A long chapter, but now I want something else."

"Such as?"

She kissed him. "You. And writing something different. I've had a novel in mind for a long time. I've just never been brave enough to start it."

"You feel brave now?"

"I do," Eliza said. "I think Hildy's right: It's good to start off a new year fresh." She leaned back and stretched her arms behind her. "But this week I'm on vacation. I'm spending all my time in bed."

David's eyes lit up. "Oh, yes?"

"It's something about winter here," she said. "All I want to do is sleep."

"Oh," he said, "sleep."

"And pre-sleep," she added, climbing on top of him and pulling her shirt over her head.

IN THE MORNING, Eliza sat in bed drinking coffee, David's head resting on her chest. He roused finally, rolled over to his bedside table, and removed something from the drawer.

"Let me see something," he said, reaching for her hand. Then without any ceremony, he slipped a ring onto Eliza's finger.

She stared at it. The round white diamond on a simple platinum setting.

Then she looked at David. "That's...it? You're not going to say anything?"

"I didn't want to make you nervous."

"I'm not nervous."

"Will you marry me?"

"Yes."

"Soon?" he asked.

"Yes."

Eliza gazed at the ring again. She tested it on her finger. "It fits perfectly. How did you do that?"

"I measured your finger with a piece of string while you slept."

"When?" Eliza asked, laughing.

"A few days after Thanksgiving."

"You're very crafty, Walsh."

"Hope you don't mind."

"Of course I don't mind." She leaned over to kiss him.

"Everything about this is perfect." Then she kissed him some more.

Finally David got out of bed, pulled on flannel pants, and casually said, "I spoke to your mother."

"Did you ask for my hand?" Eliza asked, amused.

"I did."

"What did she say?"

"That if we're getting married in the winter, she hopes it will be down there."

"Guess you'll be seeing Henderson soon, then."

"Guess I will," David said.

Eliza climbed onto her hands and knees and tugged him back onto the bed with her. "David, how long have you been planning this?"

"I told you. Since the day after the ice storm. As soon as you said you wanted me to love you forever. That was all I needed to hear."

For want of a nail, the shoe was lost; for want of a shoe, the horse was lost; for want of a horse, the battle was lost...

For want of an ice storm, Eliza thought, this moment in her life might be lost. But not just the ice storm—so many pieces had to fall into place: Moving to Careyville with Hildy. Meeting David when she was twenty, and meeting him again now. All the twists and turns in both of their lives—including Daisy's near-death experience—all leading to this moment on a bed in a sunny room with the man she loved beside her.

"Mike is going to be my best man," David said, getting up again. "I already asked him."

"When?"

"At my mother's Christmas party."

Eliza had a flash of David talking to his nephew that night while she talked to his sister.

"You don't mess around," Eliza said.

"No, I don't."

She sat back against the pillows, watching him as he pulled on a warm shirt. This was what she wanted, she thought: this kind of domestic scene, just her husband and her enjoying a quiet morning together. No fanfare, no drama. Just two people who understood and loved each other, going about their day.

"David?"

"Hm?"

"Why didn't you give this to me yesterday?" Eliza asked. "On Christmas?"

"We said no gifts." He sat beside her and lifted her left hand. He kissed the finger that held the ring. "And I wanted you to know this isn't just a gesture. It's not because of Christmas, it's how I feel about you every day."

Eliza looked into his eyes and smiled.

"Thank you, Mr. Walsh."

"Thank you, future Mrs. Walsh."

"Next month too soon?" Eliza asked.

"Not too soon for me."

~

ABOUT THE AUTHOR

Robin Brande is an award-winning author, former trial attorney, black belt in martial arts, Reiki Master, and wilderness medic. Her outdoor adventures range from the Rocky Mountains to the Alps to Iceland.

She writes in multiple genres, including mystery, adventure, fantasy, science fiction, young adult, romance, and self-help.

For more information:
https://robinbrande.com/

For information about new releases, along with special discounts on books and merchandise, subscribe to the Robin Brande newsletter: https://robinbrande.com/ pages/subscribe.